THE CARNIVAL DIVERSION

A NOVEL

Thomas Humann

authorHOUSE®

AuthorHouse™
1663 Liberty Drive
Bloomington, IN 47403
www.authorhouse.com
Phone: 1-800-839-8640

This is a work of fiction. Names, characters, places, and incidents either
are the product of the author's imagination or are used fictitiously. Any
resemblance to actual persons, living or dead, is entirely coincidental.

First published by AuthorHouse   12/3/2009

ISBN: 978-1-4490-5428-1 (e)
ISBN: 978-1-4490-5427-4 (sc)
Library of Congress Control Number: 2009912475

www.thomashumann.com

Printed in the United States of America
Bloomington, Indiana

This book is printed on acid-free paper.

In loving memory of Dawn Humann

A NOTE FROM THE AUTHOR

Not a day passes without being asked about my aviation career. Whether it's Marine Corps Supercobras in the Arabian Gulf, Marine One for President George W. Bush, or Vietnam-era Hueys into scorching California wildfires, people ask. Always happy to oblige, I've verbally regaled my audiences with tales that often times surprise me in retrospect. But even those shared with friends, family, and acquaintances can't do justice to the full story. There are too many details that delve into top-secret overseas missions and protection of the president that must be omitted. By deftly weaving between truth and fiction I've attempted to paint a more complete picture while honoring my oaths to Corps and country.

I've had the good fortune of not only traveling the world but experiencing it. Simply crossing the threshold to Marine officer meant becoming one of the few and the proud. Representing the Corps in the cockpit of Marine One was an honor that brought with it unique responsibilities. As with any other Marine Corps officer billet, I took on collateral duties. As an advance officer I worked directly with the White House staff, Secret Service, and myriad other entities to ensure smooth presidential travel. The most critical aspect of any visit was the contingency plan – what to do if things went wrong. We surveyed threats and developed plans for using the helicopter in an emergency. And did it without tipping our hand to potential enemies.

Like my military assignments, I couldn't have completed this book without help. From the characters I served alongside in the Marines to those that helped behind the scenes, I've been provided with an endless supply of ideas. Whether the experiences were on or off the clock they were equally rich. All of them provided me the opportunity to craft *The Carnival Diversion* from firsthand knowledge.

Once the manuscript was drafted the help didn't cease. I'd like to take a moment to thank Gregory Goodwin, whose keen eye and mind helped greatly with the editing process. Even though I am my own technical expert it never hurts to have your work verified by another. Thanks to Lieutenant Colonel Stephen Lightfoot for lending his attention to detail to that additional military review. Finally, a big thank-you hug to my father. Without his constant encouragement I may never have put a single word on paper. Of course it didn't hurt that he's a lifelong fan of the thriller genre and recommended a few course corrections along the way.

I hope you enjoy reading this book as much as I enjoyed writing it.

THE CARNIVAL DIVERSION

The fate of a nation was riding that night;
And the spark struck out by that steed, in his flight,
Kindled the land into flame with its heat...
In the hour of darkness and peril and need,
The people will waken and listen to hear
The hurrying hoof-beats of that steed,
And the midnight message of Paul Revere.

Henry Wadsworth Longfellow
Paul Revere's Ride

PROLOGUE

Even at the age of five, I knew this was a wakeup call unlike any I would ever have again. The morning was shrouded in darkness, voices spoke in hushed tones. Father was still home – why hadn't he gone to work yet? Mother entered my room and gently shook me to ensure I was awake. The house was still decorated from last night's birthday party. But my suitcase was next to my bed, and packed.

Mother broke the silence. "Rashid, put these clothes on, and go to the bathroom. We have a long journey ahead."

"Where are we – "

"Please, just do as I say. Your father wants to leave now." I hurried to the bathroom and quickly dressed. Father was not to be disobeyed.

As I ran down the stairs, Father was moving purposefully, bringing bags quietly to the car. Not many. Three small suitcases and his *special* briefcases. Though I was warned regularly not to go near them, I knew they housed a variety of blades and handguns. His warnings were nothing more than the exercise of parental discipline. They were always locked.

The house looked a mess, remnants of the party's food and drink strewn about without the fastidious efforts normally taken before bedtime. The lights were all out, but Father neither stumbled nor spoke. He neither broke his stride nor acknowledged my existence as I stood in wonder.

The car now packed, the paternal robot finally spoke. "Get in the car. There's food in your seat. Now. We're in a hurry." I moved without a word.

Our behemoth of a sedan waited, doors ajar, keys in the ignition, lights out. I hopped in, confused and scared, but plenty hungry to eat. Where was our driver? Where were the house guards? It was just the three of us as we pulled onto the road. I had no idea what time it was, but there wasn't another car in sight.

Father smoothly navigated the city streets as yellow and red lights flashed at intersections. The city was eerily calm, in stark contrast to the daytimes that were now filled with riots, gunfire, and deadly violence. I wasn't sure what it was about, but it had surely affected my parents. Father had become extremely irritable and disconnected. Mother remained quiet and dutiful, but wore constant concern on her face.

I never remembered driving this route before. Our house sat on the city outskirts, in the shadow of snowcapped mountains. I was in the midst of my first ski season, and had become accustomed to the drive into the hills. This morning took us the opposite direction. Within moments the city was gone, replaced by long stretches of desolate roads flanked by endless desert, highlighted by the occasional Bedouin fire. I closed my eyes and lay on Mother's lap. Nobody spoke a word as I fell asleep.

When I awoke my head was still in Mother's lap. But I was now lying across the rear seat of a running helicopter. The predawn sun cast a purplish hue across the sky, not quite enough light for normal vision. Father was seated intently in the pilot's seat. Our bags surrounded us, tied securely to the floor of the helicopter. Our car was gone.

As we lifted from the ground, I observed the vast expanse of ocean for the first time. The helo rocked forward, dipping slightly as we accelerated over the glassy water. We skimmed along low enough to be a boat with a rotor beat. Mother held me tight. I looked back and watched as the land disappeared from sight. The sun, now fully above the horizon, shone brilliantly, illuminating oil fires in the distance. The opposite shoreline and building lights materialized in front of us. From the approaching land, large airplanes rocketed into the morning sky. Father banked the helicopter in that direction.

We thumped along until reaching the outer fence of the airport, when the helicopter's nose pitched up abruptly, then leveled as we settled smoothly toward the paved area below. Father landed adjacent to a parked car that appeared to be awaiting our arrival.

Without waiting for Father to shutdown, an enrobed man stepped out of the car and walked our way. He stopped next to the right side of the still noisy aircraft, as Father opened his door. They shook hands as the man spoke into Father's ear. As he pulled back from Father, the man wailed words I didn't understand and ripped open his robes. The explosion that emanated from him instantly engulfed him and Father. Our helicopter rocked onto its side, sending shards of metal and glass everywhere. My world went black.

PART ONE

CHAPTER 1

WASHINGTON, D.C.

I lurched upright, heart palpitating. My unfamiliar bed was a pool of sweat tucked snugly into the corner of my one bedroom apartment. That damn dream was the only one I could ever remember, and I remember having it since – well, forever. The job must be getting to me.

I took a moment to catch my breath before rinsing off my body and dusting off my service C uniform. The walk out onto T Street brought welcome refreshment. I inhaled the crisp air deeply as I reacquainted myself with Adams Morgan.

I'd been away long enough that the Euro-influenced Washington, D.C. neighborhood reminded me as much of Vienna and Prague as it did of anywhere in the United States. Extensive international travel was my way of life. I relished orders to the next unexpected locale. The time away provided excitement, and made me appreciate what I had back home. It kept life fresh – like an otherwise dull marriage kept hot by the satisfaction in the arms of another.

Briefcase growing heavy, my upbeat mood slipped as I remembered how far away my car was. Available parking was one thing this neighborhood lacked.

The long walk to the car complete, it was time to sit in some D.C. traffic. That's alright. It gave me time to prepare my thoughts on my way to brief my boss. I'd just returned from a mission to South America, and had little to report. I was hoping to spin this apparent lack of work into a positive: no news is good news, right? There really wasn't much to the recent chatter emanating from Suriname. I was okay with that, but feared my boss would not share my contentment. Colonel Joe Kingman's type A personality always demanded more information.

Kingman hadn't accelerated to his position by being a slacker. While I was always impressed with my own accomplishments – honor graduate from the Basic School and intelligence school, along with numerous personal awards – I was no Kingman. He was *the* poster-boy Marine officer with an extensive combat resume. Multiple trips to Iraq and Afghanistan were interrupted only by excursions to other lesser known garden spots in need of U.S. military attention. As an intelligence guru, he worked both with high-speed ground units and on solo operations. Regardless of the mission, Kingman brought relentless intensity and unmatched professionalism. As far as I was concerned, his combat boots were far too big for anybody to fill.

Having slugged my way through downtown and across the Capital Street Bridge into Southeast D.C., I was rewarded with a long stack-up at the Bolling Air Force Base gate. I'd had more than enough time to think. I was ready to get off the goddamn road.

I returned the airman's half-hearted salute and cruised onto the base, along the east bank of the Potomac River, to the parking garage. Finally.

Helicopter noise roared as I entered the Defense Intelligence Agency. The presidential helicopters flew low and loud overhead while they readied to carry the leader of the free world. I always swelled with pride at the sight of the regal white-topped Marine Corps birds. Screw the noise complainers – open your ears to the sound of freedom.

My office at the DIA was as vaguely familiar as my apartment. Pursuant the obligatory ID check, biometric verification, and removal of all personal devices, I was granted access to my office – okay, cubicle. I had no sooner powered up my laptop and begun the encrypted logon process when Kingman cast a shadow over me.

"Welcome back, Simon. Did you miss the helicopters?" Kingman asked as an H-3 passed by the window.

"It's always good to be back and see your smiling face, sir."

"Good answer. So how was the trip?"

"Great," I started, hoping to turn on the spin. "Turns out it's just the normal drug trafficking and corruption – business as usual."

Kingman seemed less than impressed. "Simon, you were down there for over a month. That's what I get?"

"Well, sir, of course there's more. I have my full report on the computer. Let's see, the DEA has solid leads on the Carazo Cartel and their involvement with government officials in both Suriname and Colombia–"

"Okay, okay. I can read that shit later. I have more important things I want to talk to you about. As fate may have it, I will be providing you with another opportunity to succeed."

"I can't wait, sir."

"Outstanding, come with me," Kingman ordered.

"Okay if I take a leak first?"

"Oh yeah, take your time. Take a leak; get a cup of Joe, whatever. I'll see you at my car in *five* minutes."

"Aye-aye sir."

Colonel Kingman was in the back seat of the already running government sedan, a baby-faced Army lance corporal at the wheel.

"Let's go, gents. We're burning daylight here," Kingman barked. We sped out of the parking lot, inched onto I-295, and sat still by the time we hit the Wilson Bridge. Kingman didn't mind. He wanted to bring me up to speed. "Lance Corporal Peete, you cleared yet?" Kingman asked the driver.

"Yessir."

"Good. Shut your ears anyway," Kingman responded. "Okay Simon, here's the deal. The chatter we sent you to investigate was legit, but we were looking in the wrong spot. May have been unclear transmission, bad interpretation, who knows? Doesn't matter now. What matters is that we have stories that are starting to collaborate, with increasing clarity. Remember how I told you the next big thing we'd find would not be al-Qaeda? Well, I guess the Shiites didn't want the Sunnis to have the only big show in town. They've decided to step up to the world stage. We think the same folks that have been backing Hezbollah have now found a new implement of mayhem."

"Iran and Syria?" I asked.

"Yes and yes," Kingman answered. "Only now it appears that instead of just being a bunch of common thugs, they have true leadership – their own bin Laden. The NSA broke some code coming out of southern Iran, near Shiraz. It displayed advanced technology we've not seen before from terror groups. It appears their leader is a guy by the name of Asad, a former agent during the revolutionary movement back in the late 70's. He got his start as a nuclear physicist working for the Shah's regime, before following the preaching of then outlawed Imam Khomeini. We don't know too much yet about his subversive activity back then, but we're pretty sure he played a heavy hand in both the overthrow of the Shah and the installation of the Shiite regime that followed. He must have gotten frustrated when Iran became more moderate in the mid 90's, because he started to spout off and build his own army of religious fanatics. He'd never been a spiritual leader before, but seemed to be able to market himself pretty well. His message resonated with a large contingent, and pissed off the government that was trying desperately to get itself out of sanctions from the West. When the pressure got too high, Asad went underground."

"Where'd he go?" I asked.

"Most of his time can be tracked to Lebanon and Syria. He cut his militant teeth with Hezbollah, learned a great deal about weapons and tactics with them. However, he didn't see eye to eye with their leadership, and had bigger plans. Sure, he hated Israel as much as the next radical Muslim, but his hatred had global span. It seems that as al-Qaeda had successes in East Africa and Yemen, Asad was inspired, challenged. His whereabouts become a little murky in the months following 9/11. I guess he took that as his final motivation to rival bin Laden."

"A competition to become the world's biggest moral degenerate. Sounds like Hitler and Mussolini – any chance of them joining forces?"

"Not likely," Kingman responded. "It's more like Hitler and Hirohito – two guys looking to achieve their own twisted goals, the fall of the West being the common one. As long as their efforts don't interfere with each other's, all the better for both of them."

"So where does that leave us now?" I asked.

"At the NCTC," Kingman replied.

CHAPTER 2

Hidden in plain view in suburban northern Virginia, the National Counterterrorism Center appeared from the outside like an office supply headquarters or a regional bank. On the inside, however, was the government's attempt to remove the stovepipes that had prevented the information sharing necessary to prevent major terrorist attacks. This intelligence nerve center was a byproduct of the intelligence failures preceding the 9/11 attacks. Where small bits of information had existed separately and were seemingly worthless, those pieces could now be assembled into the completed puzzle. The top secret facility brought together reports from the FBI, CIA, NSA, and a variety of military intelligence sources. The center's personnel could assimilate the data, making the intelligence actionable.

Only months earlier, the NCTC had gained some public notoriety by heading off a terrorist attempt in large U.S. cities. Al-Qaeda operatives had planned a coordinated attack in the Washington Metro, Chicago CTA, and San Francisco BART. The FBI traced movements of money from suspicious bank accounts in Brussels to individuals in the three U.S. cities. The NSA wire-tapping program had produced cell phone calls placed from a source in Monterrey, Mexico to the same individuals. The callers spoke in Arabic, and discussed plans only in vague generalities. Detailed plans were in place, awaiting only official clearance to proceed.

Customs and Border Patrol was informed of the plot, and they took it from there. Inserting a team of undercover agents into Monterrey, they set their trap in place. They discovered that an additional al-Qaeda operative had chartered a plane to fly his destructive cargo across the border to an isolated airstrip in southern Texas. While the operative and his Mexican pilot were inside their North Monterrey airport office discussing final flight plans, the CBP agents were on the airport ramp hiding a remote control cartridge-actuated device. The pilot and passenger boarded and departed, none the wiser of their additional cargo.

The night flight was uneventful through landing on the long dirt strip, where the plane was met by three vans. Each van carried an individual operative designated to carry out the attacks. The CBP agents observing with night vision goggles from the nearby hills could not have asked for a cleaner scenario. They had the entire operation inside the blast zone of the explosives, and they did not hesitate. With a silent nod of concurrence and the push of a button, the plane, terrorists, vans, and one unfortunate pilot were ripped to pieces by flying shrapnel, and burned by jet fuel and their own explosives. The publicly released version of the story said something about an attempted apprehension and shootout leading to the *inadvertent* explosion.

"Peete, be back here at 1100 for the drive back. I'll buy lunch," Colonel Kingman dismissed the driver as we walked toward the building.

After standard security verification, we were inside. The main room of the NCTC was a wide open space peppered with large work stations. Each oval desk was flanked by flat-screen computer monitors and plasma televisions. At each station sat a mix of civilians and military analysts. The room had an audible hum, the by-product of high activity level conducted at low volumes. It had been designed without internal walls so as to induce intercommunication – a literal interpretation of a psychologist's recommendation when aiding relationships. The images taken as a whole were as overwhelming as trying to drink from a fire hose.

It was the job of the center's director, retired Air Force Major General Kevin Moore, to orchestrate the room's cacophony into a symphony. General Moore brought a diverse career experience to this high level post: Vietnam-era fighter pilot, defense attaché, wing commander, and a variety of Pentagon intelligence and manpower duties. He was both well respected and well known inside the Beltway as a no-nonsense leader who was capable of bringing ideas and personalities together – traits essential to such a diverse operation. He had the look of an aged warrior, a former tough guy who finally accepted his fate as congenial grandfather type.

"Good morning, General," Kingman greeted.

"Good to see you, Joe," Moore responded. "Who do we have here?"

"This is J.D. Simon, sir."

"Good morning, sir," I extended for a firm handshake.

"Joe has told me a lot of great things about you, Captain. He tells me you're one of his go-to guys when DAO shops needs extra assistance. Do you know why you're here today?" the general inquired.

"Colonel Kingman gave me some background on the way over."

"Good. Why don't you gents follow me and I'll give you the nickel tour. Joe's already heard it enough times that I ought to have him give it.

Think of this room as representing the globe, with the stations nearest each other focusing on similar spheres of influence." Moore began to point around the room. "Over there you've got Europe, to its right Asia, to the left are the Americas, and right in front of us is Africa. You get the idea. The information is all linked electronically, but it helps people like me get the personal interface without wandering around like a fucking idiot. I get enough old man jokes without any help from random desk arrangement."

"Where are we traveling to today?" I asked.

"You like Brazilian women, J.D.? I hope so, because I think you may be winning an all expenses paid trip to heaven, or hell – maybe both. I did a stint in the embassy in Brasilia a lifetime ago, and I could tell stories – but they're all highly classified. At least that's what I tell Mrs. Moore," the general said with a wink and arm-slap. "Maybe when you return, we'll share war stories over a caipirinha. Well, before I get too far down memory lane, let me introduce you to someone."

The three of us walked to a desk in the *Americas section*, its seat occupied by a man diligently observing computer screens and perusing paperwork. He looked to be in his late twenties, with a disciplined and earnest demeanor.

"Vinny, I want you to meet someone," General Moore interrupted. "This is Captain Simon from DIA. He works for Colonel Kingman in their Defense Attaché Intelligence Augmentation Division. As you may know, DAIAD is a small support unit utilized to provide extra HUMINT and on site analysis when the attaché needs a little extra oomph. These guys work in conjunction with the DAO folks, but aren't easily recognized by the locals. Therefore, they can do sneaky shit the permanent attachés would never be able to get away with. Colonel Kingman's got a few of these gurus crawling around the globe at any given time, but you may not hear about it too much. They typically send their reports directly back to DIA, who then forward the pertinent shit to us. So, to me and you, they just look like any other military intel report."

Vinny popped up from his seat, nearing a position of attention. "Good to meet you, sir. Vinny Girardi." Despite his civilian attire, Girardi had an obvious military background. "Good to see you too, Colonel."

"Always a pleasure, Vinny," Kingman replied.

The general continued, "Vinny here is one of our newest hotshot computer whizzes. He'd been breaking code over at NSA for the past four years, and just got out. He's not bad for an Army man."

"Thank you, sir," Vinny responded with a stoic voice and a roll of his eyes.

"Vinny had a heavy hand in working with the British a couple years back when they unearthed that plot to hijack the airliners bound for U.S. airports. He's a regular cryptological fucking hero. We're proud to have him on the team."

"Where did you do your time in?" I asked the former soldier.

"I did my first tour with the infantry and was over in Afghanistan for a year. I guess I must have done okay with our field computers, because my squad leader recommended to the platoon commander that I get a transfer to something more technical when we got home. Either that or he wanted me off his front line – I prefer to think the former. I got some IT classes and got a transfer to an intel unit. I really took to it; I guess it was my calling. I got lucky when they needed a guy over at NSA to do some code-breaking work. Not only did it keep me at home with my family, but it was pretty rewarding too."

"You got kids?" I asked.

"Yes sir, I've been married to my high school sweetheart for eight years, and we have three girls. These are their pictures on my desk."

"Okay, so now I know you're better than I am at two things – computers and relationships," I said. "While I would love to sit here all day and exchange family histories, why don't you show me what you've got."

CHAPTER 3

With a few key strokes, mouse clicks, and screen touches, Vinny Girardi had brought up a multimedia montage of the current state of Brazilian affairs.

"Okay gents, this map on the big screen covers the entire continent of South America, with the countries in green representing those with known drug trafficking."

"The entire continent?" Kingman asked.

"Actually, sir, you will note that the Galapagos are in the clear," Girardi replied with a smirk. "As I overlay in red annual terror activity starting in 2000, you can see the trend. This area of the map that looks like it's hemorrhaging by the end of 2006 is known as the Tri-Border Area, or TBA. It's defined by the converging borders of Brazil, Argentina, and Paraguay. Let's blow that part of the map up." The computer guru pointed to border lines separating the nations. "Okay, you can see here that we have varied types of activity – al-Qaeda, Hezbollah, Hamas, going as far back as 2000. However, note that in 2004 you see a new group, al-Ayande. They have grown significantly, to the point of being the dominant force in the region by early 2006. They have more agents, more money, more weapons, and more local support than the others. It's really amazing how they have so quickly supplanted the others."

"Like a far superior virus," I added.

"Yes, and equally mysterious at this point," Girardi followed. "The U.S. has had a military contingent in the region for over a year now, working with the Paraguan government to observe activity and take action as necessary."

"How many people?" I asked.

"The U.S. only has between ten and twenty folks on site, but they are really just advisors to the federal police force. The relationship has been mutually beneficial, despite some pretty outspoken opposition from locals concerned about increasing U.S. influence in the region."

11

"So if the U.S. already has eyes on, where do I come in?" I asked.

"Well, in recent months, al-Ayande has dropped off the map, literally – see?" I nodded as Girardi pointed to the TBA blow-up, which reflected a precipitous decrease in activity during the preceding six months. "We suspected lots of different things, some positive, some negative. Did they run out of funds or support in the area? Did they relocate to more fertile ground? It was not until we got some feedback from a couple of CIA operatives in Sao Paolo and Rio de Janeiro that we had the lead we were looking for. It seems that al-Ayande was able to establish a joint venture now known as the Brazilian Future Movement, or MFB. The movement is nothing more than a fictitious cover for a local crime organization. Their escort into the neighborhood was a native gangster by the name of Antonio Armas. With the help of al-Ayande, Armas bought and brutalized his way to the top of the heap in the favelas overlooking Rio.

"How'd they find this guy?" I asked.

"Armas was a long-time lieutenant in the First Capital Command crime organization, but had grown dissatisfied with his lack of promotion. Agents for al-Ayande had been hanging around the favelas for a year or so, awaiting the right time and place to make a move. Once they observed Armas, they knew they had a chance."

Girardi continued, "It was a match made in heaven. The favelas were shantytowns that housed the eternally poor and downtrodden masses, without any hope of an improved life. The drug lords flexed their muscle through high powered turf wars, and ruled their turf with deadly force."

"So how could they get started with just one man?" I asked.

"What Armas lacked in family connections he made up for in charisma. Working with his newly found allies, he recruited large numbers of fellow dissatisfied FCC underlings to his new crime faction. Al-Ayande promised and delivered money, food, and weapons like never seen before. The unusual twist to this arrangement was the inclusion of a new religious direction. This area was almost entirely Catholic, had been forever. Al-Ayande brought with them Islam. While many were initially suspicious, reservations melted away as the poor were given hope for the first time in their lives."

Girardi removed black and white photographs from a classified National Geospatial-Intelligence Agency envelope.

"Take a look at these satellite shots we got from NGA. They show what appears to be a newly built mosque in the heart of what we believe to be Armas's turf. Let me tell you – with the amount of violence in that area conducted with high-powered weaponry, it's amazing it still stands."

"High-powered?" I asked.

"Yes sir. These guys aren't just throwing rocks at each other. We're talking shoulder-fired rockets, bazookas, 50-caliber machine guns, and then some. This surely pains the FCC and other crime factions in the area. The longer it thrives, the more momentum the Muslim movement will gain. That means more power for both Armas and al-Ayande in the favelas."

"So what does al-Ayande get out of the deal?" I asked.

"Okay, this is where we become concerned. If it just meant a more powerful drug organization in Rio, who cares, right? If Armas wasn't killing people, somebody else would – only the faces of the murderers would be different. But with al-Ayande as the backing element, the dynamics change. Let's make no mistake; this is radical Islam at its most diabolical. They're out to accomplish the same goals as al-Qaeda, and compete to do it in more spectacular fashion. That being said, it appears that al-Ayande has been working with Armas toward achieving bigger and better attacks in recent months. We suspect these may be stepping stones toward a large scale attack with wider implications and greater publicity."

"For example?" I inquired.

"This past September, on the first day of Ramadan, many local store owners received personal visits from teenagers on scooters. The youth warned them to close their stores in honor of the holy month, or suffer the wrath of Allah. Naturally, the store owners could not heed such a financially detrimental warning. The next morning, in broad daylight, Armas's henchmen drove through the city spraying automatic gunfire through any storefront windows with *Open* signs posted. Over fifty people lay dead by morning's end."

"So why haven't we heard about the connection publicly yet?" Kingman chimed in.

"Well sir, we think al-Ayande has allowed Armas to take the public credit for now, until the time is right for the *big one*. We fear this is in the works as we speak. CIA operatives in the area have reported that the attack will occur sometime in the first quarter of the calendar year. They either don't have additional info, or just have not passed it our way yet. Either way, time is running short, as the New Year is only days away."

Turning to Colonel Kingman, I asked "So why am I – "

Kingman interrupted. "Vinny, I cannot thank you enough for your very thorough brief. We can dig up all the other vital background at DIA."

"Gents, anything I can do to help, don't hesitate to call," Girardi said. "Good luck."

"Thanks a lot," I added as General Moore turned to walk us to the door.

"Joe, J.D., my door is always open – provided you can get through security." The general chuckled at his own weak humor. "Seriously, we're all one big team now, so I want to help as much as possible."

"Take care, General," Kingman responded as we gathered our electronic devices and departed the NCTC.

The drive back to the DIA was much quicker than the morning rush – the clear roads now offset by ominous skies.

"Looks like snow," Lance Corporal Peete said.

"Yeah, I heard we're gonna get about three inches tonight – should cripple the city," I replied.

As we pulled back onto Bolling, I added, "So I guess Peete and I will have to take a rain check for that lunch, eh sir?"

"Oh, I didn't forget. Nothing but the best for you hard chargers. Pull into the BK drive-thru, it's on me!" Kingman responded.

"Big spender," I said.

Once back in our building, grease-soaked bag in hand, I followed Kingman to his office.

"Sit down, J.D. Let's go over our game plan. In case you couldn't tell, our CIA brethren are playing a game of *I've got a secret*. That's why I cut off Mr. Girardi – I did not think it was necessary for him to hear my philosophy on the matter. You, however, are paid to listen to my pontifications – lucky you. So, as you know, the NCTC was created in order to open the information highway within the intelligence communities. But traffic only flows if people choose to drive on the goddam road. In this case, the CIA has continued to use the back roads so that nobody can see them. They have the benefit of using everybody else's info, but keep theirs to themselves. Anyway, they know a bit more than they are letting on. In addition, they do not want to do anything to compromise the identities of their agents in country – so we can't count on them to take action to stop any attacks for the time being. Therefore, we need to get our own information."

Once pausing long enough to take a breath, Kingman continued. "The defense attaché in Brasilia has asked us to supplement the consulate in Rio. He has two officers and a staff NCO on site down there, and they've compiled a good amount of data on both Armas and al-Ayande. However, they're recognizable in the city, and cannot get any direct access into the favelas without being obvious. I agreed to have you deploy to Rio and attempt to infiltrate the group. How is your Portuguese these days?"

"*Excelente*," I answered.

"Great. Go ahead and pull up our files on the region. Read the classified stuff, and take the rest with you. I want you to take a few days off; go see your family and friends over the holidays. Set your departure date for 2 January. Any questions?"

"No sir."

"Outstanding. Merry Christmas and good luck, J.D."

CHAPTER 4

As usual, I cringed at the thought of telling Angie about my latest travel plans. Like most girls, she was simultaneously bothered by schedule unpredictability and intrigued by occupational mystery. I was accustomed to being bitched at for the constant lack of explanation. The flip side was the way it seemed to add to her attraction to me. Like the gravitational pull of the sun, I drew her in only for her to suffer the burn. If you wanted to get laid in my profession, this was the cost of doing business.

We met at a cocktail reception at the German embassy. She was a Georgetown law student, tired of being slobbered on by drunken undergrads. When she explained to me why she and her friends had made the move away from the college bars on M Street, I handed her a wine glass and suggested that she graduate to an intoxicated Marine officer. She bit the line, and I'd done my best to keep her on the hook. However, I tend to fish in rough seas and rock my own boat on occasion.

Bad news doesn't age well. I pulled out of the DIA parking lot, put on my hands free device, and called.

"Hey gorgeous," I tried to butter her up early. I didn't exaggerate – she shared the height of her German father and the deep, rich skin tone of her African-American mother. She was classically beautiful in a suit and sexy as hell in jeans. She was refined and intelligent discussing world affairs, yet swore like a fucking sailor when I pissed her off.

"Hey mystery man, where you at? I'm ready and waiting for you!" I always loved how time away could intensify emotions. I could feel the sexual energy over the static of the cell connection.

"On my way to see you, of course. How about dinner at *Old Europe*?" The traditional German place had become our local favorite for a meal. Angie had taken me there just over a year ago, shortly after our initial meeting.

"Ooh, sounds like somebody's been missing what I have to offer."

"Oh, you know it. Hey baby, I have something I need to tell you." I could feel the nerves building to crescendo.

"Don't tell me you found somebody else," she half-joked.

"No, not today. It's about my schedule," I said.

"You asshole! You just got back last night – I haven't even seen your Arab ass yet! You have about thirty seconds to explain yourself."

"Yeah, I know. It sucks, but we've got some big things going on at work. They need me to go out of town again. But not until after the holidays."

"Alright, I suppose I'll let you live since I at least have you for Christmas and New Years," she warned.

I did not have the heart to advise her of my morning departure to Boston. Baby steps.

The mood at dinner was hot and cold. As always, the food and beer was top notch, like a quick jaunt to Bavaria. The conversation went expectedly downhill following the divulging of my itinerary – I would be spending the entirety of the holidays with family. It took two hours and four pints of *dunkel* to achieve the reprieve I was seeking.

The loss of time and cost of the meal was worth every penny. While Angie could get upset – okay, fucking livid – she realized that she had chosen to date an intelligence officer. By the time we walked into her studio in Georgetown, I was back in good stead. I was in the kitchen getting a glass of water while she put on some music. By the time I had turned from the sink she was standing in front of me in all her glory – and it was glorious. She had long lines and voluptuous curves, and knew how to use them. She grabbed my empty hand and guided it to a large, firm breast. Her nipples were dark and erect. Instantly, so was I. Most times we made love – slow, sensual, candlelit, jazz music-on-the-radio love. That night we had sex – passionate, hard, sweaty sex. I took her: over the sink, atop the kitchen counter, across the living room floor. I'm not sure what her neighbors thought, and I could not have cared less. She screwed me so I wouldn't forget her, regardless of how long I was gone. At least I think that was her intent. Whatever the reason, I enjoyed the ride, until my alarm went off.

Boston's Logan airport, lacking any semblance of organization on a regular day, was a mob scene on Christmas Eve. I couldn't wait to get outside, or at least that's how I felt until standing on the sidewalk. After a month in equatorial South America, the wind-whipped snow of the Nor'easter stung like razor blades. I couldn't remember being as anxious to see the old Volvo wagon as I was that morning. As it rolled to a stop, I could see Mom, already excited to see me. She always looked at me like I was some long lost relative. Perhaps I was.

Amy Simon was an elegant woman who aged like wine. Persian heritage had not only graced her with bold exotic features, but dark youthful skin. She treaded on the fresh snow, and slid across the sidewalk to where I stood and smiled. "Welcome home, J.D.!" She threw her arms around me, and I hugged her back.

"Is this your only bag, son?" Dad asked. It was. I always traveled light.

Alexander Simon was a kind man and good father, but we were never close – and very different. I had a linebacker's build; he was a string bean with glasses. He was the timid, professorial type; I was resolute and aggressive. My mother was as stubborn as me, but her Persian upbringing kept her from being comfortable in an authoritative role. The result was an undisciplined son. I had been more than they could handle, a devil child they couldn't explain. Somehow I survived through just enough intelligence and an iron will.

It must've been love that kept our family together. It certainly was not religion. Though born of Jewish descent, my father was not an overtly religious man. He was more concerned with professional and economic pursuits, and focused on providing for our family. My mother had long ago been disillusioned by the hatred often bred by religious fervor. That made me an Arab-Jew raised in a secular family. With both races often subjected to widespread prejudice, my parents decided to settle in an area that was accepting of at least one.

We drove to my boyhood home in Brookline, Massachusetts. The only thing whiter than the fresh blanket of snow on the ground was the town's wealthy populace. A mix of Jewish and Russian immigrants dominated the neighborhoods. Boston's not exactly overrun with Persian communities, so my father moved our family here in order to at least have some commonality with our surroundings. While it succeeded in keeping him from being subjected to discrimination typical of Jews elsewhere, he was the light-skinned member of the family. I had inherited my mother's darker features and suffered the consequences.

"Have you talked with any of your friends?" Mom asked while busying herself with holiday meal preparation. I forgot how much I missed the aroma of a turkey in the oven and wood in the fireplace. "How about Scott or Douglas?"

"No Mom. Haven't had time," I answered absentmindedly as I thumbed through the Boston Globe sports section. Imagine that: the Bruins are in first place during the regular season, readying their fans for another playoff disappointment.

"Too bad. They're good boys, and good friends," she said somewhat to me and somewhat to herself.

"Yeah, great guys," I responded without really thinking about it. The truth was that I hadn't done nearly as good a job of keeping in touch with them as I should have. Scott was the Puerto Rican kid in my class, Doug the only black one. It didn't matter to the other kids in school that we were all of similarly high socioeconomic status. The three of us looked different and that was enough to make us the recipients of childish bullying. We bonded together to create our own defense system, becoming unlikely brothers of circumstance. I really needed to touch base with those guys.

"What about Matthew?" Dad asked. He had been quietly hovering in the background, struggling to install a deadbolt on the back door and getting nowhere. My father may be an esteemed political science professor at nearby Boston College, but he was no handyman. I sensed that he was merely trying to appear busy while eavesdropping on my conversation. This allowed him to inquire about subjects that he didn't have the gumption to ask to my face.

Matthew Bannen had gotten me my first job, stocking shelves at the Harpoon Brewery. He also taught me how to fight. Raised by a boxer in Southie, Boston's blue-collar Irish neighborhood, he practiced his burgeoning skills on me. By the time we had become regular sparring partners I was bigger than him. Tired of beating each other to a pulp, we turned our aggression toward other restless youth in his neighborhood. My father never liked or trusted Matty, and did everything within his power to prevent my association with him. It hardly should've mattered now that I was an adult living 500 miles away. But apparently the distaste had lingered.

"I hear he's finishing up his surgical residency at U Mass Med," I answered, as deadpan as possible.

"Right. And I suppose he'll next be considered for Surgeon General?" Dad posed as he straightened from his work and began to leave the room. "Maybe he's looking to improve his skills with a blade," he added as he disappeared toward his study.

I hadn't intended to drive him away with my sarcasm; I just knew what he was driving at and didn't want the hassle. Whatever. I always enjoyed my mother's company more anyway.

"We're so lucky to have you here," Mom said, having learned to ignore the soft jabs exchanged between Dad and me.

"Yeah, Colonel Kingman allowed me to stay through the New Year – then it's off again."

She mustered a half-hearted smile. "Please be safe, sweetheart. You and your father are all I've got."

I realized at that moment that I knew almost nothing about our family. A history major while at Boston University, I knew more about the personal relations of the Hapsburgs than the Simons. I was too tired to ask now. Besides, my mind kept wandering to thoughts of Angie and last night.

CHAPTER 5

DAKAR, SENEGAL

Adorned in a slim brown Parisian suit, metallic briefcase in hand, Martin Breaux straightened his tie and entered the gendarmerie headquarters. "I'm here for a meeting with Mr. Decroix," he said to the secretary in French.

Despite French being the official language, most native Senegalese spoke in tribal Wolof, and struggled with the finesse of French. The secretary was obviously school-trained for such a position. Breaux did not divulge his Wolof fluency.

"Mr. Girard?" the secretary asked, to which he smiled politely and nodded in return. "Please have a seat. Mr. Decroix will be right with you."

Breaux sat impatiently, rehearsing his speech, until he was allowed to proceed. "Mr. Decroix will see you now. Follow me."

Georges Decroix stepped from behind his enormous mahogany desk. An ivory white grin clamped down on a lit cigar; his mammoth figure cast a shadow across his office entrance. Decroix, with a career that began in the military, had worked diligently during his ascendancy to chief of the department, with little wealth to show for it. His government had a history of moderate leadership, prided on honest dealings. Senegal was an island of calm in a sea of turmoil. Decroix had seen first hand the devastation in the surrounding areas, acting as a soldier during peacekeeping in Rwanda, Sierra Leone, and The Gambia. He found it ironic that his country had the stable political development despite the relative lack of natural resources. With an economy dependent on fishing and iron, Senegal lacked the oil and diamonds that were pervasive in other areas.

What stood in front of Decroix represented a chance to provide for his family like he never had before. "Mr. Decroix, thank you for taking the time to see me today," Breaux began. "My company in Paris is excited to have the chance to foster this relationship. France is quite proud of its historical brotherhood with Senegal. Just as the French liberated the Senegalese from the Dutch, we want to continue the job of development. This time as equals."

"I seem to remember from my history books that the French took far more than they gave to the Senegalese," Decroix said, less than impressed. "What will be different this time?"

"Good point, sir. The world is different now – smaller, flatter. The imperial France is no more. We are fully aware of the realities of the world economy, and are prepared to work within this new world order. For decades, Senegal has proven itself to be the model for democratic stability in the region. However, you have always struggled financially due to a strong central government tying the hands of the entrepreneur. The circumstances have changed somewhat with the advent of new leadership. President Diap has liberalized the system, relinquishing control to localities, allowing freedom of movement within the business world. This is just what was needed to give you the opportunity to make your own fortune. Now you are in control for the first time."

"Okay, so what is your offer, Mr. Girard?" the chief inquired. "And please get to the point. I'm a busy man."

Breaux had hoped he could set the pace of the negotiations. He had a plan to ease cautiously forward, testing the waters as he progressed. It became immediately clear that it had to be an all-or-nothing moment of truth. The ceiling fan spun slowly overhead, doing little to move the stuffy office air. He swallowed hard, hoping his nerves weren't perceptible.

"To establish a partnership. We know that you now have the ability to acquire large quantities of inexpensive diamonds. We have the ability to liquidate those for you, in exchange for Euros and weapons – valuable commodities in your line of work."

"What kind of weapons...from where?" Decroix replied with circumspection.

"Machine guns, grenade launchers, explosives. Tell me what you need, and I'll arrange it. Where I get them from is my business. You don't ask me, and I won't ask you what you're going to do with them. Understand?" Breaux asked, going on the offensive.

"I understand," Decroix said, somewhat more at ease, though not fully convinced.

"I'm going to leave my briefcase here, Mr. Decroix. Inside you will find 10,000 euros, a sign of good faith on our behalf. You are making a good business decision. I am confident that this will become a long, prosperous friendship. Thank you for your time, sir." Breaux stood up to excuse himself. "I must be at the airport soon for my return flight to Paris."

"Very well, Mr. Girard. We will talk soon." Decroix watched as the Frenchman departed his office. Turning to a guard adjacent the front door, he said "Have him followed to the airport…see what flight he boards. I want to know if our new friend is really on his way back to Paris."

During the drive to Senghor airport, Breaux could sense he was being followed. He was not surprised. He was nervous during his performance in Decroix's office, concerned that the intimidating chief could see right through him. He did his best to maintain calm focus while he completed his mission. He held the steering wheel with one hand, secure PDA in the other. His message was simple yet clear:

Package delivered and accepted

The message was sent then deleted from the PDA's memory. He arrived at the airport, returned his vehicle, and checked in for his flight – the nonstop to Charles de Gaulle on Air France. He breezed through gate security, pondering about how relaxed the standards were compared to the U.S. He was able to wear every article of clothing and keep every electronic device inside his carry-on bag. It was not until he walked through the magnetometer that the process slowed to a halt.

"Sir, over there please," the customs agent said as he pointed to a separate inspection location. *So much for smooth sailing.*

"Is there a problem?" Breaux asked, sensing that this may not be random.

"Standard procedure, sir," the agent said. "Please, through this door." Breaux entered a windowless room as the door closed behind him. The agent followed him in, bringing the number of agents in the room to three. It seemed excessive. "Sir, you will need to remove your outer garments. While you undress we will be searching the contents of your bag."

"Why do I need to remove my clothes?" Breaux asked.

"Are there any dangerous items in your bag?" the agent ignored his question.

"What's the problem here?"

"We will ask the questions, sir. I expect that if you want to go anywhere, you will answer them." The lead agent maintained his professional bearing, knowing that he was in control of the situation.

"Fine…the bag is safe, and I am in my underwear…happy?"

The agent who appeared to be in charge instructed one of his cohorts to conduct what Breaux knew to be an unnecessary body search. *Pure harassment package – and the ACLU claims we have problems back home?* Once the agent finished being far too familiar with Breaux's body, the attention was turned to his bag.

"What's this?" a second agent asked, holding up the secure PDA. It did appear different from the publicly available versions, due to its additional capabilities: encryption, global positioning, emergency beacon. It had a thick extendable antenna on the top, and a rugged all-weather case.

"It's my dildo. You want me to show you how to use it?" Breaux knew that these cretins would not be able to find anything out by searching his bag, and deduced that they were under instructions to send him a message. He knew that he would appear guilty if he showed apprehension, so he refused to cower.

The lead agent grabbed the device, walked over to Breaux, and smashed it against the wall next to his head. Breaux flinched, but did not break eye-lock with the agent.

"Whoops. It seems I'm not ready to use this machine," the agent said. "Maybe I should see if I have better luck with your other items," he said, perusing Breaux's laptop computer and satellite phone. He sauntered over to where Breaux stood nearly naked against the wall. "Or should I check if your skull is stronger than your machine?" he asked while tapping his night stick on Breaux's forehead.

Just as Breaux was beginning to wonder if offense might have been the wrong tactic, the agent changed his tone. "Get dressed and gather your things, sir. Enjoy your flight to Paris, or wherever you are going." The agents walked out of the room, while Breaux composed himself and went on with his travels.

Seated onboard the Boeing 777, glass of champagne in hand, Breaux made mental notes of the intelligence he gathered during his month in Senegal. While the U.S. originally supported the new Senegalese president's policies of liberalism and free market, the result was fragmentation beyond the control of his government. Decentralization relinquished authority to regional governments, some of which were incapable of controlling local forces. The worst was the southern Casamance region, subjected to rebel tendencies even during times of stricter control. Now armed with more freedom of movement, rebel forces arranged to work with smugglers from neighboring Guinea. Intense international scrutiny limited the ability of Senegal's southern neighbors to legally sell their diamonds harvested under inhumane, even murderous conditions. The rebels in Casamance had solved this problem by providing a safe haven to move these gems to buyers, minus the stigma.

Blood diamonds moving through Senegal were problematic. Never before tainted by the stones, the country was moving down a path to violence and organized crime. There was an added twist to this scenario, however. Piquing DIA interest was a recent increase in the Iranian population in Dakar. Already comprised of ninety five percent Muslim population, Senegal was now experiencing its first influx of radical elements. The Shiites now inhabiting the city had suspected connections to al-Ayande. The question was why?

Martin Breaux was dispatched to determine the answer. An Army captain, Breaux was both innovative and energetic. Born in New Orleans and raised in nearby Hammond, he knew what it was like to be black and poor. No paternal presence in his house, his mother had instilled in him the drive to succeed. She did it with the discipline he would later revisit during military training. One of the few to rise above the poverty of his upbringing, hard work landed him acceptance into Louisiana State University and an ROTC scholarship to cover the expenses. After graduation he was accepted to the Army's intelligence school, where he excelled. He knew what it meant to have an opportunity materialize where there once was none. It was something that he would not allow to pass. He knew that Georges Decroix would do the same.

Breaux was selected for this assignment due to his African-American heritage and his French fluency. He was raised in a traditional Creole household, his family descendants of slaves and tenant farmers. His mother passed on with pride stories of their roots that had been passed on to her. Literacy a scarce commodity, this history consisted of verbal anecdotes, hearty recipes, and soulful melodies. She played music and sang loudly as she toiled in the kitchen for Martin and his two younger sisters. The children danced wildly underfoot, unaware of all they didn't possess. Martin never failed to appreciate all that his mother did for her family. He was determined to make her proud, and take care of her someday.

The defense attaché in Dakar had contacted Colonel Kingman with a request for additional support in the region. The CIA chief of station position had been vacant for more than a month, and the DAO lacked faith in the remaining unsupervised agents. One such agent, Jack Stark, had been embedded in the local Muslim community for an extended period of time. In the weeks following the COS vacancy, the amount of actionable intelligence from Stark had dwindled to nearly nothing. The attaché was left to assume that he was either lazy or incompetent, or both. It was known within military intel circles that Kingman's people were sharp and hardworking. Breaux not only exemplified these traits, but was an ideal fit for a mission to Senegal. He was a French-speaking black man, who quickly added some Wolof and Pulaar to his linguistic repertoire before his assignment.

Stark would be flown to an alternate location to meet with someone not associated with the embassy. That *someone* was Martin Breaux, the alternate location was Paris. Neither man knew the other, but both sensed that they were fellow passengers on the same flight.

CHAPTER 6

PARIS, FRANCE

The meeting was set for nine o'clock at the Buddha Bar, at Jack Stark's request. Stark spent the better part of the last two years as a CIA operative in West Africa, after getting his start in Iran. The only escape to civilization he ever enjoyed was an occasional diversion to Paris. Senegal still had many economic and cultural ties to its former colonial ruler, making France a convenient getaway spot. Assuming his departures from Dakar were under surveillance, he traveled in full Muslim garb, changing clothes and shaving his beard only once lost in the Parisian crowds. The Buddha Bar, just off the Place de la Concorde, was nearby the U.S. embassy and always crowded with foreigners and tourists attempting to be chic. Stark chose the upscale lounge for his rendezvous since he believed it was best to mask himself in a crowd. Not to mention he enjoyed the scenery.

Martin Breaux dressed down from a business suit to charcoal wool pants and a fitted black sweater, arrived at the Buddha Bar promptly at nine, and entered the dark, cave-like confines. Candles were all that shed light on the surroundings, a mix of teak wood idols and fashionable clientele. The upstairs balcony made a narrow ring overlooking the downstairs dining area, like the rim of a fishbowl. Breaux worked his way through the crowd to the bar that lined the back wall. At the far end of the bar, Breaux observed a man sipping a beer and dividing his attention between the lovely mademoiselle to his right and Breaux. *He doesn't look like anybody on the flight from Dakar.* Breaux stared back at the man. He looked like an olive-skinned European in his dark jeans and blazer, long cigarette hanging from his lip. *Maybe this guy just has a thing for brothers?* Then Breaux saw it in the glint of the candlelight. His eyes – the same cold, deep set pair that previously had been framed by beard and turban. He approached his contact.

29

"Jack Stark here, good to meet you. You must be Martin," Stark greeted with a firm handshake and overly congenial grin.

"Nice to meet you too, Jack," Breaux replied, wondering if this was an act.

Jack turned to his lady friend at the bar, "Martin is the guy I'm gonna buy all the wine from. Back in NYC, they say he's the best dealer in Paris. Most of 'em are supposed to be real jack-offs to us Americans. I guess they think we're all just back there drowning ourselves in white zin and can't tell the difference between Burgundy and Bordeaux." Jack kept talking long enough for Breaux to understand that he was to be the local in this conversation, so he spoke French.

"Good evening, I'm Martin," Breaux greeted the young lady with the porcelain skin and long brown curls.

"Enchanted, my name is Nathalie," she replied with a friendly nod and delicate handshake, but did not stand.

Jack stood and turned to the girl. "Hey beautiful, I gotta go for now – business before pleasure. Will you wait for me?"

"That depends on how long you're going to make me wait. There will surely be other strapping American men here to sweep me off my feet," Nathalie played.

"Not as funny and good looking as me, though."

"Alright, we'll see. But don't take too long." She blew him a kiss as the two men walked off to find a table.

"Man, you work quickly," Breaux said. "No wonder you like coming here."

"Yeah, I guess the whole AIDS-infested Senegalese prostitute thing just isn't for me. That place is just my office...this city is my playground."

The waitress approached and asked for their drink order. "Grey Goose martini, please," Stark ordered. Breaux ordered the same.

"Thirty-two euros please," the waitress said. Before Breaux's jaw could hit the table, Stark had handed her a fifty.

"Keep the change sweetheart," Stark told her.

"Whoa man, how can you afford to drink at this place?" Breaux wondered aloud.

"I don't get out much," Stark answered. "I guess the money adds up."

The drinks arrived, and the talk turned to the real business at hand – which was anything but the cost of shipping cases of champagne across the Atlantic. "So how did you break into the Muslim community in Senegal?" Breaux asked.

"When I first got to Dakar, I moved into an area of town inhabited by Lebanese immigrants. It was a good fit for me, since that's my mom's heritage. My arrival in the area coincided with an influx of Iranians, so I went unnoticed. I had been in the Iranian arena for five years, so I was just another Iranian immigrant moving into the neighborhood."

"Why all the Lebanese and Iranian immigration to Dakar?" Breaux inquired.

"The Shiite community has always been welcome in West Africa, which is dominated by the religion. Many Lebanese had moved to be part of the lucrative import-export business linking West Africa to the Middle East and Europe. The native Africans didn't possess the means to make these deals happen, so it was an untapped resource. Of course, some of the businesses were more legit than others. Raw materials and hand-made goods were one thing, blood diamonds were another. It was the latter that got the attention of al-Ayande, which saw a means to move large amounts of worth without the traceability of traditional monies. The terror group was coordinating the operation without getting their hands sullied. Like mafia bosses, they coerced otherwise innocent Middle Eastern businessmen into less than aboveboard practices. Those that resisted were shaken down, injured, murdered – made the example of what not to do."

"Was it all just business and money laundering?" Breaux asked.

"At first, but it soon moved on to tapping into another resource. The on-site leaders of al-Ayande began to recruit operatives. Mostly young men and boys, but some girls too. They did this in a somewhat more subtle way than other groups were known for. You have to understand that al-Ayande's modus operandi is to maintain a low profile until they're ready to strike. There's not a lot of shit-talk about how they're going to destroy the West like you get from al-Qaeda. These guys are trying a different tack; a kinder, gentler killing machine. They believe they'll achieve more widespread support and operate more freely in moderate Muslim areas if they're not so outwardly radicalized. It's pretty clever really; more insidious than their predecessors – like a virus that can lie dormant for years before making its infection known."

"So what's your interface with these guys been?" Breaux continued the line of questioning. He was trying to keep Stark focused on subject, but was distracted by the agent's constantly wandering eye. *Was he trying to watch his back?* No. He was locking onto each and every piece of ass that sauntered by their small bar table.

"My involvement has been two-fold. On the business side of things, I am in there acting as an importer-exporter, though only a small-time one. I've dabbled in the export of iron and gold, mostly to European and South American markets. In return, I move more valuable currency and some other unavailable resources into the area. By working freelance for some of the bigger fish in that pond, I have been able to get wider exposure, while remaining a relative unknown. Some of these guys are involved in everything, from the benign trade of hand carved furniture for food, all the way to three-way deals involving diamonds, drugs, and weapons."

"Really? I'd guess that the drugs are from South America somewhere, but what about the weapons?"

"You may be right on the first speculation, though I cannot safely divulge my sources at this time. I still need to work with these guys to get more info," Stark warned.

What do you mean you can't tell me? My whole purpose of being here is to be read into the big picture! "Please let me know as soon as that changes. I need everything I can get my hands on if I'm gonna help us solve this problem," Breaux took the diplomatic approach for the time being.

"I understand, and will do everything I can to help," Stark answered. "There is more that you may be interested in, though." Breaux gave a thumbs-up of encouragement to continue as he sipped his martini. "As a local Shiite businessman, I became ensconced in the local community, which is wholly intertwined with the religious community. In this culture, the social, the religious, the business, there are no separations. I began to seek counsel from the imam regarding bettering myself in the eyes of Allah. I knew that Abdoul was not only a well-respected Shiite leader, but also an active member of al-Ayande. I made it clear to him early on that I was a businessman, and that my participation would be limited to peaceful activities. He almost seemed offended that I would infer that he was involved with violent activities. He mildly chastised me that al-Ayande was about bettering the lives of Muslims worldwide, that violence was only to be used as a last resort. Not unlike the preaching of modern Christianity or Judaism. He commended my desire to help, and suggested that I could provide an example to the young people of the mosque. It was his version of the *Big Brother/Big Sister* program. I told him I would be more than happy."

"So you took trips to the park, shot hoop, went to girl scout meetings?" Breaux said as he flashed a wide, pearly-white grin.

"You laugh, but it was not too far from that at first. I told you they were subtle. It was not until I'd been doing that sort of thing for a few months that I was exposed to the underlying objectives. Sure, it was clear early on that there was a bias against all things non-Muslim. I could deduce that from the very first meetings, held in the mosque. The preaching was not overtly revolutionary in tone, but certainly played to the circumstances of the audience. These people were impoverished, yet could see that the Westerners that visited had money. They had no idea what capitalism was, only that *Whitey* had something they did not. The clerics filled in the rest."

"I'm feeling that," Breaux said mockingly of his own skin tone. "Maybe you should be my *Big Brother*."

It was at this time that Breaux felt like he was being watched. There was a man, cast in enough darkness to preclude an adequate description, sitting in a lounge chair, drinking an overpriced bottle of water. Sitting alone, he smoked a cigarette and perused a magazine. *There is no way that guy can read a magazine in this light.* Breaux was not sure, but the man appeared to be either southern European or Middle Eastern, average build, and perhaps in his mid-forties. While he could not discern his specific appearance, Breaux knew one thing for sure: this guy wasn't there for the food or ambience. He repeatedly looked over at their table, and neither ordered a cocktail nor spoke with a soul. *As subtle as this guy is, why hasn't Stark noticed? Some CIA agent…he's more concerned with his booze and women than his own butt!*

Stark was still pontificating about the wayward children he had been pretending to guide in Dakar, but Breaux had ceased listening. "Man, it's getting late. I think I'm gonna head back to the hotel," Breaux stood to excuse himself.

"You sure?" Stark asked. "I've got some more info for you if you want."

"That sounds good. I'll be back and forth between Paris and Dakar quite a bit in the coming months, and we can make sure our paths cross in one city or another. I'll even buy the drinks next time."

"Well, Mister Breaux, it was a pleasure to meet you, and I look forward to our future business," Stark added with a bit more volume in case he could be heard.

"Until next time," Breaux responded in French, now back in character.

The pseudo-Frenchman departed the Buddha Bar and ducked into an alleyway across the street. He waited, expecting to see his mystery observer follow him into the streets. He waited, and waited. *Am I just being paranoid? And where the heck is Stark?* It was not until 0200 that Breaux got the answer to his second question, then the first. He could hear the loud southern accent, now a bit drunker, before he saw Stark meander out the front door – his left arm around Nathalie's waist. *What could she possibly see in this fool?* Breaux wondered if her intentions were any more than simply an American fetish.

The couple-for-the-night was nearing the street corner as the unidentified onlooker casually walked out from the dark bar entrance into the relative light of the city street. He looked both ways, and abruptly turned in the direction that followed the operative and his lady friend. *I thought he was looking at me, but it was Stark this guy's after.* Breaux followed at a distance, knowing that his presence could easily be detected given the current lack of life on the streets and sidewalks of Paris. All that shared the night were a handful of homeless people and privacy-seeking couples scattered throughout the adjacent Jardin de Tuileries. By the time they turned away from the mammoth garden that fronted the Louvre, they were alone. The Place Vêndome's broad cobblestone echoed eerily with footsteps and oblivious laughter. They walked – the apparently unaware couple, the mystery man, and the fake wine merchant – in a loose chain all the way to the Hotel Westminster's small lobby entrance. The place was refined, yet understated enough to be discreet for someone to come and go unnoticed. Except for tonight.

Breaux stopped short of the hotel and stepped into a phone booth to see if Stark was about to have more than just Nathalie as company for the night. He debated what his next action would be if the follower walked into the lobby. *Is Stark in danger? Maybe. Should I go after him? Not yet. Should I call the police? Absolutely not. What the heck am I going to use as a weapon?* Breaux's mind and heartbeat worked overtime until the other man walked right past the hotel entrance to a parked Smart Car. He opened the door, stepped in, and drove down the street, disappearing beyond the Opera House.

CHAPTER 7

RIO DE JANEIRO, BRAZIL

Traveling as an average tourist so as to avoid any extra attention, I moved at a snail's pace with the rest of the herd passing Brazilian customs. The terminal was packed with an eclectic mix of international tourists and wealthy locals. I passed the time in line reading a travel guide book. I'd traveled extensively throughout South America, but this was my first jaunt in Rio. A virgin trip into an area where I'm not sure I could've found one. I'd be far too busy to enjoy *all* the area had to offer. Nonetheless, my interest was piqued by the thought of all the beautiful natural scenery, terrestrial and human alike.

Finally outside. The air felt like a warm, moist blanket; an instant mood improver for a traveler exhausted by a cramped overnight flight. There's something that beckons one to slow down and relax when the sun beats down and the humidity takes over. Perhaps the worst suit-wearing weather, I was comfortable in my shorts, sandals, and silk shirt – my uniform for this environ. I pulled my suitcase through the parking lot until I found the 1999 Honda Civic staged for me by the DAO. I found the keys hidden under the bumper, tossed my bags in the trunk, discovered my assumed ID in the glove box, and followed printed directions sent to me by secure fax.

The drive introduced me to the dichotomy of lifestyles in Rio. Moments from the airport, while passing through the industrial area north of downtown, favelas loomed in the hills to my right. Their drabness was contrasted by the sheer beauty that emerged on my left. As the coast drew closer, the sun emerged from behind majestic Sugar Loaf Mountain. The light shone through morning clouds, highlighting crystal blue water and white sail boats in the marinas. What a cruel twist to have the city's poorest people look out their windows onto the affluence below – just the opposite of most American cities. At least they monopolized the best view.

The U.S. consulate had arranged an apartment for me in upscale Leblon. Just north of Ipanema Beach, it was used by the U.S. government as a surveillance post to observe the unscrupulous wealthy, a hideout for intelligence agents, and possibly an interrogation room. I was told the building was owned by an expatriate from El Paso, Texas who decided to sell his chain of Mexican restaurants and retire to a land where his money would carry him to the end, and the ride would be an enjoyable one. The Tex-Mex man I knew only as Treff didn't seem to take an interest in his clientele. Perhaps he'd been advised at one point it was in his best interest not to. He appeared satisfied to keep to himself and his live-in girlfriend Samantha. She was part Portuguese, part African, and all Brazilian. I couldn't blame Treff for being content.

Apartment 311 was on the top floor, and faced a small courtyard enclosed by the building. The two-bedroom, unremarkable at first glance, featured native décor, worn furnishings, and a dated television and stereo. It was the second bedroom, its entrance masked with a faux wall panel, which had been transformed. The walls were soundproofed, and contained wiring to the roof, providing connectivity to satellites orbiting one hundred and fifty miles above. The room held a bevy of communications equipment: satellite communications radios, remote listening devices, secret internet capable computers. Opposite the one-way glass window was a closet which was now a weapons safe. Therein ran the gamut of small arms: handguns, modular shotgun, sniper rifle, submachine gun, grenade launcher, explosive devices, and associated ammunition. If this place burned, it'd be a helluva fireworks show.

I unpacked and inventoried the kitchen. Fully stocked. A unique perk of tropical travel was exotic produce rarely found fresh in the U.S. I sat down on the couch with a papaya and knife, and picked up a tattered newspaper off the coffee table. With a few hours before my first meeting, I caught up on some of the news that never made the talking-head shows back home. The section of paper I had was from even further south than Rio, and in Spanish. A low-budget periodical out of Buenos Aires called *Página 30*, its radical leftist bent was likely not endorsed by the Argentinean government.

Cocaine and Guns on Both Sides of Law

Buenos Aires
Max Nogales

Argentinean citizens had their long-suspected fears confirmed this week. Federal police are deeply involved in the trade of drugs and weapons with local crime organizations. On Tuesday, two officers were murdered in cold blood while on patrol in the crime-ridden neighborhood of La Cava. Notes affixed to their bodies served notice to other would-be betrayers that the bosses would not be crossed.

The officers had allegedly facilitated the movement of automatic weapons and ammunition in exchange for cocaine. Apparently, the officers became too greedy for their own good when they began to conduct this illicit business with rival crime bosses. Once discovered, someone decided to make a deadly statement that this type of double-cross is not tolerated.

Little detail is known at this time, given that both victims are deceased. However, the government, concerned about international opinion, wasted no time in addressing the controversy. Attorney General Manuel Ortega said "the Argentine government is extremely disturbed by the possibility that any of our officers could be involved in criminal activity. You can rest assured that this behavior, if confirmed, is an aberration. Our federal police are consummate professionals whose number one priority is the safety of the people." This defensive posture by a high level official is consistent with what appears to be a trend towards greater influence of organized crime in the region.

Later in his statement, Ortega went on the offensive. "As we speak, investigators are aggressively pursuing leads in order to make swift apprehensions. We cannot and will not allow our great nation..."

Blah, blah, blah. Politicians spew the same shit everywhere in the world. This guy wasn't close to catching anything more than a cold, and he certainly wouldn't know what to do if he did nab someone. Things often seem hopeless in the U.S., but at least the government was still ultimately in charge. Our criminals caused neighborhood-sized problems, but didn't yet threaten the national fiber. Enough jaded political analysis for one morning. I had a couple of hours before I had to make my next stop. For now, it was nap time.

CHAPTER 8

I awoke on the couch, soaked with sweat and heart pounding. Another nightmare. Sometimes I could remember it vividly, but this time I only had an unnerved feeling instead of memory. I got up, changed into a dry shirt, and walked out to my car; but not before I holstered my Glock 33 under my shirttail. I had paid a pretty penny to have my personal .357 modified so that it was undetectable to airport security screeners. It held seventeen rounds in its six inch length, those I had to wait for until I got in country. Dubbed my *American Express*, I never left home without it.

The U.S. consulate in Rio spent most of its energy assisting tourists in trouble, from stolen passports to incarceration assistance and everything in between. I covered my tracks by standing in the visa line that snaked along the sidewalk in front of the building. On the chance that I was already being observed, it would be more suspicious to saunter right in the front door. It was pleasant outside, I had nowhere else to be, so I just relaxed and people-watched as I worked my way toward the service window.

"Next please," the clerk said robotically. A sepia-skinned woman with dark eyes and kinked black hair, she didn't notice me half as much as I was staring at her. If I was to blend into this city, I had to stop acting as if every woman was the first I'd seen after a year-long deployment.

"Good day, I am here to see Staff Sergeant Davis in the DAO," I said in Portuguese. The clerk looked at me as if to say *this is the visa line, dumbass – you waited two hours to ask me that?* I continued, "Please tell him that Wolgrand is here to see him."

She phoned, and within two minutes I was being escorted into the compound by a stoic Marine corporal whose name I did not receive. To him, I was any local visiting the consulate on private business. He was trained to not ask probing questions. I volunteered nothing as we walked together, him in well-starched dress blue deltas and a high and tight, me in wrinkled beach linen and three-day growth on my face. The guard never suspected he was accompanying a fellow *devil dog*. With a passable

Portuguese accent and dark coloring, I had no trouble playing the role of the native Brazilian, especially to people only stationed here for a tour of duty.

The young Marine walked me to the DAO's locked door, where I waited as he summoned assistance from inside. The door opened.

"You must be Wolgrand. I'm Robert Davis," the staff sergeant shook my hand and dismissed the guard. I wasn't sure if he knew my real name and chose to not use it, or if he hadn't been informed. Quite often senior leadership would ensure security slip-ups did not occur by withholding an agent's true identity. Most attachés preferred not having to worry about accidentally outing the agent.

"Welcome to Rio," he greeted as we entered the office. Unlike the guard detachment, Robert Davis was in civilian attire. It was rare to catch attaché personnel in uniform, presumably because their goal was to assimilate with their consular counterparts. Nonetheless, they all appeared as unmistakable military, from the tapered hair to the tucked shirts to the creased trousers. Davis was no different, his blue polo shirt and khaki pants were an unofficial out-of-uniform uniform.

"Follow me into the SCIF for a brief," Davis instructed, then ran his identification card through a reader, passed a biometric finger scan, and heaved open the vault door. Typical of most sensitive compartmented information facilities, the room provided both security to the enclosed information and its occupants in case of attack. The walls were lined with threat maps and flat screens, a living two-dimensional display of current events in the western hemisphere. We sat at a table covered with case files and satellite imagery.

The information turned out to be a rehash of the brief I had received from Vinny Girardi back at the NCTC. I did little to cover my disappointment.

"So you don't have anything new?" I asked, still exhausted from my overnight flight.

"No, sorry bout that," Davis responded. "We had been getting regular info from the CIA agents in the field, but that flow stopped about a month or so ago. We're not even sure if they're still in the region, alive, nothing." I could tell that I had struck a nerve. Attachés took pride in keeping their finger on the pulse of their area of responsibility. This one was simply at a loss.

"Hey, don't worry about it," I told him. There was no reason to hit a man when he was down, especially if I needed his help in the future. "I will see what I can dig up out in the field, and you can count on me to push the intel your way."

"I really do appreciate it," Davis added, relieved at my understanding. He walked me out to the sentry, where I walked off alone into the unknown.

CHAPTER 9

Well, now what the fuck was I gonna do? The question resonated in my head as I returned to Room 311. I sat on the weathered coach and reviewed the files I had carried with me from D.C., devising a new game plan. I needed to take advantage of my greatest asset, my ability to blend in with the locals. My intel would have to be acquired first hand, and it would be up to me to separate fact from bullshit. The answers were hidden in the favela. I had to infiltrate the ghetto without seeming out of place. This type of plan required time, a luxury I was not afforded.

The sun was setting over the verdant hills casting a warm glow through my window. I could hear samba music coming from the courtyard. A half dozen twenty-something men drank beer and grilled meat over a fire. It sounded and smelled to me like one thing – quitting time.

I had done enough reading on the flight to make some notes on restaurants and bars deserving of my attention. While I promised myself a visit to a churrascaria, I was not hungry enough to tackle that gastronomical challenge tonight. Instead, I changed into some light wool slacks, and made the short walk to Esch Café. The Cuban lounge known for its extensive cigar and liquor selection suited my tastes well. I entered the tightly packed upscale café, bypassed the hostess, and headed for a seat at the bar.

I chatted with the bartender for a bit before settling on a glass of Johnny Walker Gold Label, sometimes hard to find in American establishments and never affordable on an O-3 salary. Instead of serving the fifteen year old scotch on the rocks, he poured directly from the freezer into a chilled high ball. Still icy cold, the masterful blend suffered no dilution. I relished the light honey flavors, the delicate sweetness and cool touch. A perfect compliment to the warm night air.

The sips went down smooth, and I decided what I was missing was a smoke. I told the barkeep I'd be back, and headed for the walk-in humidor. I was not sure if it was any more humid inside than out, but the effect was not lost on the wealthy clientele. The tobacconist was proud of his selection, and I had to stop him after about five minutes to let him know that I wanted to smoke the cigar tonight. I grabbed myself a Romeo y Julieta and thanked him for his lesson. I clipped my Churchill and drew the cool spice into my mouth. It'd been a prior deployment to the Arabian Gulf since I partook of this particular Cuban, and I looked forward to pairing it with my beverage.

When I got back to the bar, my seat was occupied. "Excuse me señor." I informed the invader that I had left only to purchase a cigar. I also shot the bartender an irritated look, feeling that he betrayed me by giving my stool away.

Instead of moving, the man on the stool requested an additional seat be brought to accommodate my ass. The help obliged, and I accepted, though I still found it odd that he was unwilling to move. He offered a friendly handshake, "Hello, my name is Max."

Max was ruggedly good-looking, vaguely Spanish with a salt and pepper beard. Though sitting, he appeared to be about my height and I could tell by his veined forearms that he possessed more strength than the average man. We conversed in Portuguese, though I had a hunch that this was neither of our first languages. I moved onto Spanish in order to test the waters. Max had no problem following. I decided to maintain the linguistic globe-hop, and began to speak English.

"Do you live in Rio, or just come here to cause trouble?" I asked with a smile.

"Some work and some play, but unfortunately not full time," Max answered with a heavy Spanish accent. I still had not decided which, but his accent was from either Argentina or Chile. "And you Wolgrand, what brings you to Rio?"

"I moved here from Brasilia a few years ago," I responded, still trying to figure out what angle I wanted to play in this situation. "For the oldest reason around...chasing pussy."

"Ha! You sucker. Where is she now?" Max asked.

"With somebody with more money, of course," I shrugged.

"Well, if you're going to lose a woman, this is the place to do it."

"Truer words were never spoken." We clanked glasses and lifted our cocktails to our lips.

"So what do you do for work?" Max asked. Test number two, but I was ready for such kinds of small talk when undercover.

"I had been driving for some of the local high end hotels until recently. One day I was going to fill the gas tank when I got stopped by the police. This guy was a real prick. He told me he stopped me for having a tail light out. When I questioned the accuracy of his statement, he walked me to the back of the car to show me. As I stood and stared at the intact tail lights of the brand new Peugeot 407 sedan, he pulled out his night stick and altered the status of the right rear brake light."

"What an asshole," Max shook his head.

"Yeah, but it got worse. He climbed all over the inside of the car, almost like he knew something. He reached onto the floor of the back seat, and came out with a clear plastic bag of white powder. He asked me to explain myself. I told him it wasn't mine; that I drove plenty of wealthy businessmen around who had more money than they knew what to do with. He wasn't buying my story, though I suspected that it was a setup from the outset. To make a long story short, I lost my fucking job as a result."

"That's typical, man," Max responded. "The police probably got a call from a minion of some business big-wig, preemptively pinning his boss's stupidity on the defenseless driver. The police have no problem taking money or drugs in exchange for biased service. The system is so corrupt. I write about it all the time, but nothing changes."

"Are you the writer Max Nogales?" I asked, remembering the article I read earlier in the day.

"In the flesh," Max responded with a small bow.

"Interesting article in that Argentine journal. I guess you really do understand how bad the police are!"

"They're really not very different from one country to the next," Max opined. He continued for a bit, as writers are wont to do. After a while he said "You seem like a good guy, Wolgrand. I want to take you to my favorite place in town: *Termas Solarium.*"

I reminded him that I was out of work and could not afford too much fun in one night, but Max would have none of it. He insisted that the night was on his *real*, and he would not accept a negative answer.

CHAPTER 10

Termas Solarium appeared like any other discothèque from the outside, but inside would prove a different story. We approached a reception desk similar to that of a small, chic hotel lobby, where Max was greeted with a warm familiar smile.

"Good evening Max," our greeter welcomed as she strutted from behind the desk to give the journalist an embrace and kiss. Her face showed her to be in her mid-fifties, though her body had not followed along in the aging process. The sun's rays had augmented her crow's feet, but her knee-length skirt hugged her still tight figure and showcased her distinct calves. "Who is your friend?" she asked.

"This is Wolgrand," Max responded, with a smile that said *welcome to my world*.

"Follow me, you big studs," the lady beckoned.

She showed us into a changing room lined with hard wood lockers and plush terry robes. Looking in my direction, she eyed me up and down, and said "Max will show you around...have fun!" She blew a kiss over her bare shoulder as she disappeared back to the front office.

"Have you been to one of these before?" Max asked.

"I've been to one in Brasilia," I lied, "but not as nice as this one."

"Yeah, the *termas* here are top notch. I'll give you the tour on our way to the bar."

We walked out of the locker room into a hallway. Max pointed out the pool area through a window on the right, complete with sitting tub and sauna room. Two leathery, enrobed men lay on lounge chairs, cigars in hand and attentive young women sitting at their sides. We passed by a set of stairs that Max identified as the *stairway to heaven*, where massage would be just the beginning – the limits of one's imagination the end.

Drum and bass music loudened as we entered a large room lit by bar lights at the far end. A disco ball twirled slowly over a small dance floor. The discothèque was bordered by white vinyl chairs on three mirrored walls and stools in front of a mahogany bar. There was a smattering of older men who appeared to have money paired off with women half their age, engaged in quiet conversation. The lap-sitting girls smiled with looks that said *I don't have any interest in what you're saying, but I will be happy to take your money.*

Max and I found two empty bar stools. It appeared as if they'd been saved for his arrival. The bartender smiled knowingly and poured us each a caiparinha. There was something strange about sitting in a room accompanied by a dozen other men in robes and sandals, most hiding varied stages of erection. My increased comfort level would certainly require a proportionate intake of alcohol.

As it turned out, the ice was broken immediately as I smiled and nodded at a girl to my liking. "Nice choice," Max said as the young lady and her friend walked our way. Maria introduced herself to me as she leaned in for a ceremonial kiss on the cheek. I had never been so happy to know Portuguese.

"This is my friend Noelle," she continued as if part of rehearsed script. I did not mind.

"I'm Wolgrand, and this is my friend Max," I responded, not bothering to stand as I would for any woman I was not about to pay for sex.

Max ordered our *acompanhantes* cocktails, and they pressed their firm bodies against ours while standing next to us; Maria on my right and Noelle to Max's left. This allowed Max and me to pursue our conversation with no interruption from our exotic window dressing. Latin women really knew how to let men have what they want. If this were D.C., the girls would be standing right between us droning on about their unfulfilled aspirations of law school, or how their last boyfriend was such an asshole.

It was not long before Max and Noelle were engaged in a deep lip lock one foot from my face. I must've stared a bit too long, as Maria refocused my attention her way with a not so subtle hand under my robe. With one hand wrapped around my now rock-hard dick, she grabbed the nape of my neck with the other and pulled our faces together. We kissed long enough that I began to forget that I was in a room crowded with old horny men and not just one beautiful young woman. I opened my eyes, and released our embrace just long enough to take a long drink. With my glass drained to the ice, I ordered us another round. This party was now underway.

There was less talk and more physical contact; there was less inhibition regarding my surroundings as liquor flowed into my belly and blood flowed into my groin. Awkwardness was replaced by an acceptance that this was just life in Rio, and who was I to question it? Max sipped his drink, turned to me and said "Why don't you take Maria upstairs?"

"That sounds like an excellent idea, sir," I responded. I turned to my new lady friend. "So what do you think?" I asked, as if there was really much question.

"Let's go, big boy," Maria said as I stood, trying to keep from jutting out of the front fold of my robe. As we began to walk away, she added "But only if we take Noelle. I don't go anywhere without her."

I turned to Max. "She's your girl. Why aren't you taking her?"

"She's not my type," he winked. "Besides, I'm not ready yet. I'm still shopping. Go on, make me proud up there!"

The *suite* upstairs was austere, an odd combination of pure sexual function and hospital-room sterility. Holding no furniture except a sheet-covered queen sized bed, the headboard was a mirrored wall. In the corner sat only a phone and a clock that began ticking down time like I was commencing a football game. The ball had already been kicked off.

My two *acompanhantes* began to undress each other while I watched. They continued to caress each other's naked bodies, each the picture of perfection in their own right. My robe dropped to the floor. Maria walked to me and took my hand. She stood nearly six feet tall, chocolate-skinned, lean, with black hair, dark nipples, and a small patch of trimmed hair pointing down to her lips. She led me sensually over to where Noelle lay on her side across the bed.

"I want you to start with her," Maria said. "I will join you." As far as I was concerned, she could be the director of this show. Without a word, I pressed my body against Noelle's. She was a petite, tan, blond, the complete opposite of Maria. Variety truly is the spice of life. Her ass felt tight in my hands, and her breasts firm in my mouth. Bossa nova music played melodically as we caressed each other, until I was ready for more. I motioned for Maria to join us on the bed, where the women simultaneously put their mouths on me. Max was right, this was heaven.

I moved Maria onto her back, lay on top of her, and slid inside. She moaned while I watched myself in the mirror behind her head. Noelle watched, kissed me, and fondled her friend's breasts. When she couldn't wait any longer, Noelle begged for her share. I pulled out of Maria, allowed Noelle to take my place and stood up as they kissed each other passionately. With Noelle now lying on top of Maria, ass in the air, I approached her from behind and entered her while standing up. My world was spinning with pleasure. The phone rang.

"Time's up, asshole!" a voice yelled as the door flew open. Noelle leapt off of me and the girls scampered toward the wall then out the door. I was left standing in the middle of the room wondering what the fuck was going on; and what the next move was for a naked man with a hard-on.

Before I could formulate a cohesive plan, a masked man in jungle camouflage utilities lunged toward me. He shot straight for my legs, presumably trying to take down the taller man. I side-stepped and parried him away with a quick strike to his exposed left shoulder. I moved a few paces back from him as he quickly rolled back onto his feet in a low crouch. No words were spoken, but I knew exactly what the tactics would be. We possessed opposite body types with opposite strengths. He was short and sinewy, well-designed as a grappler. I was taller and bulkier, with the skills of a puncher and kicker. I needed to keep distance and strike using my reach advantage.

The masked man moved in slowly this time, waiting for me to make a move. I didn't. I waited until he reached for my right shoulder. He already knew my right fist was my chosen weapon. He held a weak grip – I tried to surprise him by not pulling back. I rotated my left hip toward him and hammered his exposed right mid-section with a left knee. He lost his grip and regrouped.

I capitalized on his moment of weakness. I followed with a left leg kick, driving my shin hard into his right thigh. It wouldn't take him down, but I wanted to soften him before going in for the kill.

I couldn't see his face, but his lack of movement and wide eyes told me that I had a window of opportunity. I was getting fatigued and a bit intoxicated – my window was closing.

Rearing back, I stepped forward with my left foot and thrust my best right punch forward. Time slowed as I watched my hand sail over my attacker's ducking form. Having put everything into my ill-advised haymaker, I could do nothing to stop from leaning forward into an off balanced stance. For a split second I could see Matty Bannen shaking his head in disapproval.

Camouflage Man allowed himself to fall onto his back as he rolled underneath me. I was an aged redwood looking down at an experienced lumberjack, helpless against the inevitable. He grabbed the back of my left knee with his right arm as he rolled instantaneously onto his left side. He wrapped up like a boa constrictor, hooking his right shin across my left thigh and swinging his left thigh through the back of my left leg. I went from leaning forward to falling backward before I could react.

I was flat on my back – exactly where I knew I did not want to end up with this guy. He had a strong leg on either side of my left, to which he added upward pressure with his hands to my ankle. I could do nothing as he held me vice-like in a wicked leg bar. I tried to keep from wincing as he slowly added pressure to the vice. He knew he had me.

Our eyes locked in silence for a moment filled with questions. Who is this guy? Why didn't I work harder to achieve more Marine Corps Martial Arts Training? Where are my clothes? This really sucks!

CHAPTER 11

WASHINGTON, D.C.

Melanie Chang sat alone at a worn, nondescript desk in her cramped office. Sharing the space with nine others during daylight hours, she'd recently become accustomed to being the last to leave. Those two hours after most had departed the Eisenhower Executive Office building were the ones that had propelled the twenty-seven year old Chinese-American to a permanent position on the White House advance staff. She had worked for President Estevanez back when he was the governor of California, as a part time volunteer helping coordinate events. She was a student at the University of CA at Davis, her daddy a major campaign contributor from San Francisco.

Melanie had spent her first four years after college as a naval officer, having graduated from UC Davis and receiving a commission from the cross-town NROTC program at UC Berkeley. Her father had plenty of funds that he could've used to pay for college, but believed that the military would help Melanie develop necessary life skills. She agreed, so long as daddy would help her with her follow-on career.

Ensign Chang was pleasantly surprised at how much she enjoyed her selected specialty of naval intelligence. She served her four years with vigor before it was time to move on.

Old man Chang arranged to have Melanie brought on as a volunteer with the Estevanez White House, and covered her living costs in the expensive D.C. area. After little more than a year on staff, she'd proven herself to be far more than just daddy's little girl. Melanie put to use the skills she'd honed as a junior officer, working more hours and accepting more travel than her fellow staffers. She was rewarded with a paid position, which brought with it increased responsibility and operational knowledge. Because the paltry salary did not match the job's prestige, her father's money continued to supplement her income.

Eyes glazed and red from staring at a computer screen in the poor light of the outmoded government building, she powered down and packed her laptop, painstakingly dressed in preparation for the arctic wind chill that waited outside, slung her backpack over her shoulder, and headed out onto Pennsylvania Avenue. The street was empty, excepting the omnipresent uniformed Secret Service agents and a young couple taking photographs of the White House through thick iron gates. Melanie took pause near the couple in order to share their admiration of a nighttime view of the illuminated Aquia-sandstone. It was amazing how the fatigue of a long day and the brutal weather could be suspended by the regality of this presidential palace. Just seeing it reminded her of the honor she felt to be so young and work so near the heartbeat of this great nation.

The crowd in the front room of Old Ebbit Grill was a mix of political power brokers and tourists. Those that wanted to be seen and those that wanted to be seen with them. The majestic Old Bar's high ceilings, glossed mahogany, and polished brass were matched only by the quality of food and drink served on them. Melanie worked her way through the ogling crowd of self-important men to Grant's Bar in the back of the establishment. This turn-of-the-century style saloon had a more intimate feel, with lower ceilings that compressed the smoky air and emboldened the large nude painting behind the bar.

The bar area was jammed with familiar faces, most halfcocked from spending the last three hours powering down pints of microbrewed beer and highballs of single malts. As Melanie approached her coworkers and acquaintances, a young man in a silk shirt and wool slacks sprung from a booth opposite the bar. Hooking her waist with his arm, he slung her into the booth with him. She gasped audibly for air as she fell into the high-backed leather, turning quickly to view her abductor. She smiled openmouthed and laughed with delight.

"I thought you were going to be studying late tonight?" Melanie asked, now sitting on Silk Shirt's lap.

"I could not bear to be without you another night," he smiled. "You are barely ever around as it is. I have to take advantage of it when you're actually here."

"I know, I know," Melanie said with a coy smile as she flipped her wavy black hair away from her face. "I just thought you had a test tomorrow. Besides, I'm counting on getting all the answers from you when I finally go to law school."

"Oh, and what are you going to do to for me? You know how it works in this city – give a little to get a little," he responded with a suggestive grin.

"You know I've been on the road a while, so I bet you can guess what you'll be getting in return. I think I can arrange an advance payment tonight!"

"Alright, now we're talking. How about a drink?"

Melanie nodded, hopped up and pulled her man toward the bar. She approached a group of three friends: two were thirty-something men in dark suits and closely cropped hair, one was an older woman with too much make-up and not enough skirt to cover her shapeless legs.

"Hey guys, I want you to meet my new man," Melanie said. "Andy, Barry, Shirley, this is Steven." Hands were firmly shaken, smiling pleasantries and nods exchanged. Steven was well dressed in his silk blend button-down and starched black slacks, yet stood out without a tie and jacket among the post-work, government crowd.

"Steven, what do you do?" Barry asked.

"I attend Georgetown law."

"Oh great," Shirley responded like a cougar on the prowl. "We can always use another young lawyer on the staff."

"Easy there, he's mine for now," Melanie chided and pulled herself close to the aspiring lawyer, her head resting on his chest.

"Can I get you a drink?" Andy asked, devoid of any emotion.

"No thanks, somebody's got to watch out for this one," Steven said, pointing down at Melanie. "What do you guys do?" Steven asked of the group.

"These two hotties are Secret Service, and I'm on the staff with Melanie," the cougar said. "I'm sure you've heard all about me!"

Steven smiled as she rambled on about all the people she'd befriended during her years in D.C.

Steven was far more interested in hearing from the agents, but they were not in a talkative mood. He tolerated an hour of Shirley's stories and Melanie's overindulgence in cosmopolitans before he broke. "Mel, I do have to get up in the morning. Did you want me to drive you home, or do you just want to fend for yourself?" He was hoping for the former, but was losing patience. It was never easy being the sober boat awash in a drunken sea.

"Take me home!" Melanie declared before hugging what seemed like the entire bar patronage goodnight. Steven shook hands with Andy and Barry; cordial, yet he sensed a warning to take care of the naïve California girl. He endured a hug from Shirley then escorted the slightly inebriated staffer through the waning crowd.

The roads were empty as Steven drove his Volvo S-60 past the Jefferson Memorial and across the 14th Street Bridge into Arlington. Melanie was passed out in the passenger seat. He parked outside Melanie's red-bricked townhome in Fairlington, and carried her inside. The vast clusters were originally built as defense department quarters during WWII. The area had since become a desirable neighborhood, based on its safe, suburban feel only minutes from downtown D.C. Her father had arranged the rental with a business associate.

Once inside, Steven carried his female luggage upstairs and laid her in bed. He kissed her forehead, placed a glass of water on her bed stand, and descended the stairs with Melanie's backpack in hand.

Steven went to the basement office and, with flashlight clamped in his teeth, rifled through the bag. While her laptop came to life, he spread her papers across the floor, pulled a digital camera out of his jacket pocket, and photographed each document: official letters, printed schedules, handwritten notes. He repacked the papers and turned to the computer. The floor creaked. He closed the laptop, pocketed the flashlight, and slid to the foot of the stairs. Nothing in the house stirred. Melanie's neighbors were returning from their own Thursday evening festivities.

The law student moved back to the table, and began to hack into her password protected computer. It was a two-step process, and Steven had witnessed them both. He fished her identification card from her purse and slid it into a card reader on the side of the machine. It recognized Melanie Chang as the registered possessor of the machine, and requested her password. Without missing a beat, he typed *CaliMel85* and hit *enter* – *Welcome!* Steven smiled while he envisioned himself standing behind Melanie, massaging her neck observantly while she slaved away on her Dell.

After copying as many files as would fit onto his 4 GB thumb drive, Steven shut down the machine. He repacked everything as he had found it, placed the bag by the front door, and disappeared into the cold clear night.

Suspecting that it would draw more attention to have a cell call intercepted in Farsi, the call was placed in English. It was answered on the first ring.

"Yes, Nabil?" the voice on the other end queried.

"Let's meet for lunch tomorrow. I have a present for you," Nabil Bousa answered as he drove his Volvo back to his Foggy Bottom apartment.

CHAPTER 12

Nabil descended the half flight of stairs from New Hampshire Avenue and approached the door to Simurgh restaurant. As he grasped the loose handle and opened the creaky door, Nabil was met by the smell of saffron and onion. It flashed his memory back to the first time he had met Ahmed, three years ago in this very spot. It was exactly as he remembered. Ahmed, a restaurateur in his mid-fifties with a wife and four children, had lived in D.C. for five years. He had struggled for years as a cook in Tehran, unsure how to support his growing family in a declining economic environment. He was approached by al-Ayande with an offer to provide for his family. Ahmed would receive enough money to cover his family's move, costs of running the restaurant, and living expenses. The catch was that he would have to uproot and move to a foreign land. His entire family lived in Tehran, and he spoke little English. However, he could not bear to watch his wife and young children suffer. He accepted.

Upon his arrival in the U.S., Ahmed followed instructions to contact a man he was to know by only a first name. Billy was an African-American who had converted to Islam while in prison for an assault he committed when he was eighteen at a party in Southeast D.C. Now thirty years old, he had been a free man for over eight years. Billy put to use his lifelong knowledge of the D.C. area in his capacity as a logistician for al-Ayande. It was his responsibility to find everything from computer equipment to rental apartments to used automobiles. He had discovered Nabil's current residence and the available lease for Simurgh.

Nabil, like Billy, knew little of others' responsibilities within al-Ayande. The leaders of the movement figured the less each person knew beyond their own scope of work, the less possibility of important information or plans being compromised. This further enabled al-Ayande to purport itself as a movement of peaceful, gradual change. Ahmed had been entrusted with more responsibility because he had proven himself to be diligent and reliable in the past, and with a family of six, he had more to lose. He had been promoted to a position in future plans and operations, whereas Nabil was merely an intelligence gatherer.

Ahmed heard the bell jangle from above the opening door and felt the rush of cold outside air. He came out from behind the counter to greet his young friend.

"Hello Nabil, it is so good to see you," Ahmed said.

"You too, Ahmed," Nabil responded as the two men hugged and kissed hello. Ahmed stood more than a foot shorter than Nabil, both due to height and posture. Ahmed suffered from polio, his back and legs were ravaged by the disease. It was a testament to his determination that he was able to walk and conduct the heavy lifting required of his job.

"Please sit down. We will have coffee and lunch together," Ahmed pointed toward the empty chair opposite the one in which he seated himself. He called in the direction of the kitchen, "Sasha, could you bring us two coffees, please?" Without verbal response, a svelte olive-skinned Persian waitress appeared with a tray holding the requested coffee and its accoutrements.

"Sasha, I want you to meet Nabil Bousa," Ahmed said without standing.

Nabil stood and greeted the young Persian.

"Sasha is my oldest daughter. She will be twenty five this year. Isn't she beautiful?" Ahmed posed to nobody in particular.

Nabil smiled and nodded. Indeed she was, yet he was unsure how he was supposed to answer the question without offending his friend's conservative sensibilities.

"Aren't you the same age?" Ahmed asked Nabil.

"I'm getting there. I am twenty-three," Nabil responded.

"But you are a mature twenty-three. You will need to be if I am to allow you to marry my daughter someday," Ahmed said with a belly laugh that rocked his head back. "Okay, okay. Enough playing matchmaker for one visit. Time to eat. Sasha, bring us each some kabob and rice."

As Sasha glided away, Ahmed moved closer to the table and spoke in hushed tones. "So what did you find, my friend?"

Nabil handed Ahmed the memory stick. "This is straight from the White House advance planning office," Nabil explained.

With raised eyebrows, Ahmed asked "How did you – I don't want to know, as long as it's good information."

"It's from a very reliable source. The best part is that they don't even know that they are a source," Nabil smirked.

"So it is a resource that can be tapped again. Excellent. I look forward to reviewing it," Ahmed shook the stick slowly in his hand before sliding in into his pocket. Sasha returned with two bowls of saffron rice and lamb kabobs as Ahmed changed the subject. "So Nabil, how is school?"

"I'm doing well. I have learned an incredible amount about the U.S. legal system. It is amazing how forgiving it is for the criminal; it seems that they have all the advantages, and that the victim must overcome to achieve justice."

"A valuable tool…you will be quite an asset to our people once you have completed your education," Ahmed observed. "I am very proud of you, Nabil. I love my daughters very much, but I would like to have a son such as you."

"Thank you, sir. Since my parents were unable to move to the U.S. with me, they have appreciated that you have been like a close uncle."

"You know I am always here for you, my friend," the older man said.

"Thank you," Nabil said as he stood. "Unfortunately, I must be going. I have to get to a seminar, and you know how traffic is getting over to Georgetown."

"Yes, it's so close to here, yet takes so long. Someday the city will build a Metro station there," Ahmed said.

"But that would only invite an influx of lowly minorities like us," Nabil laughed.

"Ha, they can have it then," Ahmed chided. "Anyway, it was good to see you as always."

"Until next time," Nabil bid his old friend adieu.

Ahmed stood and watched the young law student ascend the stairs back to New Hampshire Ave. He daydreamed of him taking Sasha from him someday, and smiled. As the door rattled closed, however, he was shaken back to reality. The smile now replaced by stoicism, he reached into his pocket and gripped the memory stick. Without removing it, he told his family that he would be indisposed for the afternoon. They would be shorthanded for the lunch rush. He had bigger fish to fry than the citrus salmon sizzling in the kitchen.

CHAPTER 13

The two levels above Simurgh restaurant were formerly apartments occupied by the Chinese immigrants who operated the previous establishment. The business had been shutdown for publicly unknown reasons, and its occupants unceremoniously disappeared. Within two weeks, Mandarin cuisine was replaced with Persian. Little else was done to stylistically affect the change. The structure was untouched. Finely woven Arabian tapestries replaced paintings of the Chinese countryside. The second floor had also remained the same, providing sufficient yet simple living quarters for the Simurgh family. The third floor, however, had undergone an overhaul.

Ahmed stood in front of what had the outward appearance of a closet door. He unlocked the door, which opened to stairs leading to the top floor. Only he possessed a key, and his wife and children dared not defy his instructions to keep out. He locked the door behind him, and climbed quickly now. At least as fast as his debilitated muscles would carry him. He was excited. It had been some time since he had any real information to provide his superiors. While he did not have any personal interest in the intel he gathered, the quality and quantity had a direct impact on the money he received.

The top-story apartment was three rooms, yet only one was authorized for use. In order to provide a sufficient sound buffer to the neighbors on either side, the two end rooms had been sealed shut. This left the center room, a windowless eight by ten foot space, which was really more a foyer between two bedrooms than an actual room. Crowded by a large desk littered with computer and communications equipment, and lined with tall, thin wall safes, the makeshift office was far more utilitarian than it was comfortable. The worst part for the polio-stricken Ahmed was the lack of a bathroom, which had been rendered inaccessible by the sealed doors. He worked quickly to shorten his time spent in isolation.

Ahmed seated himself at an inexpensive faux-wood desk that he and Billy had pieced together along with the rest of the office furnishings that they had purchased at Staples. He plugged the stick into the USB port and waited with anticipation. The E:\ drive opened and displayed a litany of intriguing folders: Excel spreadsheet schedules, PowerPoint event diagrams, Word document after-action reports. Ahmed dug deeper to determine how much pertinence could be discerned from this apparent gold mine.

It appeared that Melanie Chang's most recent trip had been a multiple city swing through the Midwest. There was an after-action detailing the logistics of a rally at the Saint Paul River Centre, a fundraiser at a mansion in the Chicago suburb of Naperville, and a speech to servicemen at Dayton's Wright-Patterson Air Force Base. The president had an aggressive travel schedule, which meant that Melanie and every one of her coworkers had an aggressive schedule. The attention to detail involved in the travel and event preparation was staggering to Ahmed. The attached PowerPoint slides displayed each location that the president of the U.S., or POTUS as the files abbreviated, was to encounter. If there was to be movement in that room, arrows depicted the exact footpath to be followed. If there was to be either a standing or seating arrangement, numbers specified who would be positioned where. Every aspect had been accounted for.

The written reports highlighted which airports had been utilized by Air Force One, which hotels had hosted not only the staff but POTUS as well, and some even included motorcade routes. Ahmed read from one of the after-actions:

> POTUS arrived at MSP onboard AF-1 at 1450 after a morning event in Lincoln, NE. Traveling without FLOTUS, his entourage included Senators Robbins and Smith, COS, WHMU, Milaide, and USSS. The airport arrival was open-press, and included a meet and greet with local volunteer organization. No problems. (See attachment 1)

> POTUS departed airport via motorcade, which was 15 vehicles including press vans. Minneapolis PD provided motorcycle escort along route, from I-494 to I-35E to St Paul. The lead vehicles broke off and entered the River Centre from rear, underground entrance. Press and remaining vehicles parked outside. The lack of room for all vehicles prevented coverage for a brief time, and caused POTUS to wait in hold for 10 minutes. (See attachment 2)

> POTUS entered stage right without working rope-line

and moved directly to podium. Lighting was excellent, but sound was too loud at first and had to be reduced to optimal level. POTUS was unfazed, but more attention to detail by WHCA required for future events. Speech delivered on benefits of international business ventures as a means of improving U.S. image abroad. Well received, except for two hecklers. USSS had them quickly escorted to rear exits for questioning. Speech was concluded and followed by POTUS working the rope-line for 15 minutes prior to departure.

While the report continued, Ahmed did not need to finish. He already believed he had information that his superiors would find beneficial. Not to mention he was having some difficulty understanding the multitude of acronyms. Somebody else could translate. He opened another file, this one a spreadsheet.

Travel Schedule (Tentative)

01/19A ADW – ETD: 0800 BOS - ETA: 0930 (AF-1)
Boston University, Mass General (motorcade)

01/19B BOS – ETD: 1300 JFK – ETA: 1330 (AF-1)
NYSE, Ground Zero (helo lift)

01/19C LGA – ETD: 1900 ADW – ETA: 2000 (AF-1)

01/20A WH – ETD: 1500 CAMP – ETA: 1535 (M-1)
Camp David weekend

01/23A CAMP – ETD: 0800 ADW – ETA: 0845 (M-1)

01/23B ADW – ETD: 0900 MGE – ETA: 1045 (AF-1)
Home Depot, Dobbins AFB (motorcade)

01/23C MGE – ETD: 1700 MIA – ETA: 1830 (AF-1)
(RON) Coral Gables fundraiser (motorcade)

01/24A MIA – ETD: 1400 ADW – ETA: 1600 (AF-1)

01/25 Ft Belvoir (motorcade)

01/26 Bethesda Naval Hosp, physical (helo lift)

01/27A   ADW – ETD: 0800 LAX – ETA: 1030 (AF-1)
UCLA, LAPD (helo lift)

01/27B   LAX – ETD: 1400   MCC – ETA: 1530 (AF-1)
CA capitol building (motorcade)

01/27C   SAC – ETD: 1900 Res – ETA: 1945 (M-1)
Working vacation at Tahoe residence

02/06A   Res – ETD: 0700 RNO – ETA: 0720 (M-1)

02/06B   RNO – ETD: 0745 **TBD (overseas)**

The president's schedule did not forecast beyond February 6, but it was clear that he was leaving the country. Ahmed was unsure whether it was more useful to have detailed itineraries within the U.S. or vague hints of foreign exposure. He took solace in the fact that it was not his decision to make. His task was to sift through the vast amounts of leads accrued in the region and forward those deemed relevant.

Ahmed perused the remaining documents with diligence, though for the most part discovered nothing of significance. Such was the nature of intelligence gathering – many hours spent in the hopes of a few invaluable seconds. Then, just as it was time for a much needed bathroom break, there it was. The letter was entitled *Request for Pre-Advance Travel: European and South American Sites*. Ahmed immediately printed the document as if it would disappear from the screen. He snatched it and the other relevant papers and shuffled to the secure fax machine. He dialed 011.98.21.312.6284 and hit send.

CHAPTER 14

DAKAR, SENEGAL

Martin Breaux returned to Africa more confused than when he departed. He was fairly certain that he had Georges Decroix figured out. Here was a man with no political or religious agenda. He was merely a man seeking a higher standard of living for himself and his family, and was willing to use his position and some unscrupulous means to achieve these ends. Jack Stark, on the other hand, posed more intricate questions. Quite enigmatic, Stark seemed to feign both ignorance and a cavalier attitude. But was there more to his story?

Since his voyage to Paris days earlier, Breaux had observed an apparent change of heart in Decroix. The same man who had ordered his apprehension and harassment at the airport had e-mailed him twice since to request updates for future business. Given the state of the rest of the world's currencies, the euro proved a strong aphrodisiac. Breaux had not responded, but chose to play hard to get. At a minimum, there would be no more free appetizers. If Breaux were to present any more cash laden briefcases to the corrupt police chief, it would bear fruit.

What had not changed was Decroix's paranoia. He did not feel it appropriate to meet Breaux in his downtown office on a repeated basis. He was a well recognized figure in Dakar, and while he often conducted business with high-level officials and foreign businessmen, he desired to remain one step ahead of anyone who may be trying to ensnare him in controversy.

After an uneventful flight from Paris, Breaux approached the long, disorganized customs line with a wheeled suitcase and canvas briefcase slung over his shoulder. Outfitted in a dark gray suit and open-collar shirt, he appeared as any other Parisian businessman coming to Dakar to both seek fortune and enjoy the tropical setting. He scanned the area, trying not to appear nervous, though hoping this venture through the airport would proceed more smoothly than the last.

Beyond his periphery, a hand the size of an oven-mitt grabbed his right arm. *"Monsieur Girard?"* The hand was attached to a large Wolof man wearing western-style casual clothes.

"Who wants to know?" Breaux asked, his cool demeanor belying his internal apprehension.

The conversation continued in French. "I am Deputy Adama Gueye. Chief Decroix dispatched me to make sure that you had no problems here at the airport. And to get you checked into your hotel."

Well, this is a pleasant change from my previous visit. The giant Wolof hoisted the suitcase from the faux diamond merchant and the two men breezed by the outskirts of the customs line. Knowing nods were exchanged between Gueye and the armed customs agent. Breaux looked around for anyone from his previous customs encounter, but saw none of them. *Perhaps they were in a back room molesting some other poor sap.*

A burgundy Renault Sport Saloon awaited the two gentlemen adjacent to a police checkpoint. A boyish uniformed guard stepped out from the confines of the booth to open the doors and trunk upon their arrival. Decroix had obviously sent one of his higher ranking deputies to make this rendezvous. As Breaux sat down in the rear seat of the sedan, a cloud of mosquitoes engulfed him. He worked to keep them from flying into his mouth, nose, and eyes; all the while wondering how natives survived without the malaria medication he had been taking since his U.S. departure. Gueye climbed in the driver's seat without a second thought about the little bloodsucking monsters.

The drive out of the airport and onto the main road could not come soon enough. The dark car, even as it sat with open windows, had accumulated sweltering heat. It was the midst of Senegal's hottest season, and Breaux had not yet acclimated due to his winter time departure from D.C. Gueye maneuvered onto the open road and employed whatever he could muster from the 1.6 liter turbo under the hood of the small French sedan. The hot air was at least quite dry this time of year, and as they approached the coast there was a salty sea-breeze that Breaux could taste on his lips. Gueye did his best cursory job of playing tour guide as they whirred along the well worn two-lane road. The city's most upscale casino was not much more than the size of an American bar and grill, and was absent the typical neon glow of those Breaux was familiar with. The city's best pizza place blurred by on the left; as it did, Gueye hooked hard right onto a single lane driveway.

The view that opened in front of them was breathtaking. As the Hotel Méridien President came into view, Breaux could see the rocky coastline that jutted out into the Atlantic Ocean. The waves crashed hard, and the wind exaggerated the white foam that beset the deep blue water. The scene created an interesting dichotomy of natural and human circumstances.

The hotel itself held an aging regality, symbolic of the former French control of the region. It still provided a desirable tropical getaway for European travelers seeking a beachside retreat at less expense than the Mediterranean. However, it had clearly seen its zenith some years ago, much like the French nation that once was an international empire. The natural setting of the coastline was as beautiful as anything Breaux had seen in his travels. The dark rocks and sand were reminiscent of the Maine coast, while the hot and dry climate with desert-style greenery drew images of Baja, Mexico. The irony, as is often the case in such locales, was that the native inhabitants were both downtrodden and financially poor. Breaux recalled the stories his mother had told him of his roots that led back to Africa. His predecessors had lived in what is now Côte d'Ivoire, and had enjoyed similar settings. Breaux was sure that the legend had been greatly romanticized, yet he could not help but hearken back to a time when his family enjoyed life prior to enslavement.

Breaux checked into the hotel under his assumed name of François Girard, and presented identification and credit card in that name. He was handed a note by the girl at the registration desk. She appeared to be a native Senegalese yet spoke flawless French and English. This was typical of the young professionals hired by high-end international hotels. It also provided a forum for those young up-and-comers to hone their linguistic skills as a precursor to entrance into the business world. The note indicated that he was to join Decroix at the outdoor restaurant adjacent the pool.

Breaux took a few moments to freshen himself in his room before his poolside meeting. The room was surprisingly roomy for its French construction, but reflected the worn look of the exterior. It was surely not worth the 200 dollars per night, but it did have a great view and air conditioning. He splashed water on his face to both cool down and wipe away the grunge of traveling all day in the heat. He looked in the mirror one last time and motivated himself for the aggressive bargaining session that was about to take place. He knew that Decroix was not going to like his proposition, so he would have to be on his game.

Breaux walked out the back door of the hotel onto the expansive patio area that incorporated the large pool and a covered open-air restaurant. The lunch crowd had thinned by this time of afternoon, leaving most people by the pool. With all the white Europeans lounging in chaises or frolicking in the ice blue water, Decroix's large black figure was clearly recognizable as he sat alone at a table in the shaded restaurant. His back was to Breaux as he took in the ocean view and enjoyed a cigar.

Decroix sensed Breaux's presence behind him. "Good afternoon, Monsieur Girard," he greeted without standing, or even turning his large bald head. "Please join me, enjoy some of Senegal's best views."

Breaux took a seat across from the head of the gendarmerie. "Do you mean the beach or the young topless Françaises by the pool?"

"Yes," Decroix answered with that now familiar smile of large white teeth gripping a Churchill. He was sipping a tall drink mottled with mint leaves. "Do you know how hard it is to find good bourbon in this city?" Breaux figured that it was a mint julep. Here he was a world away from his home with a man that could have been a long-lost cousin of his, watching him sip a beverage that held such historical prevalence in the southern U.S. "Ever have a mint julep?"

"I've heard of them, but it's not real common in France," Breaux feigned. "I'll try one."

Decroix snapped his fingers, waved his hand slightly, and a fresh round of cocktails appeared as if from nowhere. "Santé," the two men clanked glasses. Decroix sipped his drink and daydreamed of a better life. Breaux sipped and was instantly home in Louisiana with family at a backyard barbecue. He was unsure how long he had been in his own world when he was snapped back to reality.

"Let's get down to the business so we can each enjoy moments like this for the rest of our lives," Decroix said as he did a complete head turn to clear the area of would-be listeners. "There is a shipment coming in from the south that will include a large amount of what you are seeking. As the only one who can get access to the quantity and quality you need, I would like to make you an offer."

"I'm listening," Breaux answered, as the two men began to haggle back and forth over prices. This was standard jousting. The numerical gap and flamboyant disagreements were merely cultural norms, and as expected they melted away as the deal was struck and hands were shaken.

"Great. So that's it, then," Decroix declared.

"Well, there is one additional issue," Breaux prepared to broach the subject at what he hoped was the right time. He did not want to scare off the chief before he had hooked him with the bait of another euro-filled briefcase.

"What?" Decroix seemed puzzled.

"My bosses have insisted that I get a firsthand view of the mines," Breaux responded.

"Out of the question," Decroix crossed his arms, symbolic of his suddenly closed off demeanor. "It's too dangerous for both of us. I cannot have some French businessman running around the countryside. Do you realize that there is rebel activity in that region? They don't give a shit who you are or how much money you have. Actually, if they did know you had money, it'd probably be worse!"

Breaux expected such a response, but attempted to reason with Decroix.

"I understand your reservations, but you must appreciate the perspective of my bosses," Breaux said. "The market has been flooded with fake stones, and they are getting more and more difficult to identify. The best way for me to reassure them is to view the site with my own eyes. I know you can arrange it – provide the necessary security. You are a powerful man, and could soon be a very wealthy one as well."

Decroix knew he wanted this deal, but had too much at stake to budge for one deal. No matter how lucrative.

Breaux did not truly expect the chief to cave, but instead was testing him. By pushing him to the brink of losing the deal, he had learned what he had wanted.

"I am sorry that we have been unable to strike an agreement here," Breaux said with furrowed brow. "I would be willing to readdress this with my superiors to see if they will change their minds. Perhaps we can figure out a different path to the same end state."

Decroix was still visibly upset. "We'll see." He was not a man who was accustomed to hearing the word *No*, and made little attempt to accommodate it. He did not make eye contact with Breaux as he stood, his figure looming large. "You can contact me if your stance changes. I hope it does." Decroix turned and walked away, followed by a trail of cigar smoke. Without looking back he said "Bon voyage, Monsieur Girard."

Martin Breaux now hoped that his next steps went as according to plan as the first just had.

CHAPTER 15

Breaux didn't check out of the Hotel Méridien, yet removed some essential items from the room before he departed. He wanted to leave the impression that he was not going anywhere anytime soon. He still had all the money he had arrived with, and was about to put it to good use.

It was no coincidence that Breaux took Adama Gueye's phone number prior to parting ways at the hotel registration desk. Breaux pulled out the cell phone he had purchased during his last trip to Dakar. He regularly acquired phones with long term contracts that would not raise the suspicion of a short term phone. The phone usage never exceeded two weeks. He paid cash to avoid the ability to track the repeated purchases. Breaux had yet to use this phone that had come free with the calling plan. He activated it and placed its first call.

"Deputy Gueye," the officer answered.

"Good afternoon, deputy. This is François Girard – the guy you dropped at the Méridien earlier today."

"Yes," he responded with a predictably circumspect tone, surprised to hear from the diamond merchant. "How may I help you?"

"As it turns out, I need another ride. I know you're not a taxi service, but I think you will want to provide this ride yourself. Can you be at that pizza place across the street in one hour?"

"I suppose," Gueye spoke slowly, still trying to figure out where this was going.

"Oh, one more thing. You must tell no one of this rendezvous. You should go home sick and expect to be out of work for a few days. I think you're beginning to feel quite ill."

Breaux sat alone in the corner of *Rallye Pizza's* enclosed back room. There were two lunch-time groups partaking of the city's most upscale Italian-style brick oven pies. The native businessmen sat in an open air courtyard, oblivious to the stifling heat and omnipresent large black flies that hovered over every dish they could sniff out. All other things being equal, Breaux might have selected to sit inside purely for purposes of anonymity. In this instance it was more for the cool, somewhat less infested air, than it was for tactical reasons.

The out-of-place Creole enjoyed a draught beer and pretended to eat some of his margherita pizza while he waited. He had already gotten his fill from the extensive seafood buffet at the Méridien, courtesy of a hopeful Decroix. That was before their meeting had abruptly ended. *At least I got something out of the deal.*

Adama Gueye found his way to the back of the small pizzeria, avoiding contact with both staff and patrons. He had never been inside, and was impressed with the contemporary décor and aromas wafting from the kitchen. While there was certainly African influence to the construction, the confines reflected the Tuscan roots of the owners. Gueye rarely made the trip out to this more expensive area of the city's outskirts. He would never be able to part with his hard earned money to pay for a specialty like pizza. Like most typical Senegalese, he dined at home on meals such as ceebu jen, a traditional fish and rice dish. Meats other than chicken were a rarity in Dakar, enjoyed mostly by the wealthy European transplants. Small fish like flounder and mullet, served whole with onions and sauce, were the common man's diet.

After finding Breaux, the deputy slouched into the chair opposite him, making sure to keep his back to any would-be onlookers. He was pleased that the foreigner at least had the good sense to be discreet with his location. The last thing that Gueye wanted was to appear that he was disobeying the chief. Decroix maintained a jovial outward appearance, but ruled his department with an iron fist. On the occasion that he was crossed, he did not allow opportunities to pass without making an example of what not to do.

Last month, two of his officers that worked in the downtown Plateau area of Dakar had become a bit too lackadaisical in covering their tracks while inventing their own form of justice regarding the city's prostitution problem. The two young men had started to aggressively patrol the neighborhood while undercover, presumably in an effort to clean it up. They scoured the streets to find each lady of the night that walked her own beat through alleyways and outside nightclubs. Once found, however, the girls were afforded the opportunity to work off their debt to society. The officers accosted working women and escorted them to a nearby hotel that rented rooms by the hour. The night manager was promised added police protection and a few extra francs for his discretion and assistance.

While nobody personally divulged the late night activities of the horny officers, their night supervisor started to see a trended reduction in the arrest activity amongst prostitution. A natural cynic, he did not believe that the proliferation of paid sex had simply subsided due to diligent police work or changes in social mores. He set up a sting operation to observe his officers' behavior. When he busted them, he was left with no option but to forward his discovery to Decroix.

The dictatorial chief decided to send a message that would both dissuade the offenders and teach an irrefutable lesson to the rest of the force. He immediately jailed the guilty party. After leaving them in prison for a few days, he paid them a visit. He had them brought into a large cell with a handful of other police guards present. With the offenders still shackled, he delivered a brief tirade designed for the entire audience. He then had the guards bring in two of the facility's resident sex offenders. One man was serving a life sentence for a series of sexual assaults he had committed while a school teacher; the other had raped and murdered his neighbor's wife. Decroix unsurprisingly explained that these two prisoners could represent the future of the officers if they did not cease their deviant behavior.

Not as predictable was the manner in which he decided to hammer the point home. When he ordered the two convicts to act out how they had taken their sexual liberties, using the captive officers as their props, the crowd of guards, officers, and prisoners stood in stunned disbelief. They collectively waited for Decroix to bluff. He didn't. Instead, he unholstered his pistol and aimed it in the direction of the two hardened rapists. His weapon cocked, he demanded that the convicts pull theirs out and follow orders. The minutes that followed were the makings of legend. The guards were forced to witness a sexual act so twisted and gruesome, it would be burned into the collective memory of those that had to witness it, and the story would spread like wildfire. There were screams, there was blood, and there was permanent trauma amongst all participants.

"I hope this is important," Gueye initiated as he sat. "If Decroix finds out that I'm working with you behind his back, he will be far from happy."

"Listen. I have as much reason as you to avoid any further attention from the chief." Breaux tried to allay any fears. "You and I each have something the other can benefit greatly from, and neither will reap those benefits if Decroix gets wind of our alliance."

"And just what is it that I have that you need?" the deputy inquired.

"The ability to get around without being stopped. There is no way that I could move through some of the outer reaches of Senegal without being accosted. You can provide the kind of access I need."

"Outer reaches? Where are you thinking about going, and why?"

Breaux explained the same request that had been summarily rejected by Decroix. Gueye was cautious, but appeared to leave an opening.

"I'm not sure that this is such a good idea," Gueye said. "What are you offering in return? Obviously not enough to convince my boss that he should partake in your plan."

"I'm prepared to up my offer since I know you are risking your butt," Breaux said. "I think the chief was afraid to help me because of his public position. You are less known and should have less to fear. That being said let me ask you a question. You are recently married, and hope to have children someday, right?" The deputy's eyes closed slightly as he cocked his head, nodding slowly. "Let me presume that it is difficult to provide for a growing family on the income the government pays you." Breaux continued before the deputy could respond. "What would you say if I told you that I could solve that problem for you?"

"I would tell you to go on," Gueye answered. "And that this had better not be bullshit."

"What if I could provide for you and your wife a move to Paris, and give you enough money to live comfortably on until you got settled?" Breaux knew that the deputy already spoke the language, and that there were Muslim neighborhoods in the city that would be a possible fit. However, he had no real way of guaranteeing that he could generate the kind of money necessary to make this happen. But he had baited the hook, and had a large fish biting. He had no intention of letting the tension off of the line. Those details were something he would worry about when the time came, once he had accomplished his own mission.

"How do I know you will come through with what you promise…if I even agree to it?" Gueye did not want to seem too eager.

"How are these stones, for starters?" Breaux pulled a small box from his pocket and opened it. It held six clear diamonds, about one carat each. He knew he could provide more, or some cash if needed, but believed that he could buy the deputy for relatively small funds given his current financial situation.

"How do I know they're the real thing?"

"Have them appraised. Go do it now if you'd like. Just remember that you may raise suspicion depending on who sees you do it. In addition, I am on a tight timeline, and will not be waiting around for you. I can always take my offer elsewhere. Your call," Breaux had him on the ropes.

"I guess you were right. I think I do feel a bit ill. I had better call in and take the next few days off." The deputy was not completely convinced that he was making the right decision, but his job would never provide even close to what he was now holding in his hand. It was a risk worth taking, and he liked the thought of the adventure.

CHAPTER 16

Breaux stood outside Senghor Stadium and smoked a wretched tasting cigarette. At least that's how it tasted to a nonsmoker trying to blend in with the locals. He had been waiting and meandering through the decrepit parking lot for forty minutes. The large multipurpose stadium had been standing since 1985, and was still in respectable condition. The surrounding area did not reflect its modernity. This was typical of Third World infrastructure, or lack thereof. One was likely to find a new building appearing much like a diamond in the rough. Deciding that pacing the parking lot nervously may draw attention to himself, he returned to the vicinity of the will call gate and sat on the ground. The wait was killing him, yet he tried not to show it. He pretended to be an interested patron by occasionally asking for tickets from those that were entering the stadium. There was to be a club football match here in an hour, and the crowd was growing.

Deputy Gueye had instructed Breaux to sit and wait as he departed the restaurant. After ten minutes, he was to request a taxi from the host. This taxi was to take him to the stadium under the presumption that he was going to attend the game. Meanwhile, Gueye was going to disappear for a while, just in case anybody was observing them. Gueye liked the idea of a pickup in the large crowd of the stadium parking lot. People would be busily filing into the arena, and there was less chance of being noticed. Gueye realized that if he were spotted in an isolated area picking up a foreigner and driving off, it would certainly raise questions, and possibly a call to Decroix.

Breaux rocked back and forth as he searched the lot for the Renault. Seconds later an older model Toyota Land Cruiser pulled up only feet from the curb Breaux was occupying, passenger side door in his face.

"Your chariot awaits. Get in." Breaux stood as his head went light for a second, hoping it was not Decroix or one of his henchmen. The feeling passed, replaced with relief at the sight of Gueye in the driver's seat, nervous smile on his face.

"I needed to get us a ride that would make the journey. The roads we'll be on can get a little rough, and that's if we're lucky enough to have roads the whole way," Gueye said.

"I like it," Breaux responded. "I will have to change on the way, but my clothes are still in the hotel room."

"No problem, my friend. I already thought of that, and you looked like you could fit into my little brother's clothes. Besides, it's better to have your bags remain in the hotel room for when somebody decides to get nosy."

Breaux was impressed with this guy's smarts, and with his renewed enthusiasm. He pulled the creaky door open and hopped into the passenger seat.

"Your suitcase is one thing, but that briefcase is another," Gueye said with a point and smile. "It's still full I hope."

"Don't worry about that, big man," Breaux answered. "You worry about the driving and I'll worry about the briefcase." He did not fully trust the deputy yet, but liked his style.

The Land Cruiser pulled out of the lot and accelerated onto the eastbound highway.

"This rendezvous puts us onto the road out of town. There will be no heavy city driving, and therefore no curious eyes. Once we get past the outlying neighborhoods to the northeast, it will be open roads for quite a while."

Breaux did his best to keep the conversation off of himself, so as to avoid either contradicting his story or running out of things to say. He had given much thought to being François Girard, but figured it was not worth the risk spewing unneeded statements. Lucky for him, Gueye seemed perfectly content to sit through extended periods of quiet, with only the warm breeze blowing into the cab. Breaux presumed that Gueye was still a bit nervous about saying too much, that anything he said in front of this stranger could still be used against him in the future.

It was dusk as they passed through the poverty-stricken areas north of Dakar. The roads were extremely dusty, and barely identifiable. They were crossed as much by sheep, goats, and foul as they were automobiles. Most of the vehicles they did observe were buses, painted with psychedelic patterns and colors, and overflowing with people. They appeared as though their past lives as hippie-mobiles in the U.S. were three decades passed, and had been handed down through Goodwill. Breaux was careful not to make any disparaging comments regarding the state of affairs.

"This is the neighborhood where I grew up," Gueye mentioned without expression.

"Do you still have family here?" Breaux asked.

"Yes, I have some cousins, aunts, and uncles just up the road," the deputy pointed across the dashboard to his right. "My family has been here for as long as any of us know. Most of them work at Rose Lake mining salt."

"Do a lot of people work there?" the questions continued.

"Yes, that's where many of the buses go to in the morning. They return in the evening, and then do it again the next day. It's a simple life, but they are content. The crime level is not as bad as other major cities in this part of the world, and the mosque supports the community."

"Mmm," Breaux nodded. He could not help but ponder the irony of people happy with their life in such squalid conditions. He thought about how people in the U.S. would be outraged with the same. He thought about the random selection of those that were shipped off to the West as slaves, while others were left behind in Africa. He wondered if his family would be happier now if they had been spared that brutal journey.

The drive continued past dusk and toward darkness as the two men and their Land Cruiser left the confines of the city for the open spaces that lay in front of them. As his eyes adjusted to the oncoming night sky, Breaux could vaguely make out the landscape. It was flat and dry, and the scenery was dotted by baobab trees. Looking like a fifty foot bottle with a multitude of scraggly arms emanating from its body, this trademark plant was not only Senegal's most useful, but most respected. The omnipresent tree's fruit was used for food and cooking, the bark used for rope, and almost every remaining bit for some sort of homeopathic remedy. The tree itself was often referred to in folk lore and as an almost religious idol for the way it provided.

Before he could ask Gueye if he was okay to drive through the night, Breaux was asleep. He was not sure how long for, but awoke suddenly worried. After all, he was traveling through an unfamiliar area under heavy rebel influence, with a driver that he barely knew and wasn't sure if he could trust. Just before he opened his eyes, he had a vision that his briefcase had been taken, and that he was left on the side of the road to fend for himself. These were always Breaux's least comfortable situations, when he knew that he needed to sleep because he had been moving nonstop with no time to rest. Yet his circumstances dictated constant vigilance. He must stay awake. No sooner had this thought crossed his mind that he was out again.

While asleep this time, Breaux imagined that a bright light shone out of the darkness, blinding in his face. He opened his eyes to see that it was no dream. With squinted eyes, he looked left and right to see what appeared to be guerrilla soldiers armed with rifles, while one pointed a flashlight into Gueye's face. The deputy appeared calm.

"Where are you going, and what is the nature of your business?" the soldier demanded in Wolof.

"We are on official government business, and not to be interfered with," Gueye responded, as if from a script as he presented his federal ID.

The rebel soldier looked at the ID and its owner suspiciously. "We do not normally see federal police in this region. Are there more of you?"

"No, we are simply transiting the area, and have no interest in causing any trouble in Casamance," Gueye said, somewhat more conciliatory this time.

"And your friend, who is he?"

"Monsieur Girard is a respected businessman from Paris," Gueye said. "There are a lot of powerful people who would be quite upset if something were to happen to him."

Breaux sensed this may be the time to play the role of nonviolent merchant. He reached into his briefcase. He then heard two rifle bolts slide back and chamber rounds in the barrel. He did not remove his hand from the bag, but spoke Wolof instead.

"You two gentlemen look like capable, intelligent young men. Perhaps you would like to make a little extra money while simply doing your job."

The soldiers did not respond, but continued to listen with rifles pointed at the automobile occupants.

"The deputy speaks the truth. We are merely trying to drive through the area, and cause no disturbance. However, I think that you two young men could provide us a service for which you could be well compensated. May I remove my hand from the bag?" Breaux asked.

"Slowly," the soldier adjacent to the driver's side window warned.

Breaux pulled out the same box that he had used to convince Gueye earlier in the day. He removed two stones, fondling them in his hand.

"I'm betting you could use these," Breaux said. "They could be yours right now if you agree to provide our escort."

"Escort to where?" the soldier asked as he reached for Breaux's hand. Breaux clasped it shut.

"The border of Guinea," Gueye intervened.

"Too far for the price," the soldier shook his head, his demeanor turning sour.

"I can afford to give you each one additional stone, but not until we are safely escorted to the border area," Breaux said as he continued the bartering process. He had known this would transpire, and therefore started his offer low.

The soldier nodded and smiled, and his cohort followed suit. "I have a question. What is to stop us from shooting you both right now, taking all of the stones for ourselves, and not having to provide any escort?"

"If the chief of the gendarmerie were to discover such a thing, the Casamance rebels would face trouble they aren't ready for," Gueye said, though he was not really sure if that were the case. The rebels had been able to exert influence in the area, and it was doubtful the federal government was able or willing to do anything about it. Either way, Gueye was betting that these two bullies would have no way of knowing this political reality.

"Everybody knows the gendarmerie has no power in Casamance," the soldier laughed, emboldened. "I think you are looking at a couple of rich rebels, at least for a few more seconds."

"If you eliminate us now, then you only get what I have on me right now," Breaux said. "If you work with us, you can be paid with an additional reward upon our return trip. We will certainly be seeking your services for the trip back through Casamance. Think about the future, gentlemen."

The soldiers looked at each other, quietly conferring as to whether or not the offer was legitimate and worth the risk. The senior rebel ran through some scenarios in his mind, and determined these intruders were going to need help returning to Dakar. The only way they would not return to Casamance was if they decided to take a more circuitous route through Liberia or Sierra Leone. These options posed numerous pitfalls for the deputy and his merchant companion. The negative attention those areas had garnered as a result of their involvement with the blood diamond industry had made them all but impossible locales from which to smuggle the tainted stones. These two outsiders would almost certainly be in need of a return trip escort.

The silence seemed like an eternity. Sweat built on Breaux's brow in the sweltering night air. Distant sounds of insects and animals emanated from the surrounding jungle. It was the first time he'd noticed that the scenery had changed so drastically. They were no longer in a semiarid climate, but instead were ensconced in lush tropics. Dense greenery encroached onto the dirt road and humidity thickened the air. The starlight that peeked through the overhead canopy was enhanced by the jet black sky behind it. The absence of ambient light served as a reminder that they were far from civilization. Very far. Breaux's body tensed at the thought.

"Okay, we've got a deal," the wary soldier started. "But don't think for a second that you'll be able to get back to Dakar without our help. We can make sure you have an *accident* on the way."

CHAPTER 17

NEAR THE SENEGAL – GUINEA BORDER

The two soldiers led the way for miles, through increasingly hilly and then mountainous terrain. The air remained humid despite the higher altitude and more arid ground. At a spot that appeared unidentifiable to either Gueye or Breaux the lead vehicle stopped. Gueye slowed to a stop adjacent the rebel SUV, and the driver handed Breaux a tattered map through an open window.

"This map will take you the rest of the way," the rebel said. "We cannot take you any farther without personal risk. You can meet us right here upon return, as long as you tell us a meeting time."

"We will be back in twenty-four hours," Breaux said.

"At twenty-five, we will be gone."

"Not to worry, he's in good hands," Gueye reassured. "Back when I was in the military, I used to patrol these areas. I know where to go and who we can talk to."

"Good luck. We hope to see you return safely, with more stones."

Gueye saluted the rebel soldiers, hoping they would keep their word.

Gueye navigated the unmarked trails rapidly through the hills despite the darkness.

"I didn't know you were former military," Breaux said, more as a question than a statement.

"I served in the army for four years prior to joining the police force. I helped to quell rebellious activity in the Casamance region, probably against the same rebels that are helping us today. The uprisings spilled back and forth over multiple borders: The Gambia, Guinea-Bissau, Guinea. I lived in these areas sporadically for two years, and know the roads, villages, and diamond mines well. Let's just say you picked the right tour guide, my friend."

Breaux nodded with an approving smile, wondering if the *friend* reference was sincere. This was such an overused term in foreign lands, almost tongue-in-cheek sarcasm at times. Figuring that beggars could not be choosers, Breaux decided to trust his escort while keeping a watchful eye on him.

It was still pre-dawn when Gueye slowed the Land Cruiser and turned off the trail, maneuvering between the trees. He didn't stop until they were one hundred meters away from the road.

"We will leave the car here," Gueye said as he pulled the keys from the ignition and began to step out of the vehicle.

"Where are we?" Breaux asked.

"We're about a hundred kilometers east of the city of Mali. Not too far from the border with the nation of Mali," Gueye answered.

"Are we near the mine?"

"Not far. Most of the older mines are further south, under heavier control from the federal government of Guinea. There are large companies, mostly European, that have struck agreements with the government. Up this way the federal government has lost control due to splintering rebel activity. These rebel forces have sought autonomy from Conakry, the capital, for decades. Once they discovered diamond mines in this area, they found a way to fund their efforts. However, they didn't have the technological or logistical means to turn their discovery into wealth."

"So what did they do?" Breaux asked.

"Well, somehow they met people in Dakar who knew how to take advantage of the opportunity. I don't know who, but good contacts. You'll see how well-built the facility is, and the surrounding camp."

"Weren't they afraid they'd fall under control of the Senegalese government?"

"I didn't say they were working with the government, just people in Dakar. This deal has nothing to do with the president or anybody else in his regime that I can tell," Gueye said with a shrug.

Breaux was developing the sense that the deputy did not have intelligence regarding al-Ayande, and did not want to broach the subject. He would view the site for himself and gather his own intel.

The two men now stood at the open tailgate of the vehicle. Breaux watched as Gueye opened both floorboard and sideboard compartments, from which he removed two sets of binoculars, two 9-millimeter pistols, and an old AR-15 automatic rifle. He slapped a thirty-round magazine of 5.56-millimeter into its holder, chambered a round, and slung the weapon over his shoulder. After slipping two additional cartridges into the cargo pocket of his heavy black pants, he offered a set of binoculars and a pistol to Breaux.

"Do you know how to use this?" Gueye asked as he held the pistol by the barrel.

"I've shot one at an indoor range before," the faux merchant lied as he took the weapon and tucked it into his waist band.

"Good. Don't use it unless I tell you to."

Breaux nodded. Gueye closed the compartments, secured the vehicle, and began to cover it with large branches and leaves. This camouflage would hopefully not be needed, as this was a remote area, and the foliage made it a challenge to see farther than a few meters. But Gueye was both diligent and a bit nervous about the unauthorized covert operation he was undertaking.

Gueye held a map in one hand and GPS in the other as he mentally prepared a plan to navigate to their observation lookout. With a silent nod to himself, he tucked the map in his pocket and unsheathed an eighteen inch blade. Motioning with the blade to Breaux, the two men started to carve a path through the dark forest. They moved slowly in order to keep as quiet as possible, and due to the limited visibility. Any artificial light would have shown like a beacon to any potential observer, so the men used only the cloudless night sky. Despite their snail-like pace, the thick brush, steep terrain, and heat provided a challenge. Each man's single canteen of water would not last long.

Just as Breaux wondered how long they would be working their way through the landscape, Gueye held up a closed fist, signaling to stop. Breaux froze as instructed while Gueye took a knee and held the binoculars to his eyes. Satisfied with what he had viewed, he allowed the device to hang from the string around his neck. Gueye turned to Breaux, pointed two fingers to his eyes then in the direction of what must have been their destination. He held up two fingers then pumped his closed fist twice: the camp was two hundred meters ahead. He motioned with an open hand, palm down, toward the ground. The two men lowered to their bellies and began to low-crawl to a rocky nook set between two small hills on either side. The sun was about to rise, and the camp was now coming into view.

Breaux had seen pictures of disorganized labor camps that had become world renown for producing blood diamonds. They were nothing more than a few tents adjacent to a pit in the ground. Young men and boys slaved at gunpoint, wading in the muck searching for stones by hand. They were often beaten, drugged, and killed in order to enforce compliance. If someone got too sick, they would be eliminated and replaced with an able body. This place was unlike any of those images.

While not a full-blown city, this camp featured semi-permanent buildings and machinery in the form of conveyor belts to assist with the work. The village consisted of fifteen modular single-story buildings similar to mobile homes. The worksite was an open mine in the ground, but had a series of belts and pulleys that appeared capable of providing great expediency to the work. As Breaux wondered how they could have possibly transported the materials required for such a venture, he observed a windsock that stood nearby an open flat area large enough for a medium-sized helicopter. They must have flown everything in and built this place from the ground up. It was an impressive site.

The two men watched in silence as daylight awakened the camp. Dozens of young men ate breakfast together under an open-air tent then took prayer together while facing what was presumably Mecca. The subsequent movement to the worksites was orderly and without brutality. The youth worked diligently for over two hours at a variety of workstations. As the heat of the day intensified, they broke for lunch at the same spot they had eaten earlier. The meal complete, the group broke up by ages and dispersed into three buildings. From what Gueye and Breaux could hear, it sounded like preaching at a mosque. It was during the sermon that two men walked out of one of the buildings. One man was of dark African skin and dressed in traditional robes, the other lighter skinned and dressed in Western attire.

"Who's the guy on the right?" Breaux whispered to Gueye, indicating the light skinned foreigner.

"I'm not sure, but I have seen him around Dakar before," Gueye answered. "I think he might be a local businessman."

"What kind of businessman?"

"Maybe an importer-exporter. He works with the local Arab community," the deputy whispered with a bit more confidence, as if his memory were coming back. "As a matter of fact, I think I've seen him speaking with Chief Decroix before."

Breaux listened, looked, and processed the information before it all made sense. He rubbed his eyes and looked again. *Yep, same guy...Jack Stark.*

Just as he was deciding whether or not to divulge any Stark-related details, Breaux's body made the decision for him. He was overwhelmed by waves of nausea, searing intestinal pain, and dizzying light-headedness. *Must be dehydration. But I haven't been out here that long.* Before his internal analysis had a chance to conclude, Breaux slumped to the ground, unconscious.

CHAPTER 18

Breaux thought he was waking up underwater. He opened his eyes in a blur to see Adama Gueye kneeling over him, pouring canteen water on his face. The water ceased when the coughing commenced. Gueye straightened his back, giving Breaux some room to breath. Breaux sat up on his elbows, quiet and confused.

"Are you okay?" the deputy asked.

Breaux paused, held one pointer finger up, craned his neck away from Gueye, and vomited. He collapsed back onto the ground.

"I'll take that as a *no*," Gueye answered himself. "Come on, I'll help you. We must get you medical assistance as soon as possible. We will go down to the camp and find the doctor."

Breaux shook his head.

"We have no water in our canteens, no medicine in the car, and we are a long way from home," Gueye said. "Depending on what's wrong with you, this could be your only hope."

Breaux mustered enough energy to speak. "Chance I have to take… the guy we saw with the imam…think he may be trouble…need to find out what he's up to without being seen."

"How do you know him?" Gueye asked.

Breaux was not about to tell him the truth, but needed his support. "He's a foreigner…radical Muslim connections…will bring violence to…" Breaux bent over and renewed his vomiting.

"So you think we need to get out of here?" Gueye asked. Breaux nodded with as much enthusiasm as he could muster. "Okay, we need to crawl a few meters to the cover of those rocks," the deputy directed as he pointed. "I will take it from there."

Gueye led the way. Breaux focused on each meter in front of him, concentrating as he inched forward. *Lift an elbow and move it forward…slide a knee forward…repeat.* Progress was agonizing and slow. Sweat mounted on Breaux's body. He pondered how long his body hydration would last.

He had lost a lot by throwing up, and had no sign of rehydrating any time soon. He started to feel nervous, which raised his tension level. A renewed wave of heat overtook him. He sweated more. The morning air was too cool to bring this much perspiration. Army training had taught him about the onset of heat exhaustion. He'd sweat profusely for a short time; then it would stop when there was no more available. *Calm down Martin. Breathe.* Breaux started to take long, slow breaths in and out of his nose as he closed his eyes and continued to crawl. His pace steadied and his body immediately calmed and cooled – even if only a bit. Every bit helped.

Gueye waited on the far side of the rock as Breaux rounded the corner. He had his GPS and machete at the ready. He had smeared dirt over his face to cover the skin oil that shined in the morning sun. He did the same to Breaux's face before hoisting him across his shoulders into a fireman's carry.

"I don't want you puking on me!" Gueye chided as he began to lope slowly through the woods. Breaux was too weak to respond but was thankful for the ride. He even suppressed his nausea during the ten minutes it took to retrace the path back to the Land Cruiser. Gueye stood Breaux back on his feet and both men got into the vehicle. There was no hesitation in starting the ignition or driving back toward the main road. Breaux leaned his head out the window far enough to not vomit on himself, but was careful not to lose his face to a passing tree limb. Gueye leaned his rifle muzzle out the open driver's side window.

Breaux sipped what was left in his canteen as he looked over at Gueye, who was stoic and focused on the windy dirt road in front of him. Breaux knew he was lucky to have such a courageous soldier with him – he reminded him of himself in a healthier state. He respected him for it, and wondered if there was some distant family connection. Probably not, but the thought helped pass the time, the nausea, and the cramps. He wanted to ask Gueye what he thought his illness was, but did not want to break his intense focus. *What the heck did it matter right now anyway?*

"How are you feeling, my friend?" Gueye broke the silence as he slowed a bit.

Breaux held up his left thumb and nodded. "Not bad."

"Good, we have a quick meeting coming up. We're approaching the border."

Breaux barely recognized the stretch of road that he was seeing for the first time during daylight. Gueye knew this area well, and slowed further as he turned right around the next bend in the road. The rebels' vehicle faced them on the right shoulder. The vehicle did not appear to be running, and as the Land Cruiser approached, it was obvious that its passengers were in the midst of a mid-morning nap. Gueye pulled over on the opposite side of the road, looked at Breaux, and rolled his eyes.

"I guess I will go roust our professional escort," he said as he exited the vehicle and began to cross the road.

Gueye strode to within five feet of the open driver's side window when he paused. He stared at the two men for a moment, then peered back and forth with a stern appearance. He approached the vehicle slowly and looked at the two sleeping men. Closer inspection revealed a lack of breathing. He reached inside the open window to try and shake the driver awake, if possible. He didn't have a chance to step away before the explosion erupted.

The blast lifted the rebel car a foot from the ground, engulfing it in flames as it returned to earth. Gueye was launched into the side of the Land Cruiser, which rocked right and left as it settled back onto its struts. Breaux forced back a wave of nausea as he reached for the driver's door handle and pulled it open. He saw Gueye slumped on the ground as he slid over to assess his vitals. They were nonexistent. Breaux mustered enough strength to drag the oversized deputy across the rear seat of the SUV. Having no idea what might happen next, he decided he wouldn't stay and find out. He scurried to the driver's seat and drove off like his life depended on it.

CHAPTER 19

RIO DE JANEIRO, BRAZIL

We lay together on the sex-room floor, wrapped together like pretzels. Had it not been for the pain of the leg bar, I might've been bothered by being naked and intertwined with another man – a masked man. Anytime I struggled to be free, additional torque was applied to my joints. My resistance continued in silence for a few minutes. I was getting nowhere and would soon need to devise a new plan.

As I was about to speak, Camouflage Man broke the silence. "I'm always looking for my next story. How would this one read? *Dumbass American Dies While Thinking With Wrong Head*...perhaps."

Max Nogales pulled off his mask, but did not release his grip.

"What the fuck is going on?!" I demanded.

"Believe it or not, I'm here to help."

"You could have helped by giving me about five more minutes to bust a nut and join you downstairs at the bar," I responded. "How do you know who I am? How did you find me? Would you mind if I put on a robe?"

"Yeah, yeah, go ahead," Max finally unwrapped himself from my legs. "Sit down, Simon. I want to talk to you about your new surroundings." I sat, relieved to be alive, though still unsure of this guy's angle. "Rio is full of dangers in places you would never suspect. I'm not here to tell you how to do your job. I know you're an experienced agent. But I've worked down here a long time, and may just be able to provide some advice."

"You had me pretty convinced about the whole writing gig," I said, now becoming aware that Max, or whatever his name was, was far more than a freelance journalist working to right the wrongs of the South American political system. "So who do you work for...Brazilian intelligence?" I asked.

"Well, I am actually a journalist. That was my first love and career, and I am still trying to fix the system. But some years ago I was approached and hired on to do some gathering for your agency. It went well, and it became a full-time thing."

"You mean DIA?" I asked. He shook his head and produced a set of U.S. government credentials. Max Nogales was our mystery CIA operative.

I did not know if I could trust Max, but he was the only lead that I had, given that the consular folks were at a loss. He detailed the extensive network of contacts he had developed in the local area, and assured me he could provide me with a cover for my time in Rio. First, however, he needed to familiarize me with the favelas that held all the answers that we sought.

Max entered Brazil as a pariah in the eyes of the government and police. They had read his previous work disparaging the corrupt police of neighboring countries and were suspicious of his intentions in Brazil. He had to provide numerous assurances to the Rio police that he would be their advocate, or at least overlook their shortcomings. Ironically, it was a payment to the Rio chief of police in the amount of $15,000 U.S. that sealed the deal. Max would be able to travel with the police as they conducted operations in some of Rio's seediest neighborhoods.

I met Max at the police station responsible for the favela controlled by the Armas crime organization. The station, which was really more of a military-style compound, had been converted from a small abandoned hotel. Once considered a more desirable area of town, the hotel's vicinity had been swallowed by the ever-expanding impoverished neighborhoods. Concrete barricades rimmed the exterior of the building, and armed guards toured vigilantly. After being nervously accosted by one of the guards, I was escorted inside for my meet.

The interior office I was taken to was windowless and dark. Max was already seated across a large desk from a grizzly looking police officer who sat with an Uzi submachine gun on his lap, and coffee in his hand. The small room was filled with both men's cigarette smoke. They both stood as I was brought through the door.

"Commander Cruz, I want you to meet Wolgrand," Max introduced. "He is the American I told you about."

"Nice to meet you, Wolgrand," the commander shook my hand. "I take it that's an assumed name."

"Yes, for security reasons. Nice to meet you too," I answered without offering my real name. "Thanks for seeing me today. Max had many good things to say about you." Actually, Max had led me to believe that Cruz was more or less a corrupt dirt bag, but I figured that introduction might not get me as far. Latin culture, even more than American, depended on the niceties of interpersonal relations, and I was not above a little ego stroking if it got me where I needed to go.

"So when you get promoted to boss here you get the center office with no windows?" I joked.

"Well, it's a matter of self preservation," Cruz said. "It happens to be the safest place in the building. We've had a couple of significant explosions outside, and sustained injuries due to blown out glass on the street-facing offices."

"As I mentioned earlier," Max turned to Cruz, "Wolgrand is here to gather more information on Armas and his al-Ayande connections. As you know, the consulate has wanted nothing to do with the situation, and Wolgrand was sent down from Washington, D.C. to help."

"Really?" I interrupted. "I was led to believe by the DAO office that they have tried to gather intel, and have been stymied by lack of communication with you. I don't mean any disrespect Max; I just want to understand what's going on."

Cruz laughed as Max responded. "Are you kidding me? I have tried to get them to help us with this shit for months now. Every time I contact them and try to either have a meeting or have them help, something comes up or they don't need the info. I don't know what they have going on that's so much more important than international terrorism, but whatever it is, it's more important than anything Max Nogales has to say."

Cruz interjected. "Anyway, Max has told me you would like to go on a patrol to learn more about the favelas," I nodded in agreement as Cruz continued. "Okay, I am taking a group out shortly. We will get you outfitted as one of us for the day. It will be nice to have another man who can handle himself with a weapon. Better than just having Max and his fucking pen along for the walk! Follow me," Cruz beckoned as he stood and walked out of his office.

We walked down a long dark hallway to a room that may have either been a vault or storage room at one point. One thing was clear when we entered through the heavy steel door – it was now an armory. Inside sat two guards, sidearms on their waists, playing cards and smoking cigarettes. They hopped up quickly upon seeing the commander, who put them at ease.

"I want you two to give *Officer* Wolgrand the tour and arm him for a patrol," Cruz ordered. "Get him a uniform while you're at it."

"Aye-aye sir," they responded in unison. One was an older man, a bit overweight with sun-weathered skin and a dark mustache. The other was a wiry kid of no more than eighteen years, with similar features. The two men could have been father and son. The old man took the lead as the younger shuffled out of the room to fetch a uniform.

"Over here we have our automatic weapons," he pointed to the shelves on his right. They were littered with a disorganized array of Israeli-made Uzis, American-made M-14s, M-16s, AR-4s, and Chinese-made QBZ-series rifles. On the shelves below them were piles of ammunition and cartridges, assorted sights, and other accessories. "Here, try this one on for size." He held up an AK-47 to my chest and nodded to himself in approval. He added two bandoliers of rounds for me to strap to myself. "Before you put all that on, you're going to want this," he said as he handed me a bullet proof vest. As we continued through the room, he contributed a holster belt and offered a Beretta pistol.

"I'm all set on that one," I responded while lifting my shirt tail, exposing my customized Glock.

"I guess you are," the old man nodded with an impressed grin, exposing his jack-o-lantern smile. "Do you need anything else?"

"Not today, but I would like to see what else you have. I'm like a kid in a candy store here."

The old man directed me to a series of large rubberized bins lining the opposite wall. In the first bin was a mound of explosive devices: hand grenades, C-4, claymores, shaped charges. The next bin held a random array of shoulder-fired launchers: mostly rocket propelled grenades, TOW missiles, and even a couple of SA-7 anti-aircraft missiles.

"Where the hell do you get these?" I asked as I pointed at the guided missiles. "And why does a police department need them?"

"Those have not been used yet – really just the kind of thing you break out in case of emergency. As for where, we confiscated them from Armas's people."

While I'd already heard Armas had been getting his hands on some pretty robust weaponry, I was still a bit surprised to see first hand evidence. Rocket propelled grenades had long been a favorite of Muslim-backed terror groups, but they were rather unsophisticated. They had no guidance or sighting systems, and were merely point, shoot, and hope-for-the-best devices. They're best employed when used in large enough numbers to saturate a target area, or as a nuisance weapon designed to cause hysteria. The weapons that caught my attention were the ones with guidance capability, and the shaped charges. The charges were similar to those affixed to the front of American-made weapons such as the TOW or Hellfire missiles. The inside of these warheads are conical in shape, and when the explosion sequence commences, build immense pressure toward the center of the cone. This pressure, along with heat that melts whatever metal the cone consists of, forces the molten metal into a stream that's perfectly directed by the shape of the cone. The liquefied metal shoots forward in a manner that can penetrate even the strongest armored vehicle. If the weaponry in this armory was indicative of the diversity that Armas possessed, his sources were both wealthy and internationally connected.

CHAPTER 20

As instructed by the old armorer, I exited the police station via a service entrance that dumped me into a back alleyway. There waited Max, Commander Cruz, and three of his officers, each smoking ubiquitous cigarettes. The warm yet crisp morning air had given way to what was rapidly becoming a steamy, hazy afternoon. Add to that my costume change from silk shirt, shorts, and sandals into a polyester uniform, Kevlar vest, and thirty pounds of steel and I knew I was in for a long day. I took a moment to remind myself how much I preferred extreme heat to brutal cold and got motivated to gather some much needed intelligence.

"You look like a native," Cruz smiled. "If the pay was not such shit around here, maybe I could convince you to stick around."

"You never know, the women are prettier and more willing here," I countered.

"Maybe so, but tell me how you feel after our little tour today. Let's go," Cruz waved his hand forward as he led the group out of the alley. He had determined that it was slightly safer to avoid using the front entrance of the old hotel for his patrols. While he figured that anybody wanting to watch him could still do so, he took advantage of any little edge he could get. His survival was a game often measured in inches.

The group's demeanor changed as we walked up the steep hill into the Armas-controlled, al-Ayande-backed favela. Good natured humor gave way to silence, stern looks, and sweat-glazed faces. The streets narrowed, pavement turned to packed dust, and concrete buildings were replaced with plywood shacks. The heat seemed to intensify despite the altitude – maybe it was all the eyes honed on our group. I could hear samba music thumping from nearby homes and could smell urine in the stale air. I took time to peer down every alleyway that we passed, clutching my AK-47 intently with my finger extended and resting gently on the trigger. Welcome to the vast mountainside ghetto known as *Complexo do Alemao*.

I felt like an unwelcome occupation force as I pondered what Max had told me about life in Armas's favela. It held the irony of being both the most dangerous and safest place in the city. Armas ruled with a stranglehold, yet vehemently protected his loyal residents. Do nothing to cross the crime lord and all of life's basic necessities were provided. Food was plentiful, medicine readily available, and schools were burgeoning. There was no opportunity for legitimate upward mobility, but life was survivable. Those with further ambition could delve into working for Armas's crime network, which brought with it greater reward and greater risk. It was Armas's goons that executed his turf wars with neighboring favelas, and he was determined to expand his sphere of influence. Al-Ayande was providing the opportunistic thug with plenty of financial backing and community support. They had built the mosque that recently became the centerpiece of a formerly ardent Catholic neighborhood. There had been initial circumspection, but that was quelled by Armas-issued threats and the realization that this new religion brought with it the first sign of progress most had ever witnessed. Al-Ayande did more than just preach; they produced. *What had the Catholic Church ever done for them?*

Following a predetermined route, our point man turned right down one of the alleyways. It was even narrower than the main thoroughfare; I could have reached out with both arms and touched the worn sheets of wood on either side. Not normally claustrophobic, I was uncomfortable with the thought that we would be like caged animals if the situation were to take a turn for the worse. But Cruz knew that he could not merely patrol the central path through the neighborhoods every day. The residents observed every movement the police made. Predictability would make it easy to hide any activity they desired to keep out of sight. Perhaps more important was the security of the patrol itself, as route diversity minimized risk of ambush. These daily patrols were as much about survival to Cruz and his men as they were about law enforcement – maybe more.

Two young boys of no more than ten years sat in the dirt near an open doorway, playing some sort of marble game. As they spied our approach, they turned their backs to us and reached into their pockets. Our point man held up a closed right fist, telling the rest of us to stop. He casually sidestepped to the opposite side of the alley, and readied his posture without quite pointing his rifle at the youth. Max had informed me that crime lords often employed young boys and girls in their violent enterprises. It was a month ago to the day that a nine year old boy in a nearby favela had jumped out in front of a similar patrol and opened fire on the group with an Uzi. He killed one officer and sent the others scurrying for cover before disappearing into another alley. The criminal investigation disclosed that the attack was conducted in order to prevent the patrol from stumbling upon a cocaine-for-weapons deal that was being finalized further up the road.

The two boys that we encountered on our patrol never did turn and fire any automatic weapon. They instead each launched small bottle-rocket firecrackers into the air. The ensuing cacophony sent my heart briefly into an irregular beat, but did no immediate damage. The boys turned back to our group, smiled, and resumed their game. The officers didn't appear phased by the act, yet maintained readiness as we passed the youth and continued. It was not until later that I was informed that the boys had not merely been screwing around. They were sending an aural signal to tip off others in the neighborhood that the police were on patrol.

The narrow alley ended as we spilled out onto the dusty road, turned left and continued uphill. Despite only being able to accommodate single car traffic, the road felt expansive after the confines of the alleyway. This street was particularly busy, mostly with foot traffic and the occasional scooter that defied all odds by dodging pedestrians despite risky speeds. Max had informed Cruz that as part of today's patrol I wanted to lay eyes on the neighborhood mosque. As we approached a plateau near the center of the Armas-controlled favela, the mosque came into view.

Al-Ayande had taken a balanced approach when funding and designing the mosque. They had resisted the temptation to create a piece of architecture that dominated the surrounding landscape. While their counterparts in Tehran were busy constructing the world's tallest new mosques, this one was comparatively understated. Its minarets did stand taller than any other building, and the construction was a step above the haphazard shantytown in which it was embedded. A concrete and brick structure with colorful accents, the blue scripted font on the façade was presented in both Portuguese and Farsi. The arched ayvan that faced the street dominated the building and gave a sense of regality. The entrance was open air, having been built both appropriate for the warm climate and in the Persian tradition.

I must have been busy making mental notes, because I didn't even notice the approaching man. He was dark skinned, wearing a well worn t-shirt, torn jeans, and a short yet nappy Afro. He had handmade jewelry draped over his left arm and a small pack slung over his shoulder. I heard someone yell *stop* as I wheeled around and found myself face to face with the grinning middle-aged salesman. He held out a selection of necklaces and offered me his *best price* as my pulse raced and body temperature increased.

I politely declined his offer as I tried to decide how strongly to react. Then he made it easy. He let the bag slide down his right arm and made a move with his left hand to reach into it. Reacting more than thinking, I poked the muzzle of my AK-47 into the shoulder loop of the back-pack, yanked it off his arm, and tossed it ten feet over my left shoulder. With the weapon still adjacent my left shoulder, I took a step forward with my right leg and thrust the rifle butt firmly into the man's chest – his wiry frame lifted off the ground and carried back a few feet until he landed on his ass. His head snapped back and smacked the hard ground. Stunned, he stayed on the ground and stared intently at me waiting for my next move. I drew on him and ordered him not to move as I stepped back and knelt down next to the bag. With rifle at the ready in my right hand, I opened his bag with my left. It held nothing but assorted knock-off jewels and the man's lunch. I closed it, tossed it back to him, and told him to be on his way. *Have a nice day!*

My heart once again back in my chest, I looked around to the rest of the team. Half-expecting to see looks of disdain or disapproving head shakes, I was met with nods of approval. It was Max who had warned me that many police had been killed in the line of duty for not acting quickly enough. Besides, there would be no public backlash. As long as the violence remained in the favelas, the general populace didn't care who was harmed or how justice was enacted. Let's just say we were not under the microscope like LAPD, and this guy would not be getting any Rodney King sympathy. I was receiving a crash course in the intensity of daily life as a beat cop in the Complexo do Alemao. In my mind I could hear Cruz repeating *"tell me how you feel after our little tour today."* As I looked around at the concrete walls I wondered about the circumstances that led to the multitude of pock marks that were unmistakably put there by gunfire.

As we walked abeam the mosque, crowds of people poured out through the ayvan onto the street. Midday prayer had just ended, and attendees were a mix of old and young, and various walks of life. There were definitely the expected poor that had long been the signature residents of the downtrodden favelas. Typical of Rio, there was no uniform skin tone associated with the ghetto. Unlike others, Brazilian culture did not hesitate to mix races. Most were olive skinned or darker, but every hue in between was represented. The only common trait in the favela was poverty. That's what made this crowd remarkable. There was an abnormal presence of a well dressed, Persian-looking contingent. It was not their dress; they wore Western attire. Nope. It was the distinctive mustaches and facial structure. The Persians walked side by side with upscale Brazilian men. There were no women in the mix at all.

We were about to start our route back to the station when I had the strongest feeling of déjà vu. Two men walked by carrying on an intense yet friendly conversation, and both were acutely aware of their surroundings. I could tell by their demeanor that they at least believed they were important men. This impression was solidified by the entourage that loosely surrounded them – a group of eight young men, all carrying automatic weapons that equaled ours. The officers on patrol with me surely had adrenaline pumping, but did not show it. Staying vigilant, they maintained their macho image by staring stoically, cigarettes hanging from their mouths and fingers on their triggers. While I should have shared their readiness as they watched their mirrors like hawks, I could not take my eyes off the two men they protected.

The man on the left was the Brazilian, and wore a light khaki linen suit with a white open collar shirt. His tan chest was covered with dark hair and ostentatious gold chains. His thinning black hair had been filled in with a poorly crafted weave. Everything about this man reeked of new money and power. The pictures I had seen of him during my intel briefs were dated, showing him in drab fatigues and a full head of hair. Antonio Armas was no longer a soldier in someone else's army, but had risen to the rank of general in his own crime family.

Armas was speaking intently to the man at his side. The other man seemed only mildly interested. It was as if Armas was trying to either impress or convince him of something. I didn't know who this guy was, but he was clearly receiving deference from an otherwise arrogant crime lord on his own turf. He had his head turned partially away from me, but I could still see his groomed mustache and goat-tee typical of many well-to-do Middle Easterners. Instead of traditional robes, he was adorned in Western style business casual attire. When our two armed groups were a mere twenty feet apart, he turned his head in our direction. His gaze crossed my way, and our eyes locked. *Did he just do a double-take?*

I'd never seen this guy in my life, yet he looked familiar. I racked my brain, filing through intel photos like a mental Rolodex – nothing. We continued to stare at each other for what had to be thirty seconds. I knew I should not have been so obviously craning my neck to continue my observation, yet I could not turn away. It was not until we had completely passed each other that he finally turned back in the direction of Armas, who had continued to talk the entire time. I had the strange sensation that I hadn't seen his photo before. I had seen him in person. Yet I had never done intelligence operations in the Middle East. I had not even been there since my time as a Huey crew chief during my enlisted days; even then, I never would have had direct contact with any local businessmen or officials.

I remembered nothing of the remaining patrol, my mind instead obsessed over this bizarre pseudo-memory of a man that had clearly remembered me too. I was sure that Max observed the eye-lock, and I could not wait to pick his brain and find out everything he knew about my Persian déjà vu.

CHAPTER 21

By the time we returned to the police station, I felt like we had been on patrol for days. I was physically drained from the heat and constant intensity of knowing that the slightest relaxation could result in disaster. I was emotionally drained from the time and effort spent pondering the man walking with Armas. I looked at my watch and was surprised to see that it had only been a bit over one hour since our departure from the station. I went by the armory to return my weapon, but I didn't bother to change out of my sweat-soaked uniform before seeking out Max.

Max and Cruz were seated in the commander's office where I had first met them before our patrol.

"So do we have a new employee?" Cruz laughed. "You handled yourself pretty well out there, Wolgrand."

"Yeah, well I've been on patrols once or twice before. However, I hear that your competition makes twice what you guys do. Perhaps it would be smarter for me to go over to their side."

"But we have better uniforms," Cruz responded as he looked at me in my salt-stained polyester. "Chicks dig a man in uniform."

"They also like a man that can provide for them," I retorted.

"I may not make much money, but I can still provide, my friend," Cruz said.

"Alright stud, I'm not here to question your manhood. I'm sure you keep the ladies coming back for more," I said, appreciative of how the Brazilians could turn any conversation into a sexual one. I sat in the only unoccupied chair in Cruz's closet-sized office and looked at both Cruz and Max before changing the subject. "It would be productive for me if we debriefed while everything is still fresh in our minds."

"Sure, whatever you want," Cruz answered.

"Good. First thing I wanted to say is that you and your men do an exceptional job under less than desirable circumstances. I would have a wicked alcohol or drug problem if I had to do what you guys do on a daily basis."

"Who's to say they don't?" Max said with a smirk as Cruz rolled his eyes.

"Don't ask, don't tell," I said, then pressed on with my comments. "I was very comfortable with the level of reaction that your men utilize. They strike a balance of when to use force and how to know when to just let things pass. It's not easy, and may be one of the biggest challenges facing police forces in the world's toughest cities. The U.S. has not been immune to these episodes – just look at Los Angeles in 1992 and Cincinnati in 2001. During each of these riots, the perception of excessive police force among locals precipitated an explosive backlash. In both cases, there were underlying conditions that were thrust to the surface. Significant racial problems were expressed through violence toward police or any unfortunate non-black who happened to be in the wrong place at the wrong time. When shit like that happens, things have a tendency to escalate. They gain momentum like a snowball rolling downhill, growing in size and speed. The longer it goes, the more it seems like it cannot be stopped. Finally, it has to crash into something at the bottom before order can be restored. The problem is that lots of people usually get hurt when that happens."

"Thanks," Cruz said with pride. "We are very sensitive to this issue, as we have had flare-ups of our own. Ours is a class system, and like racial stereotyping, carries the impression that you cannot move up in the world no matter how hard you try. This leads to frustration and criminal activity. People will do almost anything when they have nothing to lose. Unfortunately, the government puts little emphasis on the problem, since it does not directly affect the wealthiest class."

"I understand," I nodded and continued. "The same occurs around the world. There is no doubt you have a significant problem. Interestingly, the difference is that it is widely known here and simply ignored by those that have money and power. In the U.S. there is an element of this, combined with a short-term memory. I bet if I asked a hundred people in the States about the riots I mentioned, those old enough would remember 1992, but less than half would know a damn thing about Cincinnati – if they could even find it on a fucking map. Anyway, my point was that your men are doing a fine job." To myself, the parallel scenario made me ponder the future of terror groups capitalizing on the conditions like they had here in Rio. But that had nothing to do with Cruz or why I was there in the first place. That could be saved for a conversation with Max over a couple of Gold Labels.

"Is there anything else, or should I just pat myself on the back and quit for the day?" Cruz asked.

"It's not quite Brahma time yet, gents. I want to know who was walking with Armas as he left the mosque."

Cruz deferred to Max by moving both hands, palms up, in his direction, as if presenting him on a platter. "His name, at least the one he goes by, is Asad," Max began. "We do not have a full name for him yet, as he is new to the scene here in Rio."

"New, eh? It didn't take him long to get the attention of Armas," I pointed out.

"I said new to Rio, Wolgrand. Asad has apparently been behind the scenes the entire time. Rumor has it that he is the leader of al-Ayande, paying the local chapter a visit. He's been here for less than forty-eight hours."

"Why, are things not going well? Or does this guy just have a penchant for Latin pussy? Latin boys?" I couldn't help but poke fun at the stereotype of the Middle Eastern man having homosexual desires and tendencies. Cruz just shook his head and smiled.

"Actually, we have no reason to think that there have been any problems with progress. Al-Ayande has not had any open disputes with Armas that we've seen, and the Shiite community in the area has flourished at a rate greater than I expected in such an ardent Catholic region," Max added.

"So what's up then?" I asked. Cruz just raised his eyebrows and shrugged.

"My only hunch is that they're up to something," Max surmised.

"Who – and what?" I asked. Max's statement got me thinking about possibilities, but I could tell he had already thought this through, and I wanted to hear his opinion.

"Ultimately I mean that al-Ayande is driving the train, and using Armas as the muscle. It is highly unusual for someone like Asad to expose himself so publicly. Therefore, I believe that he is planning a major strike here in Rio."

"But why here in Rio, and why now? To date, al-Ayande hasn't made a large scale move to rival al-Qaeda. What makes you so sure that they are readying for one now?" I tested Max.

"Unfortunately, I'm not sure. However, I can't think of any other explanation. If you've got one, I'm all ears." I could tell Max was frustrated by the fact that he had not cracked the case yet.

"I'm afraid I'll have to get back to you on that one," I responded, thinking that I would have to kick that question back home to Kingman for an assist. "In the meantime, it sounds like we have some work to do."

Max snapped his finger and pointed it directly at me. "Exactly! We need to develop of game plan, which means I need to get you a job."

"A job?" I asked as I realized what he meant. "Of course, I need a job. Shall we meet at my place for a drink and talk over my latest career move?"

"I'll bring the lime," Max answered as he rose to shake hands with both Cruz and me.

"Big spender. I suppose I owe you for the drinks the other night. See you at six."

CHAPTER 22

The man known as Asad sat impatiently on a covered terrace that opened onto a private golf course nestled into Rio's Jardim Botanico neighborhood. The wealthy suburb was one of the city's few to contain predominantly detached residential homes. Most of the city, even the wealthy beach towns of Ipanema and Leblon, was densely populated due to the desirable locale. Jardim Botanico, with its exceedingly wealthy residents, had preserved large yards and managed to exclude any lower or even middle class intrusions. It provided the privacy desired by the celebrities that frequented the area, while affording easy proximity to all that Rio had to offer.

The mansion Asad temporarily called home was a unique blend of huge glass windows and dark wood accents. Designed by a renowned Brazilian architect for an actor that had recently died of a cocaine overdose, the residence totaled over 15,000 square feet in its four buildings. The central room was a massive open-air expanse bordered by a semicircular loft on one side and windows that reached the second floor ceiling on the other. There were two bedrooms, a library, and kitchen adjacent to the living room. Past the kitchen was a set of French doors that opened onto the patio where Asad pretended to relax on a chaise lounge. A glass of bourbon on the rocks sweated on a small table by his side, yet he sat coolly while smoking a cigar and perusing a file of papers he'd reviewed intensely a dozen times.

Antonio Armas had coordinated the rental of the house for Asad's stay. Armas had purchased a home not far away only last year, and had no problem contacting his real estate broker with a short-notice request. He needed a mansion that could accommodate six men, each with their own private bedroom and bathroom. Armas's agent had expressed just how difficult and expensive the request would be to fill. Armas explained that money would not be an issue, and that it would be in the agent's best interest to maintain a strong business rapport. Armas left the implication vague, so that it could be interpreted as a veiled threat, yet could be excused away if needed. Armas's criminal connections were widely suspected, yet never officially proven. The real estate broker, like most others, found it most prudent to accept the man's money while asking as few questions as possible.

Asad turned quickly in his chair when he heard approaching footsteps. He had been alone for more than thirty minutes now, and was beginning to wonder if he would ever get the information he was awaiting. His hopefulness washed away when he saw that it was only two of his assistants – not the ones he was hoping it would be. He had sent two others to retrieve some important information for him, and they could not return soon enough. Asad had not achieved his current station in life by being patient, and he was not about to start now. His reputation suited his self-proclaimed name of Asad, or *lion* in Persian. His given name was Hossein Zand, but having a first name that meant *good* did little to convey the aura he desired, especially within a culture that placed such gravitas on symbolic language.

"Where are the others?" Asad demanded.

"They've not returned," one of the assistants answered.

"Do you think I'd be asking you if they had?! No, they have not fucking returned!" the Lion roared. "Now sit down so we can review what we have."

The three men sat in lounge chairs while Asad took the files from his lap and spread them neatly across the oval glass table that separated the men. They were all dressed in silk trousers and shirts, exhibiting a casual tropical air that belied their seriousness. The two assistants had worked for Asad for a better part of the previous decade, and understood his nuances. They had seen the intel that sat in front of them repeatedly, yet knew better than to make mention of it. Asad was aware of this fact, and did not need to be told. This was simply a byproduct of his obsessive compulsive persona, and they had learned to accept it without question. He was the boss – end of story.

The papers were a compilation of secure facsimiles and encrypted e-mail attachments that Asad had received with pleasant surprise while still home in Shiraz, Iran. He was between scouring the internet for intelligence leads and fielding phone calls regarding potentially useful chatter when his secure fax began to ring, hum then beep with success. He scanned the documents quickly before sitting down for a more thorough review. *The devil was in the details,* and it was his mission to root out that devil in the name of Allah. The fax that arrived was from his primary contact in Washington, D.C. by the name of Ahmed. The heading atop the fax transmission read Simurgh so as to confirm source location, yet there was no return number. Before him were printouts of documents that had been lifted from Melanie Chang's laptop. Asad breezed through the after-action reports with interest, reviewed the upcoming presidential travel schedule with increased vigor, and stopped cold when he came across the letter entitled *Request for Pre-Advance Travel: European and South American Sites.* He raised a bushy eyebrow, smiled with large whitened teeth that stood out against his dark olive skin, and read.

To: Distribution List
From: White House Travel Advance Office
Subject: Pre-Advance for Overseas Travel

There are two upcoming overseas White House trips tentatively planned. The POTUS plans to visit Madrid, Spain, Paris, France, and Venice, Italy from February 6-11. The FLOTUS plans to visit Buenos Aires, Argentina and Rio de Janeiro, Brazil from February 5-10. Both visits are designed to assist in reaffirming the importance of cultural bonds between the U.S. and nations that share its Latin roots.

The pre-advance team for POTUS travel will depart from Andrews AFB aboard Air Force C-17 at 0800 on January 9. The team will consist of representatives from POTUS staff, Milaide, WHSO, WHMU, WHCA, USSS, AF-1, and M-1. Others will be added on an as-needed basis. The team will visit the planned sites before returning to Andrews AFB via C-17 on January 12.

The pre-advance team for FLOTUS travel will depart from Andrews AFB aboard Air Force C-17 at 0700 on January 8. The team will consist of representatives from FLOTUS staff, WHMU, WHCA, and USSS. Others will be added on an as-needed basis. The team will visit the scheduled sites before returning to Andrews AFB via C-17 on January 10.

Please submit names to the White House Travel Office for C-17 manifest and hotel reservations. Travel safety and medical concerns will be distributed in forthcoming e-mail from WHMU. Security concerns will be addressed via secure e-mail from WHSO. All additional information regarding local areas will be provided by appropriate State Dept officials.

Details regarding this travel are considered sensitive in nature and are not to be discussed with those without a need to know. Please stand by for further information as plans develop.

Before he had finished reading the letter, Asad knew what he would do next. With the pre-advance dates already passed, his window of opportunity was closing quickly. Asad was not rash, but he would not hesitate to act. He was able to focus his mental energy on the details and task at hand, absorbing massive amounts of information and determining the appropriate course of action without a second guess. It worked as quickly as most people's intuition, yet for him it was a fully evaluated decision. His mental focus had served him well during every step of his professional career. While others hemmed and hawed over the correct decision, or quickly made the wrong one, Asad was already running down the path to success at full speed.

Back when he was known as Hossein Zand, Asad graduated from Tehran University and worked onsite as a nuclear physicist at Tehran Nuclear Research Center. He was mentored by one of the founding physicists of the center. Dr. Tourak Alam had taken Zand under his wing after teaching him during his schooling. Zand was precocious, becoming a full-fledged physicist by the age of twenty. The two men became quite a team at the center, working on a variety of projects both public and secret. Iran was seeking to expand its energy producing capability beyond oil alone, and the U.S. government was willing to assist the friendly Shah-led government. The U.S. not only awarded contracts to American companies to build multiple reactors, but also assisted with training.

Dr. Alam was flown to the Massachusetts Institute of Technology for training as a nuclear engineer; he took his protégé with him. While the training was invaluable, Zand's experience in Boston left a bad taste in his mouth. He found the city to be extremely racist toward foreigners, and was disgusted by the open lack of morality. As he and Alam walked through Beacon Hill one balmy summer afternoon, they witnessed a disorderly mob of topless women chanting something about rebuffing the confines of their bras. He had never seen women act in such a way, and could never understand nor accept a culture that was so disrespectful toward the teachings of the Quran.

While few in the U.S. were aware that Iran was developing nuclear energy capability with American assistance, almost none knew a thing about the nuclear weapons project. Iran had purchased large amounts of uranium from South Africa under the auspices that it would be used exclusively as a raw material for energy production. Meanwhile, the TNRC had tasked Alam to head a top secret project utilizing a chemical process to extract plutonium from the spent fuel rods. This plutonium was then to be used as the centerpiece for the development of nuclear warheads. The project had direction from as high as the Shah, and the U.S. government averted its view in exchange for reduced oil prices, a market for overpriced military sales, and massive no-bid contracts for reactor construction. It was during the mid-1970's that Dr. Alam and Zand learned many of the intricacies of nuclear weaponry, and crept ever closer to final development.

Both men believed staunchly that this program was in the best interest of a strong Iran. They were each ardent nationalists, but with different visions. Alam was a supporter of the Shah-led, U.S. backed regime. He had spent four years after college working in the Shah's secret police force. The Savak had been stood up by the CIA and trained by the Israeli Mossad. They enforced the strict law with brutal force and little patience. Their primary purposes were to maintain order and preserve the Shah's power. Alam was young and full of vigor, and believed he was helping Iran move toward Western ideals through his support of the Shah. He admired capitalism and knew that his abilities would be squandered under communism. The Cold War was hot, and it was one side or the other.

While Zand considered himself to be an Iranian nationalist, he hated the Shah. The leader was nothing more than a U.S.-manipulated puppet and the Iranian people suffered as a result. Like many of his younger contemporaries, he had taken to the teachings of Rouhollah Khomeini. The exiled imam had clashed publicly with the Shah, and had inspired one too many riots for the Shah's liking; Khomeini was banished first to Turkey before he settled in Iraq. While in Iraq, he continued to preach pro-Islam messages against the Shah; the transcriptions were smuggled into Iran and read by burgeoning radicals such as Zand. Many anti-establishment types populated Islamic-based educational centers and would have no part of working for the government. Zand was shrewder. He believed he could affect more change from the inside, working quietly like a mole. His philosophy became the foundation for a lifetime of covert, underground operations.

The long-awaited assistants walked through the French doors and onto the patio. Asad sat with the others, perched over his documents like a hawk. He looked up at the two newcomers with a scowl, until a third man followed them. He instantly relaxed and sat back in his chair, a look of curiosity across his face. The man was a large Westerner, and certainly military. He wore khaki pants, a blue polo shirt, and a graying blond buzz-cut.

One of the assistants provided introductions. "Asad, this is Colonel Reynolds. He's the one I told you about." Asad remained seated while the colonel approached and leaned in for a congenial handshake.

"It's an honor to meet you," Reynolds sucked up to Asad, who nodded silently in return with a half-hearted smile.

"So what do you have for me?" Asad was not rude, but cut to the chase.

Reynolds handed the Lion a sealed envelope, which was hungrily snatched.

"The tentative schedule developed by the first lady's staff during the pre-advance visit. There may be some changes, but all the major players were here for the planning. I think the sites will remain the same. Maybe just some time changes."

"Excellent. What's next?" Asad dug into the envelope while listening for an answer, without giving the colonel the courtesy of looking at him. The colonel was accustomed to receiving respect at the consulate due to his rank and experience. To Asad he was nothing more than a paid informant – a heathen one at that.

Reynolds buried his irritation with thoughts of a large enough pay-day for him to retire in style in Brazil. He had recently sent his wife and children back to the States after endless fights over his long hours and *mandatory* after-hours social events. He did not need to deal with her anymore. She could take her American attitude home with her. The kids were ready for college and would be leaving home anyway, which would only leave him alone at home with a woman he could no longer stand. The thought of leaving all the love and attention he received from the local women in Rio in exchange for that made for an easy decision.

"The advance party for the event will be on deck tomorrow afternoon. I will have a daily report for you in the days leading up to the first lady's arrival," Reynolds offered.

Asad was satisfied. He finally stood and smiled at Reynolds. "Stay for a drink?"

CHAPTER 23

CASAMANCE REGION, SENEGAL

If he had taken the time to think about the situation, Martin Breaux would have been quite demoralized by his predicament. He was barreling down unfamiliar roads away from an unknown enemy while suffering from an unidentified illness. The adrenaline of being chased, or at least assuming he was, suppressed his nausea for the time being. Luckily, Gueye had affixed his portable GPS back onto the windshield before he paid the rebels that ill-fated visit. Breaux hadn't used this older model Garmin before, but he fumbled along through trial and error. The challenge was staying on the road's hilly switchbacks during his impromptu self-tutorial.

The road mercifully straightened as it completed its descent and the scenery became wide open flatland. Breaux leaned on the gas pedal, shooting a dusty rooster-tail behind him. As it dissipated, a second dust trail appeared in his rear view mirror. Someone was following him – *but who?* As far as he knew, nobody besides Gueye and the two rebel guards had any idea he was in the region. They were all dead. As he drove, he wondered if maybe it was just other traffic on the road. He sped up. The Land Cruiser's eight cylinders whined; Breaux wondered how long it had been since its last oil change. Breaux looked back again, and identified the white Jeep Wrangler caked with mud and mounted on oversized tires. It was getting closer.

He turned his attention to the road ahead and cross-referenced the GPS, which indicated that he was headed toward the city of Tambacounda. He began to worry about his fuel state. His tank indicated one quarter full – enough to get to Tambacounda, if he did not get lost on the way. Not to mention that if he stopped he was sure to have company. His only hope was to get into the city and lose his tail.

Breaux raced toward the city ahead and racked his mind. He'd seen that Wrangler before but something about the memory was foggy. It was the last thing he'd seen before he passed out, so he was already out of sorts. He now recalled that he had watched Jack Stark amble toward the Jeep after shaking hands with the imam at the diamond mine. *That guy never saw me! How the heck did he know I was there? Did he kill the rebels and Gueye? Why was he after me now?* The questions rattled in his head like ping pong balls in a lottery machine. If only he could get them to drop out of the bottom with answers. His concentration was broken by a searing cramp that shot through his abdomen. It was immediately followed by the feeling of impending diarrhea, the kind that would not wait.

This symptom was the last thing Breaux needed at this point. His nausea had subsided, and he had been sipping from his canteen while driving. He had been careful to drop iodine in each canteen-full of water, so he was at a loss as to why he was so sick. Whatever the reason, he had a problem. The physical pain was more than he could handle. However unsanitary or disgusting it might have been, there was no stopping the flow. Hot liquid pooled in the driver's seat. Breaux tried to ignore the feeling and the smell as he focused on the road ahead. Bothersome as it was, he felt better.

Georges Decroix sat anxiously at his desk, tapping his meaty black fingers as he watched his computer come to life. He logged on and wondered why he'd not heard from Jack Stark today. He fully expected to receive news regarding the whereabouts of both Gueye and Breaux by this time. He had kept himself a step ahead of Breaux ever since he discovered his true identity and planned on keeping it that way. He opened his web browser, dropped down his *favorites*, and linked to the GPS vehicle tracking site. The encrypted site supported the devices that he had installed into his entire pool of vehicles. The project, funded by local al-Ayande contacts that desired a little extra-friendly police service, was in keeping with Decroix's state of paranoia. He had not climbed to the rank of chief without maintaining close tabs on his people. He did not micromanage in order to ensure worker productivity, but to prevent his ouster. It's African military tradition to plot against the incumbent regime and topple it when the opportunity presented itself. Decroix was a student of history and knew this well.

A map of Senegal materialized on the flat-screen monitor, showing colored dots with numbers adjacent to them. The main cluster was superimposed over Dakar, leaving a small handful scattered through the countryside. Decroix focused his attention on the ones outside the capital city. He pulled a slip of paper out of his wallet and read the numbers on it:

U-12 and U-8. The vehicles were lettered based on type such as *utility*, and numbered as they were acquired by the department. He looked back to the monitor and found the two blue dots he was seeking. They were both in the vicinity of Tambacounda, with U-8 just behind U-12 as they progressed north. He had personally issued U-8 to Stark. He had been informed by the vehicle yard supervisor that Deputy Gueye had checked out U-12, leaving the sedan B-19 behind. He had given strict orders to the yard staff to notify him of all issued automobiles. Getting what he asked for, Decroix was regularly inundated by superfluous text messages. But Decroix knew the personnel at the yard were not the sharpest and could not be left to judge levels of importance. He'd handle the piles of information and sift through them for the grains he needed.

Deputy Gueye knew that his boss was paranoid. He figured Decroix would try to monitor the movement of all people and vehicles to the maximum extent. However, he misjudged what motivated people. He assumed that by keeping a positive rapport with people that he could inspire them to fulfill his requests. He had asked his friend at the vehicle yard to keep this particular check-out off the books, and make no mention of it. He would be back in one day and nobody would be the wiser. What he did not grasp was that fear, second maybe to sex, was the strongest motivator. Decroix understood this well. Religious belief stopped him short of using sex to achieve his goals – intimidation was perfectly acceptable. Like a mafia boss, Decroix regularly made example of those that strayed from his straight and narrow instructions. He commanded his deputies to use physical force as a means to discipline rank and file officers. His reputation was scary enough to cause most to overlook things like friendship. Gueye had not driven away from the yard more than five minutes earlier when the text was sent to Decroix.

Decroix surmised Gueye's intentions as soon as he read the text message about the sedan-for-SUV swap. He knew Breaux had recent contact with his deputy and would be looking for alternate means to achieve his goal of finding a way to the diamond mine. Breaux lacked reliable contacts in Senegal that had the ability to provide that kind of escort. His next move was a predictable one. Decroix had watched from his computer as the SUV moved to Senghor Stadium for what he assumed was a rendezvous. It was smart for Breaux not to use the hotel for the pick-up, but Decroix laughed to himself that this guy did not know who he was dealing with. He did not know about the Stark connection.

Much like Martin Breaux did under the alias of François Girard, Jack Stark had approached Chief Decroix in his office six months earlier with a financial offer. Stark had already been in bed with al-Ayande for some time when they paid him to seek a partnership with Decroix. Al-Ayande had not received negative attention in the area yet. They wanted an insurance policy to protect future activities from disruption. Neither Decroix nor al-Ayande knew Stark as a CIA operative, but as Iranian importer-exporter Kazem. Stark knew that remaining consistent with his assumed identity while in Senegal would prevent any slip-ups. He also feared that if Decroix ever had contact with the terror group, the contradiction would be a blatant red flag.

His Farsi and knowledge of Iran was sufficient to fool even native Iranians, so there was no reason to avoid this path. Stark convinced Decroix that this would be the easiest money he ever made. Al-Ayande merely wanted to ensure that their benign business ventures went unmolested. He also explained to the chief that the government needn't worry about this different brand of Shiite. Al-Ayande was interested in the financial opportunities that existed in Senegal. To threaten the government in any way would only serve to bite the hand that feeds. Stark assured Decroix that this relationship was to be a symbiotic one.

CHAPTER 24

Martin Breaux was not the only person in Senegal aware of Jack Stark's true identity. When he arrived in country, Stark received an intel update from the regional security officer at the U.S. embassy in Dakar. The RSO impressed Stark as a true professional, focused on his security responsibilities and not engrossed in the world of touchy-feely politics where career diplomats lived. Stark *almost* felt sorry for the deception he was about to commit.

"Let them worry about the international dick-sucking, my job is to make sure nobody gets their ass shot off around this motherfuckah!" he told Stark.

Danny Riordan had spent a career as a Navy SEAL before retiring to try his hand at sales for a major Beltway contractor. It was only months before he read the handwriting on the wall. He could probably pull this second career off, but not without drastic changes to his persona. He'd spent an adult lifetime as an unapologetic tough guy. He drank and swore like the sailor that he was and discovered that he was too old and set in his ways to change. One night over multiple pints of stout at D.C.'s Irish Times, an old Marine Corps friend of his suggested looking into the State Department's Diplomatic Security program.

Riordan knew it was either this or go back to Massachusetts to become a state trooper. He pictured himself sitting around with his high school buddies and relatives that had not gone anywhere or done anything with their lives. Night after night of getting drunk and bitching about the Red Sox and Bruins – no way. He'd been made to travel the world and seek adventure.

Stark and Riordan met sporadically in Dakar and other west-African locales. Both men had responsibilities spanning not only Senegal but its neighbors as well. A recent episode of unrest in Mali brought them together for some intelligence gathering. The landlocked country depended on transit through Côte D'Ivoire for international trade. Nomadic poachers from both sides of the border had been disrupting trade flow and causing outbursts of violence. Due to its extreme poverty and vast desertification, Mali already flirted with disaster. The U.S., China, and other nations that squeezed the

113

region for its natural resources did not want widespread conflict. Among others, Riordan and Stark had been covertly deployed to assess the situation and determine if overt action was required. The two men sat at a café and caught up with each other.

"So you figure these cocksuckahs will settle down or are we gonna have to come in here and kick some ass?" Riordan asked. He was not much into subtleties.

"This shit happens from time to time. Besides, nobody back home really gives a shit anyway," Stark responded.

"I ain't talking about humanitarian concern. I mean when it stahts to reach into some deep pockets of U.S. businessmen." Riordan craned his neck back and forth, checking to see if he could catch any eavesdroppers. None of the five or six locals reading papers and sipping coffee seemed to care about the foreign presence. "You really think we jumped into Liberia back in '97 cuz we're such nice fuckin guys? Hell no. We were practically running the country behind that stooge Taylor. It's no different heah," Riordan contended.

Stark had learned that every situation in Riordan's mind was black and white. There was no middle ground, which surely made it easier for him to be right all the time. Stark just backed off and let the former SEAL pontificate. The more Riordan talked, the less he had to – less chance of saying something that might give up his ulterior motives.

"Have you heard any chatter about al-Ayande moving into this area?" Stark asked despite knowing the answer was *no*.

"Mali doesn't have access to the resources those punks are interested in," Riordan answered. "They'll stay focused on the areas that have diamonds or the ability to move them. Means we'll see them crawling around Senegal, Guinea, Sierra Leone, Côte D'Ivoire, some other shitholes further south."

"So what have you heard recently about their activity in Senegal?" Stark asked. He enjoyed the way he could get first hand information from this guy without having to share much. Riordan loved the sound of his own voice. Stark might have to throw in a bit of intel every now and again, but only to keep the conversation going.

"No solid details, but something's definitely up," the RSO said as he leaned forward in his chair and narrowed his eyes. Stark knew from previous occasions that he was about to receive what Riordan believed was some important nugget. This was Riordan's serious face.

"I'll bite. What's up?" Stark inquired despite feeling confident that he was about to hear something he already knew. His main reason for asking was to get a feel for how much the U.S. knew about al-Ayande and their activities in the area.

"The intel guys back in D.C. are sending reinforcement," Riordan added.

Stark was genuinely confused. "What do you mean by reinforcement?"

"I got word they were sending some military intelligence officah over here to investigate some chattah picked up by NSA. Apparently this guy is paht of some team used by DIA when they think something big might happen."

"So who is this guy? Have you met him yet?" Stark hoped that his concern wasn't obvious.

"His name is Mahtin Breaux; he's an Ahmy captain. I talked to him on the phone, sounds like a black dude from New Orleans area – pretty thick accent."

"You're one to talk," Stark poked fun at Riordan's heavy New England accent. "I'm surprised you two didn't need an interpreter."

"Fuck off," Riordan smiled. "I'm meeting with him as soon as I get back to Dakah. You want me to get in touch with you after I meet with him? We intel types gotta stick togethah if we're gonna stay a step ahead of these assholes."

"That'd be great," Stark said as he stood. "Well, I'd better get out of here before the locals take an interest in us." The two men shook hands and Stark walked out, wondering what it was going to take to handle this *Breaux situation.*

Only hours after his initial meeting with François Girard, Georges Decroix paced back and forth in his office. In his hand was a dossier he'd just received from Jack Stark. He read through its contents and was now reviewing his options. The supposed French diamond merchant had left the chief's office and was on a plane to Paris. Decroix wondered why a U.S. intelligence officer deployed to investigate the connection of al-Ayande and corrupt Senegalese police would be going to France. That's what Stark had told him; Decroix had not seen any reason to doubt it. To him, Stark was the Iranian importer-exporter Kazem. Their business dealings hadn't incurred any problems to date.

Stark made regular payments in exchange for agreeable police services, either looking the other way or intervening when necessary. A group of concerned citizens near what had become an al-Ayande dominated neighborhood registered complaints to the police regarding disturbing trends they had observed. While there had not been a spike in violence, there was a large increase in the movement of diamonds, drugs and weapons

115

through the neighborhood. This was the trade operation that al-Ayande had established in order to accrue and launder money and gather weapons. The diamonds and drugs originated from within Africa and were sold for money, traded for weapons, or transported out of the region for other purposes.

Concerned neighbors feared that the influx would threaten their safety and tempt their children to become involved in criminal activity. Upon receipt of the complaint, Decroix took action, but not on behalf of the complainers. He dispatched his goons to the scene to assure those concerned that the issue was being watched and the situation was under control. They had nothing to worry about and should just mind their own business. Most bought the police line and went about their business. The few that persisted in complaining were convinced via more physical means. The police dragged them into the street and delivered nightstick beatings for all other potential complainants to view. Al-Ayande proceeded unmolested.

Decroix never trusted the Americans that occupied his country. On occasion, he'd been asked to work in conjunction with security personnel from the U.S. embassy during high profile visits. He did so begrudgingly in order to stay in the good graces of his own government executives who were economically joined at the hip with U.S. interest. He resented the way Americans acted like they owned the place everywhere they went. Visiting delegations expected to be treated like royalty. Embassy personnel lived in large houses protected by underpaid Senegalese guards. Marines providing embassy security strutted into local establishments and claimed the native women. In Decroix's mind, the behavior he witnessed was a derivative of that which buoyed slavery. They were a bunch of arrogant pricks that saw the rest of the world as existing to serve their own needs and desires.

The chief convinced himself that what he was about to do was, if not morally justified, at least morally acceptable. The faux diamond merchant was about to be double-crossed. *That heathen asshole lied to me anyway!* Decroix thought about how much of a stooge Breaux had become. There was a good chance his family roots led back to a long boat trip from nearby Gorée Island. Now he was a pawn of the white man sent back to Africa to further enslave his black brothers. *Not on my watch.* The world was better off without men like Breaux. Decroix opened the briefcase that Breaux had assumed would purchase his compliance. The chief figured he'd already gotten what he needed from the American pawn. He would now wait for the chance to eliminate him. His wait was even shorter than he expected.

CHAPTER 25

Georges Decroix thought back to his last meeting with the man he now knew was American intelligence officer Martin Breaux. The staff at Le Méridien hotel had become accustomed to seeing the chief of the gendarmerie conducting business at one of their dining establishments. It was off the beaten path of downtown Dakar and had the area's most lavish seafood buffet. Diamonds were not the only thing for which the giant chief had an insatiable appetite. His favorite part of the spread was the prawns. While he regularly ignored cautions from his wife and doctor about high cholesterol seafood, on this day he avoided the crustacean due to greater dietary concerns. Decroix arrived early and approached the young man who busily readied the food display.

"Psst, come with me," Decroix beckoned the young man to follow him. Once behind a hedgerow and out of earshot of the wealthy European tourists, the chief placed a small vial in the boy's palm. "You are going to empty this into the bed of chilled shrimp, drop it in the nearest garbage can, and tell no one." He added with a wink and a toothy grin, "You may not want to eat the shrimp today."

"Sir, what about the guests? This could cost me my job."

Decroix put an arm around the youth. It was at least the size of the boy's leg and its weight was intimidating. "You have nothing to worry about, son. Cholera is quite common in shellfish. The restaurant manager will catch a bit of heat from some angry patrons and then it will pass as quickly as the food through their bowels." The chief guffawed at his own quip. The boy nodded stoically but was still concerned. "Besides, what do you care about some rich Frenchmen and their pompous mistresses getting the shits?" It was a rhetorical question. The chief slapped him on the back, nearly knocking him over as he pulled a cigar out of his pocket. "Just do it – or I'll rip your balls off," he warned as he turned to walk back to his seat.

Decroix had tried to wait until he contacted Breaux. However, the chief lacked finesse and had sent two messages to the fake e-mail address that indicated Breaux worked for a company called Pierres de Gaul. Thanks to Stark, Decroix was well aware that the address, f.girard@pierresdegaul. fr, was a façade. It probably auto-forwarded to some encrypted U.S. government account; Decroix paused for a moment worried that his messages were being observed by U.S. intelligence. Before stopped by the thought of someone informing his own government of the corrupt activity, he decided that he was not worth the risk. If anything, the U.S. wouldn't want to divulge to the Senegalese government that they were secretly trying to purchase the loyalties of their own police chief.

Decroix's largest challenge during his poolside meeting with Breaux was maintaining his poker face. Far more comfortable using a confrontational approach, he found it difficult to pretend he was unaware of Breaux's true identity. Not normally much of a drinker, he ordered one as he waited in order to take off the edge. Knowing that Breaux was from the southern U.S., he decided to make it a mint julep. He would ask him about the drink – just a little psychological move to make Breaux wonder if it was just a coincidence. *Better make that a double.*

The meeting did not start as Decroix had suspected. He had begun to wonder if Breaux would ever broach the subject of going to the mines. He prayed to Allah that he was not poisoning this man without reason. Decroix mulled over what he would do to Stark if he had spread bad information. Meanwhile, Breaux shoveled back the shellfish like a true Creole. A plate of empty prawn shells in front of him, Breaux finally pushed back from the table and wiped his mouth. Then he did it. He asked for an escort to see where his diamonds came from the earth.

Decroix's blood pressure subsided when he confirmed Breaux's true intentions. Breaux did not care at all about the quality of the diamonds for his boss in Paris. He was merely seeking the path of the diamonds and money, and their connection to al-Ayande. Decroix knew where he would try to go and how he would try to get there. The challenge was going to be how to stop him without word getting back to the U.S. He needed to avoid a public episode – the takedown would have to take place well away from Dakar. Unfortunately, this meant outside his sphere of influence. To Decroix's chagrin, his federal gendarmerie's power had been eroded by rebel forces that splintered from Dakar during recent years of relaxed central governmental rule.

Not one to relinquish control unless absolutely necessary, Decroix reluctantly placed the call.

"Hallo," Stark answered his local cell phone. By no means an expert, he had become increasingly confident speaking French. He was comforted by playing the role of an Iranian; his French accent would never be questioned.

"Kazem, it's Decroix. We have a situation," the chief paused as he readied to say the words any micromanager hates. "I need your assistance."

"Of course, my friend. What do you need?" Stark had a strong suspicion it had something to do with their American interference.

"It's Girard, or Breaux, or whoever the fuck he is," Decroix said. "I don't know how you learned so much about him, but you were right. He's trouble. The good news is that I no longer have any use for him."

Decroix proceeded to tell Stark exactly what he wanted done. Stark would ready himself for a trip to the diamond mines across the border in Guinea. Meanwhile, Decroix would do some digging and find out the logistics of Breaux's travels. Once he did, he would provide Stark with a vehicle and the weapons he would need. However, Stark would be on his own once he left Dakar.

"No problem," Stark answered. "I have all the contacts outside the city that I'll need. Is that all?"

"No. I have a feeling that our boy will not be traveling alone. He will likely be escorted by one of my deputies – a man by the name of Adama Gueye."

"You know, it will be more difficult to take care of only – " Stark was interrupted.

"Kill them both!" Decroix bellowed. Stark cringed, hoping nobody was listening to their unsecured cell phone call. He never liked to speak this openly without encryption. The odds were slim that anybody gave a damn in this part of the world, but he was trained to worry about such details.

CHAPTER 26

TAMBACOUNDA, SENEGAL

For a moment Martin Breaux hoped that the dilapidated town coming into view was not Tambacounda. The so-called city appeared to be anything but. A quick glimpse at the GPS confirmed his fear. He had begun to worry that he might have to seek medical attention for his deteriorating physical condition. He could not keep any liquid in his system; it came out one end or the other just as fast as he could drink it. It didn't matter that he had no food with him – his body would have rejected that with more fervor than the water. His remaining strength was waning. His legs were weak and shaky, his stomach ached, and his esophagus and rectum burned.

As he approached the rundown village, Breaux knew his options were limited. The streets had been paved once, but were now mostly red clay with hints of asphalt poking through. The buildings were French colonial, but had not been kept up since they were built. The streets were lined with vendors selling an assortment of handcrafted goods. Road traffic consisted of more livestock than vehicles. The occasional bus or truck moved slowly amongst the goats, sheep and cows. Breaux passed a series of small shops and a school before he saw the medical facility.

Had it not been for the presence of a ramshackle ambulance adjacent the nondescript single-story building, he never would have recognized it. This was the moment of decision. He glanced back at the approaching Jack Stark in the white Jeep then back at the clinic. The building was overflowing with people and reminded him of the homeless shelters back in New Orleans. If outward appearance meant anything, this was not the place he wanted to stop for help. Breaux assumed that Stark would wait outside and give chase after his discharge, but could not be sure. He couldn't think of a way to evade Stark if he stopped. He took another look at the pathetic facility and sped up as much as the bumpy, animal-laden road allowed. It was time for plan B, as soon as he thought of one.

Breaux scanned the area for a gas station. He knew it would be risky to stop with Stark so close behind. *How bold would he be? Would he try to take me down right here in front of everybody?* Breaux had no way of knowing if Stark had enough connections with the local police to pull off such a brazen attack. He was approaching the center of town and running out of gas. With each passing second, Breaux could feel his options slipping away. He had to choose quickly unless he wanted Tambacounda to be the last place he ever saw.

Jack Stark fancied himself a black panther pursuing a wounded gazelle. He'd done this sort of operation numerous times before, and liked his odds. He knew that Breaux was probably violently ill by this time. Decroix had ensured that by infecting his food. Stark was the type of person that avoided an even fight if he could find one slanted in his favor. He watched carefully as Breaux slowed in front of the clinic. If he were to stop and seek assistance, Stark was prepared to conduct a stake out; Breaux would have to leave sometime. When Breaux bypassed the clinic, Stark second guessed how sick he was. Stark suspected Breaux would need to refuel and this was the only place to do it. There was certainly no way for Breaux to make the entire journey back to Dakar on one tank. Even if he had extra gas cans in the back of the Land Cruiser, he would not be stupid enough to stop by himself on an isolated stretch of road between here and Dakar. *Maybe he didn't plan to go to Dakar. What if he went to the nearby airport and tried to secure a flight out of town?* Stark listed the possibilities before he convinced himself to just stick close and be prepared to react. There was virtually no way for Breaux to coordinate a flight, even if he were lucky enough to find the decrepit single-building airport on the outskirts of town. It was almost time to close in for the kill.

Jack Stark had long been trying to prove his abilities to himself and others. As a boy, Jack grew up in the large shadow cast by his father. The Stark Law Firm was synonymous with corporate law in Dallas. John Stark, Sr. had built his firm's clientele from contacts he made as an Army judge advocate general. He associated himself with the best and brightest officers, many of whom became successful business moguls after their military careers. When they needed legal services, it was only natural for them to turn to their trusted friend. A handful of significant court victories created an undercurrent of interest in the former JAG. Originally from Fort Worth, he moved his bride and young son to Dallas to be close to extended family. With clients spread throughout the country and beyond, he could work from anywhere, traveling as needed to provide consultation.

Whenever home, he groomed young Jack for his eventual inheritance of the firm's reins.

Jack shared his father's freewheeling spirit yet lacked his focus. He performed well enough in school to progress toward college acceptance but had no desire to put forth the effort necessary for law school. Besides, he wanted to be his own man, not just John's son who was handed a career on a silver platter. He was going to make it on his own. Whereas Senior played football, Junior opted for soccer. Jack lacked his father's athleticism and size, standing only five foot eight inches, and weighing 150 pounds in high school. He made up for reduced stature with aggressive attitude. He fought often in school and struggled to achieve social acceptance. His father was disappointed to learn that Jack would not likely follow his footsteps to the Bar. His disappointment turned to angst when Jack chose to shun his father's alma mater, the University of Texas, for rival Texas A&M. Jack's mother had to convince a bitter father to fund this spiteful choice of further education.

Father and son compromised on the collegiate arrangement when Jack agreed to join the Corps of Cadets. Even though it still pained John to see his son in that Nazi-looking uniform and hollering *Gig 'em*, at least he would receive some much needed discipline. Maybe he would even end up an Army officer just like his old man. John's hopes remained buoyed for an entire four-month semester before Jack was run out of the Corps. He had neither the discipline nor the grades to meet the strict standards. Jack knew right away that he was ill-suited for the conformity required by that lifestyle.

He meandered aimlessly toward a degree in liberal arts during his freshman and sophomore years. It was while taking *European Governments and Politics* that his course focused. His professor, a thirty-something woman from Paris, noticed his adventurous spirit and interpreted it as unbridled energy. She invited him for tea at her off-campus apartment. Jack had a fetish for French women and eagerly agreed. Using her sex appeal to maintain his interest, she asked if he'd ever considered a job with the government. He shrugged it off, more concerned with how well she manicured her privates. She noted that the son of John Stark was destined for greatness. He predictably responded that he was not his father. She acknowledged his free spirit, and categorized it as ideal for work with the CIA. Jack wondered what the hell an elegant Parisian professor knew about covert operations. Now intrigued by more than just the smell of her hair and skin, he sought as much information as he could squeeze from her. While she never said for sure, Jack deduced she'd done some extensive work for the Agency in connection with her homeland. She instructed Jack to seek out the CIA booth at the next job fair at Reed Arena. Jack agreed. He also tried to get her to open up for him; she never gave up any more information, or anything else.

Inspired for the first time to achieve productivity, Jack Stark pursued acceptance into the CIA. He graduated as a political science major with a focus on Middle Eastern studies, passed the myriad of background checks, and moved to the Washington, D.C. area for training. Old man Stark was not enamored with the idea, but knew there was nothing that would stand in the way of a son who shared his own stubbornness. He took solace in the hope that perhaps Jack's younger sister would carry on the legal legacy.

Jack found success quickly during his career as an operative. With a natural aptitude for linguistics, he learned both Farsi and Arabic and was deployed to the Middle East. His superiors reported his progress glowingly, recommending increased responsibility and predicting further successes. While most would have been thrilled to be in a profession they relished and offered upward mobility, Stark soon became unfulfilled. Sure, he was pleased that he'd found his niche. He had a job in which no two days were alike; it offered him the freedom of movement he knew he would never have under his father's tutelage. Despite this, he still found shortcomings.

He often made contact with people that had staggering amounts of money. They regularly offered him the opportunity to partake in the riches – of course there would be a moral cost. For years Stark had rejected the offers. His conscience succeeded in keeping him faithful. As time passed, however, he became jaded. He witnessed offenses committed by his own government that supposedly acted in the name of freedom and democracy. The beneficiaries were large corporations and the government officials that followed them like puppy dogs. *Why should they be the only ones to get a piece of the action, while I risk my ass to make it happen?*

Soon after Stark had posed that self-probing question he was approached by al-Ayande. He was still sneaking around Iran at the time and had many in-country contacts. He was known to Iranian intelligence as a talented but disgruntled agent. If timing was essential to a successful relationship, this was a match made in heaven. Stark convinced himself that al-Ayande rhetoric was no worse than the imperialist attitude of U.S. efforts in the Third World. Both sought to better their own position at the brutal expense of others. *With one side no worse than the other, why deny myself the opportunity to make my life a little better? Good people are going to keep getting hurt regardless, so I might as well be properly compensated for my efforts.* Stark could put forth a convincing argument, and he was able to convince himself that this was a suitable course of action. Casualties such as Martin Breaux were just the cost of doing business. *Sure he was a fellow American, but he's no more valuable to the human race than anybody else – right?*

Jack Stark continued to close in on his prey. Traffic slowed as he and Martin Breaux approached the center of town. A shepherd led a flock of sheep and goats across what passed for the main artery. A bus slowed abruptly to a stop, causing its occupants to lurch forward. The driver honked the horn and screamed obscenities, which were met with a defiant wave of the shepherd's hand. During the chaos, Stark maneuvered past two cars stopped in traffic. He was now only five cars back from Breaux, who was at a complete stop behind the overcrowded bus. The wide load and opposite direction traffic significantly limited Breaux's ability to pass the bus. He was trapped.

The livestock cleared the road and traffic began to move again. Stark looked down at his speedometer to see he was motoring along at about forty kilometers per hour – about twenty-five miles per hour. Given the large number of vehicles, animals, and pedestrian traffic, he presumed this was about as fast as they would get while in town. The stop and go traffic provided him with moments of opportunity to leapfrog past a car, inching ever closer to the Land Cruiser. Stark smiled to himself, confident that if he did not reach his prey while still in town, Breaux would be faced with open road and an empty tank. Stark had refueled his Jeep from gas cans back at the diamond mine; his needle indicated a plentiful three-quarters full tank. It had developed into a win-win situation for the pursuer.

Stark's attention was yanked back outside with the sound of crunching metal and smashing glass. The bus had stopped dead, felling unsecured passengers and partially crumpling the Land Cruiser into its backside. Stark no longer saw Breaux's head through the rear window – the impact had either rendered him unconscious or at least knocked him down onto the passenger seat. Either way, the crash shouldn't have been deadly, given the relatively slow speed.

Stark knew that Breaux could've been stunned or hurt, but would snap back to life shortly. Hasty action was a must in order to take advantage of this fortuitous development. Stark put the Jeep into park, grabbed his pistol from its resting spot in the console, and affixed a silencer that had been in the glove compartment. With the silent weapon securely tucked into his waist band, he left his car and strode toward the mishap vehicle. Before the inevitable crowd could swarm the Land Cruiser, Stark calmly motioned for all to stay back, assuring bystanders that he was a physician. This gave him unimpeded access to the driver's side door. He pulled it open as he drew his pistol, out of view of any would-be heroes.

From the comfort of his oversized leather desk chair, Georges Decroix watched the chase unfold on his computer screen. He would've preferred to personally handle this situation, or at least with his own men. He'd been forced to relinquish much control when the mission moved deep into the Senegalese countryside. He was not sure that he could trust Stark. But he was sure he could not trust Deputy Adama Gueye. At least he was confident that Stark wanted to maintain a positive relationship, if only for personal gain. Some of the most effective partnerships were based on this type of mutual interest.

Decroix was unaware of the fate that had already befallen Gueye. He would have been far more confident in the outcome of the chase if he had known that his wayward deputy had been eliminated. Stark had not provided him with any update. While this made him uncomfortable, he knew that Stark would not have consistent cell coverage. As long as Stark's vehicle was still giving chase, he hoped for the best.

As it was, the U-8 on his monitor had closed significantly with the U-12. Stark had all but merged with the target vehicle. Decroix's intensity built as the icons on his screen came to a stop next to each other in the middle of Tambacounda. The car chase over, this situation would be resolved in short order – hopefully followed by a phone call from a successful Stark. Decroix smiled broadly and lit the cigar that he'd been chewing nervously for the past hour.

CHAPTER 27

CLARENDON, VIRGINIA

The rain poured down, driving a throng of young hipsters and aspiring urban politicos off of Wilson Boulevard into Murky Coffee. Melanie Chang thanked God that she had beaten the rain and the rush as she sipped an almond latté. Tables were always at a premium in the street corner house turned coffee shop; that was only exacerbated by inclement weather. She had sneaked out of the office early to get some work done without constant interruptions. Never completely free from her electronic leashes, she ignored them temporarily. It was impossible to ignore the parade of questioners that cast a constant shadow on her desk.

The line of sopping wet customers played a game of musical chairs as they purchased drinks and sought places to sit. One by one the chairs were filled until the only one remaining was the one across the small table from Chang. It was comfortably holding up her feet while she avoided eye contact with any potential sitters. She felt like she'd been transported back to her office as a shadow loomed over her. She looked up, knowing her little game was over.

He was the clean cut government-type that was standard issue in the D.C. area – fit, conservative, business casual dress, maybe thirty years old. She recognized him as a regular but had never introduced herself.

"I see you saved me a seat. That's so sweet of you," Mr. Clean Cut said as he set his briefcase down adjacent the table. He was clearly making himself at home.

"Oh, I was waiting for you of course," Chang responded with a sarcastic yet friendly grin. "Please sit down." She removed her feet and averted her view to her computer screen.

"I recognize you from somewhere," the man said. "Are you someone famous?"

"Yeah, I'm Lucy Lui," Chang was deadpan as she flipped her shiny black hair over her shoulder.

The guy pressed on, unfazed. "Aha, I remember now. I've seen you from time to time on screen with the president. You're on his staff, right?"

"Not bad, Columbo – but I'm supposed to stay out of sight during those events, so don't tell anyone, okay?" Chang requested.

"Your secret's safe with me," he assured. "So what's your real name, Ms. Lui?"

"Melanie Chang," they shook hands across the rickety wooden table. "And you, mystery man? You must be some anti-government hippie by the way you look."

He paused momentarily before laughing at her stoic sarcasm. "Does your Mom know how much of a smartass you are?"

She nodded with a flirtatious grin. "Who do you think I got it from?"

"I'm Vinny Girardi...nice to meet you."

"So I'm no longer just the pretty brunette who's too good to talk to anybody in the café?"

"Still pretty, but the jury's out on how good you are," Girardi shot her a less than innocent look.

A BlackBerry buzzed its way across the uneven tabletop. Chang looked at it, deciding whether or not she needed to answer the call.

"Excuse me, I've got to take this one," she shrugged.

"Kind of defeats the purpose of being at the coffee shop in the middle of the day, but okay," he said as he opened his own laptop and powered up. He had not even logged on when Melanie slapped her computer shut and popped up from her seat.

"I guess I jinxed myself by leaving work early," she said with a frown. "This court is going to have to go to recess. I'll have to find out more about my mystery government man later."

"You want to have something to look forward to in life, right?" Girardi tried to match her wit.

"I may not sleep until then," she responded as she pulled the hood of her raincoat over her head and began to walk past Girardi toward the door.

"It could be worse. It could be snowing instead," Girardi consoled.

"Goodbye Vinny," she said, feeling that he would continue to talk to her indefinitely unless she cut him off.

She was out the door when Girardi turned back to his work and spotted a folder on the floor. It was a regular government-purchase manila one, so he checked his briefcase to ensure he hadn't dropped it. With his accounted for, he picked it up and perused. It was mostly a mix of benign personal paperwork: a travel claim for a recent trip to New Hampshire, a cell phone bill, an interoffice memo regarding the usage of unauthorized space heaters, a note with letterhead from the Office of the U.S. Ambassador to France. *Wait, the Office of the U.S. Ambassador to France?* Girardi stopped flipping through the paperwork in order to read the letter, dated January 5.

Ms. Chang,

> This letter is in response to your request to have the President remain overnight at the Ambassador's residence on the nights of February 7-8. I am pleased to report that Ambassador Jenkins and his wife Betty are thrilled to have the President stay with them during his upcoming visit. They wanted to express that they would miss not having the First Lady present, but they will be sure to take great care of him in her absence. Please advise me of any particular requests that can be filled in order to make his stay as comfortable as possible. Ambassador Jenkins is hoping to host a dinner party in the President's honor at the residence on the evening of February 7. French President Chevalier would be present.
>
> We are looking forward to having you and your team in Paris next month. I'm sure we will be in touch regularly between now and then.
>
> Sincerely,
> Marilyn Taylor
> Executive Secretary
> Office of the Ambassador

Girardi was well aware of the sensitive nature of the documentation. By nature, he scanned the area to see if he was being observed and tucked the folder into his briefcase for safekeeping.

"Do you drink tequila?" Asad asked Colonel Reynolds.

"If it's good stuff, sure," the colonel responded as one of Asad's assistants presented the men with high balls on the rocks.

"It's Don Julio Reposado, my favorite. I can't get it back home, so I always enjoy it when I come to the West."

Reynolds nodded his approval as he raised his glass. "Cheers!" The two men sipped. "Hey, this is great! I'll have to get me a bottle." Reynolds made the type of small talk that people make when they're uncomfortable with their surroundings. Asad increased his discomfort by giving mostly monosyllabic responses. He was not a small talk person, especially with men that lacked his character. Reynolds knew Asad's reputation as a brutal leader that would not hesitate to kill coldly and efficiently. He hoped to have his drink and be on his way.

Asad allowed himself to take a break, retiring to the back patio to share a drink with the man who had borne fruit for him regarding the upcoming first lady visit.

It was a rare occasion that he stopped to observe his surroundings in a non-tactical manner. Comfortable that he was many steps ahead of any potential problems, he looked out over the lush greenery that surrounded the large yard. It was an uncommon sight for him; he was far more accustomed to the dry rugged terrain of his homeland. *It's a shame that a land so beautiful was infested with such a derelict people.*

The quiet of the afternoon was broken as one of Asad's assistants entered the room hurriedly, papers in hand. "These just came in via the secure fax," the assistant breathed heavily as he handed the transmission to the al-Ayande leader.

"Where is it from?" Asad asked as he began to scan the document.

"I did not recognize the name. There was no number either," he responded.

With a stoic façade that belied his internal excitement, Asad read the word Simurgh atop the fax page. There was no name indicated, yet Asad recognized that it had been sent by Ahmed. His D.C. contact rarely delivered anything but useful intel, so Asad read quickly. He raised his eyebrows and nodded to himself with satisfaction before he spoke a word.

"Colonel Reynolds, I'm afraid that you will have to be finishing your drink and leaving. Something has come up that I must tend to without delay. I look forward to your updates regarding the first lady's travel plans. You have my permission to provide them to my assistants, as I will likely be leaving town in the morning." Asad stood, more to hurry Reynolds out the door than to display any courtesy. Reynolds wondered what could be so important, but was more relieved to be leaving the presence of the Lion.

With Reynolds out the front door of the house and driving away, Asad gathered his men. "We have just received more detail regarding the U.S. president's itinerary while in Paris. He will be spending two nights at the ambassador's residence. That may be our best opportunity. Najid and I will be departing for Paris tomorrow. Do we have any American contacts in Paris?"

Najid answered, "Not full time, but we do own an American agent who travels frequently between Paris and Dakar. His CIA background includes much time spent in Iran prior to his deployment to West Africa. His name is Jack Stark."

"I want to meet this Jack Stark immediately after our arrival in Paris. Make it happen," Asad barked before leaving the room to pack for Paris. His grand scheme appeared to be coming together.

CHAPTER 28

RIO DE JANEIRO, BRAZIL

I'd rarely been so happy to return to a cramped, run-down apartment. After sweating all day from the heat, humidity and intensity, the air conditioning provided a welcome reprieve. I sat on the dingy couch and got a head start on Max by cracking open a cold Skol while I waited. I spent my alone time replaying the day's events, mostly thinking about Armas and Asad. I swigged the last of my beer when I heard a knock at the door. Without even needing to think about it I had my Glock in hand.

"Who is it?" I asked in Portuguese while standing offset from the door frame.

"It's your papi," the male voice answered in English. I answered the door without hiding my pistol, since I had no problem identifying who it was.

"Welcome to my palace, Max," I waved him in, Glock in hand.

"That's quite a warm touch," he said as he sauntered in and pointed at the weapon in my hand. "You must do really well with the women that way."

"Makes it hard for them to say no. Not all of us have the money to pay for it like you."

"I only pay for it because I don't want the strings attached. You should be careful too, Wolgrand. The last thing you need while on the job down here is some girl following you around."

I hated to admit it, but Max was right. Normally this was not a problem, but Rio was not a normal place, and did not have normal quality women. I would need to keep myself focused if I was to succeed on this mission.

I opened the refrigerator, grabbed a refill and one for Max, and sat opposite him in the only other chair in the room. My government had really spared no expense in furnishing this rat hole – what the furniture lacked in quantity it made up for in poor quality. I guessed they didn't want to provide additional encouragement to go AWOL for those on temporary deployment.

"So Señor Max, have you found a job for a fired driver?"

"Ha!" Max laughed at the yarn I spun for him the night we met, not realizing he already knew who I was. "Do you think you can manage to keep from carrying cocaine on the job?"

"If I get into trouble you can come write a story about it," I mocked his assumed profession, though I was still unsure if he was more journalist or secret agent.

"Don't worry. Your story wouldn't be worth my time. I prefer to write about people that readers would find interesting," Max smiled. "As for the job, how do you feel about driving something a bit slower than a sedan?"

I waved my hand in a tight circular fashion indicating that I wanted him to continue.

"How about a forklift?" Max inquired.

I skipped right over the questions about licensing, knowing that Max would have that aspect covered. "What the hell good does it do to have me slaving away in some warehouse? If this were a long term project I could comprehend wanting to maintain a low profile. Having this type of blue collar cover would be appropriate. However, with Asad in town our timeline is compressed."

"Easy big boy," Max tried to calm me, motioning both open palms slowly downward. "Your new gig is at the international airport moving cargo for *Infraero*. They're the government-backed company that handles air cargo for every major airport in Brazil. I figured we could use the access to our advantage, since every significant flight that comes in or out of Rio transits Galeão airport."

I could see Max was impressed with himself by his smug appearance. He continued by alternating positions on the couch, back and forth as if holding a two-person conversation by himself. "Gee Max, that's brilliant! How did you ever pull that off? Well, it's a rare combination of intelligence and resourcefulness – and that's above and beyond the good looks. Maybe Wolgrand could show a bit of gratitude and fetch some fresh beer?"

I rolled my eyes but couldn't help smiling as I stood to retrieve two more Skol.

"I'd better stand up, it's getting pretty deep in here," I derided despite being impressed with his efforts. I had mentioned in passing to him earlier that I thought it would be potentially lucrative to gather intelligence at the airport. I wasn't sure if he'd take note or heed the recommendation, since I provided no justification other than making it seem like common sense. The truth was that I'd recently received an encrypted e-mail from Colonel

Kingman. While it was more brief than informative, it did highlight that an American delegation was to conduct a planning trip for a visit by the first lady. The scheduled arrival was tomorrow afternoon via a U.S. Air Force C-17 cargo plane. I wasn't sure where on the airport the arrival was to occur; I would cross that bridge when I got to it.

"Okay smart guy, so what next?"

He began pulling papers out of the folder in his hand. "Here are your certifications to operate either forklifts or airplane tugs, straight from the Brazilian government. Take these with you tomorrow for your first day on the job. Your supervisor's name is Carlos. He is a friend of mine who knows better than to ask any questions. He will give you a pretty loose rein over there, since he's aware that this may not be a permanent career move for you. Just try not to hang yourself with it."

"Is your friend Carlos going to be of any other assistance?" I asked, wondering if this was just dumb luck that Max had arranged for me to be at the airport only hours before the C-17 arrival. How could he have known? It must have been a coincidence.

"No, he'll stay out of the way. He's happy to take a small *gift* every so often and keep to himself. He has a family, small house and modest goals." Max anticipated that I was about to ask further questions. "I do, however, have another contact at Galeão with far more juice and ambition. She could provide us with information that we may be able to use." Max stopped his explanation, as if I would accept that with nothing further.

"Okay, I'll bite. Who is she and what could she provide us with?"

"Her name is Lara Costa; she's the head of Infraero in Rio. They not only control the air cargo, but also all equipment related to air traffic control, telecommunications, and meteorology. They're a public company, so they have some autonomy from the government – at least enough so that their every move is not monitored."

"How did you meet her? No wait, let me guess," I started.

"I know it would be surprising to think of any woman resisting this," Max said as he pointed inward at himself. "However, I have the self control to not mix business with pleasure."

"Like when you brought me to the *Solarium*?" I asked.

"It wasn't me who got caught with his dick in the honey pot," he smirked as I gave him a conciliatory nod. "To answer your first question, I wrote an article a while back that highlighted Costa's rise to the top levels of a male dominated industry. Brazil tends to be misogynistic throughout its corporate world – aviation even more so than the rest. During the research I had the opportunity to get a tour of the inner workings of their facilities at Galeão. I saw what they have for aircraft tracking and communication capabilities – quite impressive really. We should have no problem knowing who is coming and going, which should help show us what we're up against and when. Not to mention we will be able to do so without any unwanted government surveillance. You never know who you can trust around here."

"So what makes you think you trust this Lara?" I asked the obvious.

"The power of the pen. Infraero landed three new contracts in the month following my article. She knows there's more where that came from," Max added.

I was sufficiently convinced that Max had done his homework and had the situation under control. I decided to lay off the grill session and make lighter conversation. "So how did Ms. Costa get to where she's at now?"

"She comes from family wealth and attended the best schools. That prepared her intellectually while her mother added the polish necessary for upper class lifestyle. Her father was a career airline pilot who also owned his own airplane. When he retired he taught his daughter to fly – she fell in love with aviation. After college she took her privilege and finance degree up the Unibanco management ladder. She was a successful regional supervisor with a promising future but an unfulfilled dream – to return to the world of aviation. She knew she would never become a commercial pilot like her father, since they were mostly former military pilots. Infraero was the next best thing."

"Quite a success story. Maybe you could retire someday and make her your sugar mama," I said.

"Maybe you could retire for the evening so you don't look like shit your first day on the job. I'd like to keep Carlos as a friend," Max said as he got up, drained his beer and headed for the door.

"No problem, I'm a model employee. Let me know if you hear anything and I'll keep my eye out at the airport."

Max gave a wave as he departed. "Sweet dreams, Wolgrand."

As long as my day had been, it did not take long for me to drift in and out of a sleep state. I was physically and emotionally drained and knew that the next day would present new challenges. Trying to unwind on the couch, I polished off my final adult beverage of the evening. I wished that I had a good book to clear my head, which flashed with images from the day's events and what needed to be done. I tried to think of anything other than my mission in Rio.

I couldn't help but remember what Max had said about Lara Costa's life and love of aviation. While it was intended as meaningless small talk it had struck a nerve deep within me. I hearkened back to my teenage years as a fuel truck driver at Hanscom Field. My father had a friend who managed the Fixed Base Operator at the airport and was proactively trying to find me employment to replace my current warehouse job at the Harpoon Brewery.

I was about to get my driver's license and the thought of me commuting through downtown Boston to work and get drunk on the job with my hoodlum friend Matty was more than my conservative father cared to contend with. He landed me the job and a 1982 Ford Escort to drive there. What he didn't know was that I told the manager I could only work weekends, allowing me to keep my night job at Harpoon and maintain my desired level of tomfoolery. The manager agreed with my story that my studies were too important for me to work midweek, and my father was none the wiser.

Fueling aircraft all day didn't sound like the job of a lifetime when I started, but it opened a pathway to the skies. I chatted regularly with pilots that spent their weekends burning holes in the skies over Boston's suburbs. I learned about a variety of light aircraft, a bit about aircraft maintenance, and picked up some pearls of flying wisdom.

During the summer going into my senior year of high school, my boss Paul bought his first plane, a 1975 Cessna Cardinal. He had slaved away on other people's planes for years to save money. But it was his mother's death that provided the down payment for the plane he name *Carol* in her memory – he even dropped her ashes from it. Shortly after I had to wipe down the stray maternal ash from the tail, Paul offered to take me on a flight. I wasn't sure if he felt guilty that I had to clean up remnants of his mother or if I was just a swell guy – I was going flying and didn't care either way. I took to flying quickly and soon became proficient at takeoffs and landings, simulated emergencies, even instrument flight. Paul was a single thirty-something guy who had little more than his work and I think he appreciated the company.

I used most of the money I earned from my two jobs to pursue my private pilot's license. Paul recommended I see the folks at East Coast Aero Club, and allowed me to adjust my work shift to accommodate late afternoon training flights. Despite Paul's encouragement and due in large part to financial constraints, it took the better part of four years for me to get licensed. By that time I was going into my senior year at Boston University.

I continued to work for Paul on weekends during college, and even began to bring my girlfriend with me once I had my license. Becky studied in the FBO lobby while I came and went fueling, towing, and parking aircraft. I pretended to study with her in between chores, but I was usually daydreaming of flying or picturing her naked body on top of mine.

Becky was an English major from a well-to-do Westchester family, and the main reason that I ever completed any lengthy writing assignments. She exhibited the refined outward appearances of her privileged upbringing, yet behind closed doors she was passionate in every way. Her unbridled Irish temper raged at times but was frequently offset by her equally energetic sexuality. She rebelled against her strict Catholic childhood using her petite yet curvaceous body to its maximum. I did my best to ride out the passing anger storms in order to revel in the fruits of her loins. Besides, it's not like I was an easygoing angel. I wasted plenty of time running around with the boys drinking and fighting, generally activities which Becky frowned upon. We enjoyed each other's company and believed we'd be happy together forever.

Paul promised me that once I earned my pilot's license he would let me take his plane out as a reward for my hard work. I accepted his offer and decided to share that moment with Becky, who had never ridden in a small plane. We were both so excited for that flight; she was like a young child going to Disney for the first time; I felt like a responsible adult for the first time.

I still remember the flight with painstaking detail; the automatic terminal information service reported that winds were calm, no observed ceiling, unrestricted visibility; it was a perfect day for flying. We taxied for takeoff; I called the tower for clearance, and smiled at Becky when the controller responded 'Runway five, cleared for takeoff.' We climbed up and away from Earth as Becky squealed with delight. I pointed out sites that she had only seen from the ground as we headed east to the coastline before following the beach southward. Without telling Becky, I'd packed an overnight bag for us and reserved a bed and breakfast in Yarmouth on Cape Cod. Her biggest surprise was to be when I proposed marriage to her before landing at Hyannis airport.

Dutifully playing aerial tour guide, I had just pointed out the Mayflower II as it rocked gently in Plymouth Harbor when the windscreen suddenly went grey with oil. There were a few puffs of smoke, unusual engine surges, then silence. Becky looked at me in horror as I scanned the ground for a spot to land – a challenge with no forward visibility and nothing but water to my left. The Cardinal glided agonizingly down from 1500 feet, the altimeter needle ticking down like the sand in an hourglass. I saw no viable open areas on the shore before spotting the narrow sandbar peninsula that formed Plymouth Beach. I wrenched the yolk hard left so as not to waste another foot of altitude in a last ditch effort to execute an emergency landing. I issued a *Mayday* call on the radio and hoped that we would have enough glide range left to make it across the harbor to the beach.

When I could see land again through the passenger window I turned right to line up with the length of the beach; Becky had her eyes closed and was nervously repeating *the Rosary*. I could see almost nothing in front of me, yet slowed for landing and hoped that weekend beachgoers were busy getting the hell out of the way. The last things I remember was the ground rushing up, the fixed landing gear catching the soft beach sand, and the sensation of tumbling forward. When I came to, I was hanging upside down in the seat harness, there were about a half-dozen people trying to get the doors open, and Becky's head was lodged in the windshield. Her harness had failed to hold her in her seat during the impact and she'd been launched forward – her death was instant.

Paul never forgave himself for what happened, though I never blamed him. We remained friends and I continued to work for him until my college graduation. That day changed me forever. More distant from family and friends, I promised myself I'd never have my heart broken again.

CHAPTER 29

It felt like Max had just walked out the door when there was another knock. I would have assumed he'd either left something behind or forgotten to provide some additional unsolicited advice, yet something told me it wasn't him paying me this unexpected visit. The weight of the rap on the door was too light for Max's ego – men with his self-assuredness gave solid pounds on door frames. This was more surreptitious.

I repeated my routine from earlier in the evening, Glock in hand and body shielded away from any potential blast through the door. I asked who it was, my mind working quickly as to who it could possibly be.

"Samantha," the female voice answered in a raspy yet sultry whisper. Who the fuck is Samantha? My mind pushed through the sleep fog, searching for names and faces. As my delayed response became a pregnant pause, it donned on me. It was the landlord Treff's girl. Now the question was: what the hell was she doing outside my door at this hour? I wasn't going to figure that out without either speaking up or opening the door.

"What do you want?" I asked, realizing that it sounded a bit defensive, but presuming she should expect the attitude.

"Can you open the door? I'm alone."

I could see that she was, or so I thought by looking through the fish-eyed view of the peep hole. I asked her to wait a moment so I could get some clothes. I was completely dressed, but scurried to the secret surveillance room to verify her assertion of solitude via my security camera monitor. She was.

"Sorry for the wait, come in," I said as I opened the door with a forced smile. "Are you okay?" I asked her not only due to the hour and because I'd never spoken a word to this woman, but also due to her physical appearance. While she still exuded pure Brazilian sensuality, her hair was unkempt and eyes bloodshot and glazed. Her attire consisted of a miniskirt that barely covered her privates and a tank top that hung loosely enough to view all of her chest but the nipples. She tripped as she crossed the threshold and fell into my grasp; I could feel her firm breasts as she inadvertently leaned onto me.

"You want some blow?" she asked, ignoring my initial question yet answering it at the same time.

"No thanks, I'm good. Why don't you sit down? I'll bring us some water."

"That would be great," she smiled as she plopped onto the couch that I'd just been sleeping on moments earlier. I went to the kitchen desperately trying to figure what had precipitated this late night visit. Did she have a fight with Treff and decide to try and get back at him? Did she have a thing for American men and few scruples about it? Was it something else? I filled two glasses of ice water since I was a bit dehydrated from my own earlier libations.

When I returned to the living room there was no Samantha, yet I had not heard her leave. The toilet flushed as she came from the bathroom, still sniffing the remnants of her latest line of cocaine. I wondered why she had not just done it on the coffee table. It wasn't as if she were trying to maintain any semblance of sobriety.

"Sit with me. It's Wolgrand, right?" she asked what seemed like an odd question from someone who'd made themselves so much at home in my apartment. I did not answer her question, but instead stared at her trying to figure her intent. She beckoned me to join her with a long slow wave of her hand. I obliged.

She wasted no time in wrapping an arm around my shoulder and mounting a bare leg over mine. She kissed my neck, face, and mouth. Samantha's body was long and lean, her skin dark even compared to my own. Her tightly curled hair smelled of cocoa butter and marijuana. I tried to kiss her back but her sloppy physical state made it difficult. Something wasn't quite right, but I was not sure what it was. It was not as if I'd never been with a girl who was a bit too intoxicated for her own good. Not to mention I didn't ask her to come in and throw herself at me. Nonetheless, the situation made me uncomfortable.

"Samantha, don't you think this is – " I started to ask about the strangeness of the situation when she stopped me with a kiss on the mouth. She followed with a firm hand on my crotch. My mind now clouded by blood flow to my erection, I grabbed a handful of surgically enhanced breast and kissed her back. She aggressively pushed me back on the couch and slid down between my legs. It wasn't unusual for Brazilian women to be so forward, so I sat back to enjoy. She pulled down my shorts and took me in her mouth. Despite the intense pleasure, I still felt as if something were wrong. Was I gaining a conscience? I briefly pondered the irony of finding morality while receiving a blow job from my landlord's harlot of a girlfriend.

I came close to climax before pulling Samantha up onto the couch. She seemed confused as I slid a hand up her long leg and under her skirt. She smiled and pushed my hand away, playing hard to get. I persisted until finding what I was looking for yet hoping not to – a cock and balls!

Samantha's look of shock turned to fear instantly as I clamped down on a handful of testicle. *He* screamed in pain before I could muffle him with my other hand over his mouth.

"Are you out of your *fucking* mind?!" I asked rhetorically. Without waiting for an answer I reared back with a right fist and delivered a crushing blow to his solar plexus. He gasped for breath that refused to enter his lungs before lurching forward onto the coffee table. He slumped onto the table and groaned weakly as I stood over his flaccid form and reached down for a handful of black mane. I stood him upright and doused his face with water.

"Come with me," I ordered without the option of refusal, since I pulled him to the bathroom by his hair. I really didn't care what he thought at this point, other than I wanted him to be afraid, very afraid. When I get to this stage of anger I'm capable of serious damage, so instilling fear would not be a problem. Restraining myself might be, and I had some investigating to accomplish. Despite wanting to kill the son-of-a-bitch without delay, I had to accomplish the mission. Times like this brought out mental clarity that enabled me to conclude things most could not. I needed to take advantage of it.

"Where is it?" I demanded as I added *Sam's* right arm to my grip, folding it behind his back and yanking it upward. I could hear his shoulder tearing out of its socket as he yelped in pain, tears now streaming down his pathetic face. This asshole had better not make me beat this out of him!

"Where is what? I don't know what you're talking about," Sam responded while shaking his head. Not only could I tell he was lying but I knew he'd be easy to break. This guy didn't have the will to hold out, which meant he had been sent here to do someone else's dirty work. There was no vested interest that I could see in his face or body language.

"Look at me, asshole. I'm gonna tell you this one time. You're lucky you are even alive right now to hear me bitching at you. I promise you if I have to ask you again nobody will ever know what happened to you." I waited all of five seconds before reasserting my grip on Sam's right arm and hair, turning him away from me, and forcing him toward the bathtub. He tripped clumsily over the edge of the tub and fell facedown into the hard porcelain basin. I transferred my grip to his right hand and wrenched down on his wrist as I stood and extended his arm upward behind him. I kicked the faucet on and the drain latch closed as I watched his limp body wriggle to life in a renewed effort to survive. I applied a slight downward pressure, moving his palm toward his wrist, countering his effort with excruciating pain. Sam had waning moments to decide whether to talk or drown.

"It was his idea! It was his idea!" he began to repeat in between defeated sobbing.

"Who? To do what?" I demanded through clenched teeth. By this time he was desperately trying to keep his mouth above the rising water. He was beginning to breathe in and spit out water as he tried to speak.

"The bug – behind the toilet," he sprayed water from his mouth as he spoke. I thought for a moment about checking for it myself before wondering if this *bug* were not an explosive instead.

"Get up," I commanded, hoisting him out of the water. "Show it to me. Get it yourself. Do it slowly or I will have no problem ending you," I warned as I released him and pulled out my Glock, ready to fire. He fell to his knees, crawled to the toilet, and reached his left arm behind it. I aimed at his head while already planning on how to dispose of the body. His hand emerged with open palm holding what certainly appeared to be a small listening device, its dimensions akin to a nine-volt battery, with a wire antenna the length of a pen.

"Who sent you here?" I repeated my request, knowing there was no possibility Sam had done this for his own purposes. My pistol remained honed directly between his eyes.

"Treff," he whispered, reminding me that this freak was supposedly the girlfriend of the landlord. The scenario, however disturbing to me, at least served to justify why Treff had relocated; Rio was widely known for its convincingly attractive transsexuals. His perverted dreams would have likely remained unfulfilled during three lifetimes in El Paso.

My mind's eye flashed with a disturbing image of the two having transsexual sex before I could refocus on the issue at hand. It was improbable that this small time landlord would risk his life and that of his lover unless he was being compensated from outside sources. That was obvious. Less clear was who had set up the botched surveillance operation. By the technique, I surmised they weren't trained professionals. The other question that stuck with me was: who knew I was here?

I tried to envision the conversation between Treff and Samantha in order to determine her level of knowledge. Treff was approached by someone with a proposal to make some easy money; all he had to do was plant a device in an apartment. This someone probably didn't divulge the identity of the target. Treff may have pushed a bit, may have even been told; it didn't matter either way. He accepted the offer and hatched a plan to access the one apartment for which he didn't hold a copied key. That was part of the deal he'd struck with the U.S. government when they agreed to pay him an exorbitant fee in order to modify and have exclusive access to the apartment. Treff could think of no way to break in and therefore decided that the tenant would have to be home to allow entry. To him the least obvious method would be to have his *woman* feign sexual interest.

Chances are that Sam was not too keen on being the one to run the gauntlet. Sure, he wanted the money as much as Treff. Sam probably envisioned himself swept away by the stereotypical wealthy American, and had become disillusioned when that dream faded. This opportunity might be a way to recoup a bit of that lost dream, but he wouldn't believe the proposition without some evidence. Sam would demand to know who was behind the offer as a method to verify its legitimacy.

Treff would resist but cave in eventually. What Treff did not anticipate was that Sam's nerves would cause him to take in too much coke, thereby clouding his judgment. He was supposed to plant the bug, play a little bit physically, then regain his senses and get the hell out. Instead, his hormones got a bit carried away and he ended up fully exposed.

"Who paid Treff?" I asked. When I received nothing but a silent scared stare, I fired a single shot, inches above Sam's head. He cowered on the bathroom floor as bits of plaster flew, showering down into his hair. The noise of the gun blast would draw no attention; people in this city had learned to mind their own business as a matter of self-preservation. I wanted its volume to inspire talk from Sam.

"Some guy named Reynolds. He works at the U.S. embassy or something."

I consciously worked to maintain a straight face as I nodded slowly. Reynolds! That's the goddam DAO! What the fuck was he doing trying to keep an eye on me? Max had told me that this colonel had been no help with counter-terror efforts in the region. I had assumed it was just laziness, but perhaps it was something more sinister. It was imperative to follow this trail quickly; it might lead to further unraveling of some tightly wound scenario. Meanwhile, it would be essential to keep him from discovering that he'd been outed.

"Let me make this very clear to you, *Samantha*," I leaned into his face and spoke slowly and clearly. "You will leave here now and go home. You will tell Treff that you did just as you were told and had no problems. You will *not* tell him anything else. Is that clear?" I asked as he nodded and said yes. "Excellent. If you do anything else, I will find out, and kill you both."

He continued to nod and say he understood and thank you very much as I shoved him out the door. I went back to the refrigerator, reached past the beer for the vodka, and poured a tall glass on the rocks. I drank until I was able to pass out and resume my dream state.

CHAPTER 30

For most foreigners visiting Rio, the drive to Galeão airport is a journey through an art museum. The mesmerizing beauty of the waves crashing against the surf, the mystery of the Sugarloaf partially shrouded by low-hanging morning clouds, and the majesty of Corcovado's Redeemer watching over this *cidade maravilhosa* – marvelous city – normally provided me with an energetic morning boost. That was on days when I wasn't running late for my first day of work and navigating typically heavy traffic congestion. Due to my night's bizarre events, I was unable to achieve any restful sleep until finally settling down about thirty minutes before I was set to rise. Four angry smacks of the snooze button later, I was in a frantic rush to get out the door. I reminded myself that this job was a short term gig and that I did not need to be Carlos's model employee. I had another job to do, one that put me on my own schedule.

Once I had resolved to adopt a more Latin approach to my morning, I worried less about punctuality and more about quality of life. I stopped by a *boteco* which I'd become accustomed to frequenting for a late night snack and nightcap. The open-air Leblon bistro stayed open until the early morning hours in order to accommodate late night revelers, so I found myself the sole person starting his day rather than ending his night.

Amused by my surroundings, I ordered a cafezinho, a shot of cachaça, and a plate of empadinhas and sat at a small table adjacent the sidewalk. A couple of bloodshot-eyed patrons philosophized in a drunken last ditch effort to bed their female companions. Another group of three older men sat at the bar, yelling at the football match on the television and drinking chopp they surely didn't need at six in the morning. I poured the sugarcane-derived liquor down my throat and chased it with the dark, sweet coffee. I'd never noticed how dirty and rundown this place was. I finished my miniature chicken pies and thought about my fellow customers sleeping off hangovers all day as I walked out onto the street, found my car and joined the disorder of morning rush hour in Rio.

Traffic lightened as I left downtown and merged onto the highway BR-101 north to the airport; my Civic crept up to the speed of adjacent cars. My commute took me past the foot of the favelas housing the tools that would be used to execute any local terror plot. For them to achieve success, however, would require external support, which was why I was glad that Max had arranged for me to conduct surveillance at the airport. It was the most likely port of entry for additional resources, both man and machine. The portable GPS on my dashboard provided the last of the turn-by-turn directions that led me directly to the Infraero Air Cargo sign standing at the parking lot entrance. I parked far enough away from the hangars so as to make for a direct departure if necessary, yet not at the very far end to avoid being obvious. I locked the GPS in the glove compartment and reluctantly stowed my Glock in a holster-like slot just below the dashboard, where it was out of view but easily accessible in time of need.

As I walked toward the facility's gated entrance, into clearer view came the main reason I'd decided to temporarily part ways with my trusty sidearm. The private security guard, like most of his couterparts worldwide, posed with overt self-importance as he watched my approach. I wondered what kind of cursory weapons training he had undergone before being authorized to wear the hand canon that hung from his belt. I had the impression he would not hesitate to employ his pistol, having not been infused with the same training that I had, not to point my weapon at anything I did not intend to shoot. I made sure not to approach in a threatening fashion, and he was at least willing to help once I had provided a name and ID that he was able to validate on his access roster.

"It says you're new here," he said with a deadpan delivery that exemplified either his tough guy image or sheer boredom, maybe both. He continued without comment from me. "We'll take your picture inside at the administrative office and have an Infraero ID made for you. Come with me," he said as he led me into the hangar's front offices.

"I'm Wolgrand, nice to meet you," I extended a hand as we walked.

He shook my hand and responded, "Officer Lupi."

"Officer – what an interesting first name," I decided to be a smart-ass to see if I could get him to lighten up. Perhaps it was the cachaça acting as lip oil; perhaps I knew I wouldn't be here long and therefore did not give a shit what this uptight jackass thought of me.

"My first name is Alfredo," he offered with a forced smile. He probably evaluated who I was and concluded that if there was a chance I was someone important that he should swallow his pride and play along. I would never have any power over him, but he didn't know. Fine with me.

I always enjoyed playing mind games with people and sometimes did so in situations of no import just to stay sharp.

As usual, Max proved to be man who knew how to get things done. With the exception of Tough Guy Rent-a-Cop, I was greeted with the type of expectant enthusiasm that only accompanies prior coordination. The ladies who assisted me with the necessary paperwork and processing were all smiles, pleases, and thank yous. Wolgrand's new ID hanging around my neck, I smiled to myself as to what else besides a favorable article Max may have given to Lara Costa to achieve this level of cooperation.

Rent-a-Cop Alfredo made a point to escort me through the entire registration process, which concluded with a walk onto the hangar floor. The hangars that comprised the Infraero air cargo complex at Galeão were typical by modern U.S. standards, making them an impressive sight by Brazilian standards. The massive structures were part warehouse and part aircraft hangar, a combination of steel beams, heavy corrugated metal skin, and enormous electric doors that allowed access for even the largest of air cargo jets. The interior featured state-of-the-art motion detectors and robust red piping that contained Aqueous Film Forming Foam systems in case of fire. I had also noted during my approach to the guard shack that the hangar's roof held infra-red sensors and the presence of at least two roving armed sentries. While precautions to protect big business were certainly warranted for anti-crime and anti-terror reasons, it reminded me of how this class-separated society chose to protect the haves from the have-nots rather than attempting to improve the status of the latter.

A man in faded blue coveralls and a look of seemingly permanent irritation on his face approached me and my new accessory Alfredo. He glanced down at my ID, looked at my face to make a match, and dispatched Alfredo with a silent wave of his hand. My new boss introduced himself and we exchanged cordial handshakes. Carlos Gil was wiry and tall, with creased leathery skin that showed decades spent chain smoking on sun-drenched airport ramps. His voice raspy and his grip vice-like, he'd spent a lifetime working hard and playing harder, in classic Carioca fashion.

"Max told me what you need for work, so I am here to help. All I ask is that you do what needs to get done when we have flights and you'll be able to make your way around the airport as needed."

"Sounds great to me, thank you," I appreciated his candor, but wondered just how much Max had told him. I had come to trust Max's judgment, so I decided to trust him in this case as well. I would not volunteer any information and I figured that Carlos would not ask.

Carlos toured me through the spaces, breezing quickly by the offices that would only serve to expose me to more people that did not have a need to know about my temporary employment. The restroom and break room followed, both filled with ubiquitous cigarette smoke, before we walked onto the hangar floor. Carlos gave me a brief class on the operation of the hangar door and manual override, how to activate the fire suppression system in the event it did not do so automatically, the location of hazardous material personal protective equipment, and had me display my ability to operate the tug and forklift. I did so with no problem, due to my previous life as an enlisted Marine.

When I graduated from high school in Brookline, MA, my parents had their high hopes for me dashed when I informed them of my decision to forego college for the Marine Corps. I was in no way ready to focus on college courses and likely would have failed miserably. At least that's how I'm able to justify my rash decision to this day. The truth is that I would've probably gone to college if my father had recommended enlistment.

Once I began basic training, it did not take long for me to realize which direction I desired. After I had spent my high school years working around airplanes and the pilots who flew them, I knew that aviation was the route for me. Of course, knowing what I wanted and getting what I wanted were not necessarily apt to coincide, due to the *needs of the Corps*. Despite long odds I finished strongly enough in my recruit class to land myself an MOS of 6174 – Military Occupational Specialty as a Huey crew chief.

The venerable Vietnam-era helicopter was older than I, yet remained the utility workhorse in the Marine Corps stable. It was the job of the crew chief to perform a variety of mechanic functions while having the opportunity to fly as an integral member of the crew. Once I had become qualified to perform significant maintenance on the turbine engines and rotor blade systems, I was allowed to ride along in the front seat during maintenance flights. The more appreciative pilots shared their flight time by giving me some stick time and providing the instructional know-how to takeoff, hover, and even land the machine.

I wore my qualification as a Huey crew chief like a badge of honor around the squadron and beyond. My cohorts and I were jacks of all trades, able to diagnose and fix the widest variety of discrepancies, load and employ multiple automatic weapons fired from the open cabin doors during flight, and even fly the ship on occasion. I was qualified to handle hazardous materials, maintain our flight equipment, and operate machinery such as the tugs and forklifts. I would have been perfectly content to grow old in that role had it not been for a burning desire to be the pilot in command, and make a few more dollars in the process.

Carlos's cell phone rang; he answered, nodded as he okayed the caller, and closed the flip phone. "Sounds like they're ahead of schedule. Let's go," he began to walk toward the flight line without amplification.

"Who?"

"The Americans – we have a C-17 inbound. It's about to get busy around here, and not with the kind of cargo I prefer," Carlos added with a scowl.

"Why is the U.S. Air Force coming here?" I asked, simply to find out if Carlos knew what I already did.

"Who knows? I just know we have some so-called important diplomats arriving from Washington, D.C. What it means to me is more people walking around with itchy trigger fingers on shotguns and rifles and a bunch of people wearing expensive suits, each one thinking they're more important than the last." I nodded to show interest, yet remained silent to encourage the man of few words to continue. He did.

"You see that guy over there?" Carlos asked while pointing out onto the flight line. "He's from the U.S. consulate in Rio – some colonel who's been coming out here for the last few days making sure that everything was all set. I guess he figured that something would change from day to day," Carlos added with a roll of his eyes. The man looked familiar to me but it was tough to tell from our distance. I wanted to get a closer look, but waited for a better opportunity.

"Like what?" I asked only to keep him talking while we waited. The longer I could keep Carlos rambling, the longer I did not have to say anything that might give me away, and I could continue to assess the area.

"Like nothing! Nothing is going to change. He is just a nervous, anal retentive officer who is concerned about getting his star and figures he cannot trust the backward Brazilians."

I was beginning to figure Carlos out. "Were you in the military?"

"Yes, I was a loadmaster on C-47 Skytrains. I spent twenty years moving heavy shit around while pilots sat on their asses and took all the glory. Now here I am doing the same shit as a civilian. What about you, were you military?"

"No. I'm too much of a pussy," I said with a straight face. He gave me a look that wondered if I was screwing with him or not. I couldn't help but throw in the sarcasm, purely for my own benefit. The awkward moment was disrupted by the sound of the C-17's engines smoothly flowing into reverse thrust after touching down on the 12,000 foot runway.

Carlos placed a call on his radio and whistled shrilly inside the hangar, causing workers who had previously seemed to be either in slow motion or a coma to spring into action. One awoke already seated comfortably on the forklift, wiped the drool from his mouth, and started the motor. Another manned a tug, apparently unaware that the only cargo would be walking out on foot. It did not surprise me that the workers had not been informed of the nature of the flight.

Carlos turned to me and asked, "Do you want to see where we park these monsters?"

"Of course."

"Come with me," he said as he led the way out of the hangar doors, which were in the process of being fully opened. The combined sound of the massive turbofan engines and the hangar door alarm was deafening even for a former helicopter crew chief. I wished I had ear plugs while Carlos seemed oblivious.

While I never personally had the desire to fly something as large as the heavy jet rolling slowly toward me, I had to admit it was an impressive sight. Carlos stood in front of me and slowly raised his hands and crossed them over his head, signaling the pilot to stop. The aircraft nose pointed toward the hangar and left just enough room for the pilot to make a tight left turn when it was time to depart. The C-17's tail was labeled with its home base markings from Travis AFB, filling me with a bit of pride about the global reach of the U.S. military. The engines slowly wound down and the hydraulic ramp dropped open under the tail.

I was accustomed to seeing camouflaged troops and military cargo empty out the back, so the sight of a dozen conservatively dressed government types with briefcases and sunglasses was a little out of place. But I had been told this was a customary means of travel for White House advance planners, since it afforded enough room for the entire team, direct travel, and the added layer of security of not being exposed to the public while carrying sensitive information.

We were now close enough for me to recognize that the graying blond-haired colonel was none other than the DAO in Rio, David Reynolds. I hadn't personally met him, but was familiar with his photo from the consulate walls and pre-brief information from DIA. As he scurried toward the exiting team, I couldn't help but think he seemed like a real suck-ass. Despite the monochromatic suits, I could tell the team was a mix of military, security, and civilians. It was easy to identify the ones that were with the Secret Service and military, which left the rest to be the staffers.

One of the three women in the group was tied closely to an older, heavy set, balding man who had outgrown his light gray suit. The pair walked with a purpose in front of the group and exchanged handshakes and smiles with Reynolds. I would have recognized Fat Man as the staff lead even without advance intelligence; he had an air of confidence bordering on arrogance as he conducted the introductions. However, Kingman had attached a photo of Curtis Pierce with his latest e-mail, advising me that the Kentucky millionaire had volunteered to represent the administration during the planning of the forthcoming FLOTUS visit.

It was common practice for the U.S. to utilize older, distinguished business tycoons in this role to exert influence during negotiations with foreign counterparts. The young woman with him may have been an assistant under training for future responsibilities. She was striking in her fitted brown pantsuit, which hugged her slender body as she moved. Her skin was golden and glowing, her wavy black hair loosely pulled back from her face and neck. She appeared Latin, yet something Asian hinted in the background. It was good to see that the U.S. would represent itself well amongst the local talent.

CHAPTER 31

"Are you the supervisor here?" Colonel Reynolds barked in our direction. Carlos's stomach must've churned at Reynolds's tone as he addressed us peons, but in true soldier form didn't show it.

"Yes sir," Carlos answered slowly in heavily accented English.

"I'd like you to help us then. I'm Colonel Reynolds, United States Air Force, head of the defense attaché office." Carlos had informed me that Reynolds had been by numerous times, rendering his latest introduction the oversight of someone too arrogant to recall those he'd met repeatedly, or perhaps an opportunity to tout his own grandeur. The upside was that he was likely too self absorbed to ever recognize me, if he'd even seen my picture. I suspected that he lacked the attention to detail required to adequately perform the security aspect of his job, focusing solely on the pomp and circumstance surrounding VIP events. He never addressed me and barely even looked in my direction. I remained mute, conveying that I lacked any comprehension of English.

Reynolds continued his instructions, presumably in order to show the White House staff that he was a man in command. In typical American fashion, his English was spoken slowly and loudly in order to enhance foreign understanding. "These folks are here for a future VIP visit. They want to use this hangar as the arrival point. We have questions about how best to conduct the arrival and departure." Reynolds leaned forward and squinted to read Carlos's nametag, confirming he had no idea who he was, despite having previously met him. "Señor Gil, this is Curtis Pierce." Carlos reluctantly shook Pierce's hand, which had been laid in front of him as a baron would accept acknowledgment from a peasant.

"Mr. Gil, my staff and I thank you for your hospitality and flexibility. We know this is an interruption to your daily routine and wish to cause as little disruption as possible. Any assistance you can give us in order to make this as smooth as possible will be greatly appreciated." I had to admit, Pierce may have been a cocky old bastard, but it was clear that his silver tongue must have been an attribute as a business man. He used his southern drawl to his charming advantage.

"I have been told I am here at your disposal…sir," Carlos spoke in a way universally understood by enlisted military men – compliant words, yet clearly he was only following orders. His pause before adding the *sir* at the end of his statements was meant to indicate that it was a mandatory afterthought. Having delivered such statements numerous times during my enlisted years, I noted Carlos's timing to be impeccable. Pierce and Reynolds were oblivious.

"Great," the staff lead said. "We'd like to do a quick walk-through of this site to determine its feasibility. Today's concerns are just big picture. We can work on the details later, during the days just prior to the event. Understand?" Carlos nodded. I gave an empty, illiterate stare while I absorbed the rest of the group's activities.

Our gaggle, led jointly by Curtis Pierce and Carlos Gil, ambled around the ramp area in front of the hangar, measuring distances for wingtip clearances and scouting spots advantageous for press pens. Meanwhile, I concerned myself more with the machinations of those in dark suits and sunglasses, cropped hair, and stern faces. The security detail for the advance party, comprised mostly of Secret Service, quietly discussed while pointing surreptitiously at key vantage points and exposed sight lines. I doubted Reynolds noticed what they were evaluating, but wondered if he had anybody else observing their observations.

Pierce was a man who knew he had to maintain a tight schedule due to limited time. He turned to his young female assistant occasionally, asking her to make a note of something or another. She dutifully obliged. I enjoyed her every movement; I'd never seen a woman appear as sensual while taking notes and sweating in a wool suit. I was sorry to hear it when Pierce announced that he had all he needed. He thanked Carlos profusely, presumably to encourage future cooperation during the visit. He turned to Reynolds and indicated that his entourage was ready to depart for the next site.

Keeping true to their security discipline, nobody in the advance party gave any indication as to where that next stop would be. I excused myself and walked to the men's room. It was empty, so I placed a call to Max. He answered on the first ring.

"Hello, Wolgrand. How are you feeling this morning? Did you make it to work or are you calling from your apartment?"

"Blow me." I thought about launching into a tirade about the late night visit from the skirted man, but decided against it. I didn't want to take the time, nor divulge that I had been inadvertently intimate with a man. "I thought you might like to know the group is complete at my site and will be departing this position momentarily."

"Where to?"

"I was hoping you might know since you seem to have your finger on the pulse around here."

"Even the great ones aren't perfect every time."

"My image of you is ruined forever. What good are you to me now?"

"Well since you asked, I do have some good news for you." Max was never at a loss for words.

"You're buying dinner tonight?" Neither was I.

"Only if you put out," Max answered. His comment sent disturbing images of Samantha and *her* extra appendage through my head. While I knew Max was joking, I could do without the homoerotic humor for now.

"You're not my type. I prefer a little less chest hair," I said.

"Oh well, I guess you'll have to settle for my other good news. I'm nearby and already moving into position to trail the group as they depart the airport. What are they driving?" Max asked.

"Charcoal Peugeot sedans," I responded. "How is it you always seem to be in the right place at the right time?"

"Need I remind you again that you are working with a professional? Actually, your question leads me to the other update I have for you. I just completed a rendezvous with my other airport contact, who informed me that there is a departure scheduled this afternoon that is of interest to us," Max teased.

"And what might that be?" I asked, now becoming accustomed to Max's habit of holding back the key piece of information in order to beg the obvious question.

"Asad's G-IV is set to takeoff at 1500 local time, with him onboard. His flight plan is nonstop to Charles de Gaulle and he will have only one other passenger and a crew of two pilots with him."

I didn't know off the top of my head, but I did not think that a Gulfstream 400 would make a nonstop to Paris, at least not without landing on fumes. Surely they would be stopping somewhere to refuel, but where? Maybe it didn't matter, but I would either try to find out or pass this on to Kingman. One thing I'd learned during my relatively young career as an intelligence officer was that it paid dividends to follow available leads, even if they were not obviously useful. They could be few and far between; I might just find a diamond in the rough.

"I'll check out the plane and see what I can accomplish," I said, already planning what I might be able to with the jet. "As for your day's activities,

I think we ought to try and see if the group is being followed by anybody other than yourself. If Asad or Armas is aware of the team's presence they may try to find out what they're planning. Then again, if they knew about an upcoming visit and gave a shit, why would Asad be leaving this afternoon?" I asked more to myself than aloud to Max.

"Good question," Max confirmed. "I'll try to find out. If they're being followed, you can bet your ass I will know it."

"Just don't show your ass to them in the process."

"Uh huh. How about 1800 at building number five?" Max asked, referencing a hasty list of locales we'd selected based on their varied qualities and geographic locations. It was not very sophisticated, but I was only planning on being in the area for a brief time and this method would suffice in the short term.

"See you there. Good luck," I said as I hung up and walked back into the hangar, which was empty, save the resident work force which had returned to their natural state of rest. I walked through one of the hangar's eight rollup doors designed to fit the trailer of an eighteen wheeled rig; it led to the road access side where I had parked my car earlier. The advance party was still in the process of climbing into their caravan of vehicles. This provided Max with ample time to maneuver into trail position, and gave me an opportunity to check out Pierce's number two as she bent down to climb into the Peugeot. Just because I was here to do a job didn't preclude me from enjoying the scenery.

As they drove away I turned to Carlos, who was standing nearby smoking a cigarette and ensuring all the Americans had left his area.

"Would it be possible to complete our tour of the area before I get to work?" I asked.

"No problem. Come with me," Carlos answered. I assumed his enthusiasm was directly linked to what Max had told me about their arrangement. We hopped into a golf cart modified to carry tools and equipment in its converted metal bed and puttered away from the hangar down the flight line. Carlos pointed across the runways and told me that the other side was all commercial aviation, dominated by flights to and from Sao Paulo. Our side consisted of air cargo, corporate aviation, and some military.

Carlos rambled on about his days in the Brazilian air force as he identified two Eurocopter Super Pumas on the flight line. The large French-made helicopters were camouflaged with swaths of brown and green paint. The open crew doors on either side featured 50-caliber machine gun mounts. Both aircraft displayed the words *Forca Aerea Brasileira*, yet this was no military base.

"Do those helicopters live here?" I asked Carlos.

"No, they're from the base in Afonsos," he answered without saying whether or not he knew why they were here. I was satisfied that they had something to do with the upcoming visit and did not feel the need to pass my presumption on to Carlos. If he did not already know, it was none of his business. I was already planning on investigating the extent of security precautions to be taken while the FLOTUS was in Rio. I was sure that they would be comprised of a combination of U.S. and Brazilian forces, but I needed to obtain the details in order to evaluate their reliability.

Beyond the section of military helicopters was a high-end FBO with a handful of expensive aircraft parked in front. There were two G-IV's parked on the ramp, but only one lacked a tail number that began with PR, the prefix for those registered to Brazil. The other number was B-5611, which I didn't recognize, but assumed that the only foreign Gulfstream was Asad's. I'd try to verify through Max or Kingman before taking any further action on the plane. As we cruised back to the hangar, I noted that the scheduled departure was a mere four hours away.

CHAPTER 32

Staff Sergeant Robert Davis reacted like I'd dropped off the face of the earth when I called him from the hangar. I had spoken to him only once, the day I arrived in Rio. I had been disappointed with his lack of intel, but he was the only consular contact I trusted. I doubted he had the information I sought, but I had to give him a shot.

As it turned out, he possessed a decent rundown of security plans for the FLOTUS visit. Of course, he provided the caveat that the plans were subject to change as the situation dictated and based on forthcoming input from the Secret Service. Unlike some other foreign nations, the Brazilian and U.S. military had a strong rapport and would be coordinating security hand-in-hand. The U.S. would hopefully not divulge all the details of the first lady's travel plans, at least not too early. It was possible to provide the Brazilians with areas of concern without compromising her safety with excessive detail.

The scheme involved a defense in depth with multiple layers of assets providing overlapping coverage. The local police force would work at the disposal of the Secret Service, which lacked the numbers necessary to provide adequate protection. There was nothing abnormal about this methodology. The Service, paid to be paranoid, would augment its capability by shipping in vehicles for the motorcade. As I surmised, the Super Pumas that I'd seen earlier were in town to receive threat briefs and acquire local area knowledge in order to provide airborne defense during the visit. Fixed wing fighter support was to be in the form of two Mirage-2000s standing a strip alert seventy-five miles away near Sao Paulo.

Davis confided in me that there was likely more to the plan, but that Colonel Reynolds was keeping that closely held. Davis, being the good soldier, indicated that the colonel was minimizing exposure of the plans. His voice and my intuition indicated otherwise. At a minimum, Reynolds was a micromanager relishing the spotlight – at a maximum he was up to no good. I didn't get the impression that his staff sergeant held any suspicions of evil. Not wanting to stir up questions that may have led to extra attention from Reynolds, I let the issue be for the time being. I'd take action into my own hands and work with Max to gather available intel.

My lunch break was nearing its end, and I was getting hungry. Time was working against me, so I had to forego eating. I finished my phone call to Davis before rummaging through the trunk of my car for some needed equipment. Into a small briefcase I placed the Glock that I would have preferred to have on my hip, a satellite phone for encrypted calls back to the States, and some other electronic toys. I grabbed three listening devices and slipped them into my pockets.

Carlos was trying to stir his lethargic work force back into action when I approached him.

"Hey boss, I think my cell phone slipped out of my pocket during our tour of the flight line. Is it alright if I take a cart and go look for it? I just paid for that fucking thing and I can't afford to buy another one…especially on my wages."

"Fine. Just don't take too long. We have a flight departing this afternoon that needs to get loaded up, and we'll need all available bodies and equipment to make it happen."

"No problem," I answered, already knowing I needed to work expeditiously to reduce my exposure.

I started the cart and drove past the helicopters to where the executive jets were parked. Earlier, there was nobody around the G-IV, which would've made it relatively easy to sneak in and out without notice. Presently, however, the aircraft was being fueled by a man in a short-sleeve cotton button down shirt and khaki shorts, the uniform of the FBO personnel. This gave me the window of opportunity I needed. I'd done his job before and knew that this guy wouldn't care if a fellow airport minion took a peek.

I waved to him as if we were old friends, and he waved back with a smile and hello at the recognition of my Infraero uniform.

"That's a beautiful bird! Mind if I take a look?" I asked the fueler.

He shrugged, "Just try to keep the carpet clean. I hear the guy that owns this one is a real asshole."

"Yeah right. No problem, I'll take my boots off," I reassured him so he would not worry about his own hide getting skinned. Boots off, I was inside scouting for the optimal hiding spot for listening devices. I skipped over the cockpit since Asad would not be flying and tracking the flight would be accomplished by air traffic control. My concern was the content of any private conversations involving Asad.

I slipped on a pair of latex gloves and fished around the luxurious cabin. I felt around the maple paneling seeking any hideaway spots and finding only a fold-out table. A cursory survey of the cabin furniture included two large captain's chairs and two couches. Unsure if Asad would be in the mood to sleep on a couch or work in a chair, I reached under the most centrally positioned seat and affixed a small listening device to the bottom. This would allow monitoring of conversations between Asad and his travel companion.

Because the distance his plane would be traveling was well outside the normal coverage of most devices, this device was equipped with an additional feature – its ability to record eight hours of audio on a continuous loop. This audio feature was not constant, but instead noise activated by decibel modulation. The sound of the jet engines would initially trip the sensor but discontinue after one minute of constant noise. After that, the varied sounds of voices would activate the sensor for thirty second intervals. If a conversation were continuous the recording would also be continuous. The only catch was that it would not be real time information; someone would have to retrieve the device post-flight.

I reached into the cushions of the Portico leather seats and discovered a phone receiver tucked under the armrest of a captain's chair. It was the only handset I could find, so I planted an additional device in the arm of the chair. I worked quickly with my multifunction tool, removing the phone from the arm. I carved a hole in the bottom of the arm's interior large enough to house the device, a black box the size of a compact disc. Once plugged into the bottom of the phone via a telephone wire, both sides of any phone calls could be monitored. Once I'd connected the wire and reassembled the chair's arm, nothing would be outwardly discernable. This telephone monitor would activate with any call connection and automatically broadcast the contents via a discreet high frequency, capable of being heard cross-continent. While this would be real time information, it would only be gathered if a phone patch was connected. Neither device was perfect but between the two we could garner all of Asad's utterances; not to mention I liked the redundancy of two devices in case one failed.

I was back outside in less than five minutes; the fueler was just disconnecting the grounding cable from the plane and hadn't thought anything of the passed time.

"What a great plane. I think I'll buy one someday," I joked. "I only need to save for about two hundred more years." The fueler laughed and nodded in agreement as I mounted the cart without further delay. While he didn't appear suspicious, I wanted him to have as much trouble as possible providing my physical description, just in case anyone ever asked.

CHAPTER 33

I returned to work and watched the clock closely until the next scheduled break. It was difficult to focus on moving crates from loading docks to the FedEx cargo jet destined for Miami. The crates smelled faintly of coffee, but I cared more about getting the chance to place a call than whether I was moving *Mundo Nuvo* or *Bourbon* beans. The second the master clock hanging high on the interior hangar wall struck 1400 I was out the door and back to my mobile office in the parking lot.

I powered up the satellite phone and waited as it acquired sufficient connection with repeating devices that orbited the earth. The phone had an encryption device that would be automatically unscrambled by the matching phone on the other end, but would sound like garbled white noise to any would-be interlopers. Once the display indicated that it was call-ready I dialed Washington, D.C. There was a momentary beep and delay that preceded the voice on the other end, indicating that the call was properly connected and encrypted.

"Colonel Kingman," the voice on the other end was not only delayed but a bit distorted by the encryption device. Nevertheless, I recognized my boss – he possessed an unmistakable tone that made me imagine him standing upright in a crisp uniform at all times.

"Sir, it's Simon," I had already cleared the area to ensure that my true identity would not be compromised.

"Good to hear from you J.D. To what do I owe the honor of your call? Do you need bail money? I'm not sure it will help you where you're at."

"No sir – not yet. Besides, I thought your wife controlled your money," I jabbed. I thought for a moment that I had pissed him off until I heard his chortled response. The long delay on this phone made witty banter uncomfortable. Time to get down to business. "The advance party is on deck and has departed the airport. They are currently being escorted by the DAO to meet with other consular folks and local government officials. I am having them followed by a friendly contact. The other news – "

"Why aren't you doing it yourself?" Kingman interrupted as I was about to answer his question. While he might have done this under normal conversational circumstances, his tendency was emboldened by the inability to time a normal pause on a delayed phone transmission.

"As I was saying sir, there is something happening of interest here at the airport." Kingman was not quite impatient but definitely direct, so I continued without pause. "Al-Ayande *Actual* is departing onboard his G-IV at 1700 Zulu." I used the military term *actual* to indicate that I meant the commander of the organization. The use of Zulu time, universal in the aviation world, allowed for discussion of times without reference to time zones. Someone has only to add or subtract the number of time zones they are away from Greenwich Mean Time to figure their local time. This technique avoids the otherwise inevitable confusion as to whose time zone someone is referring to, making it a common worldwide clock language.

I told Kingman about the number of crew and passengers; I passed on the tail number and flight-planned route; I explained about the planted devices; I provided him with the high frequency that he could use to monitor phone calls; I informed him of the location of the hidden device that could be retrieved after landing. He assured me that he would have the HF monitored and the recording device retrieved; I knew I didn't have to question his methods. But I did have a couple of remaining concerns.

"Sir, that tail number prefix is unfamiliar to me. I'm not sure if it matters, but it may be worth having someone research its registration."

"I'm on it," Kingman's strong voice warbled over the satellite connection. "Second question?"

"I'm not sure a G-IV can make it to Paris on one fuel load. We may want to monitor the flight to see it goes as filed."

"Consider it done, stud. Anything else?"

"Not at this time sir," I was brief with Kingman since I knew he would be itching to get started on this project.

"Alright then J.D., I'll let you get back to work and whatever else you have going on down there. Just watch your back," Kingman added.

While I was sure that he trusted me to accomplish the mission, there were some ways in which Colonel Joe Kingman knew me a little better than I would have liked. Our history dated back to my years at Boston University when I enrolled as a freshman, still on active duty as an enlisted Marine. I had been accepted for entry into the Marine Enlisted Commissioning Education Program after successfully weathering a stringent application process for this sought after career path. Unlike other enlisted-to-officer programs offered by the military, MECEP assigns you to a college campus for four years, where you continue to accrue time toward retirement, earn promotions and receive a paycheck; the latter being the most valuable to a college student. I was the only one of my drinking buddies going to the ATM for beer money instead of the couch cushions. The result was perhaps a tad higher ratio of imbibing to studying than would be recommended by most educational counselors. While I maintained grades sufficient to keep in good stead with the program, my extracurricular habits did not go unnoticed.

Kingman became the Marine officer instructor of the NROTC unit at BU as I entered my sophomore year. He had already been selected to pin on major when he took the reins of the Marine Corps portion of the Navy unit, bringing with him ten years of experience in the fields of intelligence and infantry. An intelligence officer by MOS, Kingman had worked diligently to become part of an elite Marine recon unit as a junior captain. He spent untold months humping through the mountainous terrain of the Balkans, gathering intel to be used during subsequent NATO operations. He conveyed to our class of zealous officer candidates the merits of striving to be part of such a unit. After all, *every Marine officer is an infantry officer.* This mantra was the graduate version of the one I grew up with, that *every Marine is a rifleman.*

Kingman took an immediate interest in his only MECEP student; I was expected to help set the example of what it meant to be a Marine. For the most part I fulfilled his expectations; I led the way during arduous physical training sessions, wore the crispest uniform, and provided leadership and guidance to the regular ROTC midshipmen. Most college students that participated in my ROTC unit tried to make up with motivation what they lacked in experience.

They were bright-eyed teenagers who arrived as varsity high school athletes, big fish in their own small ponds. Entry into the Marine officer corps would serve as a wakeup call for many, as Parris Island had for me. Having this common knowledge with Kingman partnered us in an effort to mold the others in preparation. It put me in the unusual position of being teacher and student at the same time. While I may have been able to provide the example in many ways helpful to the other *middies*, a part of me remained the young punk that had shunned college upon high school graduation.

One such episode occurred during a Thursday night road trip to the post-industrial city of Worcester, MA. It also happened to be home to the College of the Holy Cross, the liberal arts institution where my friend Bobby Pacheco's girlfriend studied physics. The Jesuit school on the hill, isolated from its surroundings by its ominous black iron gate, regularly drove its students out into the seedy city streets in search of dive bars with cheap beer and liberal ID policies.

We picked up Cindy just off campus after our lack of residency prevented access to the protected campus. When we arrived at Maguire's Pub, it was already sweaty and wreaking of stale beer that slicked the floor. The three of us, along with a selection of Cindy's friends, ordered multiple rounds of the current beer special to wash down copious amounts of Jägermeister.

My mind was a bit fuzzy when the confrontation occurred, when two preppy students decided that they warranted the attention of Cindy, whether she liked it or not. Bobby was relieving himself of some Pabst Blue Ribbon, so I intervened on his behalf. The exchange of words led to some shoving amongst the wall-to-wall crowds, which led to our collective expulsion from the establishment. Once outside, the two that had been so tough inside lacked much of their bravado. A smarter, more sober man would have let them swallow their pride and slink home. I however, decided to jump into my car and follow them back toward campus. There was some cat and mouse played as we sped along side each other on the narrow streets, complete with colorful language and hand gestures. Having decided that enough games had been played for one evening, I wrenched my steering wheel hard to the left, crunching their right door panels and sending their car off the road and into an embankment.

When I returned to the bar, Bobby and Cindy were in the parking lot with quizzical looks. With no explanation as to where I'd been, I cheerfully told them to hop in and drove them back to the school. Unable to spend the night, Bobby kissed his girl goodbye and we drove back to BU in a drunken haze.

All was well until I got called into Kingman's office the very next morning. He asked me how my night out was and let me squirm for a few minutes before divulging that he had received a call from the Worcester PD. Not finding myself in a position to be asking too many questions, I kept quiet while Kingman berated me. When he was done he ordered me to get out of his face. Nothing ever came of the incident with the authorities. He never told me why, and I never asked.

While my behavior strayed from time to time, Kingman knew he had a dedicated, motivated Marine with much potential. He rode me hard to test my limits; I must have performed to his level of expectation. He took an interest in my personal and family life, and became friendly with my parents, who adored and respected him as much as I did.

Four years after my commissioning, I was pleasantly surprised but not shocked when I got the call from Kingman concerning a career opportunity with a new team he'd be leading at the DIA. He acknowledged that there were others within the intelligence field that possessed more experience, but he was seeking players with high aptitude, personal drive, and varied backgrounds. He indicated that he liked that I had experience in aviation and had operated in hostile environments. I did not know who the other players on the team would be and did not care. I assured him that I would be honored.

CHAPTER 34

SOMEWHERE EAST OF DAKAR, SENEGAL

Only Jack Stark's mind raced faster than his Jeep Wrangler as he sped along the treacherous highway from Tambacounda to Dakar. He had done everything correctly, had Breaux exactly where he wanted him. Without a doubt, his prey was cholera-weakened when his Land Cruiser crunched into the back of the bus in front of it. From the time of the crash to the point he opened the SUV's driver side door, Stark had never taken his eyes off of the vehicle. *How in the hell did he just disappear?*

Now without the benefit of any tracking device, Stark had a decision to make: comb through Tambacounda hoping to find Breaux or retreat to Dakar where he could regroup with Decroix. He was confident that if Breaux was slinking around Tambacounda, he would attempt to seek medical attention. He also knew there were a very limited amount of clinics in the city, making the search a brief one. But if Breaux had somehow departed the city, Stark would lose him. Allowing Breaux to reach Dakar first was a chance he couldn't afford to take. Even if Breaux were seeking assistance nearby, he would return to Dakar soon. Despite his intuition telling him that he was very close to the infected soldier, Stark decided his only viable option was to make preparations for a future takedown.

Stark drove through the night, arriving in Dakar in time for the morning rush hour. He hemmed and hawed as to whether or not to phone Decroix. He did not want to give Decroix time to plot his demise, so he decided to tell him face-to-face in the public forum of his office. That way, no matter how upset he became, he would have to swallow his anger and work with Stark to develop a new game plan. At least that's what Stark was hoping.

Knowing Decroix's controlling personality, Stark figured he'd arrive in the office early and be checking his computer to track vehicles and otherwise satisfy his paranoia. Decroix's computer program would display

Stark back in Dakar, but not Breaux. He would wonder why, and likely not with a pleasant demeanor. Stark passed the presidential palace and looked for a place to park. Decroix's office was in a large government building one block past the palace. Like many capital cities, the leader's pristine white residence stood in stark contrast to its rundown surroundings. The palace was ornate, the office building utilitarian. Stark looked past the cliff-mounted palace and admired the view of Gorée Island in the distance. He thought about the Senegalese president standing on the veranda, looking at the island – an everyday reminder of how one man could enslave another. *Not me, I'm nobody's fucking slave.*

Stark entered the building and had no problem negotiating the security system, which consisted of one listless guard that listened to about half of Stark's explanation before waving him through. Decroix's office was separate from any other police facility, since his position was largely political and required interface with other bureaucrats. He couldn't relate to them; they had reached their positions through nepotism and had never gotten their hands dirty in their lives.

To his pleasure, Decroix was able to secure himself a private suite away from the unworthy prisses. He had a small reception area where his secretary sat and worked on her nails more than paperwork or phones. A side door led to a short hall into his large corner office. The privileged that dominated the government were equally happy to ostracize the knuckle-dragging, low-society cop. Stark was oblivious to all of this as he walked the long linoleum hallway to its end. At this early hour, the halls were silent except for his footsteps. It gave him an ominous feeling, like he was walking the gauntlet to the gallows and the ill-tempered chief was the executioner.

When he arrived outside the office door, Stark could see the lights were on. He opened the door and leaned in cautiously. There was no secretary behind the desk, but it was still not even eight in the morning – much too early for the government workers. He issued a soft hello before proceeding through the door to Decroix's office. He knocked on the door, which was ajar, yet not far enough to see inside. He pushed the door open gently and stepped inside, only to be greeted by the barrel of a silenced pistol. The real surprise was that the hand holding it was not the color he had expected.

"Good morning, Jack – or should I say Kazem?" Danny Riordan leaned forward in Decroix's oversized leather chair and rested his elbows on the mahogany desk. His pistol remained trained on Stark's chest. "What's a mattah, cat got your fuckin tongue?"

Stark was frozen. Not knowing how much Riordan knew, he did not know how to react. If he made a break for it, he would certainly confirm his guilt; not to mention he would have a hard time eluding the former SEAL. Riordan's Irish skin was red and venous as it struggled to contain his aged yet rippled muscularity. There was little doubt in either man's mind that gun or no gun, Stark would not survive a fight. Riordan's now silent stare bore down like a grand piano on Stark's quivering shoulders. If there remained even a modicum of hope for survival, Stark would need to begin talking his way out of this mess. Surely he could spin this into some sort of misunderstanding.

"Danny, to what do I owe the honor?"

"Don't play fuckin games with me Jack! I know you're in bed with Decroix and I wanna know what other shit you've got going on."

Think, Jack. Dammit, think! "Well of course I had to get wired in with the local police force to get anything done around here. Decroix is without a doubt the boss. With my background in Iran, it was best to play the role of Iranian businessman." *Not bad. Keep it going.* "Pretty simple really, and quite prosperous I might add…in an intelligence gathering way, I mean." Stark corrected himself, hoping he didn't wince visibly.

"That's about what I expected you to say, you fuckin weasel. Only thing that pisses me off more than what you've done is I didn't figure you out soonah. You're a worthless piece a shit!"

Stark came to the realization that his spin was not going to bear fruit. He wasn't sure how Riordan found out what he was involved in, but he obviously knew enough to warrant overbearing confidence. He needed to stall Riordan long enough to think of a way out of his predicament. Maybe keeping the conversation going would help. He could discover how Riordan had cracked the case. Maybe that would give him an opening. *Maybe.*

Stark looked down for a moment to gather his thoughts in preparation for his next words of defense. He hadn't noticed it when he walked in, but he saw now that he was standing on plastic laid atop the carpet – presumably to keep the carpet clean and dry. *Maybe not.*

Already in trouble, the sight of protective floor covering made his heart sink. Stark swallowed hard before raising his head and facing the music. Riordan was now standing with arm extended, ready to play his own kind of percussion. Before Stark could even think to move, Riordan flipped the safety and squeezed off two rounds into the now *former* CIA operative. The double-tap into Stark's torso was designed to kill instantly, sending two violent waves through his body. The human body is more than seventy-five percent water, so each bullet creates ripples like a stone tossed into a pond. When the two opposing ripples meet, there is internal chaos that tends to shake up internal organs beyond a survivable condition. Stark collapsed onto the plastic and rested permanently in a growing pool of blood.

Danny Riordan exited the office building via the same routing he used to sneak in earlier that morning. The only aspect of the trip down the fire escape that proved more challenging was the added weight of Jack Stark's bagged corpse draped over his meaty shoulders. It was still fairly early morning by Dakar standards, but Riordan was not going to waste time waiting around. Not that anyone was going to miss Stark, but the sight of a burly white man carrying a human-sized bag down a building's external ladder was likely to draw sideways looks – especially once it was discovered that the chief of the gendarmerie was missing. A close examination would've divulged that there was no way Decroix would fit into the same body bag as Stark, but that detail would be irrelevant if Riordan were accosted.

Despite leg and lower back muscles burning with lactic acid, Riordan walked calmly and methodically until he reached his Ford Ranger pick-up. He crossed the street in broad daylight with the heavy bag across his shoulders, confident that he would not be bothered once on the street. So long as he looked casual nobody would question him. He stood at the rear bumper and used one free hand to unlock the hard tonneau cover. He thrust the cover open with his right hand and used his left arm and shoulder to launch Stark's dead weight into the truck bed. A muffled whimper emanated at the impact. Riordan cracked a slight smirk at the sound and greeted the bound and gagged Georges Decroix.

"I thought you might be lonely so I brought you a playmate, big boy." Riordan never made much effort to learn French and defaulted to English whenever agitated, regardless of how little was comprehended by his audience. "Turns out your boy Kazem was fuckin with both of us. To you he was just some pawn that could help you eliminate some problems. Frankly, I don't really give a shit that you had him knock off your deputy, but I got a little problem that you had him take out an American serviceman. Just so you know, his real name was Jack Stark – the *CIA operative* who turned on you when the heat was turned up on him."

The truth was that Riordan never did get any useful information from Stark. It was from Decroix himself, not savvy enough to cover his electronic tracks. Riordan hoped it would anger Decroix more to think that he'd been double-crossed by one American rather than outsmarted by another.

Decroix struggled briefly in a futile attempt to free himself. It must have seemed ironic to the chief to be victimized in the very city that he policed with ruthless efficiency, especially as he caught a fleeting glimpse of his own building just before Riordan returned him to darkness. Were it not for the outside noise and motion of the suddenly moving truck, laying in darkness pressed against the deceased Stark would have given Decroix the feeling of being buried alive.

Riordan had no sooner begun to execute the next leg of his mission to avenge Breaux's death when his cell phone rang. It was one of the Marine security guards from the embassy, all of whom fell under his tactical command as RSO.

"Sir, I have someone here says he knows you. He has no ID and looks real sick. He come in on a beat up motorcycle. Looks like one the locals might drive 'cept he claims he's American."

Riordan was confused, but had an optimistic hunch. "What's his name?"

"He says it's Martin Breaux. But sir, he has no ID."

"Yeah, I heard you the first time. Is he a black guy, about six feet tall, thin build, short hair?"

"Yes sir. What do you want me to do with him?"

"You said he appeared ill, so I want you to escort him to the infirmary and get him taken care of."

"Sir, I still need to search him for weapons – and how do you want me to log him in with no ID?" the Marine inquired diligently.

"Yeah fine, go ahead and search him, whatevah. Just record his name and have someone stay with him while he's at medical. I'm on my way."

The guard acknowledged his orders with typical Marine Corps fervor and Riordan hung up. *Goddam these guys are inflexible! Whatever happened to adapt and overcome?* Riordan still had not become fully accustomed to the way his embassy guards operated by the specific letter of every standard operating procedure. Despite the occasional frustration, he admired their dedication to duty and didn't want to have anyone else following his orders. He had complete confidence that every one would be executed flawlessly and without complaint. True, his former SEAL teammates exhibited skills and abilities beyond normal human comprehension. But they did have a tendency to take matters into their own hands. There were times when this was necessary to react to changing scenarios, but it was reassuring to Riordan to know that his current men would simply do as they were instructed.

Riordan smiled at the sight of the Army captain, resting placidly with eyes closed and an intravenous line disappearing under the wool blanket that covered him. He approached the embassy infirmary nurse and asked about his condition.

"I can't believe that he's alive," she whispered. "He's completely dehydrated from a terrible bout with cholera. He exhibited signs of delirium and could no longer focus his vision, but his vital signs are stable. Once his body replenishes, he should be good as new." She shook her head and smiled in disbelief. "Who is this guy?"

"He's a friend," Riordan covered the agent. "He went on a sightseeing voyage into the countryside. I guess it got a little more exciting than he had hoped. I'm glad that he'll be okay. Thanks for all your help."

"All part of a day's work, Danny...anytime."

"It's good to hear you say that, Jennifah, because I have a request."

The nurse's smile dissipated. "What?"

"I need you to stay here with him overnight. I don't want him sent to a hospital. He's been through enough and I want him to recovah right here – in your capable hands." Riordan took her hands in his in an effort to butter her up.

She rolled her eyes. "I don't know what you're up to, but I know better than to ask too many questions. You'd better make it up to me."

"I'll take you to that German restaurant on the beach you like so much," he offered.

"Be ready for me to drink enough beer to make it worth my while!" she responded.

Riordan said he looked forward to watching her try to out-drink him. As he walked out the clinic door he thanked the Marine who stood watch over the mystery man inside. Riordan conveyed to him that the staff sergeant in charge of the Marine security guard detachment would be coordinating for him to be relieved at 1800. There was a requirement to have a guard posted outside the infirmary overnight due to the patient remaining in place. Riordan knew there was no security threat, but also knew that the Marines would be more amenable to standing additional duty than leaving an unidentified guest unsupervised inside the compound. Riordan had to depart the area in order to take care of pressing business. He had a few loose ends to tie up.

CHAPTER 35

Though it had been some years, Danny Riordan found himself in a familiar position as he waited in the driver's seat of his pickup truck. He had conducted innumerable missions similar to this one during his Navy career, though it was rare that he operated without any fellow team members. He repeated his forthcoming steps over and over in his head to ensure perfect execution, knowing that he could not write anything down for fear of leaving evidence.

A time check verified that it was now after two in the morning, there had not been a single sign of life for more than two hours. Normal working hours at the port of Dakar were limited to daylight, leaving only an occasional passerby for hours afterward. Just after midnight, Riordan was mildly entertained by the silhouette of a man sidled up next to a building while a lady of the night performed fellatio. The final stragglers he saw appeared to be two locals conducting a drug deal. Riordan made sure to stay put not out of fear from these criminals, but to ensure he remained unseen.

The docks were shrouded in darkness, save for the dim bulbs marking boats that swayed gently against their moorings. *It's go time.* In fluid, well-rehearsed movements, Riordan slipped into wetsuit and booties, strapped on knife and Heckler & Koch pistol, and affixed night vision goggles atop his head. The tonneau cover opened, he slung the soon-to-be decomposing body of the late Jack Stark over his shoulder and without a word closed the top. The muffled noises made by an increasingly desperate Decroix were drowned out by gently slapping waves and clanging boats.

Riordan shuffled silently down to the spot where the police kept a small patrol boat, one that he'd found the key to in Decroix's office. He dropped Stark's dead weight on the deck and hurried back to the Ford to retrieve package number two. He may have had Decroix bound and gagged, but the giant police chief was not about to proceed agreeably with the psychotic American. While Decroix wriggled, Riordan slid into the truck bed and wedged himself in behind the chief. With one arm wrapped around Decroix's neck so that his forearm pressed against the carotid artery, he hooked that hand into the crook of his other arm. He put a hand on the back of Decroix's head and squeezed until the chief went limp. Knowing Decroix would wake soon, Riordan moved quickly to hoist the three hundred plus pounds onto his shoulders. He could not rush for fear of collapsing under the weight, so he focused by repeating a mantra he instilled in his young sailors during his days as a SEAL instructor. *Smooth is fast. Smooth is fast.*

Both men finally in the police boat, Riordan started the engine and puttered slowly away from the dock. Decroix was now awake and watched as Riordan guided the chief's own vessel away from Dakar and into the waters between the port and Gorée Island. He cut the engine and allowed the boat to coast in silence. He estimated that they were approximately a half-mile from the coast, well beyond sight from the city but not too far for an easy return trip. Riordan removed his backpack and from it pulled a plastic bag of small fish and dumped it overboard, stirring the water as he did so.

Within thirty seconds the water around the boat came alive with an unruly swarm of lemon sharks, devouring the appetizer of fish and indiscriminately nipping at each other. The shallow, warm coastal waters were a natural breeding ground for the shark pups, which usually found themselves the hunted when it came to human interaction. Rarely known to attack people, these fish often ended their existence as leather goods and shark fin soup. *Not tonight.*

If Danny Riordan was acting out of vengeful anger, he didn't display it. His actions were efficient, his demeanor stoic. From the wheel of the vessel he stepped aft to where he had tied Decroix to a bench at the stern. He unsheathed a six-inch Gerber from the front of his shoulder, lunged his left foot forward, and plunged the entirety of the blade into the chief's flabby abdomen. The former SEAL stabilized his victim with a sturdy grip on the right arm while he lifted the knife vigorously, cutting a deep swath into the rib cage. The whole motion occurred so quickly that Decroix never reacted with more than widened eyes. If there was any consciousness remaining, he would have guessed he was the main course.

Knowing that it was now safe to do so, Riordan removed all that had bound and gagged Georges Decroix and allowed him to slump over where he sat. Turning to the bagged CIA turncoat, Riordan unzipped him, placed the blood-stained Gerber in his right hand and rolled his corpse over the edge. The water around the boat erupted once again as dinner was served. With the lemon sharks occupied, Riordan pulled from his belt the

.38 Smith and Wesson that he'd used earlier that day to help Stark meet his Maker. He turned back to Decroix and placed the pistol in the chief's hand. It fell harmlessly to the deck. *Thanks for letting me borrow it, but you can have it back. I don't need it anymore.*

Riordan pulled flippers out of his pack and put them on over his booties, neatly rolled the body bag into the pack, and dove overboard opposite the feeding frenzy. He pushed away from the boat with powerful dolphin kicks as he headed back toward the shore in complete darkness. He was mentally prepared when his path crossed with a lemon shark that had strayed from the pack. He cleared his path with one strong punch to the animal's nose, sending it in search of a softer target.

Riordan did not stop swimming until he was more than a hundred meters from the wayward police boat. He treaded water long enough to observe as it bobbed in the bay, unguided by its slain captain. Decroix looked like a dead king atop his throne, surrounded by crazed gators in a moat. With no emotional response, Riordan ducked into the blackness and made for the lights that glinted on the horizon.

If investigators were lucky enough to find any remnants of Stark's body, they might be able to tie his gunshot wound to Decroix's pistol. In the unlikely event that they discovered the knife, its role as the other murder weapon would be verified. It had been taken from Stark's vehicle, leaving no suspicion or connection to Riordan. He was an amphibious ghost that would be allowed to continue his job providing regional security unimpeded by the local authorities. He would continue to be a respected ally of the Senegalese security forces with whom he shared limited amounts of intelligence.

CHAPTER 36

Martin Breaux stirred to life in an unfamiliar bed. He was taking in his surroundings, which appeared to be a former office space converted into a small medical clinic. Even though he had little recollection of his arrival, the IV tube reminded him of his recent travails. It had been more than fifteen years since he last awoke alone in a hospital bed.

He had just turned ten years old and as the oldest of four siblings, was the man of the house. His father disappeared without explanation before he could remember, leaving Uncle Richard as his male role model. Young Martin had taken to hanging around with Richard, who talked to him like a man and allowed him to cruise with him in his Chrysler Cordoba. Martin's mother had long been suspicious of Richard, who had been a derelict most of his life. But she permitted the friendship against her better judgment since she lacked the energy to control all her children. At least he was getting some male influence.

While most evenings were spent driving in Richard's behemoth around sleepy Hammond or nearby Slidell, one nighttime road trip took them to New Orleans. As a passenger along for the ride, Martin had little idea of his exact location. But the size and density of the city buildings that approached only added to the excitement of a night out with Uncle Richard. They exited the highway before reaching the area with the biggest buildings and the brightest lights, and Richard stopped the car outside a row of three-story apartments. Richard got out and told Martin to follow him as they entered one of the apartments.

Once inside Martin was both amazed and horrified. His own family was poor, yet his mother had performed tirelessly to maintain the house. This place was dark, had little furniture, and endless holes in the unpainted walls. Smoke and stench filled the air. There were people strewn about in various states of undress and consciousness. Small pipes passed between some while others lay openly naked, touching each others' private places. Uncle Richard ignored the activity around him as he approached an older black man seated in the corner, next to a duffel bag and a large bottle of beer. Martin stood behind his uncle while the seated man pointed a disgusted finger in his direction and became more animated with Uncle Richard. Richard pulled out his wallet and showed its emptiness before nodding repeatedly and placing his hands together in an act of prayer. He had no sooner done this than he reached behind his back into his waistband, brandished a gun and shot the seated man in the head.

The room burst into chaos. People ducked and rolled into dingy corners – others sprung up and revealed weapons of their own. Uncle Richard was not about to stick around and compare calibers. He grabbed Martin's hand and screamed for him to run as he blasted their way out of the apartment. They were almost to the relative safety of the tank-like Chrysler when Martin, who was doing his best to keep on Richard's heels, watched his uncle collapse in a heap. Martin nearly tripped over him as he continued to run amongst a hail of bullets that flew by him and smashed into their car. He was scurrying around the large steel bumper when he felt a searing burn in his leg. He looked down to see a stream of blood staining his pants before he passed out from the pain and trauma.

When Martin woke up in a bed at New Orleans Children's Hospital, he was alone, confused and scared. He thought he was dead and in heaven. It was not until the angelic nurse entered and informed him that the police had arrived on scene just as he lost consciousness. The drug dealers scattered like cockroaches and he was rushed to the hospital in an ambulance. With no ID or any companion, it took the police a few hours to figure out who he was. The Cordoba had been stolen and resold to Richard, who had registered it under an alias. As a result, Martin's mother had only minutes ago been informed of the status of her missing child and would be on her way ASAP.

Breaux's present day feeling of déjà vu was augmented by the arrival of another angelic nurse, who greeted him with a jovial smile.

"Good morning sunshine," the nurse began. "You look a hundred percent better than when you got here."

"Yeah, looks like I even got my color back," Breaux pulled an arm out from under the blanket and held it up as proof.

"It figures you'd have a sense of humor to be friends with Danny," she shook her head. Breaux had to rack his brain for a moment to recall who she spoke of – Danny *Riordan*. He wondered what Riordan had told her, since the two men barely knew each other. Breaux kept quiet on the subject so as not to conflict anything he may have said. A smile and nod was a safe response.

"So does this mean I'm gonna live?"

"I'm afraid you're doing so well you may even be expected to go back to work; whatever that is for you."

"Any idea how I got so sick?" Breaux did not bother to relay the story of losing control of his colon. He could see and smell that he had been bathed – she must have figured it out for herself.

"Cholera. Pretty common around this area; usually from bad seafood. Did you eat any?"

"More than any one man should – I love me some shellfish."

"Yeah, well you might want to take it easy on the prawns for a bit. They are truly filthy animals..."

It was during the nurse's speech that Danny Riordan slunk in and stood quietly behind the nurse, mimicking her like an adolescent before breaking into the conversation.

"I see you met our house muthah. She always gets excited when someone new shows up that hasn't heard her lekchah series yet." The nurse scowled at Riordan, but he remained unfazed. "Good morning, Jennifah. You look lovely today."

"You know Danny, you're lucky I'm a Christian – or else I might have to belt you."

Riordan waved a hand and gave a gruff smile as acknowledgment. "Truth is Mahtin, you're in great hands. Hey Jen, is my boy heah good to go or what?"

"For his own sake I hate to release him into your custody, but yes, he should be fine. I just need to check his vitals again in about an hour." She turned to the patient. "Do you need anything hun?"

"No ma'am, I'm good."

"Well, then I'll leave you boys alone to catch up for a little while," she said as she pulled the door closed behind her.

Riordan turned back to Breaux as his demeanor became serious. "What the fuck happened to you, man?"

"Like I told you before, I was going to check out the diamond mines. I had a hunch that some bad stuff was going on connecting them to al-Ayande. I tried to con Decroix into helping me take a look, knowing that when he said no it would confirm his involvement. So I hooked up with one of his deputies and we took a trip to the mines in question. We were conducting a visual recon of the area when I got smacked by this sickness. Hit me like a brick wall, man. We had to get the heck out of there. On our way out we got ambushed, the deputy got taken out."

Breaux shook his head. "Poor guy...just trying to help. So sick as a dog, I had to figure out how to get back. I started driving and saw I was being chased. You know what? It was a CIA agent who was chasing me! Real slick white cat by the name of Jack Stark. I had seen him meeting with an imam back at the mine, and I'm pretty darn sure he did the ambush. Now as for the cholera, I'm not so sure. I did eat me a boatload of shrimps during my meeting with Decroix, but that was at the Méridien and they should have clean food for such a high end place, right?"

Riordan nodded and opened his mouth to speak when Breaux continued like a man who had been near death and not yet shared with a soul his ordeal.

"Anyway, I drove until I got to Tambacounda, then it was decision time. I was low on gas, sick as a dog, and had this jerk right on my tail. So I ducked down real low while in traffic and dove out the door. The SUV I was in kept rolling into the bus in front of me – caused an accident and a big commotion."

Breaux shrugged as if to say *sorry about that* before he continued. "Meanwhile I scampered over to where this guy was straddling his motorcycle. I ran over to him too tired and sick to explain that I needed his ride. So I summoned everything I had left and socked him in the jaw. He went down like a sack of potatoes. I felt terrible about decking another brother who didn't deserve it, but I had no choice. What was I gonna do?"

Once again Riordan tried to break in with a raised hand, but to no avail. Breaux had a lot inside and needed to purge his emotional state, like his body had done the cholera.

"So to make a long story short I fooled that guy and hauled butt back to Dakar. I knew it wasn't safe for me to go to any local hospitals since Decroix would have 'em staked out, so I guessed that right here was the safest place I could find where they had a doctor. I barely remember even getting here on account of how sick and dehydrated I was. But now I'm feeling pretty darn good, thanks to Jennifer – who, by the way, has some booty on her."

"Yeah, well she's a bit thick for me, but I'm glad to see you're feeling good enough to check out a piece of ass. Well you were certainly right about Chief Decroix; he's about as dirty as they come. As soon as you and I met, I put my best techno-geek on the job. Within no time he was listening in on cell phone calls – which apparently people around here don't seem to know how easy they are to monitor. We heard him passing instructions on how he wanted to see you and Deputy Gueye eliminated. It was during those calls that we learned Stahk was in on it – that little fuckin prick."

"Unfortunately, we had a hahder time hacking into Decroix's computah," Riordan continued. He figured he'd better keep talking now that he finally got the floor. "He's got a system to track all his vehicles, so we saw you and Stahk hightailing it back from Guinea. By the time we hacked in, Gueye musta been gone cuz you didn't stop until Tambacounda. Then your car just stopped, died right there on the screen. We were sure that Stahk had nailed you, since he just continued back to Dakar. I think he was out of cell range for most of it because he nevah checked in with Decroix. Eithah that or he was afraid to be the bearah of bad news. And from what I could tell, that Decroix's a fuckin bear."

"You know Decroix won't accept the answer that I just disappeared. He won't rest until I'm found – dead or alive," Breaux said. Riordan nodded stoically.

"I don't think he'll come looking for you, Mahtin," Riordan contended.

"You don't get the same read off him that I do then, man."

"Oh it's got nothing to do with that. You just didn't heah the news this morning. Some fishahmen reported that they found his police boat floating aimlessly around the port. When they got out to it, the chief was sitting there gutted like a tuna."

"God blessed! How'd that happen?"

"The police are pretty tight-lipped so fah, but it's not like he lacked enemies," Riordan dodged a direct answer to the question.

"That's true – I can't say I'm gonna lose any sleep over the fatso. Even so, Jack Stark is still slinking around. That snake will come after me as a matter of self-preservation – now that he knows I know who he really is."

"I wouldn't worry about him eithah," Riordan began.

Breaux was starting to realize that Riordan would never have known so much so quickly unless he had personal involvement. It was certainly well within his abilities to eliminate both men, especially when the circumstances involved water, where Riordan was more comfortable than most humans. Rather than force an admission from the former SEAL, Breaux moved on to the business at hand.

"Okay, so what next?" Breaux began before answering his own question. "The way I see it, we have a solid location on the mine that al-Ayande is using to launder money, and I got a pretty good look at the imam who's running the place. These guys typically hide behind spiritual words and robes, while all they really care about is the money and power. I should know. I grew up in the Bible belt, seeing all those jive preachers doing the same thing to their Christian congregations."

"Yeah, I guess the only difference is that the ones back home aren't trying to bring about the end of civilization as we know it," Riordan provided a minor distinction. Breaux nodded.

A buzzing and ringing came from the corner of the room. Breaux recognized it as his satellite phone.

"That's mine – it's over there. You mind grabbing it for me?" Breaux asked as he held up his arm to reaffirm its attachment to the machine adjacent to his bed. Riordan began to dig through the heap of clothes when he straightened up, phone in hand and a contorted look on his face.

"What the fuck is that smell?!" Riordan demanded while scowling at the soiled garments.

"Man, you don't even wanna know," Breaux shuddered at the thought of liquid pouring uncontrollably from his anus while he tried to focus on his frantic escape from Jack Stark. He reached and took the secure electronic device. Besides himself, it was the only thing that had survived his ordeal. It remained his only link to the outside world. He entered a password to unlock the device and listen to the message that had been left from the missed call. He made a writing motion in the air to indicate to Riordan that he needed a pen and paper.

While he listened he jotted:

- *Flight arrival 1300 / G–IV / tail # B5611*
- *Asad to pick up <u>Stark</u>*
- *Follow on to Paris*

Breaux hung up the phone and Riordan asked, "What's up?"

"My boss back in D.C. Looks like our small-time diamond mine imam will have to wait – the king of the al-Ayande jungle is paying Dakar a visit."

CHAPTER 37

The military base on the south side of Senghor international airport would have appeared abandoned if one were to only look at its condition. Dusty, unkempt grounds surrounded ramshackle buildings. The government had forsaken the facility, dumping any available airport funds into the civilian side, the only part ever seen by visiting tourists with money.

Riordan and Breaux were meeting with representatives of the Senegalese air force to perform a site survey for future military joint operations. At least that was the line they fed them. None of the officers appeared the least bit surprised to see Riordan, who made regular visits to the military base that occupied the southern half of the airport grounds. He did so to ensure that the U.S. maintained logistical support for military aircraft and personnel that visited the area. He also did so to spy on them. He was able to disarm them with his appearance as a barely literate oafish warrior. They poked fun at his inability to learn French, figuring him to be somewhat harmless and therefore sharing with him more than they ought to.

The truth was that Riordan was sharp as a tack when it came to all things military and government, yet his xenophobia caused him to take a boorish approach to learning foreign languages. Purposeful or not, he took full advantage of foreigners who let their guard down. Breaux, who had been introduced as a new member of the embassy's DAO, impressed the natives with his fluency in both French and Wolof. His deft tongue drew mock scowls from the upstaged Riordan.

It was a contact at the base that had informed Riordan about a Gulfstream IV that was making the unusual move of stopping over on the military side of the airport. Without much prodding from Riordan, the contact volunteered that this arrangement had been made by the late Georges Decroix. The chief's justification had been to assist a high profile visitor avoid attention from the commercial side. Not to mention the faster service that could be afforded with military assistance. Breaux figured that it was to help Jack Stark avoid being observed meeting with the leader of an international terror organization.

The G-IV touched down and taxied hurriedly to the south side of the airport. The pilots that flew for Asad and his cronies were accustomed to exceeding performance specifications and ignoring safety concerns; it was less hazardous than incurring the Lion's wrath. It was legendary temper that had convinced Dakar's premier imam that it would be inappropriate to send a minion to break the news of Stark's disappearance. He sweated nervously in his car as he watched the jet lurch to an abrupt stop. Its wheels were chocked for a quick refuel and passenger pick-up.

The air-stair door lowered yet nobody emerged; the intent was for Jack Stark to be ready and waiting to hurry out to the jet for boarding. When Asad had been informed by his pilots that they would likely not have the fuel to make it all the way to Paris without stopping, Asad had decided it would make the best use of time to stopover for Stark. He had already requested that the mole be in Paris upon his arrival; this way Asad could receive an extensive briefing and formulate his next plans, all before touchdown.

The imam stared at the open door, second-guessing if he should even get out of his car. Heat rose from the Rolls Royce turbofan engines, causing the red stripe on the side of the plane to dance like flames. He thought of the anger that would soon be fuming from Asad. The jet waited as it received fuel and the pilots prepared the cockpit for the next leg of their journey.

The imam reminded himself that this was not his fault. He'd cautioned the man he knew as Kazem from too close an association with the hot-tempered Decroix. He hoped Asad would understand as he stepped out of the car and walked briskly toward the jet, his stare focused on the open door.

Out of the imam's view, hidden by the tinted cabin windows, a confused Asad watched. He turned to his assistant and asked, "Who is this man? He is not the one from the pictures. Our informant is a thirty-something of Iranian descent, this man is a fifty-something African."

"I don't know, sir," Najid shared his boss's quizzical stare. "Should I turn him away?"

"Of course not, bring him to me – once you're sure he's not armed," Asad said with the paranoia of someone who knew that any man, known or unknown, could bring his life and his mission to an instant end. Nobody would be capable of carrying on his legacy should he fail.

The imam did his best to maintain his dignity while being searched like a common criminal by Asad's henchmen. He thought to himself about how backward his world had become; a world in which a spiritual leader could be shown so little respect by supposed followers of the religion. Sadly, he conceded that he had helped to foster this new world order by allowing this animal into his house of Allah. He felt dirty in Asad's presence, knowing that he had made a deal with the devil. Al-Ayande had initially purported to be a movement of innovation and peace, but the imam kicked himself for being fooled. Anecdotes of Asad's violent past were well-circulated; the imam had allowed himself to be convinced that lore had exceeded reality. As he stood in front of the Lion, he wondered how many evil things he knew nothing of.

Asad's stare remained fixed, his face stern as he listened to the imam tell of Stark's disappearance. His breathing intensified, his blood pressure rose to a crescendo. In his youth he would have stood and struck this messenger down, leaving his corpse as a message not to cross him. He still had a horrific temper, but had learned to harness his anger and focus his energy toward his goals. He dismissed the imam with a wave of his hand.

"Who is that?" Breaux asked as he lowered his binoculars.

"I nevah met him, but I think he's the imam at the mosque known as *1459*. It's on the southwest coast of the city," Riordan answered as the two men observed the airplane ramp from an empty third story office in an abandoned military building.

"How do you think he took the news?" Breaux asked with a smirk. He was satisfied knowing that Stark was no longer among the living.

"Well, the guy's still walking for now, but who knows what the fuchah holds. He didn't do anything to cross the boss. So long as the imam remains an asset, helping al-Ayande laundah money, he lives." Riordan nodded to himself as if to confirm the solidity of his argument.

The two men speculated on Asad's next moves while the G-IV finished taking on fuel. The pilot conducted a cursory walk-around inspection, hopped up the air-stair and climbed into the cockpit. He joined the copilot, who was finishing up his flight plan. Their pace was the aviation version of a NASCAR pit crew – *almost* fast enough for their impatient cargo.

"Well, we'd bettah get your ass on the road. I don't think he's gonna wait for you," Riordan said. "Besides, your chariot awaits."

"Speaking of which, what's my ride?" Breaux asked. He had told Riordan that he was afraid he'd lose track of Asad if he took a commercial flight. Besides the check-ins, boarding, and other inevitable delays, the nonstops to Paris were all landing at De Gaulle airport. Asad had arranged to land at cross-town Le Bourget.

What Danny Riordan lacked in finesse he made up for in resourcefulness. He cashed in a favor with his military contact at the airport, who cashed in a favor with his military contact in Paris; all in order to make a mirage appear in front of Breaux's eyes. Unlike the ones that played tricks with his mind during his desert race back to Dakar, this was a Mirage 2000N – the two-seat bomber the French had modified for nuclear missions. Less than one minute after the G-IV taxied from the military ramp toward the runway for takeoff, a French fighter pilot finished his cup of coffee, shook hands with his Senegalese counterparts and left the pilots' lounge. He walked into the blazing heat of the ramp and readied the modern warbird for an unusual flight.

Breaux looked down at his small carryon bag then at the jet, hoping he could find a place to stow it. He was already a bit disappointed that he was forced to leave his suitcase and a majority of its contents behind, in exchange for the backpack that Riordan gave him for his journey. The anticipation of a supersonic ride to Paris helped compensate. The pilot helped Breaux shoehorn his bag into a small compartment and climb into the rear seat. After a quick safety brief on what would happen in case of emergency, the pilot climbed in and fired up the Snecma M53 turbofan.

Breaux had been explicit with his concern that Asad had gotten a head start and that he needed to arrive in Paris first. The pilot chuckled with arrogance as he explained over the intercom that they would be traveling at more than twice the speed of sound; Mach 2.2 as compared to the G-IV's Mach 0.8. They would lose some time during the two aerial refuels, but the airspeed difference would more than make up for it. They would have time for a leisurely espresso or two before the G-IV's arrival. Hidden from view in the backseat, Breaux rolled his eyes and wondered what could be haughtier than a man who was both a fighter pilot *and* French. He was pulled back into reality as the pilot proved his point with 21,000 pounds of afterburner thrust; until he momentarily grayed out from the intense g-force.

CHAPTER 38

Asad stewed as he watched the earth move below. From an altitude of 35,000 feet, his view seemed endless. It mirrored his internal desire to have that kind of expansive power. To achieve those lofty ends would require relentless hard work and the will of Allah; the latter was why he questioned this latest development. Jack Stark was his conduit to operations in Paris and he had been eliminated, leaving Asad to regroup. It was not beyond his capability – he had adapted and overcome much larger challenges. But when setbacks occurred he could not help but wonder why.

Back in the days when Asad was known by his given name of Hossein Zand, life held hopeful promise. He was the youngest protégé of the eminent nuclear physicist Tourak Alam. Together they were going to bring Iran into the nuclear age and join countries like the U.S., France, China, and the Soviet Union on the highest levels of the world stage. On a personal level, he was courting a young Persian woman by the name of Ariana.

She worked at the U.S. embassy in the visa processing office; her bilingualism and cheery demeanor made her a natural for the challenges of such a job. She was forced to deal with people at their worst – traveling or working abroad from the U.S. and having to contend with visa expiration, loss, or theft. Many of these people were high-powered American businessmen who all believed that they were priority One. She had been raised in a wealthy Iranian family that infused her with a combination of traditional Muslim values and an education rare among native women. She was accustomed to handling men's tempers with grace and had the intelligence to multitask with the best.

The Shah-led government made many efforts to parade its best assets to the Americans whose backing was essential to the regime's existence. Ariana's employment at the embassy displayed how Iranian culture had progressed while still preserving its values. Another way for the government to show itself was to host lavish dinner events at the Shah's palace. It was to one such event that Dr. Alam had been invited to be honored as the country's top scientist. As a means to inspire and cultivate his protégé, Alam brought Zand as his guest.

Among the many dignitaries that Alam introduced to Zand was an older man by the name of Omeed Agassi. Alam explained that Mr. Agassi was a revered academic with a vast history of scientific study both in Iran and the United States. Once a prolific scientist, he had been rewarded by the government with an assignment as director of the University of Tehran. During his tenure, Agassi did much to represent his homeland during visits with foreigners; he honed his political skills to match his scientific ones. Now retired to enjoy his wealth and hopes of becoming a grandfather, he took this evening's opportunity to introduce his precious daughter to potential husbands. Ariana had been groomed since childhood to someday be married off to a man whose greatness was deserved of association with the Agassi family.

Hossein Zand aggressively pursued everything he wanted; this was no exception. He quickly broke away from his mentor in order to seek a more private setting with the stunning Ariana. He had been instantly smitten when old man Agassi introduced her to him and Tourak. While the two elder scientists reminisced of past times, Ariana slipped away to socialize with more youthful guests. Hossein followed – under a spell cast by her large dark eyes, her lustrous black hair, her sensual mouth. His mind wandered to images of what her body must have looked like under her flowing evening gown. He accosted her before she could become engaged in other conversation and immediately made his move. She was not only taken by his rugged good looks, but impressed with his confidence and intelligence. To them it felt as if nobody else was in the room: they conversed easily, unaware of the passing time until Father reappeared to take her home.

Omeed allowed his daughter to continue seeing Hossein despite reservations about his personality. The young man was too brash, too arrogant. Sure, Tourak Alam wouldn't have taken him under his wing had he not shown vast potential. But Omeed thought that Hossein ought to keep his eyes open and mouth shut at a higher ratio than he did – especially under the tutelage of the great Alam. Nonetheless, he loved his daughter and trusted her judgment. Not to mention she had become a strong, independent woman. He admitted to himself that he had raised her to be educated and questioning; he allowed her to work at the U.S. embassy. The result was a young woman that would not be told what to do. She would have to learn for herself.

Hossein and Ariana's courtship was intense in every way. They enjoyed each other's company and spent every available moment together. They planned regularly for their marriage and future life together. They disobeyed social mores and engaged in passionate premarital lovemaking. They argued over Ariana's unwillingness to become a stay-at-home mother. Despite Hossein's attraction to her strong personality, he had difficulty accepting Ariana's exposure to other men in the workplace and public in general. The closer they became the more he desired to hide her away. The fights continued but always melted away into makeup sex. The two love birds were mere months away from wedding bliss when circumstances began to change.

Hossein noticed that Ariana had begun to seem more distant, her normal exuberance toward him cooling, her loquaciousness turning to quiet brooding. His mental energy became torn between his long hours of work and obsession with getting his fiancée to open up to him. She refused, dropping only vague hints that there might be trouble in paradise.

Fearing Hossein's notorious temper, Ariana picked a public setting to break the news. Hossein could hardly keep down his coffee as he listened to the love of his life tell him it was over. She had met someone else, had been seeing him on the side. All those recent times that she had been unavailable, not answered his calls, she had been in the arms of another. His head went light. He sweated profusely. He didn't know whether to be irate or distraught – he was both. She had blatantly lied to him about what she had been doing. She had been assuring him that she was spending much needed time with her family, to show them that she was not losing them just because she was getting married.

They were all lies...*all fucking lies!* He could not decide which was worse; that she betrayed him or that she displayed no qualms in how she misled him. Following self-defensive instinct, he focused on his anger in order to suppress his stabbing sadness. He demanded to know who had stolen her heart. Surely it was someone that had no idea that she was engaged. *Nobody would be so fucking stupid to cross me.* With tears streaming down her face she resisted, assuring him that it did not matter. He pressed harder, threatening a violent outburst in the absence of immediate truth. She broke down and told him...she had fallen in love with Dr. Tourak Alam.

Hossein Zand had been raised with high expectations; his genetic intensity merged with parental demands to create a young man that refused to accept failure. At this moment he was faced with not only the earth-shattering pain of losing the person he loved most, but also the realization that he had lost her to another man – the man who claimed to be his mentor, his caretaker, his friend. He had never felt so betrayed, so alone. He realized at that moment it was him against the world. He would never allow himself to feel such devastation; he would never be made to look like such a fool.

Zand stood from the café table. Ariana remained seated and tried to avert her eyes from the enraged beast before her. He leaned forward and placed his hands on the table, moving his blood-filled face within an inch of hers. In a whisper, he demanded that she look him in the eyes and promise him that she would not alert Alam that she'd divulged his identity. It would be better for all parties involved – the scientists could continue to work together, if only on a professional basis. And she could avoid further confrontation. Her rational thought blinded by fear, she agreed.

That moment of betrayal sprouted the roots that would transform Hossein into Asad. As he sat comfortably in the G-IV's cabin, he smiled to himself at the thought that he always came out on top. He left that bitch behind and walled himself off from any other intruders – the simplicity gave him clarity. He had moved on to bigger and better things, refusing to allow personal interactions to distract him from his global plans. His focus, now as sharp as a scalpel, readied him for his next steps; ones that would be executed methodically, with surgical precision.

———————

Martin Breaux tried to relax as he sat in the rear seat of the Audi sedan. He still reeled from the remnants of cholera and the air sickness from the Mirage ride, but was comforted by the arrangements that Riordan had made for him. Upon his arrival at Le Bourget, he was met by a Marine from the U.S. embassy in Paris who would be assigned as his driver for the duration of his visit. Among other equipment, the Marine handed Breaux a radio tuned to the air traffic control frequencies necessary to monitor Asad's arrival. The radio traffic was busy, but Breaux clearly heard B-5611 check-in for approach and landing. Among all the heavily French-accented transmissions, their calls stood out. The pilot sounded distinctly *Asian*.

Breaux and his Marine driver watched as the G-IV gracefully touched down on runway two-one. Not sure what would happen next, Breaux knew it would happen quickly and that the stakes were high. Once again, he would have to suppress physical illness in order to accomplish the mission at hand. He took a deep breath and told himself aloud that it was game time.

PART TWO

CHAPTER 39

LAKE TAHOE, CALIFORNIA

Richard Estevanez situated himself in a chocolate brown leather Barca-lounger, his handlers double-checking his hair and makeup. He'd been in front of television cameras for the better part of his fifty-one years, yet it still gave him a rush of adrenaline. He looked past the ready camera and took in the comfortable surroundings of his mountain getaway. The five-bedroom lakefront cabin, partially obscured by tall evergreens adjacent Lake Tahoe's Emerald Bay had become his family's favorite place to escape the relentless attention. He chuckled as his wife attempted to corral their four children out of the family room in preparation for the fireside speech.

Born Ricardo Tomas Estevanez Jr., his father began calling him Richard as a young boy; not to differentiate from himself, but to make it easier to integrate into their lily white surroundings. Old man Ricardo had accrued a fortune developing the largest Spanish-speaking television network in the U.S. and had uprooted his family from East LA and planted them in the hills of Bel-Air.

Despite a privileged upbringing, young Richard had been taught that the U.S. was the land of opportunity. It was the responsibility of every citizen, no matter how rich or poor, to defend it. Richard carried that mentality with him through his time at Stanford and decided to serve his country as an Air Force officer for a tour before joining the family business. Mildly disappointed to not achieve a slot to fly attack jets or bombers, he nonetheless enjoyed his six years as a KC-135 pilot. The large aerial refueler, while not as sexy as the F-15 Strike Eagle, required a crew that brought with it camaraderie not found in the business world. However, he knew he could not play forever and his family had its long term expectations. He served his time and resigned.

Richard's vision saw no limits. Not content to merely inherit his father's business and live an easy life of luxury, he took the risk of creating the first major market bilingual network. Naysayers chastised that people only wanted to watch television spoken in one language. But he knew many Spanish Americans that regularly switched back and forth between the language channels to experience a greater variety of entertainment. He further believed that it would help unite the people of a land growing increasingly segregated by divisions of language and culture. If he had achieved any measure of success with the latter was subjective and nebulous; the former was without question. Richard Estevanez's Spanglivision was a monster success, bringing with it billions of dollars and international celebrity status.

Estevanez was not only the business mogul running the machine, but also the face of the network. He typified his Spaniard roots with tall stature and dark features. He exemplified the ideal first-born American of immigrant parents with his refined polish and business acumen. No actor could hope to play the role better. He took full advantage of his image by making himself constantly visible to his viewers and those he hoped to earn in the future. He was both a shrewd decision maker and a leader that motivated his people through personal empowerment. His management style, made possible by surrounding himself with the right people, enabled him to spend more time interfacing with the public – which led to other grandiose plans.

Once believing he was sufficiently well-known and respected, Estevanez made a breakthrough run for the governorship of his home state of California. What made his attempt unique was his decision to run as a Republican, a Hispanic Republican. The state's only prior Hispanic governor was also a Republican. During the 1860's, Romualdo Pacheco's political focus was the solidification of the Union against divisive forces. Pacheco was well-educated and bilingual, a judge and businessman, and used his bilingualism and polish to draw votes from both Anglos and Hispanics. Similarly, Estevanez figured that despite his ethnic heritage, his strong business foundation and views on social issues best aligned him with conservatives who desired to keep the money they earned. His hope was to inspire and enable other minorities to make their own American dream come true. His tactic was to steal enough traditionally Democratic Hispanic votes to win the election. Despite having to wait for his dreams of an ideal U.S. to come to fruition, his unorthodox campaign decision proved shrewdly successful in the short term.

During his years as governor, Estevanez made no secret of his strong patriotism and ardent Catholicism. He remained true to his pro-business stances as manifested by fiscal conservatism. He developed numerous welfare-to-work programs in order to help the unemployed provide for themselves. He instituted state-subsidized health savings accounts in order to shift some of the burden from employers to individuals who were now responsible for their own decisions. His no-nonsense attitude was softened just enough by his charisma for him to not only remain the man in charge, but to become a media darling.

The phenomenon of Richard Estevanez appeared unstoppable. But he knew that nobody remained indefinitely popular in politics. After two terms as governor, he needed to strike while the iron was hot. He and his family knew that a run for the presidency would be grueling, given the deeply rooted bigotry that still remained woven into the American fiber. Undeterred, he took on all comers, including a certain female senator from Iowa. Margaret Duncan was a career politician that used her numerous lifelong connections to try and mudsling her way to the nomination. Her people used subtle scare tactics to infer that a Hispanic president would most certainly focus efforts on *his own people*, while forgetting about *the rest of hardworking Americans*. Estevanez was forced to retaliate, which his campaign did by presenting a laundry list of pork-filled legislation that Duncan had placed her heavy backing behind. By contrast, he displayed how he'd remained true to his political promises to the greatest extent possible, which rang true with enough Americans of all races to win not only his party nomination, but also the White House.

Once in office, President Estevanez allowed more of his personal biases to show through. While he remained supportive of businesses and averse to raising taxes or increasing the scope of governmental intervention, he made no secret of where he placed his international allegiances. Like a modern day James Monroe, Estevanez supported strong ties to Latin America and showed circumspection toward other troubled regions. Lukewarm to some traditional allies such as France, he was more than just privately wary of China, Russia, and Muslim nations. He believed these nations had their sights set on worldwide expansion, a goal that would only be achieved at the expense of U.S. power.

Advisors to the president were often skeptical about the plans he devised; they cringed at the thinly veiled slaps in the faces of nations that Estevanez resented. They had attempted to redirect his idea to celebrate the traditional Catholic holiday seasons of Mardi Gras and Lent in such public fashion. While he sometimes bent, the president was insistent on sending a message – his advisors were promptly rebuffed. He was excited at the opportunity to share his upcoming plans with the nation and Catholics worldwide.

"Good evening my fellow Americans. I join you tonight to share a bit about what it is that makes this nation the greatest in the history of the world. In recent decades, it has gone somewhat out of vogue to openly embrace, or even discuss, the virtues of organized religion. Many modern intellectuals often refer selectively to the First Amendment when they speak of freedom of religion and the separation of church and state. In their teachings it is as if there is something evil about organized religion; that it ought not be acknowledged by public officials. This could not be further from the truth. Just take a look at the Founding Fathers who developed the Bill of Rights and Constitution."

"It was John Adams who said 'Jesus is benevolence personified, an example for all men. Christianity is the religion of reason, equity, and love; it is the religion of the head and the heart.'"

"It was Samuel Adams who told us that 'the right to freedom' was a 'gift of the Almighty.' That 'the rights of the colonists as Christians may be best understood by reading and carefully studying the institutions of Christ, which are to be found clearly written and promulgated in the New Testament.'"

"It was Benjamin Franklin who said 'the most acceptable service we can render to God is doing good to his other children.'"

"Finally, it was George Washington himself that implored to non-believers: 'you do well to learn our arts and our ways of life and above all, the religion of Jesus Christ. These will make you a greater and happier people than you are.'"

"None of this is to say that the practice of religion is required, or that there is only one proper choice of religion. Our Constitution does indeed protect every American's right to practice, or not practice, whatever religion they so desire. However, it does so only if that religion does not engage in either hate speech or acts of violence toward others. When these occur, the laws of the land are violated and must be prosecuted regardless of whether or not one attempts to hide behind religious freedom."

"The Founding Fathers were attempting to strike a delicate balance between freedom for all people and fostering a society of good and honest citizens. It was their personal belief that organized religion could provide the guidance necessary for people to lead the kind of lives that would preserve our nation. It is no coincidence that we have constant reminders of these tenets, such as 'one nation under God' and 'in God we trust.' They exemplify the wisdom that religion can inspire people to do right in life without having their freedoms restricted by authoritative governmental rule."

"Certain religions have a rich history of providing a common link to people of all races and financial status. While atrocities admittedly have occurred throughout history in the name of God, the Catholic Church has inspired innumerable acts of charity toward humankind. Through its spirit of community, Christianity has given hope to even the most desperate both here in the U.S. and abroad. Compare for instance the state of affairs in the Americas and Africa. Tribal differences without any unifying forces have long resulted in brutal, genocidal violence in Africa. While there are still many problems of poverty and corruption in Central and South America, widespread destruction has been curtailed by religious commonality. It is inherently counterintuitive for people of Christ to hurt one another. Sure, there are evil people in this world that would hurt others regardless of religious affiliation. However, those people such as drug lords and organized crime leaders would be that way no matter what church they belonged to. The point is that their influence is limited by the masses of people who remain true to their faith and refuse to bow to the criminal elements that strive for power in their countries. It is that common bond among citizens that enables certain nations to persevere, where others crumble."

"While the United States is not officially a Christian or Jewish or Muslim nation, it does have a tradition of Christian values that help steer the ship through sometimes troubled waters. There are instances in our celebrated history that exemplify this value system. The Civil War and the abolishing of slavery, the voting rights of women, the work programs of President Roosevelt during the Great Depression, the Civil Rights movement, to name just a few. Each of these successes came as a result of the country being presented with a challenge to either its freedoms or its very existence. As during those tumultuous times before, we are now with great challenges of grave consequence. We must not wilt in the face of these dangers; we must instead focus on our common bonds and work to preserve our great nation. One manner in which to do this is to once again utilize our Christian heritage and its values of human decency."

"For some time now, the world has been faced with radicalized segments that claim to be associated with the Muslim religion. These people twisted the religion's tenets to serve their personal goals of power and destruction. For decades these movements existed only on the fringes, displaying their fervor through occasional act of terror. Today however, they have made significant inroads with the vast majorities of numerous Muslim-dominated areas. Those that once hijacked the occasional airliner have managed to hijack a religion. Like those that fought back on the ill-fated United Flight 93, it is time for the good people of the world to protect themselves from the forces of evil. It needs not be a violent battle, but instead one of united acts of kindness and goodness."

"It is essential for the people of the United States to come together against the forces of evil in this world. During World War II we were faced with fascist forces that threatened the freedoms we hold so dearly. Our society came together on all fronts in an effort to defend these freedoms. The efforts went beyond just the deployment of military forces overseas. Women back home went to work in factories and grew food at home in *victory gardens*. The symbolic examples of unity and sacrifice were as important as the military effort; they showed the world that our states truly were united, and that we would not compromise our freedoms."

"One way for us to show this unity in defense of our way of life today is to display our compassion for fellow man, aptly displayed through traditional Christian values. We have an opportunity and a moral obligation to help our people help themselves in time of need. One prominent example of this is the ongoing effort to rebuild and renew the iconic American city of New Orleans. This city still suffers the effects of Hurricane Katrina and its people must know that the nation cares for all its people and desires to enable all its citizens to have opportunities to succeed. The best way for this to happen is to encourage the efforts of the Church, which calls on its members to help others in need. This idea of philanthropy is in keeping with the original intent of our nation's foundation, as it limits the involvement of the federal government and encourages individual citizens to combine efforts as they help their fellow Americans."

"While it may be essential for us to collectively come to the aid of those Americans in need, it is not enough to overcome all that our nation faces today. We need the strong alliance of other like-minded nations in our struggle against evil forces that are actively attempting to destroy us. The most natural allies in this struggle are those people that share our values found in our Christian heritage. While these religions may have originated elsewhere, today these values are strongest in our own hemisphere. The nations of the Americas – North, Central and South – are the ones that are most closely aligned with us both geographically and culturally. We are all people that have a common history of Christianity and have often fought to defend our own freedoms from outside oppression. The attacks that are now taking place require us to reinvigorate these alliances; they give cause for us to tighten the bonds that we have. Only by uniting can the people of the Americas survive against outside forces of evil."

"Do not mistake this call that I make tonight. It is not a call to arms. Instead it is a call to unite culturally and morally; it is a call to support our fellow man. It is always true that the sum of the parts is greater than the numbers of individuals. As such, I am imploring each and every one of you to give of yourselves; I need for each of you to realize that your input is important to the greater good."

"I plan to lead the way in these efforts by kicking off a campaign of goodwill this week. I will be using the Christian season of Lent to represent the collective sacrifice necessary to make this society persevere. The kickoff for this traditional holiday season is of course Fat Tuesday, or Mardi Gras. While this celebration occurs worldwide in a variety of Catholic locales, its most revered U.S. site is New Orleans. Therefore, I will be in the Crescent City during the upcoming Mardi Gras in order to raise awareness for my plan to strengthen our society. I will be side by side with the good people of a city that, by no fault of its own, has had to endure difficulties that most of us have not had to face in our lifetime. I will convey to the nation that these people are no different from any others, and that their strife is our strife."

"Meanwhile, the first lady will extend our goodwill to fellow Christian nations by paying a similar visit to another largely Catholic city – Rio de Janeiro. Christina is excited at the prospect of being able to share this very special time with people that we have so much in common with. By focusing on our cultural commonality, we can work toward preserving that which we have worked so hard to build. The way of life that we hold so dear in the West is not to be taken for granted. It took the sacrifice of thousands of lives to establish, and is not guaranteed for the future. We must actively participate and come together if we are to be assured a promising future as a free people. This symbolic gesture is just a starting point, from which we can build a stronger defense against those that strive to destroy us. It is our common strength that is our best asset; capitalizing on our best qualities will raise us above those that wish to do us harm."

"Please join the first lady and me as we embark on this venture of peace and goodwill. Together we can use our common forces of good to repel those of evil. We have come too far as a society to allow it to slip away – guarantee a promising future by taking hold of our nation today. Time will not wait; neither can we. I look forward to seeing all of you coming to the aid of each other as we work for a renewed commitment to America's fundamental values. Until then goodnight, and God bless America."

CHAPTER 40

RIO DE JANEIRO, BRAZIL

The thin mattress of the single bed in Apartment 311 sagged tiredly wherever it wasn't supported by wood beams. It was just uncomfortable enough to keep me from falling asleep. I lay there instead, thinking of all the possibilities of what could happen when the FLOTUS arrived in the morning. I felt the weight of the nation on my shoulders. I couldn't be sure that al-Ayande would make an attempt on the first lady, but there were certainly indicators that added to my paranoia. Colonel Kingman would not have deployed me to the area had the threat not warranted it. Asad's appearance, no matter how brief, was significant. Add to that the plans Max had shared with me over our dinner at Porcão.

Max preferred to discuss sensitive plans in a loud public forum. He believed the ambient noise made it more difficult for anyone to listen in on what he said. I think he just fancied the notion of discussing such things right in front of people who had no idea what was being said right next to them. It seemed to satisfy some perverse arrogance of his. Either way, I was happy to oblige once I had convinced him to buy dinner.

Naturally, I'd selected a high end *churrascaria* where I could eat and drink to my heart's content on his tab. Max scoffed at the idea, saying that type of restaurant was too gluttonous for any self-respecting man. It's true that the appetizer bar of salads and seafood was more than its own meal, and that the meat skewers paraded around by well-dressed waiters wielding large carving knives bordered on medieval. As far as I was concerned, the place was perfect – Max was afforded the opportunity to hear himself pontificate as I quietly stuffed my face with enough food and drink to make any over-served American proud.

As Max began, he provided the caveat that he needed to protect his source for future use, even though I hadn't asked. Most of what he presented, while quite detailed, was not earth shattering. It was an administrative rundown of the FLOTUS itinerary while in Rio, starting with the airport arrival and proceeding through a press photo op at the Christ the Redeemer statue atop Corcovado, a public relations visit to the Museum of the Republic, followed by afternoon coffee at the mayor's residence. All of it seemed perfectly acceptable and safe; it was the next portion of the plan that bothered me. She was scheduled to take a tour of the Complexo do Alemao, the very favela that Armas domineered with the backing of Asad and al-Ayande.

I half-choked down a pleasantly salted hunk of sirloin in order to rhetorically ask Max why in the hell the FLOTUS's people were allowing her to take that kind of security risk. Knowing he had no answer, I allowed him to continue before retracing our steps back to details of security and potential pitfalls. Her evening would take her to the Sambadromo, the site of the Rio Carnival Samba Parade. That would also prove to be a security nightmare due to potentially unruly crowds and widespread debauchery. But it wasn't as blatantly hostile as Alemao. Her trip would conclude the following morning with an Ash Wednesday mass at the Nossa Senhora de Candelaria – if she made it that far.

So I lay in bed, uncomfortably full, wondering why the staff and Secret Service would agree to expose the first lady to a known terrorist hotbed. I was almost asleep when there was *another* knock on the door. I never got this many visitors back in D.C. Now becoming accustomed to the ritual, I slid adjacent the door frame with my Glock.

"Who is it?" I asked, assuming it was Max, but too unsure to throw open the door.

"Treff...the landlord," the male voice on the other side responded. I did not recognize the voice as either Max or the oddball transsexual Samantha.

"Hold on a minute," I answered as I scurried to the back room to get a visual from the hidden camera, just as I had done when his partner made *its* late night visit. Sure enough, it was the expatriate from El Paso. I ran back to the door and opened it. Unlike during Sam's visit, I made no effort to hide my sidearm.

The Hispanic Texan sauntered right by me into the apartment as soon as the door was ajar. "You know, we don't allow firearms in the building," he said without looking back at me. He was far more interested in taking in the surroundings. He began to wander toward the spare bedroom, the one filled with all the secret toys.

"That room's private," I cautioned him without making any move toward him. I wanted to see if he would heed the warning, or if I needed to flex a little muscle. Even if he was the landlord, that didn't give him the right to barge in and conduct his own impromptu inspection. At least not as far as I was concerned; and I was the one packing the heat.

"Why? Is that where you keep the bondage devices?" Before I could address the twisted irony of his sexual innuendo, he continued. "Or is it filled with state-of-the-art surveillance equipment and weapons cache?"

We locked each other in a stare, two poker players trying to melt the other's will. *What the hell did this freak know about me, and how?* Based on my recent visit from his partner, I was fairly certain that he was also in bed with Colonel Reynolds, if only figuratively.

"First of all, it's none of your business what I have in any room here." I could feel myself losing my temper, and I was starting not to care. It was late, I was under a lot of stress, and I did not see why the hell I was getting a late night visit from a landlord who I'd never spoken with. "Second, I paid my damn rent. Third, what the fuck are you doing here anyway?"

"I thought you'd never ask, *Wolgrand*," he said while inviting himself to sit on the couch. He motioned for me to take a seat. Supremely suspicious but still confidently armed, I sat across from him in the armchair. I was determined to figure out his angle and hoped that maybe he would be stupid enough to reveal his connection with a corrupt DAO.

"So have I been playing my music too loud?" I asked, not hiding my sarcasm.

"Probably, but I don't really give a shit. What I do care about is the company you've been keeping."

"If this is about Samantha – " I began as Treff cringed in mock pain.

"No!" he cut me off. "It's about your friend Max."

"What about him?" I asked, though I was beginning to have a sense where this conversation was leading.

"He's not who he claims to be."

"And what does he claim?" I did not want to divulge anything I did not have to before I knew who he was or what he knew.

"I'm talking about the CIA part," Treff responded. I could sense he was getting a little frustrated with my ignorant act, but realized that I wasn't going to volunteer anything. As far as I knew, he was a man on the take.

"Alright smart guy – who is he? And while you're at it, who the hell are you? I find it hard to believe that a guy who runs an apartment building has good cause to know who is and who's not a CIA operative."

Treff nodded and took a deep breath before he spoke.

"Max Nogales has had a sordid history in this part of the world. He is a journalist, a mercenary, a government subversive, and even a CIA informant. Whatever the role, the one constant is that Max serves one master – Max. He first caught the attention of the Agency with his inflammatory anti-government writings, some of which have incited violence. The U.S. has worked hard to establish rapports with left-leaning regimes down here and doesn't want to risk losing them because of some self-serving vigilante."

I thought back to the Max Nogales article I had read on the day of my arrival in Rio. Was it possible this guy was for real?

Treff continued. "An agent that preceded me in Rio made contact with Max about five years ago, to offer him a deal. In exchange for a healthy sum of cash he would provide the Agency with information on organized crime elements in the favelas. With no loyalty to either the government or organized crime, Max was a cheap buy with a wealth of intel. The agent in Rio knew they were not getting all the info that Max had, but the price was right and the Agency figured that he would never be in a position to double-cross them. That was before the stakes went up."

"How so?" I asked, still cautiously fingering the trigger of my Glock.

"Al-Ayande of course. Everything changed when they hit the scene – more money, more weapons, more potential for disaster. We believe that's when he made contact with Armas."

Treff pulled an envelope from his pocket and emptied its contents onto the coffee table. The photos were grainy, black and white, and only four-by-sixes, but the picture was clear. Each one showed Max with Antonio Armas: seated at a café, stepping out of a limousine, shaking hands, smiling. The varied hair styles and facial hair, along with different weights of clothing, suggested that this was a long-standing relationship.

"That son-of-a-bitch," I muttered as I began to realize there was a real good chance that Treff was delivering the straight scoop.

"Exactly. Max was taking money from both sides and supplying info to both as well. We also know Max found out that his CIA contact discovered he was tied to Armas. Not long after these pics were taken, the agent's torso was dropped on the steps of the U.S. consulate. We had to write the poor bastard off as a wayward tourist that got himself involved on the wrong side of the local drug scene. It was a horrible way to eulogize a good agent, but he would have understood."

"Is that when you got this plum assignment?"

"Almost. I was working in Brasilia at the time. The chief of station up there decided to come down to Rio for a while to make his own assessment after the murder. He was going to determine how to handle this Nogales situation. Do we keep him alive or eliminate him? What he found out both shocked him and answered the question at the same time."

"What was that?" I asked.

"The corruption ran deeper than just one unscrupulous journalist."

"Was the other agent dirty?"

"Nope. You can't pin this one on the Agency. This guy is one of your fellow military brethren."

"Reynolds."

"Jackpot."

"I knew there was something wrong with that asshole." I relayed to Treff how he kept Staff Sergeant Davis completely in the dark and otherwise micromanaged everything in the DAO.

There was something that still did not hold water with Treff's story. I had to change the subject to address my concern. "Okay, so let's assume I buy all this stuff you're selling. That still does not explain my late night visit from Samantha. What's the story there?"

"Did you really fuck that thing?" he asked.

"Don't try to turn this on me. That's your bitch, man. I don't even think I want to know the whole story. I'm only interested in knowing why that thing showed up at my door. And don't try to tell me that Max is somehow behind this too," I said.

"Alright, alright. I did send her up here, but I had no intention of her coming onto you. I have been paying her to pretend to be my girlfriend around here for some time. I found it was less trouble for me not to have a real woman around to distract me from my job. This way it can be purely a business relationship. I admit my intent was to have her plant that bug so I could verify that you could be trusted. My mistake was not noticing that she was getting so coked up that night. That's what really brought the plan crumbling down. Her making a move on you was her own libido-fueled ad-lib."

"So then why did she throw you under the bus by saying you were tied in with Reynolds?"

"I guess she just got freaked out when you nearly shot her in the face. I've done a pretty good job of keeping most things from her, but I'm sure she's picked up on a few things from conversations over time." Treff shrugged. "If it were to get too bad, I would make her disappear."

I was kicking myself for not being more thorough on my background check of Max; a mistake I would not repeat with Treff. As soon as we concluded our conversation, I would be placing a secure call back to Kingman in order to verify Treff's credentials. He would be able to contact the CIA offices in Langley through private channels that I did not possess in Rio. I would skip the part about making a mistake in judging Max Nogales. It was water under the bridge that could only muddy Kingman's confidence in my abilities. He may have understood that I was still a somewhat green intelligence officer, but I didn't feel the need to validate any doubts he may have had.

If Treff proved to be the real deal, I knew the mission could be salvaged with his assistance. Now I had to hope that Kingman would be able to access the information in the middle of the night, on extremely short notice. I also hoped my concerns didn't show on my face. I had no intention of sharing them with Treff, just in case I got bad news from Kingman. It would be easier to remove Treff from the equation if he never saw trouble coming.

"Okay, I believe you," I began. "So here's what I want to do now. I have good reason to believe that something big is going to go down tomorrow. The FLOTUS's life may be in danger and we need to act quickly if we want to have any chance of stopping an assassination attempt." I skipped the details for the time being, pending affirmation of Treff's identity. "We'll need some added firepower, since there are only two of us and a virtual army under Armas's command. The best place to quickly get an armed force of our own will be to work with Commander Cruz and his boys. They have their finger on the pulse of Alemao and will know the best way to prepare for and counter any plans of attack. Going directly to Cruz will also bypass the bureaucratic mess of trying to get support from the federal police and limit the hysteria that would surely ensue."

Treff nodded with satisfaction. "Name the time and place."

"The police station at 0600. We'd better get some rest. We're going to need it."

CHAPTER 41

Sleepless with anticipation, I played scenarios in my head and prepared reactions for every fathomable contingency. Every half hour, I checked my encrypted e-mail account for a response from Kingman. Each instance overnight displayed no new messages, increasing my consternation with each login. I had made numerous attempts to connect with him via satellite phone to no avail. Without time to troubleshoot what may have prevented the call's success I settled for e-mail. Despite my impatience, my only hope was to await a response via the computer. It was not until I was readying to depart my apartment for the police station that I made one last check.

There was one new message:

> *Treff is legitimate and deemed a reliable agent.*
> *Good luck with mission.*

I e-mailed the boss to acknowledge receipt and thank him for much needed confidence in my new association with Treff. I made no mention of Nogales. I logged off, tucked my Glock into my holster and hurried out the door to get started on what was sure to be the most significant day of my intelligence career.

The station was the same worn building from which I had toured the Alemao favela with Commander Cruz and his men. As before, the cool morning air belied the impending heat of the day. It was as if each day in the favela began with renewed hope before succumbing to daily oppression. As I approached the converted hotel there was something distinctly out of place. The quiet of the morning was a bit too quiet. In fact, the area was virtually devoid of activity.

The armed guards that had been present were no longer on patrol. The windows of the building that had been previously lit were shrouded in darkness. Even passersby on the street crossed to the opposite side as they neared the compound, as if repelled by some unseen evil. Reaching behind me to the small of my back, I took hold of my Glock. Normally, I might have been concerned about being observed walking into a foreign police station with a pistol openly on display. This time, however, I brazenly pulled the slide back and allowed it to chamber a round as I moved with a heightened awareness of my surroundings. I wished that I had body armor as I entered the building.

The halls inside were dark and quiet except for the street noise that carried in from the awakening neighborhood. I methodically cleared each room that I passed, my blood pressure spiking with each entry. My intensity increased and I could feel sweat running down my back as I neared Cruz's office. I assumed that his office held some clue to explain the eerie silence. Even if Cruz had taken his men out on an early morning patrol, two guards would have been present and the offices lighted.

For a moment I wondered why I had not had any sign of Treff, but it was just now turning six and he may be following me inside soon. That is unless he had something to do with the reason it was so quiet right now. I would find out soon enough; Cruz's office was just ahead on the right.

The door was closed as I slid against the wall and ducked low to the floor. Just in case someone was inside and heard me approach, I did not want to present an easy target for random shots taken through the wall or door. I rose to my knees and reached for the door knob, only to discover that it was locked. Dammit! So much for subtlety.

I rose quickly and without hesitation raised my booted foot and thrust the bottom of it into the middle of the door with all the force I could muster. It must have been many years since its last maintenance because the entire door flew off its hinges and fell with a thud onto the middle of the office floor. Despite the aural commotion and wood splinters that filled the air, my attention was drawn immediately to the commander's desk, or more specifically the chair that sat behind it. Seated serenely was Cruz himself, staring intently in my direction. I might have believed that he had nerves of steel if it had not been for the bullet hole in his forehead and the blood and brain matter splattered on the white wall behind him.

While I desperately wanted to know who had murdered the local police chief, it was not the most pressing question that needed answering. This was a fluid situation, and I was likely in danger at the current moment. The blood on the wall was still fresh – at most a mere hour old.

Without a doubt, the place that I needed to go next was the armory. If I were making a move on the facility, I would be very interested in looting the armory, especially if I were associated with either Armas or al-Ayande. After all, a majority of the weapons cache present had been confiscated from them. With increased pace, I moved down the long dark hallway to the large converted vault. The chances were that the room never contained so many valuables when it performed its originally designed hotel duties. I paused just outside the heavy door, took a deep breath, and checked to see if this room was also locked. To my surprise, the door was not only unlocked, but slightly ajar. I wished I had a flash bang with me so that I could toss it into the room and at least temporarily stun or disable any potential threat. I had only my trusty sidearm, but was not about to turn back now that I was possibly so close to whoever had put a bullet in Cruz's head.

I gave the door a healthy shove with my left arm and dropped to one knee as I centered myself in the doorway and raised my pistol to firing position.

"Whoa! Easy big fella," a voice responded from the shadows, in English. It was unmistakably Treff's Texan twang.

I kept my pistol up.

"Don't move a fucking muscle!" I warned. As my eyes slowly adjusted to the darkness I glanced frantically for a light switch. I ran my hand across the wall behind me until I found one and changed its position only to realize that it did nothing.

"They cut the power," Treff said.

"Who?"

"Whoever did this."

"Did what?" I asked as I saw a glint of black metal in his hand. "I told you to freeze."

"It's alright, man. Just a flashlight. I pulled it off this guy," he said as he pointed it toward the floor to his side and turned it on. The beam illuminated an officer that lay in a pool of blood. It was the old man who had armed me during my prior visit. Next to him lay the younger officer that could have been his son. Now the two generations rested in peace together.

"You're lucky that people back in D.C. vouch for you. If not, I wouldn't have hesitated to fill you full of lead," I told him.

"Good morning to you too, Wolgrand," he answered.

"I'm just saying that you may want to be more careful. You should have waited for me outside, or at least told me you were heading in. Communication is the key to any successful relationship, you know."

"Well, the building looked abandoned and I wasn't sure I was in the right place. Maybe I should have waited for you until the meeting time. What can I say? Curiosity got the better of me," Treff said. "I guess it got the better of you too, since you checked up on me with your sources back home."

"Just doing my homework," I countered. "I didn't have a transsexual coke addict freak to do it for me."

"Fair enough. Now that we're all good friends here, can we get back to work?" I concurred as he continued. "Whoever paid this early morning visit was quite busy – look around," Treff said as he slowly panned the room with the flashlight. I counted at least eight uniformed bodies, all soaked with fresh blood.

The obvious suspect for the murders was Antonio Armas. The police and the crime lords were in a constant state of war, sometimes hot and sometimes cold. It was a violent game of cat and mouse. The police sporadically staged offenses into the favelas in order to quell the rampant crime and slow the ever-growing power of the gangs. At least that was the publicly stated justification. The truth was that the measures taken by police coincided with either a political campaign by an incumbent wanting to appear tough on crime or a dip in tourism due to international fears. In the midst of Carnival this may have been a preemptive strike by a proactive crime organization. It was often questionable as to who was more of a threat to the safety and sanctity of life in the favelas – the police or the gangs.

With al-Ayande backing him, Armas may have felt emboldened enough to take the fight to the police. It would certainly show the federal government that he was to be reckoned with; perhaps he hoped that it would convince the police to leave him alone. This would also allow al-Ayande to progress unimpeded in Alemao. My theory was reasonable, but something about it didn't hold water.

Every act of violence in the favelas, by either police or gang, reflects the machismo of the Brazilian culture. Each one upstages the previous in scope and scale, designed to compel the opposition into inaction. The irony was that neither side seemed to recognize that the upstaging only elicited a stronger reaction. Ironic observations aside, this attack, while plenty bloody, lacked the flamboyance of its predecessors. I would have expected to see the building rocked to its foundation, or the fight to take place in the street. At least if Armas's men drew the police outside with gunfire, their slaughter could be witnessed by many – that's the way of violence in the favela. A large component is the show of power, a display meant not only to dispatch the current enemy but to dissuade future ones.

"Who do you think could have pulled off this operation?" I queried Treff.

"I think it's pretty obvious that Armas decided to up the ante," he responded.

I shook my head and smiled. "Good first guess, but no." Treff looked confused and opened his mouth to speak when I cut him off. "This hit was way too clean to be part of a normal turf battle. Just look around. Nobody was killed outside. I did not see any blood out there, or any on the way in here. We can certainly go double-check with the flashlight since it was dark in the hallways, but I believe that all the shooting except for Cruz occurred right in this armory."

"So who then? Al-Ayande?" Treff guessed as I shook my head.

"They don't have troops on the ground here. They are only providing support and influence. Armas is supplying the muscle."

"You don't think it was – " Treff began.

"Max? You bet your ass I do."

"That son-of-a-bitch! How can you be sure?"

"He's the only one who could have gotten unimpeded access to Cruz without interference from his guards. I know exactly how he did it – as a matter of fact, he used me as a dry run. He brought me here to meet Cruz last week and told him that I was with the U.S. government. While it may have been true, the statement was never challenged and I was never checked for any weapons. Max really put in the time and effort to develop a rapport with Cruz and his men. All so that he could turn on them in the end – that devious fuck!"

"Okay, so Max got in here with someone. How did they take down the place?"

"All he would have needed was two men with him, each concealing a sidearm. Max shot Cruz; then the three men moved directly to the armory. Max already knew that there were only two armorers, and they both knew and trusted Max. Before they knew what was happening they were shot dead. The electrical power box for the building is in the armory. Max cut the power to the building while one of his henchmen set off a small controlled explosion – just loud enough to draw attention from the other officers in the building. They would naturally assume that the explosion was tied to the power outage and move immediately to the armory to check on the power box. They must have been suspicious enough to call for backup from the outside guards, or the guards heard distressed radio traffic and decided to come in on their own. Whatever the reason, the guards also stumbled into Max's trap."

My eyes had adjusted to the lack of light in the room and I could see Treff nodding silently to himself as he evaluated my theory.

"Okay, not bad for a Marine. What next?"

CHAPTER 42

After finding the building's power supply, we had more light in the armory than we wanted. We sifted through the carnage, taking inventory of what remained. It was important for me to assess what Max had taken back to Armas and, more importantly, what was available for our use today. I took charge and worked quickly as I cobbled together a weapons cache to suit our upcoming mission.

We filled two large, wheeled tubs with semi-automatic and automatic weapons, cartridges and belts of ammunition, grenades and explosives. We took defensive gear used by the police, including Kevlar helmets and vests. I knew we were going to be outmanned and outgunned, but I had been there before.

As a Huey crew chief, I deployed aboard the USS Peleliu to the Arabian Gulf as part of a constant U.S. presence in the region. Operation Desert Storm had run its course and there was relative peace in the region, but the specter of conflict remained due to regional instability and emerging radical Muslim elements. While we conducted regular training and received threat briefs designed to maintain our focus despite lack of actual combat, it became difficult to sustain a high level of intensity.

That changed one night when we got the wake up call to report to the ready room. Our commanding officer opened by informing us that this was the real deal. An American commercial vessel had been taken over by what was believed to be Somali pirates. They had snuck up alongside the ship in small boats and climbed up using ropes they affixed to the side of the ship. The buccaneers quickly overtook the small crew, but not before a distress call had been sent out by the captain.

Our mission was to conduct a VBSS, to subdue the enemy and return the ship to its rightful operators, if they were still alive. The Visit Board Search and Seizure process was one the Marines onboard the Peleliu had practiced numerous times; not because it happened often, but due to its high-risk elements. This one would be even more challenging due to nighttime. The decision was made to deploy under the cloak of darkness for expediency and our assumed night-vision advantage. During the daylight, our CO would have recommended a large force brought in by numerous helicopters to overwhelm the enemy. Given the added risk of flying over water in complete darkness, he limited airborne assets to a minimum, thereby reducing the chance of a mid-air collision, but lowering our ratio of friendly forces.

I still remember the tension of the crews as we manned the helicopters; we quietly configured our guns and rocket pods as the pilots conducted preflight checks and the recon Marines loaded their gear into the cabins. Without further delay, the air boss cleared us for takeoff and two Hueys lifted, followed closely by an escort of two Supercobra attack helicopters. All four aircraft conducted penetration checks to ensure that weapons and defensive gear was operable. We were ready for action. The Marine Expeditionary Unit CO gave us explicit clearance to use aggressive tactics in the takeover; he wanted to send a message to other would-be marauders. We were more than happy to oblige.

The helicopters found the distressed ship and approached with infrared lights that could only be viewed by night vision goggles. The two Cobras sprinted ahead of us and made what must have been a deafening low pass directly overhead the ship before peeling off to the right. We made a slow approach astern the ship, remaining far enough away to avoid detection. The Cobras went to work. As planned, the flyby had drawn out the enemy like ants to picnic. With my NVGs I could see about ten men on the deck, firing automatic weapons in the general direction of the Cobras. The Cobras proved to be a tough target as they circled in darkness, still moving at more than one hundred knots. Tracer rounds and two rocket propelled grenades sailed harmlessly into the abyss as the Cobras rolled out of their turn. They were now abeam each other as they slowed their forward airspeed and pointed their menacing noses toward the ship. I cannot be sure if the Somalis had any understanding of the impending trouble they were facing on that dark night.

Once within five hundred meters of the ship, the Cobra pilots unleashed a barrage of 2.75-inch rockets. Wanting to avoid severe damage to the ship, the rockets employed were armed with flechette warheads. As each rocket motor burned out, an internal fuse expelled more than 2,000 metal nails that sprayed the target area. While merely scratching the structure of the ship, the nails tore mercilessly through the flesh of the pirates. I could see bodies dropping to the ground as they were dismembered by the onslaught. All movement on the deck ceased, though I knew our mission wasn't complete.

The Cobras ceased their attack and relocated to hovering overwatch positions nearby the bow, poised for another strike. The enemy had been punched squarely in the nose – now it was time to deliver the body blows that would be their end. Our Huey flew to a position just over the stern. There was no landing pad, so our pilot held a three-foot hover while six recon Marines jumped down safely onto the deck. In the midst of this tricky deployment, more attackers emerged from the shadows in front of us. They must've realized that with our Marines on deck it wouldn't be safe to further employ the Cobras due to the likelihood of friendly fire casualties. This was a critical vulnerability of any VBSS, and we were prepared.

I already had a solid hold of my GAU-17 machine gun mounted in the open cabin door and wasted no time in opening fire in the direction of the tracer rounds that were coming our way. I laid down a stream of 7.62-millimeter rounds while the other Huey employed its sniper, who used his night vision scope and laser sight to fire deep into the darkness. Our Huey took some rounds but continued to hover until all the recon Marines were safely away and hidden in the shadows. This batch of bandits subdued, we climbed away from the stern and headed for safer skies. Our most dangerous part of the mission was complete; the recon Marines took it from there and did what they do best. They methodically secured each compartment until they had taken the ship back and returned it to its crew, whose survivors had been bound, gagged and held as hostages.

That was the last combat action I had seen as a Marine prior to joining MECEP and going off to college. As an ambush, it was also the closest thing to what I was planning for this afternoon. While we would not have to contend with the hazards of darkness or over-water operations this time, I didn't have near the same size force on my side. It was me, Treff, and hopefully the Secret Service once the dominoes started to fall.

The ideal solution would have been to affect a change in the first lady's plans. This idea was stymied by the late hour and that Colonel Reynolds, who I had every reason to believe was owned by Armas or al-Ayande, was the conduit to her staff. Without time or the proper contacts to go directly to either Mrs. Estevanez's staff or her Secret Service protectors, a counteroffensive was the next best answer.

Treff and I had a solid compliment of weaponry after procuring all that we could carry from the police station armory. Now we needed an updated itinerary and a communication plan. With Colonel Reynolds working against us, our only hope was Staff Sergeant Davis.

Davis recommended meeting at a *galeto* not far from his office at the consulate. When we arrived we did not see him, so we took a seat at the counter and each ordered a rotisserie chicken for lunch. Typical of most galetos the restaurant was bare bones, consisting only of a stool-lined counter encircling an open-air kitchen that doubled as the service area. It was packed with businessmen on their lunch hour due to its location in the Centro district – just about the only area of the city that ever gave the appearance of productivity. The cook approached our side of the counter, but without the poultry. He beckoned us to follow him through the only private door in the establishment, which led to a back room that served as food storage and office. There was one table where the staff likely ate their meals in privacy – Davis stood from his seat at the table.

"Good afternoon, gentlemen," the staff sergeant once again appeared as professional as the day I met him. "Please have a seat. I hope you're hungry, because Pedro prepares the best chicken in Centro."

"Not to mention private seating. I feel so VIP," I said with a wry smile as I eye-balled the rickety table and chairs that were tucked into the corner of the undecorated storage area. "Robert, I want you to meet Treff. He's working with me on an important project with an immediate timetable."

The two men exchanged handshakes and introductory pleasantries as we all sat at the table. Within seconds the cook swept in and deposited large plates of grilled meats and potatoes; then he was gone.

"Pedro and I have an understanding," Davis began. "He provides me with an unsuspecting place to sneak away for clandestine meetings and keeps to himself; I make him feel like he's part of something important even though he never has any idea who my guests are or what the hell we're talking about. Everybody wins."

"Having people you can trust can be very hard to find," I responded. "Which is why we're here."

Treff took full advantage of not being an integral part of the conversation by wolfing down his bird. He glanced up occasionally to ensure us that he was still listening.

"What can I do for you today?" Davis inquired.

"Hopefully provide us with information that other Americans don't want us to have. I need the most up to date schedule of FLOTUS movements. I also need to know what frequencies her people are working so that I can track them in live time without being within sight the entire time."

"What is it that you're afraid will happen? And why are you coming to me?" Davis asked, but I could sense he already knew the answer.

"Frankly, I never could get a damn thing from your boss. Then I found out why."

"Why?"

I turned toward Treff, who was busy licking the grease from his fingers, his mouth still full. "Go ahead, tell him," I said.

Treff did his best to answer despite having his words muffled by chewed food. "He's dirty as a Caroica transsexual whore."

Davis shot him a quizzical scowl.

"Never mind – we just know he's up to no good," I shook my head at Treff as I answered.

Davis looked me square in the eyes. "I know."

"Really?"

"I'll skip most of the details for now, but I got frustrated enough with his secrecy to do some investigating. Let's just say what I found was disturbing," Davis shook his head in disgust as he relived the realization that the colonel he once respected had become a traitor.

"Water under the bridge, man. The only question that's important is 'what are we going to do now?'" I posed. "Can you get us what we need?"

"On one condition," Davis said with a look of resolve. "I go with you."

221

CHAPTER 43

The basement of the apartment building had been converted from individual storage units into a large multipurpose facility for Treff's non-landlord duties. There were weapons lockers, computer stations, a communications suite, and a small briefing area. Our mini-team had grown to three but our preparation time was dwindling rapidly.

"So where's your girl?" I probed Treff.

"First, fuck you. Second, I told *her* to go away for a couple of days."

"Did you get a goodbye blow job?" I could see that Treff was reminding himself that I was just trying to push his buttons. "No? You gave one instead?"

"Man, that's harsh," Davis said. "What are you talking about anyway?"

"Never mind," Treff intervened quickly before I could elaborate. He swept aside some papers to clear room on the table and motioned for Davis to take the lead.

"Okay, here's what we've got," he laid out a photocopy of the movement schedule. "I reprinted this from the memory on Reynolds's printer."

"So what he lacks in patriotism he makes up for in stupidity," I noted his oversight that copiers and printers can have their previous jobs recalled unless properly erased. If Davis agreed he was not quite ready to badmouth an officer, even a corrupt one.

He smirked but continued. "The FLOTUS is departing the mayor's residence at 1800 local time en route to Complexo do Alemao. Her arrival time is estimated at 1830 and departure at 1930."

"Does that paperwork specify where she'll be stopping? How about motorcade routes?" I asked.

"It only specifies two places and one is only in general terms." Davis fingered through the pages until he found one entitled *Vehicular Routes*. "The motorcade route comes up from downtown on Avenida Brasil and makes turns on Linha Amarela, Estrada do Timbo, Avenida Itaoca, and

Estrada de Itarare before the first scheduled stop at a community pool. She is onsite there for ten minutes before heading up the hill into the heart of the favela. There are numerous shops in the shantytown along Rua Joaquim Queiroz. Looks like she'll be stopping at one or two along the way."

"Isn't that the same road as the al-Ayande mosque?" I asked.

"You got it, but there's no way in hell she'd stop there," Treff noted. "President Estevanez is the most ardent Catholic around."

Treff's comment may have been flippant, but I couldn't help but wonder again about the choice of stops. Of all the favelas, why did her staff have to choose the only one not controlled by Catholics? It was atypical of the Estevanez administration to reach out this far to the Muslim community. Maybe he was trying to thumb his nose at them in some way. No matter which way I spun it I could not figure out a solid explanation. I surmised it was above my pay-grade and returned to the immediate task at hand of trying the preserve the FLOTUS's safety.

"What about radio frequencies? Are we going to be able to listen in?" I likely had more questions than Davis had answers, but he was doing well so far. "What about the size and description of the motorcade? Do we know who will be up on the nets? Any call-signs?"

"Here's a list of freqs. We've done plenty of work with the Diplomatic Security guys during VIP movements, so I know I've got the right handhelds in my back pack. I can set 'em up to scan all the likely encrypted freqs. I'm not a hundred percent familiar with the letter codes they have assigned to the freqs, but it won't matter with the scan working."

DS agents provided most protective services for dignitaries, both in the U.S. and abroad. They were not as specialized and perhaps not as proficient at protection as the Secret Service but they were certainly competent. Many of them were former military and possessed a wide variety of skills that made them very dynamic, an attribute that would have been useful today. I wished that I had a team working for me right now.

Davis continued. "As for the motorcade, you can be sure they'll get a police escort."

"Not from the local station they won't," Treff said in reference to the late Commander Cruz. Treff and I had briefed Davis during the ride to the apartment building.

Davis continued unfazed. "They'll come from downtown – the same ones that provide escort to the mayor when he goes somewhere. The rest of the motorcade will consist of two limos, four support vehicles, and an unknown number of press vans."

"Is that all?" I asked.

"Yes sir. Unfortunately I have no info on call-signs or who will be on the radio."

"That's alright. After a few cycles through the scan process we'll be able to figure out which freq is for the Secret Service and which one is FLOTUS staff, just by the traffic passed. I'll make notes on call-signs as I hear them and piece the puzzle together in no time." I pointed to Davis. "Select a random freq not normally used and we can use that as our default if we get separated." He nodded and began to fiddle with his Motorola.

I dictated a list of equipment to Treff and Davis as we organized our back packs, loaded Treff's old van with supplies, and armed ourselves with weapons and body armor. We were as ready as we were going to be.

CHAPTER 44

I was a bit concerned about Davis's fair skin as we neared the favela, but decided that with Treff and me as native-looking company he'd be overlooked. We still had some time to spare, so we traced the motorcade route on our drive to Alemao to check for bottlenecks, underpasses and other weak points. The route appeared clean up to the turn at the community pool; the police would have no problem blocking traffic as necessary up to that point. From there it would prove a larger challenge.

While Rua Joaquim Queiroz was the main artery through the favela, large enough to handle small trucks and SUVs, it did not allow for contingency maneuvering. There was insufficient room to turn a standard size vehicle one hundred and eighty degrees. Many of the alleyways that jutted off the sides were not navigable by any motor vehicle on more than two wheels. The only feasible way out was straight ahead – it was a Secret Service nightmare.

Treff drove his van up the hill past the ramshackle houses and shops. Even for the favela there was an inordinate number of locals crawling the streets; word had spread that a big event was about to occur. I could only hope that the event in mind was just the visiting dignitary. At the apex of the street casting ominous shadows from the setting sun stood the mosque. I marveled at how out of place such a building appeared surrounded by poverty. It was not unlike many equally poverty-stricken neighborhoods featuring beautiful Catholic cathedrals. We drove past the mosque, pulled into an alley on the right, and parked.

I went alone to check out the mosque for signs of life, assuring the other two that I would call on the radio immediately if I found trouble. My adrenaline surged as I approached. I felt naked with no body armor and only my Glock tucked into my waistband. I knew I'd never pass for a curious local if adorned with chicken plate and Kevlar helmet. So as to not seem suspicious, I sauntered right in through the entrance ayvan. As sunset approached the inside of the mosque was dark. Even so, I could clearly see it was far more ornate than the outside. The floor was lined with richly red imported Persian rugs, from which grew thick stone columns. From the high ceiling hung enormous chandeliers that during the day would've augmented the natural light through detailed stained glass windows. It was eerily quiet and empty, as if everyone was busy elsewhere – just what I was afraid of.

I hurried back to the van and unloaded the largest of the packs I had prepared at Treff's apartment.

"Looks like we're a go," Treff remarked.

"You got it, boss. Let's load up all the explosives and get inside. Keep everything covered up – there are bound to be curious onlookers. It seems like nobody around here has a job. Oh yeah, bring flashlights. The lights are out."

Nobody bothered the three of us as we made our way with our gear. Once inside, we spread ten handmade explosive devices throughout the interior of the mosque, each one linked by fifteen feet of slow-burning fuse chord. In order to achieve the desired result from the explosives, I filled gallon-sized plastic containers with a mixture of jet fuel and Napalm powder that I had discovered at the police station armory. I had procured the fuel from the airport, presuming a future opportunity to put to use an old trick from my ill spent youth. My old airport boss Paul had an Army buddy who had access to the volatile powder and used to harass Paul to get him aviation gas. When Paul asked why, his buddy let him in on the secret of how to mix a batch of Napalm gel. Breaking a vow of secrecy to his buddy, Paul taught me. If only Paul could see me now.

The batches of Napalm would burn easily from the fuse, but needed an explosive charge to splatter the fuel across the inside of the mosque. Very carefully I inserted lead styphnate charges into each container of Napalm. I used rubber gloves not so much to keep the Napalm off my hands, but to limit static electricity that might inadvertently detonate the ultrasensitive explosive. I ran the fuse chord along the floor to the ayvan, making it long enough to burn for three minutes.

"You two stay here. I'll be back in a few minutes," I told Treff and Davis. "Turn on your Motorolas so we can get a comm check. Then we'll be ready in case the motorcade is early."

"Where are you going?" Davis asked.

"I need to get some more stuff out of the van," I walked away before I could be further interrogated.

It was a potentially risky move, but with only three people comprising my team, taking some calculated risks was a necessity. I quickly identified a group of four young men who appeared to have nothing better to do than continue to mill around the neighborhood news stand smoking cigarettes and telling each other stories that were likely the subject of wild embellishment.

I approached them with directness. "Hey you four," I said as they looked at each other as if to ask 'who, us?' I continued in firm Portuguese, "Come with me. I need your help."

I could sense that they wanted to tell me to go to hell but were just afraid enough to hesitate. Perfect.

"Who are you and what do you want?" one of them asked.

"I work for Antonio Armas," I said as their attention focused with fear that I may be telling them the truth. "We're about to have some trouble here and you have a choice. You can either help him and reap the rewards or be part of the problem and suffer the consequences. As a token of his appreciation he has authorized me to compensate you for your trouble," I said as I removed an envelope from my cargo pocket and flipped it in their direction. The smallest, youngest teen in the group caught the package and immediately handed it to a tall lanky man of maybe twenty. That made him the Alpha male of the group. That's who I would talk directly to henceforth.

He tried to contain his excitement as he eyeballed more than two thousand Brazilian reais. The equivalent of a thousand dollars was surely more than any of them had ever held. I beckoned for them to follow me, which they did without further question.

I walked quickly to the van and opened the rear doors. They scurried to catch up with me and stopped in their tracks as they laid eyes on a small yet potent selection of automatic weapons. I asked if any of them had ever used such firepower before. They shook their heads in silence as I broke the news to them that today would likely change that answer. I removed an AK-47 from the back of the van and proceeded to give a field-expedient class on basic loading, firing and trouble-shooting. Whether or not they all meant it as heads nodded with understanding, I was not sure. But I didn't have time to provide expertise. I was confident they were afraid enough to not turn on me, and it was not the job of speed bumps to act as a brick wall.

"You're probably wondering why I asked for your help and showed you how to use AK-47s. The truth is that Alemao is about to come under attack. Señor Armas has gotten wind of the attacks and wants to do whatever he can to help save this neighborhood that we call home. There is a rival gang that is trying to hurt Armas because our favela has become so much more successful and productive than the others. These people are jealous and want to take what Armas has provided to us. We can't let these thugs disrupt our lives. We are arming natives around the neighborhood in preparation for the attack, which may begin any minute." I paused to observe if any of my lines were being bought.

"What are they going to do?" the oldest one asked. He was hooked.

"My fear is they will try to assault the mosque. If they do, your job will be to stop them, no matter what. Do you understand?"

"We will fire at them like our families' lives depend on it."

"Remember, do not hesitate. They will not hesitate in shooting to kill – it is either you or them." They nodded in solemn agreement. I truly felt bad that I was sending these four young men to the slaughter, but the first lady was my priority.

CHAPTER 45

My radio crackled to life. "Pony arrives, community pool." I glanced down at my radio and made a note of the frequency. *Pony* must have been the first lady's call-sign.

"Wolgrand, this is Treff. We have movement – "

"Roger. I'm on my way," I cut him off before he could transmit anything that might contradict the scenario I had painted for my new recruits. "Good luck men."

By the time I returned to the mosque Treff and Davis were outwardly anxious. Treff said, "The motorcade is already at the pool and it sounds like things are ahead of schedule. Where the hell did you go?"

"I was purchasing an insurance policy," I said. "Everything's in place. We'll initiate as soon as the motorcade is on the road again."

The radio crackled again. "Lead, this is Robinson. Move the vehicles into position; Pony is moving toward the exit. Notify the police escort that we will be on the road in three minutes." I looked at my radio display and noted a different frequency than before. This traffic was indicative of a Secret Service protective detail.

I positioned myself at the mosque's entrance and instructed Treff and Davis to return to the van. After waiting sixty seconds I said a quick prayer to a God I did not know and lit the fuse. I walked back to the van, hopped in and told Treff to hit the gas – Now!

Just down the hill from the mosque, along the worn pavement of Rua Joaquim Queiroz, was a motley collection of stalls with unusually eager crowds gathered in front. Treff confirmed this was the most prominent concentration of merchants in Alemao. He swung the van into an alley and positioned it a mere one hundred meters off the main drag.

The vehicle was no sooner in park when a burst emanated from the mosque's direction. We walked as casually as possible to gain a better vantage point. The thunder clap was somewhat muffled by the walls of the mosque, sounding more like the popping of paper bags than the detonation of a firebomb. The concussion must have blown out the windows because thin columns of black smoke rose into the sky. I hoped that nobody had entered the building after our departure. If they had, they might have been asphyxiated by the sudden loss of oxygen. Worse yet was the prospect of being able to breathe and being scorched by burning gel that clung to anything it landed on. I tried to put it out of my mind.

As my explosions continued I asked a store owner if he knew what was happening. He just shook his head and said something about things being too good for too long. The third then fourth bombs detonated as a ragtag group of armed men charged up the hill. They may have lacked the pretty police uniforms that Cruz's men sported, but they toted serious arms – a mix of Russian and Chinese-made machine guns and grenade launchers. This was the Armas army that had been reinforced by al-Ayande funds, on their way to investigate the sudden attack on their mosque. As they passed us I heard the last explosion, then the clash of opposing machine gun fire. I winced at the thought of those poor boys giving their lives for Mrs. Estevanez.

The gunfire intensified and I could now see smoke billowing from the mosque. The Napalm was going to burn for some time, possibly reducing the entire building to ashes. Armas's men and the armed locals each believed the other group had started the fire at the mosque, and were going to make the opposition pay the price. Meanwhile, we had our window of opportunity to intercept the motorcade, which was broadcasting its confusion on the radio.

"Lead, this is Robinson. We're hearing lots of gunfire back here! You got anything in sight up ahead?"

"Not yet – correction – I have smoke at the top of the hill. It sounds like the gunfire might be from the same area. Recommend you keep Pony back there until we can sort this out," the lead vehicle responded.

"I don't want to stop the motorcade – this could be an ambush," agent Robinson said.

"We can take a chance and just power our way through," the lead said. I was getting very concerned they were going to unnecessarily run themselves into a hornets' nest. I had orchestrated the firefight to give the motorcade a chance to evade Armas's outlaws, and the agents were gravely misreading the situation. Despite being afraid of their reaction I had to intervene.

"Agent Robinson this is Captain Simon, United States Marine Corps," I decided I needed to blow my cover if I was to have any chance of success. "I am on scene and have information imperative for survival of your protectee."

There was a pregnant pause before Robinson spoke. "Do you have the current authentication card?"

"No. I'm not read into your program." We didn't have time for this bullshit but I knew he was paid to be suspicious. "I am here on a separate but related mission that I can explain later. I am going to walk out into the middle of the street wearing black cargo pants and a khaki short sleeve shirt." I grabbed Davis as I began to walk, knowing that his blond crew cut was far more American looking than my dark skin and five day growth. "I have an American assistant with me. We will keep our hands in sight as you approach."

Another extended pause. "I'm not sure who you are, but let me make clear I won't hesitate to blow your ass away if we see anything funny. Lead, do you copy?"

"Copy. We've got these guys two hundred meters in front of us. They're as described; we are continuing."

As the motorcade slowly approached I noticed the radios were particularly quiet. The only traffic we copied was the two agents. I wondered why we had not seen or heard any additional assets enter the area. If those helicopters at the airport were supporting this trip, where were they? What could be a bigger contingency than this?

Flanked by six motorcycle police officers, the lead vehicle of the motorcade stopped fifty meters in front of us and doors opened. Within seconds we had ten automatic weapons honed in on us; I could not tell if the sweat pouring down my back was from the heat or the gun barrels and itchy trigger fingers. Two agents approached while the others provided cover. Davis followed my lead as I raised my hands and instructed the agents to check my right front pocket for identification. One agent did so cautiously while the other aimed from point blank range. After a long examination the agent's demeanor changed.

He handed the billfold back to me. "Sorry Captain, but this is highly unusual. Are we in immediate danger?"

"You could say that. I have them occupied for a few minutes but it won't take them long to figure out they're killing each other, while the real target is down here."

"Okay, so what do we do?" the agent asked as gunfire flew by our heads and sent splinters flying from the nearby wood shacks.

"Get in the vehicles and follow our van!" We were all ducking now as the police escort fired in the direction of the returning Armas gang. "We'll lead you out of here!"

I turned to run toward the van to join Treff, who was surely freaking out wondering how long he could afford to wait for us. An agent grabbed my shoulder.

"Sir, FLOTUS has requested your presence in the limo," he said as he pointed back toward the large black vehicle.

I nodded as I looked to Davis. "Go to the van and get ready to take us through back roads down the hill." Davis agreed and ran off underneath a growing barrage of gunfire.

As I approached, the rear door of the limousine opened and a dark-suited agent reached out to wave me toward him. I took one last glance back to see Davis disappear around the corner. Locals scattered from the street and hid in any crevice they could find. This was an all too familiar scene for people who knew exactly where to run to when bullets began to fly.

The agent yelled for the motorcade to go as the car lurched forward and took a hard left turn into the alleyway that brought Treff's van into sight. I was glad that Treff was leading the way. Only someone with intimate knowledge of the local area would be able to navigate the side streets of the favela with any hope of not getting stuck. I was equally glad we had an expert limo driver. Only someone with professional training could hope to move this behemoth nimbly around hairpin turns and through tight bottlenecks without crushing civilians in the way.

The first lady turned to me and said, "Colonel Kingman has been worried about you, J.D."

"Really ma'am?" I asked as I tried to look into her eyes. Thick blonde locks and large fashionable sunglasses shrouded her youthful face. Too youthful. I had never met Christina Estevanez in person, but knew she was a woman of at least forty years. The woman across from me appeared no older than twenty-five.

"Yes. He informed me that he lost contact with you recently and wanted me to find you."

I was truly puzzled. "That can't be right. I just received an e-mail from him this morning."

"He feared that someone was intercepting your transmissions and responding to them. That's why he sent me to help." She reached to her face and removed her glasses to reveal eyes that were far more Asian in appearance than that of the Caucasian Estevanez. She then grabbed her lustrous blond hair and pulled it from her head – revealing black shiny hair in a tight bun behind her head. She was not only beautiful, but familiar.

"Melanie Chang?" I was flabbergasted. I did not need to wait for an answer before continuing. "Could you explain to me why a staffer would be acting as FLOTUS – not to mention why she would know who the hell

I was?" I had many more questions but was having difficulty organizing my thoughts.

She looked back and forth at the two agents in the rear of the limo, as if to remind them to keep their mouths shut. "My job at the White House has been a cover all along, Simon. I've been a member of Kingman's team for more than a year now. Just like you, he never told me who else worked for him. That is until now, when necessity broke the silence. He lost comm with you and assumed that either you were dead or that someone was interfering with your ability to communicate. He knew FLOTUS was on her way here and that I would be here as well. I guess it seemed like a natural fit to have me find you."

"Okay, so that's great. You found me. But isn't Mrs. Estevanez still in danger? I can assure you Armas won't take this setback well. They have a golden opportunity to achieve a major accomplishment on behalf of al-Ayande – one that can further both of their causes immensely."

"I know, I know. That's the next step. She's still on her real schedule, which has her readying for the Carnival Parade at the Sambodromo right now. She's getting fitted into costume as we speak, unaware of the danger."

We cleared the last vestiges of Alemao and merged onto the southbound highway to downtown. I grabbed my radio to call Treff about new plans to go to the Sambodromo when Chang stopped me.

"I need to tell them about our revised plans to save the first lady," I said in opposition.

"You mean my plans, Simon. Kingman has other plans for you and time is of the essence."

CHAPTER 46

PARIS, FRANCE

The wind whipped ferociously, blowing the winter rain sideways across the tarmac. Martin Breaux prepared himself for the sour weather as he savored the last of his second cappuccino in the warm confines of the Audi sedan. It had taken him some time to convince the café barista to allow him to take the ceramic cup, if only temporarily. Parisians remained less than enamored with the idea that coffee could be enjoyed in any other way than seated for extended periods of time at sidewalk cafés. While Breaux appreciated their reverence for the finer things in life, it was no surprise to him that the French had slowly been left behind in the international rat race.

As Asad stepped from the comfort of his G-IV, he was impervious to the wind and rain; the storm seemed to accompany his arrival like an omen. With his henchmen trailing him he strode confidently to the private executive terminal. The engines were still spooling down as Asad disappeared into the building. Breaux allowed his binoculars to fall from his hands and hang by their nape strap as he downed the last of his beverage and ordered his Marine driver to take him toward the terminal building.

Breaux had expected that Asad would remain inside long enough to stretch his legs, use the men's room, and perhaps make a phone call. He had already changed his clothes into those of the catering service that resupplied the jet's food and drink for its next flight. It was an arrangement that Danny Riordan had worked out for him prior to his arrival by pulling some strings with old friends. Breaux was again amazed at how effective the former SEAL was despite his outward gruffness.

It was a technique foreign to the diplomatic Army officer who had been raised to be exceedingly polite, in keeping with his Louisianan roots. His mother insisted on the effectiveness of killing people with kindness. Elated that Martin was the first family member to enroll in college, she was

237

never thrilled with the idea that her son had decided to undergo training to kill people with real weapons. Despite his chosen profession, Martin remembered the lessons of his youth and employed them artfully as a fresh lieutenant.

After showing high aptitude throughout his intelligence training, Breaux was given the opportunity to join an ongoing operation in Southeast Asia. He completed his French language schooling in Monterey, CA before taking on the responsibility of a team of enlisted soldiers tapped with gathering intel in Indochina. Breaux hid his initial nerves and took charge, leading his men as they scoured Vietnam, Cambodia, Laos, and Thailand for evidence that the Chinese were exerting influence in the region.

It was during a venture to Bangkok that two of his young hard-chargers got themselves into some trouble with the local authorities. It was never clear to Breaux whether or not his boys were being completely forthright with their claim that they had followed a suspected Chinese spy into the massage house. He chose not to ask too many probing questions, since it wasn't pertinent to getting them out of detention. The argument focused on a failure to make payment for services rendered. The soldiers contended they had consented only for the base-priced massage, nothing extra. Breaux was forced to come up with the extra cash for the parlor, along with a few baht to grease the police – all to ensure the incident had a happy ending.

Throughout his time in Asia, Breaux learned much about not only harnessing the energies of his young soldiers, but how many foreign countries operated. He would not take for granted the safeties and liberties he enjoyed at home. He always tried to anticipate not only what would happen next, but what the worst case scenario would be, and how to counter it.

Breaux knew he must work quickly and efficiently not only to service the cabin of the executive jet, but to accomplish his actual mission of intelligence retrieval. He would perform that step first, just in case Asad and his men returned prematurely. They would be annoyed if the service were incomplete upon their return; they would be murderous if they found the caterer pilfering the upholstery for hidden listening devices. Breaux stole a glance through one of the oval cabin windows to ensure the area would remain clear for at least the next two minutes. That would provide sufficient time to retrieve both devices since Kingman had already relayed their locations. As he looked, he assumed two possibilities: Asad would be on his way toward the jet or the coast would be clear. Breaux had not entertained the third possibility: Asad and his men departing out the front door of the jet center and loading into a large sedan in the parking lot. *Their jet is in here, where the heck are they going?*

Instead of feeling relief that he now had time to retrieve the devices, Breaux knew he needed to do more than immediately recover them. The answer to his question laid within the microchip memory banks of the devices. Kingman had informed him that the device connected to the phone in the armrest of the captain's chair provided real time information back to D.C. Without taking the time to pull the devices Breaux placed a secure sat-phone call.

"This is Kingman," the voice on the other end warbled slightly.

"Sir it's Breaux. I'm in the G-IV about to retrieve the devices, but there's a problem."

"What's that Martin?" the colonel's calm was clear despite the distortion of the satellite connection. "Can you not retrieve them?"

"That's not it sir," Breaux said before realizing that perhaps they were not still in their stowed locations. After all, he had called without verifying their presence. "It's Asad – he and his men are not returning to the plane. They left in a sedan. I was hoping you might know why."

"I've been trying to put this together but I need your assistance," Kingman responded. "There was a phone call placed to the G-IV informing Asad of the POTUS plans to visit New Orleans for Mardi Gras. It did not take him long to deduce that the trip to Paris was a ruse. Seconds later the transmission was cut. Without knowing for certain I must assume that it was on purpose. I fear that somehow he discovered he was being monitored."

As Kingman spoke, Breaux fumbled hastily into the armrest and yanked the phone from its moorings. It came out easily, having already been completely disconnected. There was no listening device attached anywhere. Breaux could feel heat welling inside his body and sweat emanating from his pores despite the brutal cold outside. The churning in his gut that followed was not due to cholera. He realized he may be in deep trouble.

"Sir, it's gone," Breaux tried to keep his cool as he slid over to where the other device was supposed to be hidden. He reached under the most centrally located seat and grabbed furiously, hoping to find it.

"Martin, we have to presume that Asad has altered his plans and is on his way to your hometown. There is no way he could get last second clearance to bring that jet into the States. He'll fly commercial. If you can get the other device immediately then do it. Otherwise get out of there – you may be in grave danger if they know they've been surveilled."

"Yes sir. I'm going now. I will call you later."

"Good luck Martin," Kingman responded and terminated the call.

Breaux swept his hand across the underside of the couch, his heart pounding. His right hand raked over what must've been an exposed nail, slicing a narrow groove into his palm. Now injured, irritated, and nervous, he made one last sweep. This time more cautiously with his left hand. He felt something the size and shape of a Sharpie marker and pulled it off the fabric, knowing that nobody had affixed an actual pen to the upholstery. *Amen! I am outta here.*

Breaux tucked the pen into his pocket and practically tripped over the cart of supplies he had brought with him to the jet. Bottles of Perrier and wine, pungent soft cheeses, and fresh fruit and meats littered the cabin floor as Breaux stomped his way to the air-stair and back into the stinging cold, which provided a blast of refreshment. It took every ounce of self discipline to slow his gait to a fast walk as he put distance between himself and the aircraft. He hoped his Marine chauffeur was waiting for him just on the outside of the jet center, ready to roll.

He was only twenty feet from the automatic door into the posh jet center when time ran out. The blast erupted behind him, knocking him forward with such force that the doors didn't have time to sense his presence and open. Instead he was crushed into the heavy glass and fell to the asphalt. The deafening pain and thrust of the explosion was followed by debris: twisted bits of metal, burning rubber, and ripped upholstery rained down. Breaux took a quick glance back and saw the formerly pristine jet now broken and ablaze. It looked like a large bird whose spine had been decimated, leaving it unable to hoist its limp wings. The cabin of the G-IV had been blown to smithereens by Asad, in response to his discovery that its sanctity had been compromised.

Pushing the pain and dizziness back, Breaux picked himself up as the doors now opened, as if they had finished playing their prank and would now allow passage. All eyes within the jet center turned in his direction. The men and women in business suits wanted nothing to do with him out of fear of involvement. The two young French women behind the counter looked fearful as one raised a handheld radio and placed a call.

Breaux could hear nothing due to the massive ringing in his ears from the explosion, but sensed that he had just gone from intended victim to primary suspect. Not about to take the time to make his case of innocence, he made a break for the door to the parking lot. Breaux looked up at the door sensor as he approached, wondering if it would open in time for his departure. It did not. He banged into it hard, trying fruitlessly to knock it open with brute force. It had been remotely locked by the girls behind the counter, a security feature while help could be summoned.

It did not take long before help approached in the form of a slightly overweight security guard. Despite his adrenaline surge and immense pain from the explosion, Breaux almost felt bad for the guy. He was clearly overmatched, with no weapon but a nightstick that hung from a belt that did most of its work harnessing his waistline. He drew the stick as he huffed toward Breaux, yelling for him to freeze. Breaux could see the fear in his eyes, and assumed this was the first time he'd faced real danger on this normally placid job.

Everything moved in slow motion to Breaux as the guard raised his right arm, stick in hand. Breaux made an abrupt forward step with his right leg in order to draw the guard to act. The guard fell into the trap by swinging his arm at Breaux, clearly unsure where to hit him or how hard. Breaux had little difficulty parrying with his left forearm as he lurched forward with his left leg to get in close. In one fluid motion Breaux cocked and thrust his right arm in an open-handed punch. The heel of his right hand connected firmly with the guard's jaw, knocking him back on wobbly legs. Without hesitation Breaux snatched the nightstick – the guard was far more occupied with his loose mandible than making an arrest. Breaux had no desire to kill the man, only to make an unmolested escape. Instead of issuing a *wood shampoo*, he swung the stick low and hard into the side of the guard's unprotected right knee. The guard's body, overwhelmed with pain, collapsed onto the tile floor and assumed a defensive fetal position.

While the upscale jet center was not prepared for such violence, the airport police was a different story. It wouldn't take long before reinforcements arrived – Breaux had no intention of waiting around to greet them. With an intentionally crazed tone he screamed to the counter girls to open the door or he would not hesitate to crack the skull of the incapacitated guard. *Now!* They broke their panic long enough to open the doors without uttering a word. Nobody spoke as Breaux ran out the door and found his ride ready and waiting.

"When I heard the blast I wanted to come inside but I didn't know if I should, sir. You told me to stay put so we could roll right away," the Marine said, confused and apologetic.

"Don't worry about it. Even an Army man can handle one fat unarmed security guard. You were just following orders. Let's get the heck outta here!"

"Where to sir?"

"De Gaulle airport. I need a flight home to New Orleans."

"Going on leave sir?" the Marine asked as he ripped out of the parking lot, tires squealing on the rain slicked pavement.

"I wish," Breaux shook his head as his driver sped to merge with highway traffic on l'Autoroute du Nord for the short drive to Charles de Gaulle.

Despite mild concern about the young Marine's aggressive driving, Breaux knew he must take advantage of every second gained on Asad. Breaux diverted his attention to the faux pen in his pocket, from which he removed a memory card the size of his pinkie nail. From the same pocket he pulled out a miniscule MP-3 player and inserted the card. He put on a set of headphones and listened to the recording, scanning forward for a few seconds at a time to spot-check the context of the conversation. Thirty-five minutes into the digital recording he picked up the first outburst of anger; the tone matched what he had heard about Asad's temper. Sure enough, it was the al-Ayande leader's initial reaction to discovering that he had been bamboozled. Add to that his realization that his phone had been tapped and the G-IV could hardly contain his rage.

The recording was static-filled due to ambient noise from jet engines at max blast just outside the soundproofed cabin walls. Breaux could hear enough to deduce that Asad was revising travel plans. It was no surprise that his destination was to be the Crescent City; what was quizzical was his sudden demand to have an extended layover in Boston. There may not be a direct flight from Paris to New Orleans, but why would he mandate a stop in Beantown? Breaux paused the recording, removed his head phones and placed another secure call to his boss.

"Sir it's Breaux."

"Martin, it's good to hear your voice. I take it you have something important for me."

Breaux was always comforted by Kingman, who was always a step ahead. It made him wonder if that's what it's like to have a real father as a young child; someone you could look up to, who knew the answers to all your questions. Kingman was the closest thing he'd ever had to a Dad, and Breaux had unwavering faith in his judgment and abilities.

"I thought you should know what I heard on the recording from the airplane cabin. We know Asad is headed to New Orleans, but what's strange are his layover plans. He told his assistants to coordinate an *extended* stop in Boston. Is this significant?"

There was a long pause that caused Breaux to wonder if the connection had been broken before Kingman responded.

"Yes Martin there is, but nothing you need to worry about. I'll look into it on my end. You just keep me up to date with anything you can dig up on Asad's plans and get yourself to the Big Easy ASAP. Your best bet is to catch the next Delta flight to Atlanta Hartsfield. You will be met there by a customs agent who will hand you a packet of information. It will contain instructions on your course of action once you make your connection to New Orleans. I also need you to e-mail me the audio file before you depart."

"Yes sir."

"Good luck Martin."

The connection was broken. Breaux looked out the car window as the Marine weaved deftly through traffic. The storm outside was intensifying.

CHAPTER 47

WASHINGTON, D.C.

There were many SCIFs inside the confines of the DIA compound, each focused on its own program. Most people had clearance to only one, if any. Because of the unique scope of Joe Kingman's new counterterrorism module, he could enter a handful. This not only kept him up to speed on more events, but granted him access to a wider variety of technologies.

This particular room featured the highest tech sound equipment – better than anything on the market. Kingman and a radio technician sat next to each other wearing high definition head phones. Over and over they played the audio from inside the cabin of Asad's G-IV. The technician diligently jotted down bits of the conversation until she had constructed a nearly complete transcript of the airborne discussion. There were parts of the transmission that had been heavy with static, but the technician had honed listening skills and a robust computer program designed to identify words in multiple languages.

"Play that part again Abby," Kingman stopped the young woman, one of many civilians employed by the DIA to analyze data collected from a myriad of worldwide sources. Abigail Spencer was fresh out of college at nearby Towson State and possessed virtually no experience with world affairs. But that didn't matter as her job scope was limited. She had no idea who was on this recording or where it came from. Her responsibility was to process the intel and supply it to those with a need to know. It was this compartmentalization that helped preserve the high level of security inside the agency.

The technician reversed the recording a few seconds and replayed it for Kingman.

"Can you identify the name that he says right there?" Kingman asked. "The one where he mentions a contact inside the Beltway."

"There's only one word mentioned so I can't be sure if it's a first or last name or even a code name. However, it sounds like it might be Garvey, or perhaps Girdy."

"How about Girardi?" Kingman posed.

Spencer listened again and nodded, her auburn ponytail bobbing excitedly.

"It is Girardi after all. I think you have a knack for this, sir!"

"Thanks, but I think I'll let you keep your job. When can you have a complete transcript?" Kingman remained polite but was clearly not in a joking mood.

"It might take days to get it just right," she answered.

Kingman frowned. "How about to get it *almost* just right?"

"Within the hour, sir."

"Perfect. I'll be back in thirty minutes," Kingman was already up and out the door before Abby Spencer could retort.

Kingman sat behind the wheel of his Acura MDX as a light rain blurred his windows. He was positioned deep in the parking lot of the NCTC, far enough from the entrance to avoid observation but close enough to view the main entrance with his binoculars. So long as he occasionally ran the windshield wipers he would not lose sight of his target.

On his lap was an open file folder; Kingman sifted through the papers reviewing their dubious contents. First was a copy of a letter to Melanie Chang from the office of the U.S. ambassador to France, requesting the presence of the president at a dinner to be held in Paris during Mardi Gras. Kingman had drafted the letter himself and given it to Chang with orders to have it *stumbled* upon by Vinny Girardi. Soon after she had done so, the information was found to be transmitted to a location somewhere in D.C. Abby Spencer had been picking up chatter from a secure fax number that she was able to decrypt. She had not been able to hone in on a geographic locale for the electronic activity, but confirmed that a fax received at that number matched the letter drafted by Kingman.

Kingman had been following a hunch when he planted the *Chang Letter* on Girardi. During his previous visits to the NCTC he noticed uncanny similarities between Girardi's intel reports and chatter Spencer had gathered from her unidentified D.C. source. When the matches became too close for Kingman's comfort level, he took action. More disheartening was Spencer's ability to follow the fax from D.C. to a location in Rio de Janeiro. Not only was the city a known hotbed of al-Ayande activity, but J.D. Simon had reported that the leader of the radical Muslim group was on site. Worse yet, Simon had gone incommunicado just after that report.

It was as if someone had been listening in and decided that DIA was getting too close to Asad.

Any remaining doubt that Kingman may have had – or hoped for – that Girardi was not involved with the transmittal of information to al-Ayande was eradicated by the transcript Spencer had just produced. The recording device that Simon had planted on board Asad's G-IV for his flight from Rio to Paris had sewed the rotten fruit Kingman had feared reaping. While the recording may not have been crystal clear, it had sufficient clarity to hear Asad make reference to a source within the Washington, D.C. intelligence circle. He mentioned Girardi by name. Girardi had been using a local conduit, but Spencer had yet to identify the name on the recording. Kingman figured this other name would lead to the secure fax machine that had been sending the intel from Girardi. He would tackle that problem as soon as he sacked this one.

It was just after four o'clock in the afternoon when a dark haired man in a long olive rain coat walked out the front door of the NCTC and opened an umbrella over his head. He walked alone with briefcase in hand; Kingman recognized the gait and stature as Vinny Girardi's. Kingman shook his head as he started his SUV. *What a shame to see a young man with such potential get so lost.*

The young intelligence hotshot unlocked and climbed into a new Volvo XC-90, the silver color glistening with rain drops that beaded and gently cascaded off the paint. Kingman looked around at the interior of his ride. He was perfectly content with his five-year-old Acura, but he was a full bird colonel. Girardi was a recently resigned staff sergeant with three young children and a stay at home wife. The forty plus thousand dollar price tag seemed a bit too rich.

The two cars pulled out of the parking lot with Kingman far enough in trail that there was no way Girardi would ever know he was being followed. Not that he was even looking. Kingman knew that the kid's arrogance would make him easy prey, as it had already done with al-Ayande. Kingman's biggest challenge was not to lose him in the D.C. rush hour. *These people lose their minds at the first drop of precipitation.* The only saving grace was that it wasn't snow.

The silver Volvo merged onto the Dulles airport toll road and headed toward D.C., as expected. What was not expected was when it took the ramp for I-495 southbound at Tyson's Corner. Kingman knew that Girardi's residence was in Laurel, Maryland. His suburban home in West Laurel Acres was nearby his former NSA office at Fort Meade, and the opposite direction on the Capital Beltway. Kingman was forced to change lanes quickly to make the exit, cutting off a Dulles Flyer taxi in the process. *It's about time someone gave them a little road rage for a change.*

Volume on the Beltway was picking up as the time approached four-thirty, but Kingman had no trouble keeping up with Girardi as he moved toward the Route 1 exit for Alexandria. The supposed intel genius made no effort to evade his tail, telling Kingman that he was still unseen. But Kingman was no fool, and kept his vigilance high for any changes or traps.

The silver Volvo headed north into Old Town Alexandria and turned right and left before settling onto Saint Asaph Street amongst the tall oaks and hundred year old townhouses. It rolled to a stop and parallel parked into a tight spot, leaving Kingman no room to park. It hardly mattered, as Kingman had no intention to stay long. He pulled up next to the parked Volvo and stopped in the middle of the narrow street. Girardi stepped out of his car, assuming that this other car had stopped to ask for directions. To his surprise it was Colonel Joe Kingman that lowered the passenger window.

"Colonel Kingman? What are you doing here?" Girardi asked as he glanced quickly over his shoulders.

"I was about to ask you the same question, Vinny." The rain began to intensify and Girardi reached toward his car for an umbrella.

"Not so fast stud," Kingman said, stopping Girardi and regaining his attention. "Whose house is this?"

"It's a little embarrassing, sir. Let's just say she's a friend," Girardi answered with a sheepish grin.

"Oh, a little extracurricular activity? What's the matter? Couldn't make the basketball team?" Irritation was building in Kingman's tone. This type of behavior rubbed him the wrong way. As an officer, he'd counseled countless Marines on infidelity and the problems it caused to everyone involved. The only thing that bothered him more was being lied to – which was what he suspected.

Girardi shrugged off the comment. "She's just a friend, sir." Girardi knew he needed to break off this conversation. "Anyway, it was good to see you sir."

"I'm glad to hear that Vinny, because you're going to get to see more of me." Kingman raised a silenced Beretta 9-millimeter and aimed it squarely at Girardi's chest. "Let's go for a ride."

CHAPTER 48

Their ride took them back onto the Beltway and across the Wilson Bridge into Maryland. Kingman exited southbound onto Indian Head Highway and drove deep into the rural area along the east bank of the Potomac River. The rain turned to sleet, making the windy country roads slick with black ice. Kingman didn't slow as he steered with his right hand; his left sat in his lap with his pistol aimed at his captive. Neither man uttered a word until they pulled onto a long driveway that meandered through dense pines and oaks. After about a quarter mile, a quaint cabin came into view. The dark brown ranch backed onto the Potomac, and had a small pier with a twenty-two foot Boston Whaler tied to it. It was the perfect vacation getaway, though Girardi knew this would be no vacation.

"Get out slowly," Kingman said sternly as both men stepped out of the car. Kingman kept his weapon on Girardi as he walked around the front bumper. "Stop there and turn around."

Girardi performed as instructed. His body tensed as Kingman grabbed his left wrist. Knowing his captor would have to temporarily stow his weapon in order to secure his hands together, Girardi presumed this to be his only opportunity to escape. He spun left and swung his right leg up in a roundhouse motion toward Kingman's left thigh. The blow connected solidly, but the young computer geek immediately realized that he was no match for the wily combat veteran.

Kingman remained stoic as he watched Girardi follow the kick with a wild right-hand haymaker. In one fluid motion Kingman released Girardi's left wrist and reached across and upward to grab the inbound right arm. Kingman utilized Girardi's forward momentum as he pulled the right arm forward and thrust his own left hand onto the back of Girardi's wayward limb. Securely held in a classic arm bar, Girardi was easily taken to the ground face first. Kingman wrenched Girardi's arm back, sending a burst of mind-numbing pain through Girardi's body. Kingman was deciding whether to choke him out or knock him out with a head blow when Girardi made the decision for him. He passed out from the pain.

Kingman hoisted the dead weight over his shoulders in a fireman's carry, taking him in the front door of the cabin. The interior was utilitarian; nothing adorned the dingy white walls. Kingman walked through the main living room, which had an eclectic array of used furniture thrown together around an old television set that appeared to be equipped with satellite dish service. Kingman smiled, thinking that at least the men who occasionally stayed here had their priorities. He'd only been to this location one time, when it was used as a safe house for an outed intelligence agent who was being pursued by the infuriated drug lords that were the subject of his prior efforts. There were two bedrooms on either end of the single story building, which was no more than fifteen hundred square feet above ground. That did not include the unfinished basement, accessed via a stairwell in the back of the kitchen. Kingman moved directly to those stairs, which he descended sideways due to the added baggage on his back.

The dimly lit basement had concrete floors and walls and was littered with an assortment of advanced interrogation devices. In one corner rested a well used waterboarding device, in another was a chair with clasps built into its arms and legs. From the beams above hung chains with padded cuffs at their ends – just high enough to suspend someone above the floor. From hooks on the walls hung enough tools to do some extensive plumbing, car engine work, or ensure human compliance. Kingman was not sure how much of this was really used or how much was scare tactics. Hardcore interrogation was not the focal point of his career history; that was usually other people's job. This time, however, was a uniquely urgent and important case. Girardi was a former U.S. military member and the stakes involved the president's life. He had no intention of using the more extreme measures at his disposal, but he was hell bent on getting what he needed.

By the time Girardi awoke, his wrists and ankles were shackled to the only chair in the room, which was securely bolted to the floor. Girardi's eyes filled with confusion as he scanned the unfamiliar surroundings with increasing alarm. Seeing nobody present only added to his growing hysteria. A firm voice came from behind him, distinctly Marine.

"Good morning sunshine. Enjoy your nap?"

Girardi gasped for air in an effort to speak, but no words came.

"You know the questions are only going to get tougher as we go along, Vinny. You're going to have to be able to talk for this to work."

The room was dimly lit, but Girardi had no trouble making out Kingman's figure as the statuesque colonel walked past the chair to the wall of tools. Putting a hand to his chin as if deep in thought, Kingman reviewed his options, then reached for a foot-long black stick and a head-sized plastic bag.

"Okay, let me lay out the ground rules for you," Kingman began. "You can make this easy by telling me what I need to know. If you decide to be stupid, we will play some games. Each lack of an answer on your part will be rewarded with increasingly painful results. *Capisce?*"

Girardi nodded slowly.

"Good. So tell me Vinny; have you been busy lately with all the recent al-Ayande activity?"

There was a long pause before Girardi finally spoke. "Yes sir."

"I know you were brought over to NCTC due to your acumen in the field, so I'm assuming they've been leaning on you pretty hard."

Another pause. "Yes sir."

"How has that played with your family?"

"Sir?"

"I presumed you've been putting in some odd hours. I also know you have little ones at home. I may be old but I can still recall how my wife beat me up for my constant deployments when I was attached to fleet infantry units. So, has it been tough for her?" Kingman asked.

"She's handled it well, sir. We've been together long enough that she knows the drill."

Kingman knew that he was getting Girardi to open up, to get a bit more comfortable. It was Kingman's intent to intimidate with threatening surroundings while comforting with familiar conversation – to keep Girardi off balance until he fell into the trap.

"How old are your kids again?" Kingman continued to disarm.

Girardi glanced quickly down to his right, showing Kingman his mind was in recall. "Anna is seven, Matthew is five, and Vinny Junior is one," Girardi nearly broke a smile.

"And the friend that you were visiting – what's her name? How do you know her?"

Girardi paused as he glanced up to his left. Kingman could see him developing the answers, could almost smell the smoke coming out of his ears.

"Her name is Sally. We went to intel school together. She got out and started working for a defense contractor."

"Which one? What's her last name?"

Another pause and upward glance. Girardi knew better, but couldn't stop himself as stress heated his body.

"Roberts. Her name is Sally Roberts. She works for Raytheon, sir." Girardi appeared relieved that he was able to manufacture what he thought was a reasonably convincing lie.

"Is she a friend of Lisa's too?" Kingman asked about Girardi's wife.

Girardi looked at Kingman then away before he spoke. "Of course sir."

"Should I give her a call and ask?" he queried as he pulled a cell phone from his coat pocket – Girardi's cell phone.

"I don't think she's home right now."

"I guess I'll have to find out. Maybe I'll just leave a detailed message," Kingman said as he dialed and held the phone to his ear.

"Sir, please hang up!"

Kingman did so. "So who were you really visiting, Vinny?"

"General Moore," Girardi said as he dropped his head in partial defeat.

"Okay, now we're getting somewhere." Kingman believed the answer but was unsure as to why he resisted. *Did the complicity with al-Ayande really run to the very top of the NCTC?*

"So tell me, how long has the general been using you to do his dirty work?"

Silence.

"I'm gonna tell you this one time, Vinny. I'm already pretty upset that you lied to me about *Sally*. I've been gentle so far, but that's about to change, son. You've got about half a heartbeat to start telling me what I need to hear!"

Kingman attempted to give Girardi an out that he was just following orders. "Who did General Moore order you to deliver information to?"

Silence.

Kingman stepped so close that the two men shared the same air while he pointed the black stick directly at Girardi's crotch. He pressed a button that telescoped the baton until it struck its target. Girardi began to let out a moan. That was before the device discharged seven hundred thousand volts through Girardi's pants and into his genitals. Kingman removed the electroshock baton and stepped aside as Girardi convulsed forward.

Kingman did not relent. "This thing will take a minute to recharge until I hit you with round two. I'll ask you again – who's Moore working with?"

"I don't know sir – not exactly," Girardi tried to speak but he was still reeling from the effects of the electrical surge. "I've never met him personally – I think his name is Ahmed."

"Where is this *Ahmed*?"

"I told you sir, I've never met him."

Kingman took the plastic bag from his pocket, pulled it over Girardi's head, and held it shut around his throat. "Consider this like your *thinking cap*, Vinny. Hopefully it works before you run out of air."

The bag contracted and expanded with increasing rapidity with every passing second. Through the clear plastic Kingman could see the desperation in his captive's eyes. Girardi's world was becoming blurry as he tried to speak.

Kingman removed the bag as Girardi tried to suck in all the air in the room. His face was cold and clammy.

"You have something to say?" Kingman asked as if he'd been interrupted from the morning paper.

"He owns a restaurant on New Hampshire Ave – Simurgh. But I swear I never met the guy! He keeps himself real protected – uses other guys to do his dirty work."

Kingman stared at him for what seemed like an eternity to Girardi, who wondered if he had given enough. He had.

"Vinny, I cannot tell you how disappointed I am. You disgust me," Kingman said as he turned to walk away.

"Where are you going sir?"

"I don't have time to screw around with you anymore. I have work to do, son – a nation to save. Not all of us are solely out for ourselves." Kingman began to climb the stairs before looking back.

"Don't worry; I'm not leaving you here forever. Someone will be by to take care of you."

"Just what I'm afraid of," Girardi whispered to himself as the lights went out.

CHAPTER 49

BOSTON, MASSACHUSETTS

Air France Flight 322 arrived more than two hours late due to the inclement weather in Paris. The Boeing 747's business class section, despite being a bit antiquated for his taste, provided Asad with the comfort to achieve the rest he needed. He'd logged thousands of air miles in the hours since his departure from Rio and his body clock no longer registered the proper time of day. It took a couple glasses of brandy to ease him into the relaxation required to recharge his internal battery. He wanted to be his sharpest upon touchdown on U.S. soil.

As the jumbo jet taxied to the gate, Asad could make out the Boston skyline in the distance across the harbor. It had been more than thirty years since he was last in the city, when he studied nuclear engineering at MIT under the tutelage of the esteemed Dr. Tourak Alam. *That asshole.*

Asad pondered the use of Logan airport as a launching pad for the al-Qaeda attacks of 9/11. Both American Flight 11 and United Flight 175 had originated here. Asad conceded that it was a bold move and a massive slap into the face of the U.S.; yet he questioned the long-term effectiveness of the technique employed. He had always viewed Osama bin Laden as a showboat who placed greater import on his international celebrity than the proper goal: the expansion of Islam.

No doubt Asad was aggressive and ruthless; yet he had adopted a philosophy that purported making an attempt to win the hearts and minds of the common man before committing a violent act. His current mindset was influenced by his experience during his days as a foot soldier in Hezbollah, when he took pleasure in killing Jews yet never truly believed that his actions were affecting positive widespread change. The same had been true for the Israeli attacks on their local Arab enemies. The absence of effort on behalf of either side to endear itself to the other would forever preclude resolution. It wasn't that he was a pacifist – he was a sly realist.

He had observed many Jews that were not interested in further violence; these were the ones that he believed to be a missed opportunity. He understood that the political leaders and military would not alter their course of defiance and expansionism, but he suspected that their stance could have been weakened without the first bullet being fired. By not fostering the image that Hezbollah was an organization of peace and prosperity for all people, the movement had missed an opportunity to cause dissension within Israel.

Asad considered himself a student of history, aware that the U.S. had been both victim and perpetrator of such psy-ops. During Vietnam, the American will had been broken not due to inferior military might, but widespread questioning of the cause's validity. The effort had been destroyed from within by removing the support of the people; without that foundation the political and military structure crumbled.

Perhaps the most prolific executioner of such political upheaval was the U.S., and Asad knew it. American presidents had previously used propaganda campaigns to try and sway the populaces of nations thought to be adversarial to the U.S. There had been the support of the Contras in Nicaragua during the 1980's in an effort to eliminate the left-leaning Sandinistas. The argument was that the Contras were acting as *freedom fighters* against an oppressive, Soviet-backed regime. The truth was that the Contras were cutthroat mercenaries who cared nothing for the greater way of life for the majority of Nicaraguans. The U.S. bedded with them solely to repel Soviet influence, regardless of what was best for the citizens of Nicaragua. The irony behind the Reagan administration's efforts was that the funding for this illegal conflict came from the sale of weapons to another professed enemy of the state: Iran. It was no wonder that the U.S. was quite effective at removing foreign governments, but not so effective at replacing them with stable alternatives.

Asad's premier example of how to affect change from within hailed from his homeland. He smiled at the thought of seeing the arrogant Shah attempting to flee for his life. The U.S.-backed puppet dictator proved no match for the will of the Iranian people. It was not that Ayatollah Khomeini was a stronger man or held a mightier military force. He had developed undeniable grassroots support by showing people the real possibility of a better way. It wasn't until he secured himself in power that he unleashed the brutality for which he became feared. It was this method that inspired Asad. He viewed himself as a modern day version of Khomeini – one that would take the next step. Khomeini had done well to repel the U.S. from Persia; Asad was ready to take the fight directly to the West.

It was true that bin Laden had created fear through terror on 9/11. But he also stirred great anger. No act since the Japanese attack on Pearl Harbor had done more to unify the American people. *What was the real goal here? Was it to make people temporarily afraid or to bring down the immoral West?* To Asad, this was a simple question to answer. The complexity lay in the manner in which to make this occur. The process had multiple phases. The first was to build a solid foundation of funding for operations, logistics, recruiting and weapons. *Done.*

The second was to carve out a niche in the local populace which would be amenable to supporting the cause. Asad's approach to this was to exploit the vulnerabilities of the downtrodden. He had been successful in the Complexo do Alemao favela of Rio de Janeiro, where he had gambled that people had grown increasingly disillusioned with both the government and the Catholic Church. Al-Ayande replaced the existing lip service with action. Where others promised change, Asad's movement produced things the poverty-stricken had never seen in the favela. Asad validated his theory that if people were in dire enough straits they would put aside bullshit philosophy for tangible results. He had created a schism between the poorest people and the upper crust that consisted of the government and their wealthy supporters. By doing so, he'd implicitly made these people not care if the government were to continue or disappear. With this, the second phase was *done.*

The third phase was to capitalize upon the newfound support by removing the head of the enemy monster. With part of the body already devoid of its loyalty, the likelihood was great that the follow-on regime could be influenced in a manner favorable to the interests of al-Ayande. While Asad had employed steps one and two in Rio, he had no intention of pursuing step three at that site. Knocking off the leadership of Brazil was not worth the effort at this time. No, he would fell that domino in the future. The main prize lay in his immediate plans.

The methods al-Ayande had utilized in Rio during recent years had been equally successful right under the nose of the arrogant President Estevanez – in New Orleans. Al-Ayande had been testing the waters in a variety of U.S. cities with lukewarm results. That was until the tropical waters of the Gulf of Mexico spawned Hurricane Katrina, unleashing her fury on the ill-prepared city. With the poorest areas of the city decimated and residents at wits end, Asad finally had his chance. Unlike New Orleans's mayor, Louisiana's governor or FEMA, al-Ayande wasted no time commencing recovery efforts. Following a template developed in Rio, the Muslim movement used pragmatic results to steal away followers that previously would've never thought to abandon the Christian religion or the

U.S. government. But people will do what they need to do to survive. Asad was confident that he had done what it took to win over the loyalties of the remaining residents of New Orleans's Ninth Ward. When the time was right, he would call on them to take the next step. That time was now.

In a perfect world, Asad would have had more time to incubate his plan. But the president's change in travel plans had created conditions too conducive to pass up. He hoped that his strike on the first lady in Rio would create a diversion from his primary goal – the assassination of President Estevanez during his visit to Paris. The move to New Orleans did create some logistical problems, but mostly related to making last minute adjustments. On the up side, he had all the necessary elements in place to take action; even more so than in Paris. In addition, he relished the symbolism of eliminating the president during Mardi Gras – easily the most hedonistic holiday season celebrated by Christians and the West. It would be most poetic to make this statement to the world on this stage. Clearly this had been the work of Allah.

With the leadership removed, the U.S. would be ripe for the taking. Asad viewed Estevanez as a dictator put in office by special interests and the wealthy minority. After all, the U.S. did not utilize a direct election, but instead a convoluted system wherein unknown officials placed the votes supposedly based on the popular vote. This Electoral College was merely a means to prevent the will of the people from taking hold. Asad was supremely confident that al-Ayande could surreptitiously affect change that would be welcomed by the ever-growing lower class in American society.

Asad's assistant approached him and handed him a large white Styrofoam cup with pink and orange lettering. Asad took a sip and made a foul face.

"What is this *Dunkin' Donuts* shit?" Asad asked but continued before a response could be proffered. "I forgot how Americans like their coffee weak and sickeningly sweet."

"Do you want something different?" the assistant asked.

"No time. What about the connecting flight?" Asad was all business as usual.

"Delta Flight 661 is set for 0600. We connect through Atlanta and arrive in New Orleans at 1213."

"And the car?" Asad asked.

"We have a Lincoln Towncar in the parking garage ready and waiting," the assistant answered.

"Good. Let's go."

Having only carryons and briefcases, the men bypassed baggage claim. Across a pedestrian bridge, in one of the very front parking spots, sat their black sedan. An Arab man stepped out from the driver's seat and quickly opened the trunk as he paid his respects to Asad and his assistant. The men loaded their bags into the trunk, taking note of the additional duffel bag. Asad unzipped it and sifted through the contents, nodding to himself as he zipped it shut. The driver opened the rear door as the two visitors slid into the car to find an envelope containing ten thousand U.S. dollars, as instructed.

The driver started the car and drove out of the garage into the clear dark Boston night. An Iranian immigrant who worked in Boston as a cab driver, his help had been solicited by a leader at a local mosque. He had little idea as to what Asad's purposes were, but obediently followed the instructions of his religious leader. He deftly navigated through the confusion of Boston's streets, taking them to the Mass Pike. Tired from the night flight, Asad was relieved to be on the highway, until he saw the construction crews. Frustration mounted as they crept along, until finally arriving at the Huntington Avenue exit. Once off the highway, they sailed west along Route 9. The city lights faded away in the rear view mirror as the urban noise transformed into quiet suburbia.

They turned onto Chestnut Hill Avenue and slowed so as not to attract unwanted attention. Upper middle class neighborhoods in Massachusetts tended to be places where families knew each other and who did not belong. Greeting strangers with wariness was the norm, especially those with the wrong color skin. They turned left onto Clinton Road and slowed below thirty miles per hour. House lights were out for the night; the only light on the street was cast by the occasional street lamp and the Towncar's head lights.

Asad watched as the numbers on the mailboxes ticked slowly up – his heart rate did the same. They passed the 300s then the 400s and finally the 500s. The driver confirmed their arrival at 600 Clinton Road. Asad looked closely at the mailbox that stood at the end of the driveway – *The Simons*.

"This is the one." Asad said.

CHAPTER 50

The night air was as cold as Asad had ever felt, yet he wasn't the least bit uncomfortable. Despite the lightweight rain coat that hung over his shoulders he was warmed by building adrenaline. The arctic cold of the air was somewhat offset by its remarkable still; there wasn't a knot of breeze or a single cloud in the sky. It was a perfect night. The only evidence of the cold air was frost that formed in his nose each time he inhaled. He felt alive.

Asad's assistant joined him as he leaned over the open car trunk; the driver stood by and watched intently at the darkened houses along Clinton Road. Each man removed a silenced pistol from the duffel bag and tucked it into hip holsters. The Chinese-made QSW-06, the newest in use by the People's Liberation Army, held a twenty round box magazine – more than enough for this job. The assistant at his side took hold of a handful of zip-ties and roll of duct tape; Asad added to his repertoire a military-style knife and a key ring of lock picks, which he tucked into his coat pocket.

In this older neighborhood, phone lines still hung above ground atop poles, then ducked down to the ground. It was simple to trace their path to the side of the houses, where they reappeared and entered through small holes in the exterior. Asad chuckled as he gathered a wire bundle in his hand, sifted through them until he found the telephone wire, and cut it. His snip was followed immediately by a loud warbling alarm from inside the house. Interior lights came on soon thereafter.

Asad nodded to his driver, who took the cue silently and returned to the sedan, started the car, turned around in the cul-de-sac in front of him and slowly disappeared into the darkness from which they had arrived only minutes earlier. Left in the eerie quiet outside the Simon home were two armed men on a mission. Asad and his closest assistant knew each other's every idiosyncrasy, allowing them to operate in complete silence like two bodies with one mind.

Najid had served alongside the former Hossein Zand in Hezbollah. Even early on Zand knew he was destined for greatness and began to build a cadre of cohorts that would later form the heart of al-Ayande. Each man had proven he would fight until the death for Zand; a trait that Zand presumed would be essential in the pursuit of the greater good. During a firefight in the outskirts of Beirut in 1983, Najid covered Zand and took a bullet in the process. His actions and fortuitous survival had ensured that Zand would repay the loyalty. The two men performed many successful covert ops together. With each success the pair became more brazen with their actions and more grandiose with their plans.

Asad and Najid moved hastily to the house, slinked stealthily against its solid brick side, then trotted low to the ground until under the cover of wild blueberry bushes and oak trees beyond the small back yard. They lay down amongst the brush and waited. From their vantage point, they observed the single squad car that arrived moments later. With no backup, no lights and no sense of urgency, it was clear to Asad that this dispatch was assumed to be spurious. One male and one female officer sauntered toward the front door, casually joking with each other as they knocked. Asad could not see inside the front door but could see that it was opened and subsequently closed once the officers were inside the house. He waited less than five minutes before watching the two officers depart the Simon residence. The front door closed and interior lights extinguished one by one as the police drove away.

Just as Asad predicted, cutting the phone line triggered what was assumed to be a false alarm. The call from the alarm company was made to a cell phone, confirming the alarm. It wouldn't matter if the land line had no dial tone – nobody would discover the cut line in the middle of the night. The police likely recommended calling the phone company in the morning since there was no evidence of foul play and nobody observed outside the house. Asad looked at his watch and whispered to his assistant that they would wait ten minutes. He made a mental note of the order in which the house lights were shut off, so he would know the most direct path to the bedroom.

Without a word Asad rose and Najid followed him to a weathered set of wooden stairs that led up to a rear porch and door to the back of the house. With his knife Asad sliced the screen door. He smirked – the rear door didn't even have a deadbolt. He easily picked the single doorknob lock and eased the door open slowly. All was silent for only a moment before a jingle-jangle grew louder in the darkness.

Asad tensed and grasped his blade tightly in his right hand until he saw the shaggy figure approach into the ambient moonlight. He was relieved to see that it was only the family pooch, but could not take a chance that the dog might bark or that its chain would awaken the residents. He knelt and allowed the dog to greet him with wagging tail and flapping tongue, its toothy grin glowing in the dim light. Asad petted the back of the pup's neck gently with his left hand, breaking down any barriers before gripping it firmly and plunging the knife into its throat. The cut sliced instantaneously through the dog's windpipe, preventing any unwanted vocal reaction.

The messy pool of blood that poured onto the floor was of little consequence to Asad. He was not worried about the aftermath of this visit, only its effectiveness during the next few minutes. He dismissively dropped the dog's lifeless body from his grip, stood and wiped his blood and fur-covered knife on a kitchen towel. He looked back at the unfazed Najid and waved his arm forward to indicate it was time to move.

There was no need to turn on any lights. Asad's eyes had adjusted to the darkness and he'd already memorized the path to the stairs from his backyard view. The two intruders slinked up the hardwood stairs, making their footfalls as light as possible. Despite the occasional creak neither man slowed their ascent. They approached the recently lighted bedroom at the end of the hall. Asad and Najid could hear whispers and shuffling feet.

"What's going on?" a man's voice called from next to the bed. "Who the hell is there? What do you want?" the intonation grew more frantic with each phrase. The man's false bravado did little to hide what Asad already knew. The man was a bookish type, wholly uncomfortable with the prospect of having to fight for his life or that of his wife.

"Shut him up," Asad barked to Najid. The man armed with nothing but a pair of boxer shorts made a feeble move toward Najid, presumably to defend the honor of his wife who cowered as close to the headboard as she could. Asad's assistant watched casually as the man lunged toward him. He drew his pistol and fired a single silenced shot into his leading thigh. The man dropped to one knee and yelped, clutching the hole in his leg.

Najid took advantage of the distraction, cracking him over the top of his head with the butt of his pistol. He fell limp on the hardwood floor. Najid deftly moved the man's hands behind his back and secured both wrists together with a zip-tie. Asad's assistant repeated the process with his victim's feet and affixed a piece of duct tape over his mouth. The man lied there unconscious.

"Prop him up in that chair," Asad demanded as he pointed to an antique rocker in the corner of the room. "Wake him up."

Asad ran his hand against the wall until he found the light switch. Without allowing his gaze to leave the bed, he flipped the switch. As two wall sconces came to life above either end of the headboard, Najid reared back with his left arm and smacked the consciousness back into his hogtied victim. He grunted through the duct tape and squinted his eyes as they adjusted to the light. As the man's eyes opened fully, Asad could see fear.

The woman in the bed shrieked briefly before stopping herself with her own hand. She wanted to appear strong in the face of true evil.

"What's the matter Ariana? Did you see a ghost?" Asad asked with a devilish grin.

He turned to the man and said "So Alexander, do you have any idea who I am?"

Alexander Simon shook his head slightly to confirm that he did not. His eyes showed confusion and dread.

"Well I know who you are," Asad said. "You're the man who ended up marrying this whore." He pointed as he moved closer to the bed. "Perhaps you've heard of al-Ayande, the future of Islam worldwide. It is my movement. I am its leader Asad. I am sure that if you were allowed to speak that you would convey how honored you are to meet me," Asad chuckled.

Asad opened his coat, allowing it to drop to the floor. Ariana Simon knew she was no match for the man she once knew as Hossein Zand, so she slid out of the bed opposite him. Her only chance was to make it to the second-story window and leap to the grass below. Tears streamed down her face at the realization that even if she evaded him, Asad would murder her husband. Alex had done nothing wrong, did not even know who this enraged psycho was.

Ariana was out of the bed and across the floor to the window in little more than a second. She unlocked the latch atop the bottom half of the window and thrust the wooden frame upward. She was hit simultaneously by a blast of frigid air against her bare legs and midriff and by Asad's body against her back.

Alexander writhed and struggled to no avail.

"So you want to do this here?" Asad asked as he snatched Ariana's hair and bent her torso forward out the window. She could see her neighbors' homes so close by; she began to scream for help. Before a single note could emanate from her, Asad reached with his right hand and clutched her throat with silencing force. He leaned on her with more than twice her body weight. She felt the air being squeezed from her body against the sharpness of the window sill.

He relinquished her hair with his left hand, undid his belt, and dropped his pants around his ankles. He ground against her ass until hard. He grabbed her lace panties by the waistband and ripped them from her body in one rapid motion. She tried to yelp and struggle, but it only brought more pressure around the throat and against her body.

"Go ahead and struggle Ariana. You always were a frisky bitch." Asad turned back to Najid. "Make sure he keeps watching. I want him to know just how much of a slut he chose before I kill him."

Asad spit into his hand, lubricating himself before he violated Ariana. He plunged into her repeatedly.

"It's no surprise that you've gotten so loose over the years," he chided. Sweat formed on his brow despite the icy breeze. Hanging halfway out the window, Ariana made noise as if trying to speak.

"You have something to say? Maybe just to moan in ecstasy?" He loosened his grip on her throat just enough to allow a brief sip of oxygen and raspy words.

"You monster! I probably feel loose compared to the little boys you like to fuck!" Ariana knew that no amount of sweet talk would lead to her release. She recalled his enraged look from the day she divulged to him that she'd fallen for Tourak Alam. She closed her eyes and wept.

Asad clamped his pliers grip on her throat as he thrust with jackhammer hips in response to Ariana's comment. He grunted and groaned under his breath as he momentarily ignored his surroundings and focused solely on his climax. It had been more than thirty years since he'd been inside Ariana. He was swarmed by a myriad of emotions as he unloaded into her – lust, betrayal, anger, pleasure, hatred, love.

Now in the denouement of his personal sexual experience, Asad returned to the present and regained his clarity. He loosened his grip from Ariana's neck, but this time she did little more than breathe. She lay limp against the open window sill, her will to fight as broken as her body. She turned slowly to face her assailant with terrible sadness in her eyes.

"Why? Why? Why?" Ariana whimpered.

"I am taking care of unfinished business," Asad answered while he hovered over her. They were both still naked from the rape that had just occurred. His exposed state did not go unnoticed by Ariana, who feigned a demeanor of resignation as she prepared for one final attempt at freedom. She slumped her shoulders and hung her head slightly. She focused energy into her right leg then lifted it as hard as she could, kicking upward toward Asad's exposed groin. A step ahead of every enemy at all times, Asad shifted to his right and allowed Ariana's shin to strike the inside of his left thigh. He reached forward and grabbed a handful of thick black hair and yanked her into his chest. He twisted hard and spun her half naked body a half-turn, facing her away from him. Despite her efforts to resist, she moved like a rag doll in his meaty arms.

He glanced back over his shoulder and spoke to Alexander Simon, "Say goodbye."

Still clutching her hair with his left hand, Asad took her chin with his right. He leaned forward and whispered into her ear, "Say hello to Tourak in Hell, bitch." He kissed her cheek before wrenching her neck and snapping her spine in one clean break.

Asad lifted Ariana by her armpits and tossed her onto the bed. He spread her onto her back and ripped her night-shirt from her body. She lay completely exposed, brutally raped and murdered in plain sight of her bound and gagged husband.

Still naked from the waist down, Asad turned to the other two men in the room. Looking at Alexander, he said, "Should I do you next?"

He allowed the question, along with his privates, to hang in the air for a few seconds before bending over to pick up his pants. He slid them on and approached Alexander and Najid.

"I'll take it from here my friend," Asad waved his assistant away and unsheathed his knife.

Turning to the now shivering captive, Asad queried, "You're probably wondering what I have in mind for you, aren't you?"

Alexander did not respond except to look at the deceased love of his life, which lay sprawled on their bed. Her normally bronze skin appeared pale to him. His vantage point gave him a disturbing view of her torn vagina, oozing with Satan's sperm. He began to weep and shake uncontrollably.

"Pull yourself together, you pussy!" Asad yelled. "She had it coming. You probably don't even know that we used to do that on a regular basis before she began spreading those legs for Tourak Alam. She was taking both of us at the same time. Why don't you picture that? Make it your last thought, why don't you?"

Asad's anger intensified. "You know, I would normally torture someone like you, but I almost feel bad for you. If I had a choice I might even let you live. It's not often I find myself saying that about a Jew; especially one who spent his life screwing the woman that was supposed to become my wife. However, survival is not an option for you and time is not a luxury that I possess."

The terrorist unceremoniously plunged the four-inch blade into Alexander's belly. Asad looked into Mr. Simon's dying eyes as he lifted the blade with all his might; it sliced through muscle until it was slowed but not stopped by ribs, which snapped one after another until the knife came to rest in his right clavicle. Asad removed the blade, wiped it on Alexander's shirt, and sheathed it.

Najid broke the silence. "We'd better leave now."

266

Asad nodded in agreement as Najid called the driver. The attackers made no attempt to sterilize the crime scene as they departed, still under the cloak of darkness. Asad knew that he would be the prime suspect, but presumed that he would be out of the country by that time. *Let the Americans try to come find me.*

It was daybreak before the first vehicle responded to the Simon residence. Not a single neighbor had seen or heard a thing. The police hadn't been alerted to any disturbance. There was no obvious reason for anyone to be paying a visit to 600 Clinton Road. A tan Ford Taurus pulled into the driveway without hesitation; its driver knew exactly where he was going. Looking haggard but determined, Colonel Kingman stepped out of the car, drew his pistol and moved purposefully toward the front door.

Kingman knocked and then pounded as each passing second made him fear worse. He removed a flash bang from the pocket of his overcoat as he readied to kick in the door. He laid the bottom of his size twelve squarely into the door as it flew open. The alarm did not trip. Kingman cleared rooms quickly, almost haphazardly, knowing he may be too late.

Familiar with the layout of the Simon house, Kingman had been there numerous times before. He had become a friend of the family over the years, present for backyard barbecues and holiday parties. Images of past get-togethers flashed through his head as he took the stairs three at a time, the hardwoods bowing under the strain. He threw open the bedroom door and stepped into his worst nightmare.

CHAPTER 51

NEW ORLEANS, LOUISIANA

I was jolted back into reality by the touchdown of the Boeing 767 that provided my red-eye transportation back to the continental U.S. The jump-seat ride on the DHL cargo plane from Rio to New Orleans international airport had come as an unexpected twist. I'd barely digested my introduction to Melanie Chang before she passed to me the details of my latest mission. The dossier she handed to me in the limousine had come straight from Colonel Kingman and it was explicit in its instructions. Chang was to remain on site in Rio and assist in counterterrorism measures as they pertained to the FLOTUS. I was to proceed immediately to New Orleans to partake in the same as they pertained to the POTUS.

My attempts to either rest or focus on mission-related details were supplanted by my interaction with the pilots of the heavy jet that was my taxi out of Rio. The captain was a retired Marine Corps F/A-18 pilot who, despite his advanced age, was still much enamored with his world traveling career. Part of me hoped that I would speak so highly of my life at his age, but I doubted it.

It had been my dream to become a military pilot, a dream thwarted by a medical condition I was previously unaware of. After earning my private pilot's license and surviving my crash on Plymouth Beach, I took some time away from aviation. But my tenure as a Huey crew chief rekindled the fire. I was determined to take advantage of my commissioning as a second lieutenant by securing a spot in flight school. While attending the Marine Corps Basic Officer School in Quantico, Virginia, I worked diligently to ensure a high enough class standing to guarantee selection. I endured seemingly endless bullshit from instructors and weathered tedious days and nights trudging through the elements. I knew I could tolerate a different specialty, but my heart was set on aviation. My platoon leader, knowing my desires, warned me daily that I was destined for a career in the infantry. Just great.

Selection day arrived and brought with it the news I'd been anxiously awaiting. The assignment was an MOS of 7599; I was a student naval aviator on his way to Pensacola, Florida. I packed everything I owned – a few boxes of clothes and some compact discs – into my used Pathfinder, and moved into a rental house on the beach with three other aspiring pilots. While waiting for school to start, we spent our days running the roads and our nights running after the local ladies. I was in superb shape and was ready to take to the skies. My mind knew that failure was not an option – my body knew different.

The first important flight school event was the medical evaluation. I hadn't made it through day one of the process when the doctors of Naval Aerospace Medical Institute informed me that I had a slightly irregular heartbeat. I'd been slapped with the *NAMI Whammy* – found not physically qualified for flight status. My career as a Marine Corps pilot was over before it began.

It was as easy to find a replacement for my portion of the lease as it was to repack my limited belongings. None of this lessened the sting of failing my very first hurdle in Pensacola. My uncertain future would soon be made less so by Headquarters Marine Corps. Within two weeks, I was reassigned to attend the Navy and Marine Corps Intelligence Training Center in Dam Neck, Virginia.

In time, I overcame my disappointment and made the most of my assignment as an intelligence officer. Hell, how many people could honestly say their job involved saving the leader of the free world? I hoped that I'd still be able to make that claim by day's end.

The red and yellow cargo jet rolled to a stop and was greeted by two vehicles as the dark of night gave way to daybreak. One was an aircraft tug with two air cargo employees, there to assist with the offload of whatever cargo was in the back of the plane. The other was a sedan with Customs and Border Patrol markings. Two uniformed agents stepped out and waited for one of the airport employees to drive a tall set of wheeled stairs up against the side of the 767. The copilot opened the aircraft door and greeted the agents as they ascended the stairs and boarded the plane for a standard inspection of cargo. The older, heavier agent seemed tired and disinterested as he ran through a checklist burned into his memory by hundreds of uneventful iterations. The second agent was a black man in his late twenties that was too tall for his uniform. He remained quiet as if he was under training, but I knew better. I recognized him from the pictures in the dossier from Kingman. I could tell by his intent stare that the recognition was mutual.

He pulled me aside to speak out of earshot of the others.

"Captain Simon, I'm Captain Martin Breaux, U.S. Army," he said without tipping his hand by shaking hands.

"I know. Good to meet you. Kingman told me to expect you. By the way, please call me J.D.; I'm not your typical anal Marine."

"Alright J.D., sounds good. We should get going. Don't worry, I've already advised the CBP agent that I was under specific orders to take you with me immediately upon your arrival. I showed him some official letterhead, but he couldn't have cared less. How about these pilots...they know anything?"

"Nope. I flashed my credentials and told them I could not answer any questions. It was that easy. I think they've carried unusual cargo before," I said as the two of us excused ourselves and headed down the stairs to an unmarked car in the parking lot. Neither the agent nor the pilots minded as they continued their entry inspection process.

Obviously, it was imperative that our identities remain a secret from anyone that could potentially be an enemy of the U.S. In the intelligence world this often involves unclear lines of delineation, so it's usually better to remain unidentified to anyone you don't know. This would protect us from anyone tied to al-Ayande. What was less obvious was limiting our exposure to fellow Americans. Kingman had made it clear to me from the beginning of my tour of duty on his team that there were legal restrictions regarding our activity in CONUS. As active military members, our activity was constrained unless specifically authorized by Congress. By the time those sloths made proper authorization, everybody in the world would know who we were and whatever bad thing it was that we were supposed to stop would have long since occurred. It was clear that the same ideas had been ingrained in Breaux. Only those that absolutely needed to know would ever discover our true identities while in New Orleans.

Breaux sped along the airport access road and found his way quickly to I-10 east, taking us in the direction of downtown. As we approached, the quiet was palpable and eerie. It was just after seven in the morning on a Wednesday; most U.S. cities would be well into the throes of rush hour. While I'd never been to the Big Easy, I had read that nearly half of the city's population had been displaced by Hurricane Katrina, leaving the city at less than 300,000. Combine that with the collective hangover from last night's Mardi Gras culmination and we had no trouble cruising at better than eighty miles per hour.

We exited the highway and descended onto the city streets below, winding between the Superdome and the Louisiana State University Medical Center along Poydras Street. The dinginess of the streets, broken sidewalks, and homeless people made me wonder if I'd actually left Rio behind. I wasn't sure if what I was seeing was remnant of Katrina or a preexisting condition. Either way, it was no surprise to me that this place was an annual contender for the crown of the country's crime capital.

"Man this place is a shithole. I wonder if it was like this before the storm," I said half to myself and half to Breaux.

"It still had its fair share of problems, but not this bad," Breaux commented as he turned left onto O'Keefe Avenue. The conditions off the main drag of Poydras only exposed more decay.

"I can't imagine who would live like this," I continued.

"Well I grew up not far from here," Breaux shot me a look.

Whoops. "Sorry man. You know there are parts of my hometown of Boston that are just as bad." I was not sure if I had salvaged the conversation as Breaux nodded silently. He whipped the car deftly onto Canal Street then immediately onto Bayonne Street, pulling to a stop in front of the Fairmont Hotel.

The valet greeted us with a half smile as he eyeballed our Chevy Cobalt with mild disdain. Breaux was unfazed as he stepped out and instructed the valet to keep the car close, encouraging the agreement with a green-filled handshake. We needed to be able to roll out without delay.

I'm sure we looked like quite a pair as we entered the ornate lobby of the Fairmont, Breaux dressed in an ill-fitting CBP uniform and me looking haggard and unshaven. Inside the hotel looked more like the Arabian Gulf than the Gulf of Mexico. We walked across large Persian rugs bordered by thick square columns of gold and brown. There were tall palms and grandiose chandeliers that looked as if they would pull themselves from their ceiling mounts.

"So this is where we're meeting Kingman? Is he on a different pay scale than the rest of us?" I asked.

"Yes and no," Breaux finally broke a smile. Perhaps he was getting over my foot-in-the-mouth comment from earlier. He continued in hushed tones to limit any echo that someone might want to hear. "He's upstairs, but he's only here because this is the White House staff hotel. The POTUS stayed here last night, so this place is probably overrun with his entourage. They've got a couple of floors to themselves and security all around, so this is an ideal place to meet."

"So is the Man here as we speak?" I asked in reference to the president.

"He should be. His first event outside the hotel today is brunch at Muriel's in the French Quarter at 1000. Then he walks next door to Saint Louis Cathedral for the noon Ash Wednesday mass. After that he motorcades directly to the airport for his departure on Air Force One."

We approached the bank of elevators where a bell hop asked if we were going up. *Yes.* The door opened and we stepped in as Breaux reached forward and hit the number nine.

CHAPTER 52

The door to the ninth floor suite opened to reveal that the entire hotel had not completed its post-Katrina renovations quite yet. Unlike the palatial lobby, the room was dated, dark and musty. The only thing in the room more rundown than the space itself was Colonel Kingman. I'd never seen him appear anything less than flawless. He was wearing rumpled khaki slacks and a button down shirt that hung partially out at the waist. He was unshaven and his eyes sunken with fatigue. He looked as if he hadn't slept or as if he had seen a ghost.

"Please come in gents. I'm glad to see you both made it here safely," Kingman began as he gestured toward the couch in the middle of the living room. On an adjacent cart rested a spread of pastries, fresh fruit and coffee. "Please help yourselves to some breakfast. You're going to need it and won't have time to get anything for a while."

"When did you get here sir?" I asked as I stuffed a mammoth cheese Danish down my craw. I hadn't realized how hungry I was, nor could I recall the last time I had eaten. I washed it down with some chicory coffee and took a seat next to Breaux on the couch.

"About two hours ago. Based on recent developments, I called the Secret Service and asked them to have a room reserved for us here at the staff hotel. They did so and had WHCA – White House Communications Agency – sweep the room before my arrival to ensure that we could speak freely. That being said, I'll cut to brass tax since time is of the essence. As you are both aware, al-Ayande has been actively building support amongst some of the world's poorest communities in an international effort to create a foundation from which to build. Until recently that foundation held up the façade that the movement is one of community outreach and philanthropy in the name of Allah. Of course we all knew that was bullshit. The only questions were when, where, and how the scenario would play out."

"So we think the where is *here*? And the time *now*?" I asked.

"Affirmative," Kingman answered. "It's no secret that groups like al-Qaeda have long been trying to gain a foothold within the borders of the U.S. They've had some successes within certain mosques and even with the development of training camps in remote locations. But loose affiliations and lack of focus have hampered them. Al-Ayande has both the funding and focus to take their cause to the next devastating level."

Kingman continued, "Their leadership decided to take full advantage of the Katrina disaster, pouring a multitude of resources into the huge gaps left by the broken levees. Our government officials pointed fingers and exchanged verbal barbs – al-Ayande took action. Free from bureaucratic red tape, they funneled money quickly into the area, taking over a handful of existing brick structures that were formerly Christian churches. They were transformed into hasty mosques that became rallying points for those that so wanted to return to their homes in the lower Ninth Ward. While the U.S. government simply condemned neighborhoods and pressured natives to relocate, al-Ayande worked under the radar to provide the desired alternative."

"Why hasn't this been big news in the media?" Breaux asked.

"Publicly, they've used names of charitable organizations. Ever heard of *Americans Rebuilding America*?"

Nods from both Breaux and myself.

"Front organization," Kingman said with an intent stare. "Many faith-based groups have contributed large sums of money and volunteers to help. However, the Muslims have done a better job of assimilating into the local populace. While other churches imported their sympathetic white congregations, al-Ayande paid empathetic black Muslims from other poor U.S. cities. Human nature has drawn the displaced New Orleans natives to folks that looked and talked like them."

"Where's the FBI been in all this?" I asked. "Shouldn't this be their show?"

Kingman shook his head and broke a weak smile.

"You try to criticize anything black or Muslim publicly in this day and age."

"Racial profiling?" I asked, not really surprised.

"That's right, J.D."

"So they're getting away with this all due to their skin color? That's some PC bullshit!"

Breaux broke the ensuing silence. "It's not all about being black, you know."

"No shit, man," I shot back. "If you couldn't tell, I'm pretty fuckin dark too," I said as I raised a bronze arm.

"Easy fellas," Kingman intervened. "We're all tired and stressed. Let's stay focused. I'm friends with the senior agent-in-charge of the local FBI unit. He's been pushing intel my way in hopes that I could do things that he couldn't. He's allowed us to work the area since nobody knows us and we can maintain our cover easier."

As much as I didn't want to believe what Kingman was saying, it was beginning to make too much sense. I'd just been witness to how effectively al-Ayande gained a foothold in Rio. For some reason, however, it disturbed me more to think of it happening inside the U.S. Perhaps I viewed places like Brazil as remote lands that were a million miles from home. The sad reality was that New Orleans, Detroit, and pockets of many other American cities reeked of the same Third World stink. It raised an age old question: was it more important to attack political problems before they arrive on your doorstep or to focus efforts at home where citizens have an immediate need? Did we possess the will to do either successfully?

Breaux seemed dumfounded that this could all be occurring in his hometown. He asked, "So how does it go from some folks building houses for some other folks to a national security threat?"

Now slumped into a plush armchair, Kingman was clearly exhausted, yet took the time to elucidate. "The backers of this movement have shown great patience. They fostered a rapport with locals by providing assistance, all the while commiserating with them that the government had left them in the lurch. They showed returning refugees that Muslims were not evil people. After all, if they were so bad, why the hell were they the ones helping?"

"So this process went on for a while," Kingman continued. "People began to buy the message. The imams were tied in with al-Ayande, and they began to recruit. There was no shortage of angry young men to pick from that felt they'd gotten a raw deal from the government and society in general. The imams empowered these chosen ones by making them believe they could make a real difference. Take a look at these pics I got from NGA."

Kingman spread out a handful of blown up satellite images from the National Geospatial-Intelligence Agency on the coffee table. He looked up at us waiting for us to comprehend.

I broke the silence. "Sir, they look like overhead shots of training camps."

"Very good, J.D., but where?" Kingman asked what instantly became obvious. The terrain around the camp was devoid of any relief. The foliage was a mix of tall grass and dots of bushy trees amongst blotches of murky water.

Breaux chimed in, "The bayou – probably Louisiana, but maybe Mississippi."

"I'll cut the suspense; it's Louisiana. About ninety miles southwest of New Orleans in Terrebonne Parish." Kingman turned to Breaux as he detailed the location of the camp. "If you know where Houma is, then you know they do those swamp tours a few miles outside the town."

Breaux nodded.

"Well, it's another twenty miles – in the middle of nowhere."

"Man, that area's rough," Breaux shook his head and pursed his lips in emphasis. "No wonder nobody's been out that way to stop them."

"They've got their own gator-filled moat around the facility," Kingman concurred.

"Suffice it to say they've got quite a few soldiers in the area?" I asked.

"Exactly – quite a few trained, well-funded, disciplined, suicidal soldiers," Kingman elaborated.

"And you figure since they went after FLOTUS last night in Rio that POTUS is next? Part of some master plan to decapitate the U.S. government?" I asked.

"More or less. I don't think al-Ayande really cares one way or the other about the FLOTUS. Let's call that the diversion. Draw all the attention to another hemisphere – then deliver the real blow at home the very next day."

"Speaking of FLOTUS, any status report from Brazil?" I asked.

"She's on her way back to D.C. as we speak," Kingman responded. "The Secret Service convinced her to skip the church service today, but no such luck at the parade last night. I guess they got a bunch of extra police protection and kept an impregnable bubble around her."

"Did Chang stick around for all the action?"

"Who?" Breaux asked.

"I'll tell you later," I said.

"Yeah," Kingman said. "Did a helluva job from what I hear. Let's see if you two can do the same."

"Can't we just get POTUS to cancel today?" I hoped.

Breaux cut in. "I bet it would take too long to convey the urgency of the situation to officials here at home. We're the ones found out that Asad was going to New Orleans. We're the ones with the intel to piece the puzzle together. We're the ones who can't take a chance in waiting – hoping that someone will listen and act."

"Well, well, well," Kingman finally cracked his first smile of the morning as he sat back and interlaced his hands behind his head. "You two aren't half as dumb as you look. You know the irony is if they'd been successful in Rio, POTUS would've cancelled this trip immediately. They never would've had a chance today. Anyway, now that you know what brought us all here today, let me point you in the right direction. You're not going to save the free world from this hotel suite."

"So where to, boss?" I asked.

"For starters, up one floor," Kingman pointed straight above his head.

"Al-Ayande is right up there?" I smirked.

"No smartass, but the Milaide and the Secret Service lead are. They're expecting you. I've given them what I have for intel. They can get you up to speed on their defensive capabilities. Help them figure out if we need to get the POTUS the hell out of Dodge."

Breaux and I stood up to leave.

"Martin, you go ahead," Kingman said. "I need to talk to J.D. for a minute."

Breaux did as he was told.

"Sit back down, J.D. – I have something I need to tell you."

CHAPTER 53

Kingman's demeanor turned dour. "I need to tell you something before you go."

"What's up sir?" I asked as I plopped back down on the couch; but not before grabbing myself a beignet from the platter.

"Something horrible happened last night. There's really no easy way to say this, but I felt it was important that someone who cared about you be the one to tell you."

"What is it?"

"It's your Mom and Dad. They were attacked at home late last night while asleep in bed." Kingman paused and looked away. It was not like him to do anything but look you in the eye and deliver with bluntness. I chewed but tasted nothing.

"Are they okay?"

"No J.D., they're not. They didn't make it." Kingman reached across the corner of the coffee table and placed a firm hand on my knee. My beignet fell to the floor.

I could see Kingman's lips move but was having a hard time hearing him. His voice warbled as if we were under water. He looked like he was a quarter mile from me as he sat in the next chair. I started to discern bits and pieces of what he said.

"...telephone line had been cut...alarm disabled...at least two men..."

I let him drone on for a long time. I felt like he must have been talking about someone neither of us personally knew.

I finally broke in, but only halfheartedly. "How were they killed?"

"Look J.D., this isn't easy. I didn't want to delve into the details, but I know you won't take *no* for an answer." Kingman breathed deeply before continuing. "From initial reports, it appears that it was a premeditated double homicide. Your mother's neck was snapped – your father suffered a fatal stab wound to the chest."

"Were there any witnesses?"

"Not known at this time."

I felt that if I kept talking I would be able to hold it together. "Suspects?"

"The police have no leads yet. I'm so sorry, J.D. You know how much I cared for both of them."

I must have waited too long for my subsequent response because I was instantly overcome by a tsunami of nausea. I leapt to my feet as my head emptied of oxygen. I stumbled in the direction of where I hoped the bathroom was, tripping over the coffee table and sending the continental breakfast for an unexpected flight. The only thing that made a larger splash pattern than the coffee on the carpet was my vomit on the wall beyond it. I fell to my knees and took a minute to gather myself before moving another muscle. When you lose that much self control there's no point in hurrying to try and regain your composure.

"It's okay J.D., I'm sure this city sees a lot worse in its hotel rooms."

I actually appreciated Kingman's attempt at humor. I think I even allowed a chunk-filled smile as I returned to my spot on the couch. Kingman handed me a towel as he continued.

"You know, Martin Breaux is a very capable officer. Not only that but he's a native."

"Sir, if you're thinking that blowing chow one time is going to keep me from accomplishing the mission, you've never been on the road with me." I paused long enough for Kingman to appreciate a lightly veiled reference to my affinity for late nights and hard partying.

He did. "Okay, okay. I suppose I'll let you play."

"Sir, I do have another question."

"What's up stud?"

"You said *the police* had no leads yet. I know you well enough to know you choose your words very carefully." I tried to read Kingman but saw nothing. "Who is *your* suspect, sir?"

A headshake but no verbal contradiction. *I was in.*

I just stared with a cocked head and determined look. I was not going anywhere without an answer. Kingman knew it.

"Alright J.D., listen. This is complicated, and I already told you we're pressed for time. You're going to have to settle for the *Reader's Digest* version for now."

"I'm ready sir."

"I'm not sure how much your mother told you about her past, but she worked for the embassy in Tehran in the 70's up until the revolution," Kingman began. "She worked there with your father, who served as an FSO in the economic branch."

"Right, and when the revolution hit, Mom's family was able to sneak her out of the country. They even offered to help Dad but he refused and stayed at the embassy to take care of business. That's why he got taken hostage. They rendezvoused in Boston once he was freed. I know all this, sir. What's the point?"

Kingman motioned for me to remain patient by easing his palms downward slowly.

"J.D., your mother was not romantically linked to Alexander Simon until they met in Boston, more than a year after his release from captivity. She *was* rushed out of town by her family under the cloak of darkness... that's true. But it was her nuclear family, not her powerful father. She was married at the time to a well-respected scientist by the name of Tourak Alam. She went by the name Ariana. It was during their escape from Iran that Tourak was killed by a suicide bomber. It was a miracle that Ariana managed to evade capture with her only child – her five year old son."

I could feel Kingman looking inside me, as if to pull something from within.

"The bombing – was there a helicopter?" I asked.

"Yes."

I felt as if the walls were closing in on me. There was heat, there was cold. I saw flashes of gray, then white, then black. My mind raced with images. Most were scenes from a recurring dream I'd had since, well, as long as I could recall.

I saw a young boy being woken from a sound sleep and dragged out of the house by his parents. The family drove for hours through the desert and mountains until daylight broke. They boarded a helicopter which was piloted by the father. They crossed what looked like the Persian Gulf and landed at a large airport. That's when it happened. The dream ended the same way every time. The man who greeted the helicopter, shook hands with the father, then blew himself up. Everything went black.

Except this time – this one time as I sat daydreaming in front of Colonel Kingman. This time the boy woke up in his mother's arms. They were both bloody and surrounded by burning wreckage, but alive. The mother called to the son. When he looked at her face it was *my mother's*. It was my mother. It was my father. It was me!

"Sir, was her son's name Rashid?"

"Yes, it was. Until she escaped to the States and changed it to J.D." Kingman answered.

I was floored. It felt as if I had been kicked in the gut. I might have heaved right then had I not already sullied the room moments earlier. I wanted to ask Kingman how in the hell he knew all this, how he could be so sure. But I knew he was right. I only wished that he wasn't. It was a perfect explanation for the dream that haunted me for my entire life. I watched my own father get assassinated and repressed the memory. My mother never had the heart to tell me. Besides, she needed to cover our tracks for our own safety. She moved us to the U.S., changed our identities, and started a new life for us. It worked for the better part of three decades. Had time finally caught up with her? Why? Who was responsible?

"Sir, all of this is truly earth shattering. But what does it have to do with last night?" I feared the answer I knew I would get.

"I believe that the same person is behind both crimes."

Yep, that's what I was afraid of.

While I sat in stunned silence, Kingman proceeded to tell the story of Tourak Alam and Hossein Zand. He told how the elder Alam had mentored the younger Zand as both men worked toward the development of an Iranian nuclear program. He explained how their political views took them down separate paths; the teacher remaining conservatively in support of the U.S., while the rebellious student strove toward the radical Muslim solution. Next he told the tale of a love triangle between the two men and a privileged young woman. The young woman by the name of Ariana Agassi had dated the hot-headed Zand but left him in favor of the older, refined, stable Alam. Tourak Alam and Ariana went on to happily marry and have a healthy son.

Me.

Zand, with his legendary temper, vowed to avenge his loss. He took his first step by killing my father that day in the helicopter. He missed his opportunity to kill my mother until today. Did he have further intentions for their son? As far as I was concerned, that fucker could bring it on! It would be the last mistake he ever made. All I had to do was find him.

"So where is this Hossein Zand now?" I tried to conceal my seething hatred.

"I know what you're thinking right now, J.D. I don't claim to feel your pain or anger, but I can assure you that I want this guy too. But I don't know for sure. Rumor is that he still works out of Iran, perhaps near Shiraz." Kingman stood and leaned over me, putting both hands on my shoulders. "J.D., I need to know if you have what it takes to finish the job here...in New Orleans...against al-Ayande...*today?*"

CHAPTER 54

By the time I entered the tenth-floor suite three people were huddled around a conference table reviewing documents. Martin Breaux was the only one not wearing a suit. Opposite him stood a tall blond surfer type who appeared uncomfortable in his light gray pinstripes. His hair was short at the neck and temples but sprouted atop his boyish head. He was one of those service men who never fully embraced the discipline of the military, but did enough to stay out of trouble. Next to him was a short but solidly built woman, not heavy but athletic. She wore a pantsuit and had her hair pulled tightly behind her head. I weighed which side of the plate she swung from before Breaux interrupted.

"I wondered if we were ever going to see you again," Breaux said as he motioned toward the two suits. "J.D. Simon, this is Commander Brandon Nelson, Milaide for this visit. And this is Margaret Anderson, lead Secret Service agent."

Introductions were completed with handshakes before Commander Nelson took control of the meeting with a command presence that stood in stark contrast to his laid back appearance. It was a characteristic I'd never gotten accustomed to amongst naval officers. Marines often make a snap judgment of others' professional character by their appearance. In the Navy, however, some of the best officers weren't clean cut or polished.

Nelson began, "Colonel Kingman already briefed us on al-Ayande's background in the area, so we started showing Martin some of our contingency plans. We touched on how we plan to fly him out of town if we need to, including fixed and rotary wing assets at our disposal. There's a subsequent plan involving a group of small Navy SEAL boats moored at the Canal Street dock. For now we'll review the primary and alternate motorcade routes."

Margaret Anderson leaned in over the table to brief her piece of the puzzle. Her body language was as mannish as her voice and handshake.

"Okay gents, take a look at this street map of the city," she said as she went into an orientation of the major arteries that would serve as the city's potential ingress and egress routes. She then reviewed in detail two different routes from the hotel to Jackson Square. I was a bit surprised to see that the most obviously direct one was the primary.

I interrupted, "Why are you taking the most direct route?"

She sighed as if bothered by a moronic child. "We have our contingency motorcade taking the alternate route as a *dummy*. Anybody paying attention will not be sure which is the real deal, but might be inclined to believe that we would rather take POTUS along the more circuitous route."

I nodded in sheepish approval. Okay, so it was the not the first time I've shown my ass...won't be the last either. What's that axiom about no stupid questions?

She laid down a blowup of the square and pinpointed spots where well armed agents would be providing countersurveillance. The omnipresent balconies of the French Quarter made for ideal overwatch positions. The Service had definitely done their homework when it came to countering any threat that might emerge while the president was conducting his site visits. Their fields of fire intersected in a manner that covered as many enemy possibilities as could be hoped for given such a venue. The Quarter was ridden with innumerable nooks and crannies for people to hide in, presenting a huge security challenge.

Their plan involved a large number of plain-clothed agents on the street, armed with pistols and radios. Their purpose was to provide immediate suppression in order to make time to call in the big guns.

The major firepower would come from high-powered rifles above street level and heavy automatic weapons inside bullet-proof vehicles. The black SUVs were going to be staged on either side of the Saint Louis Cathedral, enabling rapid response regardless of where an attack emerged from.

As Anderson wrapped up her dissertation on the Service assets, the Milaide and Breaux nodded in tacit approval. I was left unconvinced, and continued to dig in spite of being mildly slapped down after my last question.

"What about those air assets?" I asked to the group in general.

Nelson jumped in on this one, either because this was his realm or he recognized that he possessed greater skills of diplomacy than his Service counterpart.

"We began to pass that info on to Martin, but we can review it for both of your benefit. We've got a layered defense, starting with some fixed wing assets responsible for intercept if anything enters a thirty mile ring of the French Quarter or the airport. We'll have an AWACS flying up top acting as command and control for all other assets and as a comm link so that we know we can get a hold of anybody at the drop of a hat. One of their primary missions is to control the launch and employment of a section of F-22 Raptors on strip alert at Keesler Air Force Base in Biloxi."

I'd never witnessed the Air Force's newest toy enter into actual combat operations, but had seen it display its unprecedented flight characteristics during some flight tests at Edwards AFB in the late 90's. Its extraordinary maneuverability, inspired by thrust-vectoring nozzles, was overkill given that there would not be any viable airborne threat on this mission. Nonetheless, the combined thrust of 70,000 pounds from its two Pratt and Whitney turbofans would make its response time optimal if it needed to bring its air-to-air Sidewinder missiles to bear. Whenever briefed on such a plan, I couldn't help but speculate as to whether or not we'd have the gumption to down an interloping aircraft over a populated area. The intercept and takedown would have to occur over the surrounding swampland before it reached the metro area.

Nelson continued with the rundown of airborne contingencies. "If we have something a little closer into the city we've got some helo support lined up. Pre-movement route surveillance will be conducted by the Service in a Coast Guard Dolphin. They'll also have snipers onboard during the motorcade movements, in direct contact with both the counter-assault team and New Orleans SWAT on the ground."

Now the plan sounded like it was really coming to together.

Nelson had more. "The Marines also have a helo at New Orleans International, just in case POTUS needs a lift somewhere he can't get in Air Force One." He did not elaborate. I figured I didn't have a need to know.

It was clear the advance team had done a yeoman's job in preparing to react to any type of attack launched against the president. We all understood that if somebody wanted to get to him badly enough that they would be able to do it. That's why the U.S. had long ago decided to establish a continuity of government plan in the event of the loss of the president. That didn't make me any less uncomfortable. It was one thing to be ready to react. That was the job of the Milaide and Secret Service. It was another to preempt an attack from occurring. That was my job. I looked at Breaux and could see the same concern in his eyes and furrowed brow.

I had to tell them what they did not want to hear. "These plans are great, no doubt. You guys are the true professionals at what you do. But I must do my job as well; which is to inform you that the probability of an attempt on the POTUS is not just possible, but likely."

I allowed that to hang in the air for a moment. "Your defenses are designed to counter possibilities. You would need a full-blown military force to ensure his safety during this visit. One that could afford to sustain collateral damage. I don't believe that's something that would sit well with the public; to see innocents gunned down in the streets in order to rush Estevanez to safety. Especially if it ever came out that we knew ahead of time."

"If we canceled every time we had a credible threat we'd almost never travel," Anderson chimed in. "The presidency would be crippled, and we'd serve no purpose. What makes you so certain?"

Breaux jumped in before I could. "Asad, the leader of al-Ayande, is in town; and it's not for the crawfish gumbo and sazeracs."

Nelson stared intently at each one of us before he spoke.

"Margaret, what do you make of this?" he asked.

"Boy this is a tough one," the lead agent pondered. "Very disconcerting. But let's noodle this through. We can make sure we limit his exposure outside; cover his every outdoor movement with vehicular blocking. He won't be happy about it but we can insist. Both sites have been thoroughly swept for explosives and secured overnight. Each and every person that enters either the restaurant or the cathedral will be run through at least handheld mags."

I wished that I had more tangible evidence to make my argument. I tried. "I just got in town from Rio. As I'm sure you know there was an attempt on the first lady last night. What you may not know is that it was orchestrated by al-Ayande. It didn't involve any high-tech weaponry, and was carried out by a force completely comprised of natives. These were homegrown terrorists and gangsters that had been secretly funded, armed, trained, and inspired by an invisible foreign force: al-Ayande. It's the same thing that's happening here; same background, same training, same disgruntled natives. You have to realize just how creative and resourceful these assholes are. They're every bit as sneaky as al-Qaeda, but have not done as much to piss people off yet. The downtrodden locals see them as people who genuinely want to help. Therefore, the locals will help cover their tracks. You may never see the attack coming until it's too late."

The Milaide responded. "I'm just playing devil's advocate here, but don't we hear this chatter all the damn time? What's different about this particular time? It's not as if these guys have been as big a problem as al-Qaeda."

"True nuff," Breaux intervened. "But I bet there were people saying that stuff just before the World Trade Center bombing in '93, or the Kohbar Towers in '96, or the African embassies in '98, or the..."

"Okay, okay, I get it," Nelson nodded his head as he pulled out his cell phone. "I'll talk to the staff lead about amending or canceling the plans."

CHAPTER 55

Satisfied that we had just done our part to preserve the presidency, Breaux and I were sitting at Café du Monde over a couple of café au laits. I was greedily stuffing my face with piping hot beignets, filling the void I had created by my earlier purge in Kingman's suite. It was the first time I'd been able to relax in days. In between bites I took in the sites. Despite the cool, damp air there was a mix of early rising tourists and wayward revelers still meandering about from the night prior. The sun was trying to warm Jackson Square, where artists set up their wares under the shade of umbrellas and oak trees.

"Who are you calling…family?" I asked Breaux as he dialed his mobile device.

"Nah, they'd never understand how I could come all the way here and not spend every minute with them. I'm checking in with the boss," Breaux said to me just before talking to his phone. "Sir, it's Martin. It looks like the trip is off, so J.D. and I are going to head over to the Ninth Ward and do some gathering. Give me a call if you have anything for us. Out here."

"Straight to voice mail?" I asked. Breaux nodded. "He must be on a plane outta here; didn't waste any time, did he?"

"That guy's a ghost, man. It's like, was he even here?" Breaux posed rhetorically.

"Yeah," I half-answered as I thought about the ghosts he had raised from my past. I was going to enjoy a few days off when I got back to Boston…after the funeral, of course. By the time I got back to D.C., I was going to be more than ready to tear into Angie. I wondered if Martin was the type of black man who resented non-black guys who dated sisters; like it diluted their dating pool. I didn't ask. I already badmouthed his home city and just wanted some peace and quiet for the time being.

That was broken by the buzz of my phone. It was a *private* number, which I hated because it could be anybody with a government-issued phone.

Begrudgingly, I answered.

"Simon. It's Brandon Nelson. Bad news, I got shot in the face by the White House staff lead. He talked to the Man, who assured him that he would not be intimidated on U.S. soil. The site visits are all a go. We're on schedule."

Shit.

"Alright. Can we help?" I asked. I had hoped for a break, but certainly wanted to make sure that I got to help if it meant protecting the president. Nelson informed me that I could drive to the Canal Street dock area to pick up the necessary equipment. Look for the black windowless van with all the antennae on top. WHCA personnel would be waiting for us.

I hung up and turned to Breaux. "Let's go." He needed no explanation; he knew exactly what had transpired during the call.

Breaux and I were outfitted with new accoutrements, most of which were to be worn underneath our casual clothes so that we would blend in with the locals. Much like the Secret Service agents who were surreptitiously patrolling the streets of the French Quarter, our only giveaway was a temporary pin the size of a quarter that we would need to show in order to gain access to any controlled area. Its specific design characteristics would also alert any agent that we were armed and authorized to be so.

Speaking of arms, we were each issued a SIG Sauer P229 along with three magazines of .357 rounds. The handgun, though not my Glock, was a welcome backup. They didn't need to know I was already packing that heat. Breaux, who had his own Beretta concealed under his shirttail, agreed the more firepower the better. A couple of pistols may not be much, but it would help us blast our way out of a jam.

Perhaps the most important pieces of gear we received were the handheld radios that would enable us to monitor every movement. Much like the Motorola I used yesterday in Rio, the radio was capable of scanning multiple channels and encrypting all transmissions. The WHCA soldier who issued us the radios provided a hip-pocket class, running down how each frequency was represented by a letter on the display, how to operate the keys, and how to hook up the ear piece and microphone. With radios and weapons neatly tucked under our coats, Breaux and I thanked the technician and headed back to our rental car.

After conducting a habitual walk-around of the vehicle for tampering, we drove the short distance back to Jackson Square. We decided to split forces so we could observe more than one locale. We were used to operating independently and there was no reason for us to be covering half the ground with two men. Breaux was going to make his way around the square and pretend to be window shopping while he observed the area nearby the two sites to be visited by Estevanez. Based on the schedule and the radio traffic we'd heard so far, the Man was already inside Muriel's partaking of a lavish brunch – and politicking with wealthy locals and government officials, of course.

As the French Quarter disappeared in the rear view mirror of my Cobalt, so did the façade that New Orleans had been resurrected post-Katrina. Dilapidation increased slowly as I cruised the back streets through the neighborhoods of Faubourg Marigny and Bywater. It was not unlike some of the rougher parts of Roxbury back home. But nothing could have prepared me for what I would see once across the Claiborne Bridge. The Ninth Ward looked like a cross between a former war zone and a desolated ghost town.

I surveyed the damage along Jourdan Avenue, which butted up against levees that had been rebuilt. These new walls, tasked with the defense of the ward, lacked the extra reinforcements that were a part of the levees rebuilt for the wealthier neighborhoods. Tall grass obscured house foundations, hiding the only evidence that there were ever residences on this street. It was obvious that no effort had been made to rebuild structures. I turned right and headed a few streets away from the levee.

Abandoned piles of wood and trash that used to be houses were strewn about at random. Cars were upside down in torn down garages; broken appliances lay atop caved in roofs. One empty house frame had a handwritten sign tacked to the front door.

Due to a lack of help from our governments this is where we stand. Nothing being done to help us. Look at our neighbood very good. It is gone. <u>Pray</u> that our people be able to come home to something a home.

It didn't appear as if any government was going to do much to rebuild. Officials had gone through each structure to search for signs of life, as indicated by the codes spray-painted on the front of each. Nothing more than a date of inspection, which agency conducted it, any pets found, and numbers of dead bodies.

As I drove east on Prieur Street, I approached an oasis of life amid an otherwise dead swamp. New modular homes sat on old foundations; lawns were mowed and young trees had been planted. As I crossed the aptly named Flood Street, I passed the centerpiece of this gentrification project; a red brick church that appeared to have been gutted and refurbished. I drove a block further before turning around and stopping a hundred yards short of the church. I unfolded a black and white photo that Kingman had gotten from the FBI. It featured an old church, converted to a mosque by al-Ayande. Perfect match.

The 1842 on the side of the building was still present, but the brick cross built into the adjacent wall had been painted over. Spartan in nature, the exterior was decorated with traditional Muslim trimmings. A sign above the entrance read *In the Name of Allah, the Beneficent, the Merciful*. There was little else remarkable about the building, which was quiet on Ash Wednesday morning. I eased the car forward when I noticed two other things. One was the telephone pole next to the building. The lack of telephone wires running to or from it was not unusual given the overall state of disrepair. But the radio antennae affixed to it were. They ran into the side of the building. The other item of note was the SUV parked at the far end. The Lincoln Navigator was far and away the highest end vehicle I'd seen within the entire ward.

I scanned the area and saw no other activity outside the mosque. My gut told me the men inside were manning some sort of command and control hub. I was hesitant to sneak in without any assistance. However, my gut also told me that I did not have the time to wait for backup. The leadership of al-Ayande was not going to come all the way to New Orleans at the same time as the POTUS, with all the assets in place, and not capitalize. Something was going to happen; something serious; something soon. I took a deep breath, chambered rounds in both my pistols, and double-checked the radio battery before leaving the security of my car for the unknown inside the mosque.

CHAPTER 56

The mosque's inside lacked the lavish flair that typified those found in the oil-rich Middle East. It was even less extravagant than what I'd personally seen in Rio just yesterday. But it was clean and neat despite its tattered exterior. Maybe they hadn't gotten around to fixing the outside, or perhaps they meant to hide the goings on held within.

I could smell the faint scent of the pale green paint that couldn't have been more than a few days old. There were only three Arabian-style rugs in the room's center; from the low ceiling hung not chandeliers but fluorescent lights and ceiling fans. It was a utilitarian haven for locals to come find a God that would not abandon them when disaster struck.

The lights were out and the ceiling fans still as I slunk slowly toward what appeared to be an office on the far end of the large rectangular space. I heard voices, some in person and others via radio transmissions.

I knew it made no tactical sense for me to approach any closer without help, but my adrenaline pulled me. I could now hear that the voices in the room were a mix of African-American and Arab men. Sounded like maybe two or three, which meant that double that number were likely in the room.

Backtrack and call for help.

You don't have time. Listen for what you can hear. Intervene only if you need to.

I stood just outside the open doorway, my back pressed up against the adjacent wall. I grasped my Glock tightly to my chest. I could barely hear the voices over the beating of my own heart. I took long, slow breaths through my nose. I heard a radio crackle to life.

"The target is leaving the restaurant," the radio voice said in a heavy southern accent. "He's well covered by people and vehicles. I don't think we can get to him."

I expected to hear a discussion in the room next to me, but there was only brief silence broken by a powerful Arab voice – a Persian voice.

"Do not fear, my brother. You will not fail. Asad is with you; al-Ayande is with you; Allah is with you. Go forth and complete your mission – now!"

Holy shit! Was I too late? There was only one way to find out, and it was not by staying out here.

I swung into the doorway, legs braced widely and arms extended forward, ready to fire.

"Freeze, assholes!"

Five men, two black and three Arab, stared back at me with weapons hoisted in my direction. In an instant I recognized Asad in the middle of the group. The only reason I wasn't immediately gunned down must have been my pistol pointed directly at the al-Ayande boss. The others likely feared that if a shot were fired I would drop their leader before I succumbed. A correct assumption.

I stole quick glances around the room. An office that housed radios and laptops, it appeared to serve double duty as administrative office for the mosque and intelligence gathering facility for al-Ayande. There was a desk in the corner with pictures of a black man and his family. In one photo, he stood in front of a congregation. He didn't wear traditional Muslim garb, but instead a black suit, white shirt and black tie, a la Malcolm X or Louis Farrakhan. The same man, in the same suit, stood in front of me at Asad's side. I wondered if he fomented the same vile innuendo as the leader of the Nation of Islam, who implied the levees had been blown up to destroy the black part of town and keep the white part dry. No doubt that would've helped convince the impoverished locals that Islam was their religion of hope. That became the foundation upon which al-Ayande had built not only new homes, but a jihadist mentality. That mentality was being transformed into action this very day – this Christian holiday.

Time was not on my side. I needed to be bold, and lucky, if this terror plot was to be stopped.

"Put down your weapons if you want Asad to live!" I barked.

Asad laughed. "Perhaps you didn't notice, but you're a bit outnumbered. Besides, if you shoot me down I will only grow stronger in death. But I don't expect an infidel to understand such things."

"I understand a lot more than you think, Asad. I know what you tried to pull in Rio, and I know it was just a ruse to get the president."

"Okay, big deal," Asad shrugged. "You're too late to stop anything from happening to your precious leader anyway. Did you think that you could just walk in here, wave a gun in my face, and have me call off the operation? Your arrogance, though enormous, does not surprise me."

Marines were known around the world to be cocksure, and I was no exception. I assumed that's what Asad meant, until he continued.

"You have the same cockiness as your father," he said with a smug smirk that peeked out from underneath his thick black mustache.

"What the fuck are you talking about?" I asked. "First off, my father's a mild-mannered professor. Second, what would you know about me or my family?"

His smirk grew to a wide smile. "Well, Captain Simon, I know more about you than you think. In fact, I may know more about you than you do."

I was getting heated by anger, but allowed the terror leader to continue. I wanted to see where he was going and how he knew my name. And I was still plotting my next step; preferably one that would keep me alive.

"I'm not talking about the *late* Alexander Simon. I'm talking about your *real* father. The *first* father of yours I killed." His smile transformed into an angry glare.

I was struck with a moment of clarity unlike I'd ever experienced. Asad was Hossein Zand. Zand was Asad. They were the same man. This man that stood in front of me had spent the better part of the last three decades trying to murder my family. Of course, that's when he wasn't busy trying to conduct worldwide jihad.

My clear mind didn't last long. Within seconds I became blinded by rage. This was going to end right here, right now. My finger was already on the trigger. Five and a half pounds of pressure later and I would be looking at Asad's head splattered on the white wall behind him. I would be gunned down immediately, so that would be the last thing I ever saw. Given what this asshole had done to my family and the world that would be fine with me. Radical Muslims weren't the only ones who could martyr themselves.

I pulled the trigger smoothly but never got off a round. The room was rocked by an explosion that knocked me out temporarily. When I came to, the room was still filled with smoke which I could only sense by smell. I could not see and I could barely hear a thing. An African-American voice spoke to me as someone grabbed me under the armpits and hoisted me to my feet.

"Man, you got some balls on you," the voice spoke, presumably to me. "I don't think I woulda just sauntered in here with nothing on me but a pistol."

"My balls always were bigger than my brains," I said while trying to blink my vision back.

"Hold on," he said while wrapping my left arm over his shoulders. He guided my way until I began to see the light that meant we were outside. I was so taken aback by all that was going on that I only now realized I didn't know who my savior was.

"Not that I'm in much of a position to question right now, but who the hell are you?"

"The name's Leon Sims. I'm an agent in the N'awlins FBI office. We've been surveilling these guys for a while, as I'm sure you know. I heard you might be snooping around these parts so I kept an eye out for you. Not too hard to miss a white dude in this neighborhood."

My vision was clearing up enough to see that we were about to get into a silver Ford Explorer. "Funny, I was never white enough for most of the people back in Boston."

Sims chuckled as he shifted gears. "Those guys in there are not going to stay down forever, and we don't stand a chance around here without big time back-up. Let's get the hell outta here."

"Where to?" I asked.

"Dunno, but not here. Got any ideas?" he posed.

"Yeah, as a matter of fact I do. How fast can you get us to the airport?"

CHAPTER 57

Richard Estevanez stood at the altar, looking understated in his dark blue suit and pale blue tie. A classic look for a man in power attempting to appear deferential to his surroundings; all the while internally enjoying the spotlight. He was no priest but was completely at ease speaking to the Catholic congregation. After all, his audience had been handpicked: old friends, wealthy contributors, power-seeking politicians. All desiring to remain in favor.

The sermon had already been delivered by the priest, but on this day it was merely an appetizer. The main course was being served by a master of the trade, a man who'd made his fortune in front of television audiences of millions. As he began to speak, the television cameras in the rear of Saint Louis cathedral came to life. Red lights aimed forward like lasers as cameramen shuffled to acquire the perfect shot. The center aisle of the venerable church made for a dramatic picture; its enormous arched ceiling bordered on either side by rows of flags and skirted by monumental stained glass windows. Situated at the heart of this city that had endured such hardship, the backdrop sent the message that through any travails, faith in God and determination could prevail.

This message was not intended for the hundreds that sat in front of the president; it was designed to reassure American citizens that their government was fully capable of responding to disaster. It was designed to address the infamous failures during the immediate aftermath of the hurricane.

"Good morning, my fellow Catholics and all faithful Americans. I'm honored and humbled to be able to speak to you from this awe-inspiring house of God. Ash Wednesday is a day with a message that transcends any one religion. It signifies the start of the Lenten season; one of sacrifice, self reflection, and spiritual redirection. We are not meant to limit our actions to one day, however. It is to serve as a reminder of how we should act everyday toward our fellow man. I will read a passage from the book of Isaiah.

"Is it not to share your food with the hungry and to provide the poor wanderer with shelter...when you see the naked, to clothe him, and not to turn away from your own flesh and blood?"

"If you spend yourselves in behalf of the hungry and satisfy the needs of the oppressed then your light will rise in the darkness, and your night will become like the noonday."

"Your people will rebuild the ancient ruins and will raise up the age-old foundations; you will be called Repairer of Broken Walls, Restorer of Streets with Dwellings."

"The word of God," the president said as he closed the Bible.

There was a long pause during which only a crying baby could be heard echoing in the cavernous confines of the cathedral.

"I am quite proud of the efforts that have been made here in New Orleans and her surrounding areas. I recognize that we still have a long way to climb to the top of this mountain. However, the sacrifices made by folks like you and many others around the country have gone a long way toward repairing the walls and restoring the streets with dwellings."

Estevanez continued, but Martin Breaux knew he was witness to little more than political spin. He had grown up watching this kind of rhetoric on his mother's small, static-obscured television set. He heard stories that regaled uplifting the poorest locales; he saw none of it in his poverty-stricken neighborhood. When a young Martin asked his mother about the discrepancy, she responded that the monies hadn't trickled down to them yet. It had dried up on the way.

"What do you think of this?" a voice whispered to Breaux. It was the Secret Service agent who had escorted him into the event. Breaux barely had time to get his name before the young black man hurried him into a nearby safehouse to change into a spare suit that had been dug up from somewhere. Agent Bruce was out of the local New Orleans office, not part of the presidential protective detail. It was standard procedure for the PPD to augment their cadre of personnel with local agents. The technique provided extra muscle and increased local area knowledge. They were typically given menial security tasks such as guarding hallways, alleys, and other access or chokepoints. Not about to be read into the extensive plans to protect the president, these agents were more accustomed to chasing down small time money-launderers than thwarting major assassination attempts. PPD agents were the elite force with the premier mission; when they rolled into town every other agent was mere support.

"Typical political stuff," Breaux responded. He had gauged that Bruce saw the world through the same colored lens as he did. Two black kids from New Orleans witnessing the same old song and dance. Promises of government money that never made it to those who needed it most.

"Amen, brother." Bruce reached over to Breaux as the two men tapped fists in solidarity.

Agent Bruce stood from his seat, slid out of the pew, and walked away without a word. He positioned himself against the side wall underneath the glow that emanated from the stained glass window above his head.

Breaux observed the agent, but his curiosity regarding the unexplained relocation was abruptly interrupted. There was a sudden outburst from one of the front pews. A large, older man of mixed racial descent stood and began to speak loudly. With spittle flying haphazardly from his mouth, his comments were aimed directly at President Estevanez. The man's girth and ill-fitting white suit had become quite recognizable on the New Orleans political scene in the days and months following Katrina.

Jimmy Ford was merely one of seven city council members, and was neither the president nor vice president. He was the outspoken representative for District E, which included the Ninth Ward and areas east of downtown. He'd made a name for himself by regularly breaking ranks with the council and chastising any and every political bureaucracy for the lack of progress being made to rebuild the city. Reviled by other officials that found his grandstanding to be counterproductive, Ford's rants resonated with the poor blacks of the Ninth Ward. These were the same people that, like Ford, had turned away from the Christian establishment that had seemingly turned its back on them. Believing that he was doing the right thing, Ford had helped al-Ayande gain its foothold in the area.

"Mr. President, the good people of this city have suffered long enough at the hands of the wealthy and powerful that do nothing more than talk and take...talk and take! You and all the rest; my fellow council members, the mayor, the governor, whoever; you talk about all the progress and all the money. But we never see it. The only explanation is that the money is being taken for other projects or to line pocketbooks. Talk and take!"

The rotund loudmouth was intent on continuing his tirade on national television. He was in the presence of Louisiana's oldest money holders that didn't know how to react to this outburst. They were frozen into inaction the same way they would have been had one of them been stopped in a dark alleyway by a menacing thief with the wrong color skin. Even the president was shocked into momentary silence.

"The time for change is now!" Ford yelled as three Secret Service agents converged quickly, pushing and shoving their way through crowded pews.

"The time is now!" He yelled again as he was taken down to the ground by the armed men in suits.

The scuffle between the fat man and the undercover agents was short-lived, but proved to be a precursory order for action. Out of the corner of his eye Breaux caught a glimpse of something small and black flying through the air. What he thought at first may have been a small bird proved not to be as it fell to the floor at the base of the altar. It clanked along a bit and came to rest only ten feet from the foot of the president. All attention was on the targeted leader and the grenade that lay near his feet. He was immediately grabbed by the agent-in-charge and yanked in the direction of a doorway to the side of the altar.

Another agent leapt from his post in the front row toward the grenade as it began to hiss and smoke. The agent decided against flopping onto the grenade once he realized that it was some sort of smoke device rather than an explosive. The stunned crowd clambered frantically to its feet as it looked with horror at the smoke.

The agent nearest the grenade began to yell, "Gas, gas, gas!" Then he started to choke and fell to the floor.

CHAPTER 58

Breaux scanned the interior of the cathedral. The crowd grew increasingly chaotic as people struggled to get to the exit. The tight bottleneck at the double doors left most looking back toward the altar in an effort to see what had become of the gas grenade and the president. Those wedged in closest to the altar were becoming enveloped by smoke; bodies began to drop as they succumbed to the noxious fumes. The few that were nearest the exit stared toward it in hopes that they could will themselves outside to fresh air. That left nobody looking anywhere else in the church. That is, nobody other than Breaux.

Breaux stepped atop his pew to get a bird's eye view. Following a hunch, he looked to where Agent Bruce had been standing only seconds ago. It was the same direction from where the grenade had been tossed. Sure enough, the agent hadn't moved from that spot. The only difference was that he was now hoisting a short-barreled automatic weapon from under his overcoat. From the distance Breaux could not be sure what kind it was. It looked to be about the size and shape of an MP5, but current circumstances precluded further investigation.

Bruce yelled something that could not be heard over the growing din of the crowd that echoed in the cathedral. Breaux drew his pistol and aimed directly at Bruce's chest. Eyes glazed over with rage, Bruce never saw Breaux. The traitorous agent had his weapon aimed at the far right end of the crowd that was fighting to escape. He had just begun to squeeze the trigger as he was caught in the leg with the first round. His trigger pull interrupted, he looked up at Breaux just in time to get slammed in the chest with round number two. Seeing he was on target, Breaux delivered rounds three and four. The agent fell to the floor as the fifth sailed harmlessly over his head.

Breaux could feel his PDA buzzing away in his pocket; the message was from Simon.

Ambush at St Louis.
They want to flush POTUS into Jackson Square.
Use other route to escape.

A bit late about the ambush thing, but I guess it's good to know the hit is meant for Jackson Square. As if on cue, Breaux heard the sounds of gunshots ringing from the square. He pushed his way the opposite direction toward the altar, holding his breath and closing his eyes as he passed by the still smoldering canister. He ran through the doorway where he'd last seen the Secret Service escort the president. He found himself in a dark, narrow hallway crowded with White House staffers, armed agents, and support personnel all loudly discussing their next move.

Breaux was able to maneuver about halfway down the corridor before he was stopped by a PPD agent.

"We're keeping this path closed off for now," the agent said sternly. Breaux had an authorized lapel pin on, but just the temporary kind that the Service issued to local agents. The agent that stopped Breaux wore the permanent pin issued only to personnel with clearance to operate in close proximity to the president. This was a sign to Breaux that he was getting close to the folks he was looking for.

"I need to get a message through to either the agent-in-charge or the Milaide," Breaux said breathlessly. The agent stared back as if to ask why. "I just received intel as to the nature of this attack and…dammit man, can you just call?!"

"I'm sorry, what was your name?" the PPD agent asked.

Breaux could see he did not have time for this. "Forget it," he muttered as he turned away. He pulled out his WHCA-issued radio and hoped that he could remember how to use it from the thirty-second class he'd received. He knew each of the frequencies had an associated letter on the radio display, but could not recall who was on which frequency. Assuming that the radio was encrypted, he used plain language.

"Commander Nelson, this is Martin Breaux. How do you copy?" he said, paused long enough for a response then flipped to the next frequency. It only took two tries before success. The Milaide asked where Breaux was and told him to hold his position.

Seconds later the tall naval officer emerged from the door that the PPD agent had been guarding. His shaggy blond hair was even more disheveled than before.

"Good to see you Martin. What've you got?"

"I just got word from Simon that they're trying to flush POTUS out into Jackson Square. We need to either keep him in here or get him out a different way."

"Come with me," Nelson said as he grabbed Breaux by the arm and guided him past the stern gaze of the agent guarding the door. Behind the door was a restroom in which stood about ten people, among them a couple of PPD agents, a White House physician, and President Estevanez.

Nelson provided cursory introductions and kept the discussion moving.

"Okay everyone, we need to decide our next couple of moves. Martin Breaux has informed me there is an ambush set up in Jackson Square, so that's a definite non-starter. We can either wait it out in here until the police can get some order restored or we can try to use the contingency motorcade. Is there any compelling reason that we should not stay right here for now?"

The president sat in silence on the sink countertop, his face buried in his hands. He may have been the leader of a world superpower, but recent events reduced him to a captive of circumstances. During such emergencies, it was protocol that mandated the Milaide run the show with input from the senior agent-in-charge.

"Yeah, we don't know what the hell's in that fucking grenade...or how many more's coming our way," said Frank Castiglione. He was the most familiar face of the PPD inner circle, the personal protector of the president during not only the Estevanez administration but his predecessor as well. Nobody knew the job better, and it showed through his demeanor. Castiglione showed the same cool, almost disdainful, tone as he did when he was a young cop walking the beat in North Philly. He'd been shot at and stabbed by perps on the streets back in the 1980's and was not about to be fazed by anybody. At least he would never show it. He prided himself on maintaining a stoic exterior and providing few words. "We need to get the fuck outta here...ASAP!"

"Anybody else?" Nelson asked. If there were dissenters, they were not willing to challenge the grizzled agent-in-charge.

"Okay, so where's the motorcade?" the Milaide asked.

"Parked out on Royal Street. I'll have 'em here in thirty goddam seconds," Castiglione answered.

"Before you call I have one more question. Where do we take him?" Nelson asked as if the president were not even in the room. "I'd recommend we call up *Nighthawk* and have them meet us at the riverfront LZ."

The Marine Corps Blackhawk variant was one of the helicopters that provided administrative transportation for the executive branch. When not operating as Marine One, its mission was to evacuate the president in the event that he was in danger or severely injured. The pilots and crew had been on standby at the airport since the president's arrival and were ready to launch at a moment's notice. The advance officer for the Marine helicopter had worked with the Secret Service to determine prearranged landing zones in the event of an emergency. The riverfront landing zone referred to an open area of grass on the banks of the Mississippi River, only six blocks from the cathedral.

Nelson continued. "They can be there in nine minutes. Then get us a couple hundred miles out of town. From there we've got other options depending on what develops. What do you think Frank?"

"If I had my choice we'd keep him in *the Beast* the whole way back to D.C."

The primary limousine was a hefty, bullet-proof stretch Cadillac DTS, designed specifically to take some hits and keep going. A luxury tank, it was equipped with not only physical survival capabilities, but robust communications gear that could keep the president in touch while in transit.

"I just don't like the idea of too many transfers into aircraft that can get knocked out of the sky. Realistically, I'd say we gotta drive to the airport ASAP and get onto AF-1."

Nelson turned to the president. "Sir, do you have a problem with that idea?"

Estevanez still appeared to be in shock as he absorbed the question. He slid from his countertop perch and stood as tall as his strength would allow. He tugged gently on his lapels and cleared his throat. "We can't let these assholes beat us. You folks have my confidence. Let's do this."

Like a pack of hungry attack dogs released from their leashes, the agents and Milaide snapped into action. The salty Castiglione grabbed the president by the arm and followed the armed PPD agents out the door; the physician scurried to keep pace.

With a single radio call from the lead agent, the contingency motorcade slipped from its spot on Royal Street and arrived just outside the iron gate surrounding the cathedral's north-facing courtyard. The PPD agents hurried their protectee past the Christ statue that seemed to give a gentle push with outstretched arms. Commander Nelson jogged a few paces behind, trying to keep up while toting the bulging nuclear football.

The barebones motorcade consisted of no more than four bulletproof Suburbans, of which the first three were loaded up with those escaping the compromised church. The fourth was already occupied by a well-armed counter-assault team. As the SUVs pulled away the CAT vehicle rode in the trail position with hatchback open and heavy machine guns directed menacingly into the city streets. Locals and tourists parted like the Red Sea as they observed the oncoming flashing lights. Despite fearing the worst, the motorcade departed the French Quarter unmolested.

Breaux wasn't surprised that he had been abruptly left behind. The professionals took the immediate actions for which they were trained, and weren't about to take along any strap-hangers. Still armed with his pistols, he ran back through the now mostly empty cathedral. The smoke that hung in the air inside was highlighted by sunlight that knifed in through the windows. It paled in comparison to the smoke and commotion that was building outside.

As he approached the double-doors that opened onto Jackson Square, Breaux was witness to the carnage that had been intended for the president. It was difficult to tell where all the shots were coming from. The square was lined with thick old oak trees; the bordering streets were ringed by balconies and dark windows. With the amount of cross-fire and smoke there was bound to be friendly fire on both sides of the battle. Breaux could see that most rooftops were mounted by Secret Service agents in black fatigues with binoculars and high-powered rifles. On the ground were also well-armed men in black; yet their blouses had the markings of New Orleans SWAT. The ground forces were flushing those they determined to be innocents from the area, while trying to corral those that were not. Despite their best intentions, the SWAT and USSS troops were having a difficult time due to the terrorists' ability to blend in with the other locals.

Hidden from outside view was an abandoned second-floor room that overlooked the square. Inside sat two local men who'd been displaced from their lifelong Ninth Ward homes by Katrina. Among the many that had subsequently been indoctrinated by al-Ayande, one sat armed guard as the other manned a command and control radio. The radio operator had been surprised at first to hear that he had been talking to the actual leader of the movement; by now he was corresponding with comfort and openness. Like those that had previously gone to battle under Asad's command, this young man had been instilled with confidence by his leadership and inspired to do his every bidding.

"Sir, I'm sorry but we ain't seen our target. We're losing folks and achievin nuttin! What should we do?! Should we leave?! Should we fight?! I just don't know what to do. I don't know what to do," the radio operator said.

"Not to worry my son," Asad replied. "I have expected that this might happen. You have to believe that those that have given their lives have not given them in vain. I do not have time to explain now, but trust me when I tell you that I have a plan for this. Allow your men to continue to bleed the enemy as they are right now. Our soldiers will occupy the enemy so that they cannot otherwise help to protect their president. It is a good and useful battle that you are fighting right now. Continue – to the death if necessary."

"Allah akbar," the radio operator answered.

"Allah akbar," Asad answered before turning to his assistants. "It is time to implement our backup plan. Call our men at the airport and advise them that our target is coming their way. This may be our last chance at success; they must not fail."

CHAPTER 59

As we raced westbound on I-10 toward New Orleans international airport, I noticed an increase in police activity and the disappearance of radio traffic on the Motorola that WHCA had issued to me. More cops meant that the motorcade was not far behind us. I was concerned enough about the quiet radio to try and call Commander Nelson. No answer. I switched frequencies and tried Agent Anderson. No answer. I called Martin on his cell. He gave a brief synopsis of the fireworks that had occurred at the cathedral. We were left to guess that comms had been taken out either as collateral damage from the battle at Jackson Square or on purpose. Either way, it was going to make getting the president safely out of town a greater challenge.

I hung up with Breaux and turned to my driver, FBI agent Leon Sims. I explained to him what I knew and we began to brainstorm as to where we could go next.

"I say we gotta go directly to AF-1," I said. "I heard the Milaide say it's parked outside of Signature Flight Support. You know where that is?"

"Yeah I know where it's at. But we'll never get close to that place right now. Even with creds they'll have that son-of-a-bitch in lockdown. No sir, that ain't gonna work." He answered.

"You got any better ideas?"

Sims thought in silence for a few seconds. "As a matter of fact I do. We can go to the cargo side of the airport. It'll be a little easier to get access."

"Then what?" I asked.

"Give me a minute," Sims said. "I'll come up with something."

My cell phone rang. It was Martin again.

He spoke as if out of breath. "J.D., we may have even bigger problems. While I was still at the cathedral I got a call from Kingman. He told me a suspicious aircraft had been tracked to New Orleans Lakefront airport. It's a G-IV that looks just like Asad's, but with the tail number B-5612."

"The next in registration sequence."

"Yeah, so I grabbed a car and started to drive that way, but got afraid I might not get there in time. So I called the tower."

Agent Sims looked at me as if to ask what was going on. I waved him forward frantically. He sped along until we arrived at an access gate to the cargo ramp. I kept listening to Breaux as I handed my ID to Sims, who did what he needed to get us through the gate. As we drove out onto the open ramp area, one of the massive hangar doors began to open on our right. I assumed that someone inside had become interested in the unmarked sedan speeding toward the taxiway. What I saw inside brought pleasant surprise and new possibility.

Breaux continued to tell me what was happening at Lakefront. "They told me that the G-IV taxied for takeoff without permission. The pilot was told he was operating inside a presidential TFR, but the aircraft neither responded nor stopped. They rolled for takeoff while I was on the phone."

I couldn't get a word in edgewise. Breaux was now talking a mile a minute. "I asked them what the heck they were gonna do about it. They were calling TRACON, where they had a Secret Service agent monitoring the airspace for interlopers. That agent would scramble the fixed wing jets out of Keesler Air Force base."

"They'll never make it in time," I muttered to myself. Asad had flown into the country on a commercial flight in order to cover the entry of his replacement corporate jet. He had it sit by quietly at a nearby airport and wait. But wait for what? The odds on managing to escape in any airplane in the midst of the temporary flight restriction were slim to none, and Asad would know that. No, this was no escape attempt. This was a suicide mission. I didn't know if Asad was onboard or not, but it hardly mattered. That G-IV was headed for Air Force One. Even if they had the clearance and the balls to do it, the fighters from Keesler would never make it in time. To make matters worse, we were all hampered by a lack of radio communications. We were taking a bite out of a real shit sandwich.

"Thanks Martin. I'll take it from here," I said as I hung up the phone.

"What's up hoss?" Sims asked.

"Pull into that hangar," I instructed as I pointed in the direction of an emerald green helicopter topped with white paint. It had the unmistakable markings of the Marine Corps' executive transport, commonly known as Marine One. This Sikorsky H-60 variant, or one similar, provided a shadow escort for the president wherever he went in the world. On trips like this one, when no helicopter flight was scheduled, the aircraft remained hidden away but always within immediate response.

Across the runway I could now see the flashing lights of the SUVs that formed the contingency motorcade. At the same time, a tug attached to the front of the Nighthawk helicopter was started. As the helicopter was pulled onto the ramp, pilots and crew ran toward it. Despite the comm breakdown, they had obviously gotten word that things had gone direly wrong. As I had expected, our vehicular approach was being confronted by a handful of armed military police in camouflage utilities.

"Stop the car!" one of them yelled with his shotgun barrel aimed squarely at Agent Sims's head. He did. "Put your hands where I can see them!" We did.

I quickly explained to the guard who we were, showing them our identification. The MP was a bit skeptical as he eyeballed my military ID, then my scruffy appearance, then my ID again. Without a salute he acknowledged my rank. "Good morning, Captain. How can I help you?"

"Sergeant, I don't blame you for doubting me," I said. I did not make a habit of divulging who I really was or what my mission was, but this situation called for frankness and clarity. "I am an intelligence officer with DIA and I have essential intel pertaining to your mission to protect the POTUS. I need to speak with the command pilot ASAP."

"Are you armed?" he asked. When I told him that I was, he requested that I step out of the vehicle. One of the other MPs frisked me and confiscated my two pistols. I nodded in approval as they proceeded to give me an armed escort toward the helicopter, which was already starting its engines. Of course, their weapons were not there to protect me. They were all aimed straight at me.

I walked adjacent the cockpit as the engines roared and rotors spun. The pilots were awaiting further launch instructions from the Milaide. However, they only had limited radio connectivity with him at this point. The only radio that was likely working at this point was the satellite radio, which must've been swamped with everybody trying to talk at the same time. Not to mention that the Milaide may or may not have known yet about the G-IV.

"I'm Captain J.D. Simon, USMC!" I yelled over the din of the twin GE T-700 engines. "We need to get over to AF-1 and get the POTUS! The jet's about to get hit and our only hope is to put him in the helo!"

Like the guard, the pilot looked at me with skepticism. "Who the hell are you again?!"

I didn't have time for a long story. "Look man, just call Commander Nelson and ask him about me! We don't have time for this shit!"

The pilot tried to make a radio call but shook his head in frustration. He then broke out his cell phone and tried a number. Once again no luck. I couldn't hear him but could see he was swearing to himself.

"Okay, hop in the back and get on ICS!" he barked. He turned to the MP. "Keep an eye on him!" The armed guard and I stepped into the cabin and put on headsets.

"Thanks. Now you don't have to believe me but I'm an intel officer who's been tracking al-Ayande activity worldwide. As I'm sure you know by now they tried to hit the president at Saint Louis cathedral. Well just because they failed doesn't mean they're just gonna take their ball and go home. They launched a G-IV from Lakefront and I believe it's headed straight for AF-1. Nobody can seem to get a hold of the Milaide or the Service lead right now, so it's your call man."

"Alright, alright," the pilot gathered his composure quickly. "Are you all ready to launch," he asked the crew, which consisted of a co-pilot, crew chief, radio operator, and two MPs. They all responded in the affirmative as we immediately lifted into a hover.

I could see almost nothing from the closed confines of the modified H-60, so I had to depend on the pilots to be my eyes.

"What are you seeing right now?" I asked.

"It looks like POTUS just finished his climb into the rear of AF-1. They're closing the door as we speak," the co-pilot answered.

"Shit! We gotta get over there *yesterday!*" I snapped.

"Yeah, yeah, I got it. Hold on," the pilot said as we rocked forward and flew low and fast across the airport taxiways and runway toward the ramp where AF-1 idled. I listened as the pilot was finally able to get through to the Milaide on the Satcom radio.

"Nelson, this is Nighthawk. We're ten seconds out from your pos. Recommend POTUS transfer at your rear door," the pilot said as he banked hard around the tail of the majestic blue and white Boeing-747. He lifted the nose abruptly before settling firmly on the tarmac.

"Negative. We're rolling for immediate takeoff," Nelson answered without further explanation.

I had to intervene. "Tell him about the G-IV!"

"I'll try," the pilot told me. He made repeated calls on the radio to the Milaide, none of which were met with any response. Their decision had been made and they were onto follow-on planning for what to do with Estevanez.

Fuck!

Through a small porthole in the rear cabin I could see Air Force One make its final turn to line up on the runway. While all eyes were focused on the venerable jet, I looked out the opposite window to see a more menacing sight. It was a white corporate jet in the distance flying directly toward the airport. I scanned the sky and saw no sign of any fighter assistance.

"Take a look out your left side!" I told the pilots. "I hate to say I told you so, but I'm willing to bet that guy ain't authorized to be zorching around out there."

"Shit," the pilot said. "There's no way AF-1 can outmaneuver that guy."

"Nope," I agreed. "So what do you want to do now? I didn't exactly notice that you guys had any armament on the outside of this bad boy."

"The way I see it we've only got one choice, and it isn't a good one. We've got to launch and intercept the G-IV...try to chase him off. Play a little game of chicken with him. Anybody disagree?" the pilot asked.

Silence.

"Lifting," the pilot advised as he pulled the helicopter from the ground and once again rocked forward and accelerated. He made a radio call announcing his intention to depart to the east, but didn't await any clearance.

As we passed the departure end of runway two-eight I could see Air Force One rolling for takeoff. I watched it disappear out of view as we continued to accelerate and climb to the same altitude as the incoming Gulfstream.

"Where is he now?" I asked.

"About one mile out and still headed right for AF-1," the co-pilot answered.

I was damn sure that whoever was flying the G-IV was on a one-way mission. The next question was if we were on one as well. With the wheels already set in motion and things out of my control, my thoughts turned to images from my past.

I pictured myself at the controls of *Carol*, my buddy Paul's 1975 Cessna Cardinal. I looked at the love of my life, Becky, only to see the fear of death in her eyes and the white knuckles on her hands as she clutched the glare shield for dear life. The engine was out, the windshield obscured by oil, and the ground rising ever closer. She had gone with me that day having complete trust in me; that I would bring her back safely. Instead I lost her forever. I never understood why it was me – the one at the controls – that lived and not her. I never forgave myself for that. I built a hard shell to protect me from the hurt. Since that day I never opened my heart to another woman. Each woman I dated since had suffered the consequence of my history. Poor Angie was just the most recent in a long line of those that had been used and tossed away by me.

I pictured myself as a young boy in the back of the small helicopter piloted by my father. Sitting in my mother's arms, I watched as a suicide bomber attempted to take all of our lives. The father that I never really had the chance to know and enjoy was gone forever. Wiped away in an instant, my mother was forced to protect me by erasing any memory of him. I didn't know why at the time, but I never fostered any connection with the man that raised me. By the time I learned who my real father was, I no longer had my mother either. No parents, no siblings, no meaningful relationships whatsoever.

I realized at that very moment I had nobody. I'd accomplished nothing of import, professionally or personally. I had misspent my youth drinking and fighting and my adulthood drinking and screwing. It was by sheer luck and a bit of raw talent that I had even gotten to where I was.

My only hope now was to be part of something larger than just one man. I was seconds away from possibly becoming at least a footnote in American history. One of the U.S. Marines who helped save the president from a terrorist-fueled assassination attempt. I was actually hoping that our helicopter would take a direct hit from Asad's G-IV. I hoped that Asad was onboard. It would be poetic for us to perish together at each other's hands. I may not have been the pilot at the controls, but I was definitely the main reason that Nighthawk was on a collision course with the terrorist jet – and history.

The pilot interrupted my wandering mind. "Brace yourselves, gents!"

I could not see our bogey, so every subsequent move was as unexpected as the prior one. We banked hard left then back to the right. Despite our best efforts, we were bounced around the cabin like ping-pong balls in a lottery machine. The nose of the helicopter rose abruptly, then to the left, so that we were skidding sideways through the air. A split second later something ripped the tail ferociously from the body of the machine.

The cabin behind us had been stripped away as if peeled by a can-opener. Just prior, I'd managed to fasten myself into one of the two captain's chairs. Air rushed in, blowing paperwork and headsets everywhere. The radio operator was tucked securely into his station. Unfortunately the two MPs were not buckled. As they slipped out the aft part of the cabin, the crew chief made a valiant effort to grab one of them. This move of heroism cost him his life as well. All three disappeared out of the helicopter and fell to their death.

Without its tail rotor, the remaining body of the helicopter began to spin out of control to the right. The pilot still had control of the main rotor and could therefore continue to apply power. But his pedals were ineffectual. He did an admirable job of keeping the aircraft upright despite the increasing rotational forces. He attempted to reduce the spinning by reducing power and entering autorotational flight. This gave him the ability to stay oriented, but sent us rapidly toward the swampland below. I think I heard him screaming a Mayday call on the radio.

As the ground rushed up at us, the helicopter rocked backwards. Our descent slowed rapidly, but the spinning came back with full force. I heard the snapping of branches and felt the cabin walls caving in around us as we tumbled forward into the trees. We were upside down by the time I felt the bone-jarring smack of the roof hitting the water.

CHAPTER 60

BETHESDA, MARYLAND

Before I opened my eyes, I could see bright light through my eyelids. I didn't recall it being quite that sunny at the New Orleans airport. Not to mention there had been a light breeze in the air that was now gone. Come to think of it, I felt like I was lying prone on a bed. I opened my eyes. Through my squint, I thought I saw Colonel Kingman's silhouette shrouded by the glow of fluorescence.

"Stupid question. Am I alive?" I asked the ghost of Kingman.

"J.D., given what you've been through I suppose I can cut you a little slack in the stupid question department. You're alive. But that was up in the air for a while. I think for your own good I'm going to have to ban you from going anywhere near any aircraft. You and flying machines don't seem to play nice together."

I was still finding it hard to believe that I had not been killed in the helicopter crash. Was I dreaming now? Was I dreaming then? I patted down my own body to make sure it was there. I was covered in a thin sheet and blanket. I had tubes sprouting out of my arms and nostrils.

"Where are we sir?" I asked the figure that I was starting to believe might be my boss in the flesh.

"Bethesda naval hospital. You've been here for three days," Kingman answered. "Right after you guys collided with the Gulfstream and tumbled into the swamp, the Coast Guard responded in the helicopter that had been flying around Secret Service snipers. Luckily, the water you landed in kept the aircraft from catching fire, but wasn't deep enough to drown you. The rest of the crew was not so lucky. None of them survived the impact."

"I'm the only one?" I asked.

Kingman nodded solemnly. I closed my eyes and wished that I had been dreaming. I wished that it could have been me that died if only one of the other Marines could have lived. It had been my idea to use their helicopter. Had it not been for me those devil dogs would be alive today.

"J.D., it's not your fault. All of you are heroes. Your actions saved the life of the president of the United States. The pilot in command, Major Tom Plant, was able to maneuver the ship so that the G-IV pilots could do nothing but run into the tailboom. Both aircraft fell from the sky immediately, staving off the assassination attempt."

I wondered if Tom Plant had a wife, kids. What about the others? Then my thoughts turned to Asad. Was that asshole on the jet? God, I hoped so.

"Sir, what about Asad?" I asked, my eyes fully open and focused intently on Kingman.

"His body wasn't found amongst the wreckage. He's gone," Kingman said. "But don't worry, stud. We're going to find him. Someone with that kind of ego can't stay hidden forever."

I tried to muster a smirk but I doubt it ever made it to my face.

Kingman tried to raise my spirits through subject shift. "The White House contacted my boss's office and thanked him for all of our efforts. He was invited to go to the White House to receive an award on behalf of our team. The offer was graciously rebuffed with a response that the people who did the work should be the ones to get the recognition. It was a bold move, but the result is that we – me, you, Martin, and Melanie Chang – have all been invited to a private ceremony with President Estevanez. Not bad, eh?"

This time I felt the smirk linger on my face. It was rather amazing what we had pulled off. We had spared the lives of both the president and first lady from coordinated attacks in separate parts of the world. We had exposed what was previously a well-masked terrorist organization. One whose leader would now certainly have his face pictured adjacent Osama bin Laden's among the World's Most Wanted. I knew full well all that I had done to help, and had a pretty good idea what both Breaux and Chang had provided. But I still knew little about how Kingman had unraveled the tightly woven enemy plot. He was a magician whose tricks I felt I needed to learn if I was to progress in this career path.

"How did you do it, sir?" I asked. "How did you figure all this shit out?"

"Remember Vinny Girardi?" he asked.

"The intel sergeant at the NCTC?"

"Yeah, that's the one," Kingman acknowledged. "Well, it turns out he's not the all-American family man he plays himself to be. He may have been the NSA's best cryptologist, but lately he's served himself more than his country."

"How so?" I asked.

"It's a classic case of selling secrets to the enemy. He was taking highly sensitive information and in some cases hand delivering it to foreign contacts in the D.C. area. We even planted some bogus stuff to see if it followed the suspected path. He took the bait."

"Are we going after these contacts?"

"Already in the works," Kingman nodded. "However, I don't expect to get too much. This guy's a radical Muslim who used his Persian restaurant in Foggy Bottom as a front. Most of what we get will come from the computers we confiscated from the upstairs office. Old Ahmed will likely just rot away quietly in a private cell at SuperMax."

"This Ahmed, how's he tied in to al-Ayande?"

"Not too sure yet, but it seems he was sending secure faxes to a number in Shiraz, Iran – the last known HQ for Asad. There was also one sent to a number in Rio last week. So I'd say he had a pretty direct line with the boss. It might also mean that Asad runs a flat command structure and likes to micromanage. Our people haven't finished digging through the computers yet, but they have found a few interesting things."

"Let me guess," I said. "This runs deeper on our side than just Mr. Girardi."

"Well, well, well," Kingman looked impressed. "You might have a future after all. Care to take a guess?"

"His boss...General Moore?" I posed.

"Why him?" Kingman challenged.

"Well, he had way too much enthusiasm about someone who was relatively new to their facility. I mean, I understand that Girardi's a rising star and all, but come on. He's a sergeant who broke one well-known case. Does that really rate the undivided attention of the commanding general? Hell, I don't know. It's just my gut."

"Keep following those instincts, J.D." Kingman said. "You're right on. It didn't take much pressure on Girardi to get him to squeal on Moore."

"How did you get – " I began before Kingman cut me off.

"Save that lesson for when you've got your energy back. Besides, I can't give up all my secret techniques yet. You'd have all the more reason to put me out to pasture." Kingman chuckled at his own dorky humor. "The important portion is what we got from Moore."

I was curious to know how he got Girardi to sing, and to know where he was now.

"Okay, no details. But is Girardi still breathing?" I asked in an effort to see how far I could get.

"Yes. And when he was confronted with a choice between treason and obstruction of justice, he finally made a wise decision."

I gave a feeble, tube entangled thumbs-up. I would let that answer suffice on the Vinny Girardi situation, at least for now.

"Now, about the general," Kingman seemed anxious to move on. "I invited him for dinner a couple of nights ago. I drove down to his neighborhood in Old Town Alexandria and met him at the Fish Market. I told him I wanted to celebrate this win over al-Ayande. I didn't want him to think anything was wrong. I had gone to the trouble of calling in sick for Girardi so that his absence from work wouldn't be suspicious."

"Did he buy it?" I asked.

"If not, he at least played along. He showed up at dinner chipper as ever, carrying on with all his jocularity and bravado. We exchanged niceties over a round of schooners before I broke the news. When I told him what I'd found out about Girardi, he did not act surprised. He was stoic and silent. It was weird."

"Was he trying to come up with something?" I asked. "Think on his feet?" I always had a decent street sense, growing up in Boston and having to watch my back. But I never had a real strong sixth sense or the analytical ability that I had always envied in Kingman. I felt different now. I could see what was happening. I just knew that General Moore was full of shit.

"We'll get there," Kingman cautioned. "Once our awkward silence was broken, Moore told me that he'd tasked Girardi with making contact with some local al-Ayande operatives. They'd been tracking them electronically and were ready to take it to the next level. Their goal was to get more detail on upcoming operations."

"Any reason why they didn't pass that off to the FBI?" I asked the question I already knew the answer to.

Kingman smirked, acknowledging that I was staying a step ahead of his story. "Moore appeared sorely disappointed that Girardi would have gone astray. 'Perhaps he was too young and impressionable to take on such a mission,' he lamented. I allowed him to wallow in his manufactured act of sorrow before continuing. I asked him why he felt the need to maintain such compartmentalized secrecy from other agencies, especially since the entire purpose of the NCTC was to integrate the intelligence community. He retorted that what he was chasing down was far too sensitive and potentially explosive to share with too many other agencies. Now, I like to think I do a pretty good job of keeping my finger on the pulse, but I have to admit that what he said next threw me for a loop."

"Yes?" I asked.

"Asad and his al-Ayande operation have been heavily funded and armed for some time now by an unlikely source, given their radical Muslim foundation. The Chinese," Kingman said as any sign of pleasantry melted away from his face.

I lied in that Bethesda hospital bed, stunned. I thought back to the weapons I'd seen in the police armory in Rio – Chinese-made QBZ-series assault rifles. I recalled the weapons that the Armas army toted through the favela – Chinese-made Type 79 rifles and mini-rocket launchers. Then I thought about the tail number on Asad's G-IV.

"Sir, B-5611 is registered where?" I asked.

"It's a Chinese tail number, J.D."

That's what I was afraid of.

Kingman continued while I processed this new twist. "The connections between al-Ayande and the Chinese government are unclear at this point. But my fear is that Moore is correct. Not only are there evidentiary links, but it helps to explain where Asad has been getting his seemingly endless funding. You see, he never had the individual Arab backers that al-Qaeda has enjoyed; he's had to go elsewhere. Like many terrorist leaders, Asad isn't concerned about whether or not his backers share his religious beliefs. First, men like him care more about power than fundamental beliefs. Second, fervent Muslims accept doing whatever it takes to achieve the will of Allah. In their minds, it's perfectly acceptable to make any unholy alliance, so long as it perpetuates the expansion of Islam."

"Wow," I said with a sigh, not able to say much else.

"Wow is right," Kingman acknowledged. "This is both good and bad news. On the down side, the U.S. intel community has a serious breach that needs to be closed. While I am almost one hundred percent certain that Moore is dirty, I have no idea at this point where else this infection has spread. Beyond that is the implication of the Chinese making an indirect attempt to assassinate a U.S. president. That is a serious charge that must be addressed delicately. On the upside, discovering the source of al-Ayande's funding is huge. For instance, we've been able to stymie major al-Qaeda plots in the U.S. largely due to cutting off financial pipelines."

"How are you going to handle General Moore?" I knew that Kingman had to use the man who at this point was his only real connection to the enemy.

"I'm still deciding," Kingman answered as he looked to the ceiling and pondered. "For the time being, I'll let Moore continue to think I believe him. I know that won't last forever, so I'll have to make a move sooner than later. In the meantime, I'll try to play like his buddy and find out what I can from him."

"So does all this mean that I should start planning a trip to the Peoples' Republic?" I asked.

"J.D., the first flight I want you on is one to Boston," Kingman said as he brought me back to reality. "You have plenty of family business to tend to before you go anywhere. I know you don't have any siblings to help you with arrangements, so I've taken the liberty of calling some of your parents' friends and coworkers to set up funeral services for this weekend."

I wasn't the type of person to outwardly express my emotional state or display any sign of weakness. I appreciated what Kingman was doing to help. Without his help, I never would have been able to coordinate a memorial service befitting two people as wonderful as my parents. He was the closest thing to family I had left.

"Sir, will you be at the service?" I asked.

"Of course," he answered as he put a hand on my shoulder. "Of course."

CHAPTER 61

BOSTON, MASSACHUSETTS

It was no surprise that I found myself bellied up to the bar at the Cask 'n Flagon. The iconic sports bar had been my favorite dating back to when it was just a crappy local watering hole. Before the Red Sox became a *nation* they had a local fan base. Before Fenway Park's Green Monster was topped with overpriced seats, the bar just across Lansdowne Street from it was filled with only those local fans. Despite changes in recent years that brought an influx of bandwagon fans from around the world, the Cask maintained a friendly, familiar feel.

Having weathered the funeral services at First Presbyterian Church in my hometown of Brookline, I was ready for a few cocktails. I'm sure it's never easy to lose a parent prematurely, but I can assert that it's dreadful to lose both in a gruesome double homicide – especially when you've recently discovered that your biological father was murdered years prior at the hands of the same animal. To make matters worse, that animal was still roaming the earth as he plotted the senseless murder of others.

Physically I was present in the loud, smoky pub. Mentally I was anywhere but. Everyone at the church had been so kind to me, so sorry about my loss. I knew they meant every word and had cared for my parents dearly, but their words echoed with emptiness. I barely recognized any of them and could not help but fixate on the thought that I was truly alone in this world. The only people that I had were Colonel Kingman and my old drinking buddies from home, all of whom sat in front of me at the bar.

"J.D., I'm going to call it a night," Kingman said before emptying the last of his pint glass. "I've got to catch an early flight back to D.C. Besides, I want to maintain plausible deniability for whatever you guys get into later tonight."

We both stood and shook hands firmly. Kingman surprised me by pulling me in for a hug. It was not like either of us to display such affection, but it seemed appropriate given the compiled emotions of all that had recently occurred. I stepped back and observed Joe Kingman, the closest thing to a father figure I'd ever really known.

My adoptive father was a kindhearted man who treated me and my mother well, but there was always something missing. I never knew what it was until learning that we were not blood related. Alexander Simon and I were not cut from the same mold. He was a pure intellectual who always sought to talk through conflicts with calm reason. I had spent my rebellious youth bowling him over with willful brute force. I never understood him as a young man, and he was never able to control me. I was a stallion who'd never been broken. That was until being ridden by Kingman.

He observed something in me that nobody else had, myself included. He inspired me to polish some of the rough edges, to focus my efforts and harness my vast energies. As I bid good night to my mentor and watched him disappear through the smoke and out the front door, I looked around at what was left surrounding me. What I saw was what I would have become had I never met the best Marine officer I'd ever known.

I turned back to the bar and the stools that my friends and I had come to treat as a home away from home. My lifelong friends Scotty, Doug and Matty were fueling themselves with shots of Jägermeister, the liquid courage they needed to deliver the same tired lines to the next batch of ladies vying for drinks at the bar. I interrupted their vain attempt at drunken love by hoisting my glass tumbler in honor of loyal friendship.

Unbeknownst to my friends, or any of the other intoxicated patrons of the Cask, was that I was toasting not only them, but myself. The harsh licorice liquor that I'd used on so many occasions to kick-start an evening of idiocy was to send me off in a new direction on this night. No slight to my hooligan comrades, but I needed to take things in a different direction. They say that all events lead to this moment, along with a bunch of other stupid clichés, I guess. The point was that I found myself at a crossroads in my life, and I knew which path I would choose. I would always love these clowns and never take their friendship for granted, but I needed to take my life more seriously henceforth. My mother and father not only gave me life, but gave their lives for me. Living a life of honor was the least I could do to honor their memory.

Against their will, I bid the boys goodnight and left them to their own devices. They fought my departure hard at first, then bear-hugged me sloppily, then probably forgot about me after either four minutes, three shots, or two ladies.

As I walked outside, the cold, crisp winter air hit me like never before. Of course I'd felt it my entire life growing up, but it never made me feel like this. Instead of making me want to hide under my collar and get to the next warm spot as quickly as possible, I opened my coat and bathed in its invigoration. I walked the streets of Boston until they were empty.

My ambling brought me past sites I'd seen more times than I could recall. Before tonight they were nothing more than locales where I had engaged in youthful tomfoolery. This was the first time I viewed them in a historical or cultural context. I walked down Marlborough Street and appreciated the architectural elegance of the century-old townhomes. Their ornate façades were framed by old-growth trees, giving the city street a remarkably suburban feel. Attention to detail was present not only in the buildings, but permeated the iron-gate fencing, the old-world lampposts, and wide sidewalks.

I crossed through the Boston Common and valued the serenity tucked into its urban surroundings. As I passed underneath the canopy of large branches that hid the surrounding skyscrapers, it felt like a garden oasis. Somewhere in the dark corners of the ponds slept the city-dwelling waterfowl for which the area is famed.

I climbed up and over the regal Beacon Hill and past the illuminated gold dome atop the Massachusetts statehouse. I continued past Faneuil Hall and through Quincy Market. The normally bustling shopping area was eerily quiet. It was devoid of ever-present tourists, leaving nobody but a handful of late-night revelers spilling out of local pubs like the Purple Shamrock and the Black Rose. I thought about the historic speeches delivered on these very grounds. Men like Samuel Adams had spurred others to action as they laid the foundation of a revolution that would change the world. I tried to picture what the marketplace might have looked like, and figured that in some ways it hadn't changed all that markedly.

With no destination in mind, I meandered into the quaint Italian North End neighborhood. Narrow streets led me past red brick apartment buildings, shops and restaurants. All the pizzerias and cafés were closed for the night, yet hints of garlic and espresso lingered in the air. I breathed in deeply as I continued up Salem Street toward the waterfront.

Before I made it to the piers comprising the Coast Guard facility, I came upon a structure that towered above the rest. The steeple of Old North Church looked out over the neighborhood like a sentry post, guarding the surrounding area from harm. Perhaps not its originally intended purpose, the church had served that very cause more than two hundred years ago.

I was far from the best student as a youth, but my interest always had a bent toward history. Having grown up in this area, my school teachers hammered us with details about colonial and revolutionary America. Upon seeing the church, I recalled studies of Paul Revere and the Sons of Liberty. My mind's eye pictured the young revolutionary risking his life for the nation he and his cohorts dreamed of. I looked up at the steeple and envisioned two lanterns lit in order to notify nearby patriots that the British regulars were coming by sea. Revere, mounted on steed, took to notifying others of the impending attack.

Revere had no difficulty identifying the enemy. That invasion occurred in a time when that was easily decipherable. They wore bright uniforms and fought in open fields. They announced their intentions, declared war, signed and honored peace treaties. I wished we had it so easy today.

We invest huge sums of money, time and people just to find out who our enemy is and what they're trying to do to us. We had gone to all ends of the earth just to track down al-Ayande's plans for taking out the president. Even after we succeeded in exposing the secretive plot, we still hadn't discovered who the real enemy was. It wasn't until ferreting out our Benedict Arnold that we unearthed the Chinese behind the conspiracy. This only served to raise a new batch of unanswered questions and open our eyes to new dangers on the horizon.

I couldn't be sure what my role was to be as we opened this next chapter in U.S. history. Regardless, I was determined to make the most of every opportunity. I needed to make this solemn vow worth more than just some words I'd uttered to defend the constitution when accepting my commission as a Marine Corps second lieutenant.

I refused to dwell on things that might have been. My family was gone. I'd never even had a chance to know my real father. He was nothing more than a passing memory in a recurring nightmare. My mother and adoptive father, who had done their best to focus my wild youth in the right direction, were prematurely taken from me. I never even told them how much I appreciated them. I'd lost the one true love of my life. My girl Becky had put her precious, young, beautiful life into my hands, only for me to end it. Even my passion for flying had brought me nothing but heartbreak. After a faulty engine had stolen my love, my faulty heart robbed me of my dreams of becoming a Marine Corps pilot. When I finally did get on board a Marine helicopter, it came crashing to the ground, killing everyone but me.

I didn't ponder these things in order to wallow in self pity. The truth was that I had allowed them to affect me, to run my life in negative ways that I had not been aware of. The deeper truth was that I needed to accept my past openly and honestly if I was ever to get past it.

I'm sure it would have been easier to have listened to others wiser than me, or perhaps to learn from the mistakes of others. Since I had chosen not to, I hoped that lessons learned firsthand would prove to be ones with staying power.

I walked the last few feet to the blackened waterfront of Boston Harbor. From a ball field adjacent the Coast Guard base, I looked out across the inlet and just barely identified the white masts of the USS Constitution. For better than two hundred years Old Ironsides has been the symbol of U.S. sea power. One only has to trace her early deployments to develop a clear picture of the expansion of American influence in the world. We'd become so interwoven with the rest of the world that our survival depended on it. We would never be able to withdraw back into the shell of our own borders. We could not afford to be overrun by competing powers lurking in the shadows. I took pride in knowing that I might have a chance to help.

The cold air burned my nostrils as I breathed in deeply. I'd never felt more alive. I nodded and smiled to myself, confident that my epiphany would lead me down the path to success. I hoped and prayed on the souls of those that had given their lives for this great nation that it too would awaken and follow suit.

LaVergne, TN USA
12 January 2010
169772LV00003B/6/P